A VAMPIRE'S GUIDE TO WORK-UNLIFE BALANCE

VAMPIRE INNOCENT
BOOK SEVENTEEN

MATTHEW S. COX

DIVISION ZERO PRESS

A Vampire's Guide to Work-Unlife Balance
Vampire Innocent #17

© 2022 Matthew S. Cox

ISBN (ebook): 978-1-950738-60-1

ISBN (paperback): 978-1-950738-61-8

CONTENTS

CHAPTER I

EMERGENCY SUSPENSION OF MOM CODE

P aranoid is too strong a word for my mood lately.

Ever since the backyard grill burst into flames and threatened us, I've been on edge. Okay, so it's not really an 'ever since' as it's only been a few days. Something's coming and it's not going to be pleasant... like Michelle surprising me with concert tickets and I'm not sure if it's for Justin Bieber or that weird clown rap group.

Oh, speaking of concert tickets... Michelle did surprise me and Ash three days ago. We saw Billie Eilish. Also, damn my strange vampire brain. Something about her music made me cry so freakin' hard and I still can't figure out what about it got me. Ash twisted my arm into breaking the rules. We took advantage of our paranormal abilities for some backstage time and got to hang out with her for like half an hour. Part of me feels bad for doing that. I mean, for thirty minutes, she thought we were friends she couldn't remember where she'd met, and now she doesn't really remember us at all.

Okay, we did it for Chloe. She adores Billie. Poor kid's a little sad we had to make her forget seeing us.

The day after that, Hunter took me on a date to see a Led Zeppelin cover band called Dread Zeppelin. Yes, a bunch of Rastafarian wannabes doing reggae covers of Zep. I'm still not sure if I liked it or not. Everyone else there except for Hunter and I were quite obviously baked, and not 'amateur baked' either. A third of the audience almost couldn't stand. If we'd been smart, we'd have brought snacks to sell there and made a fortune.

So, yeah. Paranoia.

It's not really. I mean, as a mortal, I'd been scared to go outside alone after dark or pretty much be alone in public anywhere a creep might be able to get their hands on me without witnesses. Pretty standard mindset for a girl in this society. Does it count as paranoia if the fears are legit? Thought I was done with that when I died, but nope. To be fair, I am less worried now than I used to be. Apprehension might be a better word.

I'm like my brother Sam going to the doctor to get a vaccine. Like the rest of us, he's not a big fan of needles. Unlike the rest of us, Sam never protested, screamed, or freaked out. He had a 'this is going to suck, and it's unavoidable, so let's get it over with' attitude. Poor Sophia screamed and cried like they were going to amputate her arm. Then, after the jab, she had this adorable 'wow, that's it' face.

Sierra was more devious. She tried to 'escape' or hide before going to the doctor's office. Once, she even bolted out of the building and ran down the street with Dad chasing her. I think she was seven at the time.

Me? I just cried. Grew out of it around eleven or so. Stopped crying and only trembled until the jab was over. Super silly to think about how frightened I used to be of a medical needle after I've had an *entire freaking katana* stuck inside me. If I'd have known at age six what a sword felt like, there never would've been any panic over needles. However, society tends to frown on impaling children on swords, so it's not an effective means to take the anxiety out of vaccinations.

If someone told me that becoming a vampire meant a continuous series of entities trying to kill me and I'd always be looking over my shoulder, I might've—wait. I didn't choose this. So, I'm basically like Sam. It happened and I have to deal with it. The 'it' here being whatever is trying to kill me this month, not the vampire stuff.

Dad said I'd drive myself nuts if I'm constantly bracing for cata-strophe, so I'm trying not to think *too* much about it. I mean, how seriously can death threats from a barbecue grill be taken? For all we know, it might be a few decades before the demon can muster the strength to be an actual threat. Sam said something about 'killing' a demon in the mortal world doesn't destroy it, but leaves it super weak and trapped 'back home' for a long time, unable to again break through into our world. So, yeah. Perhaps there's no need to worry just yet.

I have no doubt he's going to be a problem, though.

From what I understand demons *really* want to break into our world. They're not looking to take it over or anything like that. No, they simply want to sow chaos and misery. At least some do. I keep calling them 'demons' which carries a whole lot of folkloric baggage that isn't necessarily true. According to Sam, demons aren't anything like what various religions say they are. There isn't a 'good and bad' war going on with vast armies of angels fighting vast armies of demons. Angels are apparently not a thing. 'Gods' are the same sorts of beings as demons who appeared to humans throughout history and tricked them. So not all creatures I call 'demons' are evil incarnate.

Some are just annoyance incarnate.

Like imps, Blix excluded.

And yeah, sure, Sam is getting his information from Olmaz, who is a demon, so it's 'trust at one's own risk'. Can't think of any reason beyond 'just because' for the guy to lie to my kid brother. Still, demons do things randomly for fun.

Right, so trying not to let worry consume me and just have fun for the last few days before reality comes crashing down on summer-time. Technically, it's after Labor Day, so summer is over. I'm talking about me not having any obligations to be anywhere specific until next Monday.

Ashley and I are getting our introvert on, hanging out at home. Before the whole vampire thing started, whenever she was over here, we'd be together trying to do the same thing. Since she basically lives here now, we don't spend every waking second within arm's reach of each other. Right now, she's in her room on the computer. Likewise, I'm playing *Skyrim*. Yes, I know. It's older than hell. Just haven't found anything new that holds my interest and I'm *not* going to touch that *Fortnite* game. I'm not like Sierra. I dislike player-versus-player games.

Chloe's playing with Barbie stuff in her corner of the room. Should I think it bizarre she's happy to have such a low-tech pastime? I suppose it's what she's used to. Her horrible birth parents didn't let her have any sort of video games or electronics. I think it was more a case of them just not wanting to spend money on fun things for their kid than trying to make some sort of statement about technology.

Anyway. I pause *Skyrim* to watch Chloe amusing herself with the dolls.

It's slightly tempting to test her interest in video games. It's also kinda nice to watch her completely enthralled with such simple toys. I mean, she's seven. Not even Sierra was super big into video games that young. Amazing how much difference three years makes to a little kid. I used to think a year was a horribly long time. Like, as a nine-year-old, January sucked so bad since it was a *whole year* until Christmas. Now? A year doesn't seem like that much. The past two zoomed by. I'm sure for the 'rents, it's even worse. They probably think of years passing the way I think of months. Dad loses track of stuff that happened six years ago and talks about it like it was only last May or some such.

Okay, I'm stopping myself before I get maudlin again over not being a kid. This is really annoying. I'm not old enough to miss my childhood. That's not supposed to kick in until I'm in my forties. The heck is wrong with my brain?

My iPhone pings... then pings again before I can even grab it. Then again as I pick it up.

Texts are streaming in from Mom. She sent '911' four times, then 'plz come to my office asap big 911'.

Well, crap. It's just after three-thirty in the afternoon. I can't fly right now thanks to the fiery ball of nope in the sky. And nothing

4

about driving into Seattle from here even remotely approaches 'immediacy' in any form.

Mom has never 911-ed me before. This has got to be super serious.

How the heck can I get to Boeing 'immediately' during the day?

My thoughts fork in two directions: Sophia or Blix. Can't ask my little sister to open a magical doorway right now because the Littles are in school. Also, she'd get upset if she thought Mom was in danger, and probably mess things up and teleport me to Moscow or something... assuming I didn't become an earplug for a giant void octopus.

Do giant void octopi have ears to plug?

Bleh, no time to ponder such bizarre mysteries of the universe.

"Blix!?" I call, shattering the quiet that had been hanging over my room for the past almost hour.

Chloe jumps, then stares at me. Her expression is startled for half a second before taking on a tinge of glare. "Why did you scare me?"

"Sorry. Emergency. I think Mom's in trouble." I take my feet off my desk and sit up.

Blix appears sitting on top of my monitor—neat trick since it's a flat panel—and tilts his head at me.

"Can you mirror me to Mom's office? Something's wrong in a big way."

The imp makes this face that combines 'eek' with a sense of 'yeah, I know'. He nods, then zooms for the door, smacking straight into Ashley's face as she charges in. He clamps on as a reflex, total *Alien* facehugger moment. She belts out a muffled "Mmmf!" as he clings to her, wings flapping madly like a panic-stricken bat trapped in a house. She spins around and stumbles backward into the room while Blix struggles to disentangle himself from her thick red mane.

It's over in less than two seconds, though it seemed longer. Ashley stands there huffing at the now empty doorway. "Why did you yell?"

"Mom needs me. Gotta go. Can you watch Chloe?" I run past her out into the basement and cut left to the short hallway leading to the basement bathroom and the utility closet where the furnace and hot water stuff is.

Blix hovers by the basement bathroom door until he sees me notice him, then darts inside. Driven by worry for Mom, I sprint in there. He's levitating by the small mirror above the sink. I'm about to complain and suggest we go upstairs to Sophia's room since she has a full-length mirror inside her closet door. Between my near panic over Mom and being online in the windowless space, I don't bother. Blix has already activated the mirror. The instant he poked a tiny, clawed finger into the glass, it stopped being reflective and turned into a desaturated version of the bathroom.

I fly up off my feet, angle flat like Supergirl, and fly through the rectangular opening into the mirrorverse.

Blix takes my hand—well, he grabs one finger—and pulls me along.

We run back across the shadow of my basement. By the way, Ashley's room on this side glows like crazy. It's still charged with a bunch of magic from when Sophia created it. Hopefully, it won't collapse back into solid dirt any time soon. By the way, Ashley's room is probably the safest place in our house right now—potential magical catastrophe's aside. All the dirt that used to be filling the space where it is got compressed into the walls, more or less becoming impossibly dense stone. Her bedroom is essentially a bunker that could survive pretty much a direct hit from a nuke.

I race upstairs into a creepy not-quite-right version of our house. The similarity to normal ends the instant Blix makes a flicking gesture at the front door, which flies open. Outside is not our cul-de-sac but a stone-walled corridor straight out of a video game. It's like *Doom* but medieval fantasy.

A few seconds of running later, I realize I forgot my shoes thanks to the patter of my feet slapping stone echoing around. This leads to me realizing the only thing separating me from nakedness is a long T-shirt with a Coca-Cola polar bear on it. I'd say this is taking casual Friday at the office too far, except it's only Thursday. Yeah, I'm freaking out that Mom's in deep shit. Good thing she didn't send me that text when Hunter and I were in the middle of things or I might've brain farted so bad I forgot to put clothes on at all before rushing out the door.

In most situations, I'd like to say I handle stress well. I do tend to panic a little when my family is in danger. No worries. At least I have the long shirt. It's basically a short dress on me. As long as I don't end up getting into a tumbling acrobatic duel with the Forces of Evil™, I'll be fine.

Running through the mirrorverse is not the safest thing in the world. This place is full of all sorts of crazy nonsense. Some of the nonsense here is part of this realm. The rest comes from the plane reacting to the inner workings of our minds. Like, those enormous anthropomorphic mice who talked like British aristocracy and wanted to eat us for snacks came from Sophia's weird nightmares. The MC Escher inspired room probably came from Sierra. She's into art.

I'm not spending too much idle time thinking about randomness, so this trip shouldn't be *too* insane.

Also, I have Blix as a guide. Demons are able to traverse this place easily. I suppose that means it's a demonic realm behind the mirror... again, though, wrong connotations. 'Demons' aren't evil or 'satanic' in that sense. They're just creepy and inhuman, from another world, and love to mess with humans.

The video game dungeon corridor ends at a heavy wooden door with iron banding. Again, Blix waves dismissively at the door and it flies open by itself. We rush out to a bright, sunlit meadow. I feel like I've stumbled into a Windows 95 desktop image with the hypersaturated colors. The sky is *too* blue and the grass a nuclear waste shade of fluorescent green. Flowers dot the area, each with a babydoll head at the top of the stalk ringed with a crown of daisy petals. Yes, they're alive, and for some stupid reason, they're all laughing.

Blix picks up speed, tugging me along.

Some of the flowers uproot themselves and give chase. Not sure what will happen if they catch me. Things could range from annoying, to embarrassing, to deadly. Doesn't matter what they're planning, I'm not interested in finding out.

Thankfully, I'm a vampire. I do not get tired. Running at a full sprint for extended periods of time is no big deal. It takes me about a minute and a half to reach the top of the enormous grass hill. By the way, this 'grass' feels soft like I'm running on a gigantic angora cat. We race up that enormous green hill to the top.

I'm not ready for the sight waiting for me past the crest of the hill.

The valley in front of me looks like a farm where an insane godling on LSD is growing airplanes. Numerous large commercial aircraft protrude up from the ground at various angles. Some are warped and bent as if made out of gummi bear stuff. Giant robot battle mechs meander around 'watering' the planes. At the center of the insanity is a giant Smurf-like mushroom house.

Okay, maybe I'm more like Ashley than I admit to myself. This has to be coming from my subconscious somehow. I'm not as mature and serious as I pretend to be.

Blix pulls me down the hill, navigating around a handful of 737s, which contort their nose ends to 'peer' at me. They're kinda cute, not menacing. Like that Pixar movie *Cars,* only with airplanes. We race up to the giant mushroom house, barge in the front door... and it's a huge corporate type bathroom. Once inside, the Pablo Picasso on crack stuff stops. I'm now standing in a perfectly ordinary, sane large bathroom... except the colors are ever so slightly not right.

This is to be expected from the mirrorverse. I'm in the bathroom of a Tim Burton movie at the moment.

Blix points out a mirror on the wall, changing it from a silvery square to an open window into the real world—which seems bright, sunny, and colorful compared to the scenery around me.

"Awesome. Thank you!" I hug the little guy like a tiny gargoyle plushie, making him squeak, then Supergirl it through the hole.

The instant I'm back in the real world, I go offline and promptly fall flat on my chest in the middle of the ladies' room. Can't say I know where I am right now since every ladies' room in the Boeing building looks the same. (Or at least, all the ones I've been in on various 'take your kid to work' days look the same.)

I scramble to my feet and run for the door. Once I'm out in the hallway, I know where I am. This is the legal department, where

Mom works. I recognize the enormous painting of a meadow on the wall to the right. Mom had to tell me it's a meadow. To me, it looks like someone dynamited a paint store and this canvas happened to be sitting across the street at the time.

Nothing appears to be out of the ordinary here, well, except for me standing here with 'just got out of bed' hair in a thigh-length red Coca Cola shirt. Hey, both of my sisters have gone to school wearing pajamas on more than one occasion and they got away with it. Going to the office like this is like the grown-up equivalent of wearing PJs to school, right?

Hope whatever's going on here doesn't end up in a vampire claw fight. I really like this shirt. It's my favorite one. Super soft and warm. Screw dignity. The instant I see one claw, I'm flinging it off. Hey, maybe that will work in my favor. Who'd want to fight a naked vampire? It worked for the Celts, right? I read somewhere their guys would charge into battle totally naked to intimidate their adversaries. A person's gotta be a few shades away from bat-poop crazy to do a thing like that. Maybe the other vampire will think twice and run away.

Anyway, Mom needs me.

I run down the hall, hook a left by a giant fern, and veer through an archway into a big room full of adjustable desks. Mom's spent a lot of time complaining about the whole 'open office' thing upper management loves. They got rid of the cubicle walls, so everyone's all in the open with these desks that can shift back and forth between normal or 'standing desks.' Everyone hates it.

Mom, being in a middle-management role, still has a private office.

A few people stare at me as I rush by, likely wondering who I am or—if they recognize me—what I'm doing here. Not worrying about that now. Exercising the 'daughter privilege,' I barge into Mom's office without knocking and close the door behind me.

Mom's pacing behind her desk.

Oh, this isn't good. She *looks* nervous and rattled. I've never seen her look obviously worried before.

"Mom?" I rush over.

"Sarah..." She stops pacing—and her brain seems to short circuit as soon as she looks at me. "You didn't get dressed?"

"Five 911s. I didn't want to waste even a second. What's going on?" I dart around the corner of the desk and stop in front of her.

Mom looks down at my toes, then back up to make eye contact. "You didn't even get dressed before leaving the house? You went outside in your night shirt?"

"Pants are overrated," I roll my eyes. "And you said it was an emergency. You've *never* sent me four 911s before. And no, I didn't go outside. Blix pulled me through the mirror. What's going on? Why the panic?"

Whatever embarrassment I should probably be feeling for going commando in a long T-shirt in public manifests on my mother's face. In fairness, it's not something I did on purpose. I rushed to her without thinking since she freaked me out so much. I thought a matter of seconds could've been life or death.

After a moment of silent staring, I poke her in the arm. "Mom?"

Her eyes flutter. When she speaks again, she's barely whispering. "I need you to alter the memories of the IT staff."

"Why?" I blink, baffled. There's no way in hell my mother has porn on her work computer. What could the IT people have possibly found that's going to get her in trouble?

Mom almost gnaws on her finger, hesitating at the last second to instead grip my shoulder. "My computer sent sensitive information to rival counsel from another company, and it looks like I did it on purpose."

I cover my mouth.

"I didn't." Mom shivers. "I swear I didn't. The computer just... I don't know. Cristian may or may not believe me when the IT people finish investigating. I've got maybe five to ten minutes before security walks me out."

Oh shit.

"Okay, Mom. I got this." I take a step back. "Just wait here and try not to panic. No matter what happens, I'll smooth it over. The only 'if' here is if I can do it all right now or it might take me all night. It *will* be fixed. Don't panic."

I'm not sure what shocks me more: that Mom appears to trust me enough to calm down visibly… or that she's asked me to use my vampire powers for her benefit. Though, it's not like she's asking me for an advantage or to cover up something bad she did. External forces are at play here, I'm sure. Mom is like an ethics bloodhound. She wouldn't even let me compel Christian Fowler, her boss, to give everyone an extra few days off for the holidays. She'd never tolerate it if I did something serious like get her salary doubled.

"All right." She exhales and flops to sit in her chair.

I head for the door.

Time to get creative.

CHAPTER 2
DISINFORMATION TECHNOLOGY

We have three major problems.

The first rule of crisis management is to establish a list of what's blowing up in some sort of priority hierarchy, then tackle each item in order. Yes, I'm making that up, but it works for me. Problem one: Mom is about to be in deep shit because it looks like she sent confidential information to a competitor's legal team. She didn't tell me what the information was exactly, not that she had to. The look on her face said enough. Probably going to cost the company millions, get her fired, and they might even prosecute her if they think she did it on purpose.

I can't let this happen.

Problem two: it's daytime. This causes a split into two subproblems. Problem 2a is that it's really damn difficult to use vampire mental powers when I'm offline. Problem 2b is someone seeing me running around here could easily mistake me for a younger teenager having some behavioral issues. I could end up being carted off by security and detained, which will delay me and put Mom through more of an ordeal. If I'd been fully dressed in jeans, boots, and a shirt most likely wouldn't make much difference since I look too young to work an office job. My polar bear shirt is making it worse. Can't really fix problem 2b without mugging some random Boeing employee for her clothes like straight out of *The Terminator*. Give me your clothes, your ID badge, and that coffee. Or something like that.

I'll deal. It's not like I'm showing too much skin. This isn't skimpy. The shirt is really long. It just looks obviously like 'lounge around at home' wear.

Okay. Problem 3: I do not know where the heck the IT department is. This place is huge.

I'm going to skip problem 2b for now. I can't fix problem 1 without fixing problem 3, so I have to start with problem 3.

Luck is sorta with me and sorta against me at the same time. When I step out of Mom's office, some dude across the open work floor points at me. He's talking to a woman in a security uniform. Okay, I guess they didn't recognize me as Mom's daughter after all. The security guard, a black woman in her later thirties, blinks at me and appears to visibly relax. While I can't read her mind at the moment thanks to the daylight, her facial expression gives off a sense of confusion and concern. She probably thinks I'm like fourteen and she's dealing with a 'misbehaving kid' and not a serious threat.

Good.

I can use this to my advantage.

It's too late to pretend I didn't notice her since she saw me clearly looking right at her. I can use that, though. Doing a ninety-degree right turn and fast-walking away is basically inviting her to chase me. Like 'yeah, I know I'm doing something wrong, time to get out of here.' Sure enough, the security woman rapidly ends her conversation with polo shirt guy and comes after me. I speed up a little more but not to the point of running.

She's like fifteen feet behind me by the time I make it to the hallway outside the big open office area. Salvation is a short distance ahead of me in the form of a coat closet. There are six of them, but I only need one, so I beeline for the nearest set of double steel doors and duck inside.

I imagine the security guard wants to laugh at me for being a dumb kid thinking I can hide in a closet to get away from her. One second after I come online in the dark, the doors fly open. The woman's standing there giving me this 'you gotta be kidding me' look. She seems way more like a mom about to yell at her kid than a security guard preparing to put the smack down on a shoplifter.

Yeah, I complain a lot about looking young, but sometimes it helps.

I take advantage of the brief period between exposure to daylight and my vampire stuff shutting down. Before she can say a word, I grab and pull her into the closet. She wobbles, off balance, barking a startled yelp at my unexpected strength. It's enough to give me time to close the doors again. She reaches for something on her belt. I don't give her the chance to pull it out, spinning her around and 'gently shoving' her against the closet's back wall, pinning her there. We're nose to nose, me staring into her pupils.

The red light from my eyes illuminates her face for a second, then fades. Her willpower melts under my charm.

"Shh," I whisper. "I'm not going to hurt you. I am an authorized visitor."

She stares, unblinking.

I coalesce the idea that I'm the daughter of a 'higher up' in her thoughts. No, my mother doesn't qualify as a 'higher up.' I'm obscuring my identity here. This woman will be completely at ease with my presence in the building. She's also going to disregard my polar bear shirt and lack of shoes. Lastly, she will escort me to the IT room like she's showing a VP's kid around the place for a tour.

That done, I let go of her.

It takes about twenty seconds for the mental fog to wear off. Then she smiles at me.

"C'mon, sweetie. It's downstairs."

Acting as if it's completely normal for us to be hiding in a coat closet, she opens the door, steps out, and walks off. I follow her to the nearest elevator. Having a security guard guiding me around is perfect. No one's really paying too much attention to me now. Thankfully, polo shirt dude who called security on me didn't walk out into the hallway to see what happened. I'm sure he'd be baffled at this woman playing tour guide instead of 'arresting' me or whatever it is corporate security does to intruders. Wait, she's corporate security. If she hadn't thought of me as a kid, she'd have kept her distance and called the police, not taken me on in person.

Did I mention the elevator floor is kinda chilly?

We take it to the ground level. Shari, the guard, leads me down another hall, badges open a door, and keeps going. Gah this place is huge. It's so big I think they should give their IT people Segways to get around. We walk through a baffling series of hallways. Lots of plain grey carpeting and white walls. I have no idea how anyone can work here and not get lost.

Finally, she stops at an imposing set of grey double doors. "This is our IT office."

"Great. Can I see inside?"

"Of course, dear," replies Shari in an ever so slightly robotic tone before badging the door open.

Computer nerds are a lot like vampires in that we both have an aversion to sunlight. The main difference is that vampires aren't as averse to work. I say this knowing my dad is a programmer. He even jokes about how programmers will put in five times as much effort trying to avoid having to do something than it would take to do the something. All excuses possible to fix a bit of buggy code must be exhausted before they dive in and do it.

The IT office has no windows. It's an interior space in the heart of the building. Perfect.

Another hallway leads deeper into the server area. Where I am now is all desks (still actual cubes) and some tables full of computer stuff being set up, tested, or examined. Perfect. I pull the door closed behind us, then pause until the surge of energy ripples through my body. Good thing my hair looks like something out of a Japanese horror movie at the moment. No one can see my eyes glow red for a moment behind my eyelids.

Online.

As soon as my senses make the leap to hyperdrive, I pick up on a conversation occurring in a private office off to the left. A sign on the door says it's the VP of Info Tech in there. He's talking to one of his underlings about Mom. Both of them think she sent the information out since they can't find evidence of viruses or a hacker getting in from the outside. They're getting ready to go to Christian Fowler with their report. Also, the underling dude wants to know if he should call the police yet.

Crap with a capital c.

Gotta start with the brightest fire.

I run (a bit faster than humanly possible) over to that office before anyone can touch a phone. A late-fifties guy with silvery hair sits behind the desk. A younger, somewhat chubby man sits in a basic chair facing the desk. The older man, no doubt the VP, stops in mid-sentence while telling the IT employee to suspend Mom's access to everything, and glares at me. His face is totally saying 'who is this that dares to barge into my office without even knocking! Throw them in the dungeons!'.

I'm kinda tempted to jump up on his desk, grab a fistful of his shirt, and pull him up nose to nose, but there's no need to be melodramatic. Vampire powers have some range on them, after all. I don't have to be within kissing distance. And, there will be no kissing distance here if I can avoid it. This guy's making my eyes water. It's like he went for a swim in a vat of Old Spice before coming to work. I'll stick to minimum safe distance, thank you.

My derp hammer knocks him back into his chair before he can start yelling at me. There's something about guys like him. Whenever they get a bit of power, they believe someone who looks like me (young and female) deserves to be yelled at rather than spoken to whenever they think we're doing something wrong.

Dad told me once that IT people can develop attitudes like they're superior to everyone else at the company. Give someone access to things most employees aren't allowed to have, and it can make them feel powerful. This guy is the king of IT here, so yeah. Take that effect and quadruple it. Either that or the dude's just an arrogant prig.

Don't have time for his BS, so it's straight to the brain with the Derp-o-Matic.

I give the underling a somewhat less severe mindslap, then return my attention to the boss. For as young as I am in vampire terms, something tells me I've been doing a lot more brain surgery than most. They say practice makes perfect. Wonder if I'm getting *too much* practice for Follows Rules Girl to tolerate.

Meh. She's not complaining now, poor thing's just pacing around inside my head stress-eating Doritos. It's Mom's job at stake. And I don't for a nanosecond believe Mom did something wrong on purpose. I don't even think she brain-farted and sent confidential information out to an unauthorized party as an accident. She's too methodical. If she did really do that, there might be something like a brain tumor involved.

Ugh. I'm going to need to go diving into Mom's thoughts after I finish down here just to make sure she's okay.

Right, so... I erase this guy's memory of the entire thing. Apparently, some sort of software they have to monitor outgoing emails flagged it as suspicious, and IT began investigating. Mom found the sent email before anyone notified her. As far as the company knows, she isn't aware they know she sent anything yet.

Once I'm sure he doesn't have any memory of it, I add a lingering compulsion. If it crops back up about Mom sending emails where she shouldn't, this guy will be convinced it's the work of a virus or a hacker despite any lack of evidence. I'm hoping to erase everything and smooth it over so the compulsion never kicks in. However, it's good to have a failsafe.

Mr. Underling is next. He simply gets an erase of anything regarding Mom and email.

Since I'm here already, in a private windowless office, I bite the underling guy as soon as I finish tinkering with his memory. Oof. His blood tastes like Mountain Dew and Doritos. No, it's not him. It's my brain doing it to me, but still. Blergh.

From there, I make my way around the other IT people in the office, going from cube to cube. This whole 'chamber of info tech' is windowless. Awesome. Bow before me pathetic mortals... or something. Only one other IT worker, Jenny Larson, was aware of the investigation into the email. She's the one who did the more technical things, like checking all the access logs and looking to see if Mom did anything else suspicious (she didn't find anything).

Okay, this woman gets a failsafe as well as an erase. If anyone brings up Mom's email again, she's going to be convinced a keylogger virus got onto Mom's computer and allowed someone to access it via remote, impersonating Mom to send the email. Alas, the hacker was 'too good' and left no trace. Hmm. I wonder. Whatever little hints of Lost One powers Dalton gave me let me conceal myself from surveillance cameras and even open locked doors. Would they work on computers? No one could accuse Mom of doing it if it looks like the email was sent at three in the morning. They know—thanks to their badge access system—she wasn't in the building then. It would have had to be a virus.

I rest my hand on the keyboard of Jenny's workstation and think about exerting my vampire woo power on the machine. If I can mess with security cameras, maybe it will work on a computer, too, right? It's just electrical pulses in a board, right? Change the timestamp of the email. Change the timestamp of the email. After a few minutes of mentally repeating the phrase, I open my eyes—and nearly let out a scream. Holy shit! It worked! The logs showing on Jenny's screen show the offending email went out at three in the morning last night, not 3:02 p.m. this afternoon.

Sweet! Okay, I think I've got this fire pretty much put out.

According to the VP's memory, he hadn't yet reported the email breach to other VPs. He'd been waiting to get all the information his people could gather first. He's one of those guys who absolutely despises being made to look foolish or seem unprepared. Given the seriousness of what happened, he absolutely wanted to be thorough before accusing someone at Mom's level of that. Not that my mother is *that* important here, but she is on the legal team. Everyone's afraid of messing with the lawyers. Anyway, point is, he kept his mouth shut to protect himself from reputation damage if anyone made a mistake. This helped me immeasurably.

In reality, the email only went out a minute and a half before Mom texted me... and the IT department was about to drop the hammer on her right as I made it to their technology cave. I no longer feel like a derp for running out of the house in my sleep shirt. If I'd taken the time to get dressed, this job would've been significantly more complex. Preventing Mom from getting fired and shamed across the company is an order of magnitude easier than trying to make a few thousand employees forget that happened.

Eek. Near miss for the lose.

It's probably best if I don't get seen walking around the Boeing office in my night shirt by too many more people. Also, I'm pretty confident no one outside the IT department is aware that an email sent sensitive information outside the company. Mom said it went to a 'rival counsel.' Maybe the other lawyer is ethical and will delete the information once he realizes he shouldn't have it.

Yeah, okay. And unicorns are real.

I walk back over to the security guard, Shari, and delete myself from her memory. Instead, she intercepted a stray twelve-year-old whose parent works here but was off today and stopped in briefly with their kid in tow to do something quick. She thinks both employee and wandering tween have already left the building. A non-issue.

While she's still in the midst of the mind fog, I leave the IT room and jog down the hall to the first bathroom I see. Mom really needs to know her bacon is out of the fire. Alas, I don't want to make things worse by running around here without a security badge. If I raise too many eyebrows, people are going to ask Mom why I was here, and that puts scrutiny on her, scrutiny that might chip away at my memory erasing. I'll have to make her wait as long as it takes me to get home.

I approach the sinks and stare at my reflection in the mirror.

Eep. I really *do* look like I just rolled out of bed.

"Blix?" I whisper. "Are you still hanging by?"

Something pokes me in the left calf.

I look down.

Blix, sitting on the floor beside me, flashes a toothy smile.

Oh, he's in the real world. Guess he's been following me the whole time. Or he just appeared. Whatever.

"Awesome." I pick him up. "Can you take me to the person who received the email Mom sent?"

He cuts his hand across the air in a 'no problem' gesture, then dives into the mirror.

I climb up on the sink and climb after him like a kid sneaking out their bedroom window after dark. Only, I'm not going to a party my parents told me not to attend. Hmm. I'm not sure if the mirrorverse is safer than an illicit party or not. No one's going to roofie me in here, though I might get devoured by a giant monster. That's probably worse.

It's as if I jumped out the window of the Boeing office. I land in the grass beside the huge building. Only the eerie coloration of the world around me offers any indication I'm in the other place. Blix heads off to the right. I follow him. We cross the manicured lawn, then a massive parking lot. Hmm the planes in the not-too-distant distance appear normal now, not like they're growing out of a farm. Guess that came from my anxiety over mom. Interesting. This place is weird. I disregard most of the scenery for the sake of expedience and rush after the imp. Soon, we're on city streets that sorta resemble Seattle, but also don't.

"Nice shirt," says a distracted-sounding guy in jeans but no shirt going by on my left.

Intending to ignore him, I keep going.

He reaches for me.

I jump aside, glaring at him. "Hey."

"Shirt," drones the guy, in the manner of a zombie while again trying to grab me.

"Shirt," echoes a woman behind me... also sounding like a zombie. Yeah, she's shirtless as well.

In fact, every pedestrian in sight—some hundred people or so—are all bare-chested and staring at me like I'm the only kid in the recess yard with a lollipop and they all want it.

Crap. This is the mirrorverse feeding off my thoughts. It knows I love this shirt. It's also bizarrely tame. Shirt-stealing zombies are markedly less scary than ones trying to rip me to shreds and eat my brains. Still, I don't really want to lose my shirt here. This is the mirrorverse, not Las Vegas.

Running happens.

This place is really effing bizarre. One moment I'm running away from fashion-envious zombies, the next, I'm walking through my old high school. It's completely empty and dark. The off colors and eerie noises make it feel more like the set of a *Nightmare on Elm Street* movie than my former school. Can't be helped. Mirrorverse is going to mirrorverse.

I tune it out since I have Blix pulling me along.

A few minutes of feeling lost in an endless series of hallways full of lockers later, Blix opens a closet door between two classrooms which leads into a shadow realm version of our basement bathroom. Good grief, how did he know it would be in there? The scenery in the mirrorverse changes on a dime with no predictability or sense. Is David Lynch in charge of this place?

"Wait... home?" I stare at Blix.

He nods rapidly, making his big ears flap.

"I need to check on the person who received the email."

"Abo neirba mor."

"I have no idea what you are saying." I sigh.

He babbles again, too fast for me to even attempt to guess where one word ends and another starts.

"Blix, I can't understand you."

He points at the mirror and makes a shoving gesture.

When a demon tells you to get out of the mirrorverse, you get out of the mirrorverse. Home isn't where I need to be right now, but it's way better than here. I climb through into my basement bathroom. Blix follows. The end of his tail momentarily gets 'stuck' in the mirror. He grumbles and tugs on it. The tiny, bladed point at the end pops loose, causing the mirror to ripple and shimmer like a tray of liquid mercury for a second before returning to normal.

Blix again babbles at me.

"Will you please go find Sam and ask him to call me to translate?"

He nods and disappears in a puff of greasy, dark smoke.

Shaking my head, I return to my room.

Ashley and Chloe are playing Barbies together, with plush

unicorns involved somehow. I think the Barbie dolls are riding them into battle.

"Aww," I say.

They grin at me.

Ash is not the least bit embarrassed at acting like a child. For one thing, she wholly embraces her innocent side when she can. For another, she's entertaining an actual child. It's the same mechanism that gets big tough grown men to dress like ballerinas when their daughter wants them to be a faerie for Halloween.

"What happened?" asks Ashley. "Is Mom okay?"

"She's having a stress Armageddon. I need to tell her it's all clear." I rush to my desk and grab my iPhone.

"*Ich stecke immer noch hier fest. Wann lässt du mich raus?*" asks my Phone.

I assume the ghost is asking me how much longer he's going to remain stuck in my phone. It's super irritating how he can understand English but can't speak it. "Working on it. Sorry it's taking a while. Need the phone."

"*Um mir zu helfen rauszukommen?*"

"What?" I ask.

The screen shifts to Google Translate in a web browser. He asks if the reason I need the phone right now is to help him get out of it.

"Not yet. My brother's going to call me."

A notification pops up that an incoming call got shunted immediately to voicemail.

"Oh, come on. Don't be like that." I sigh at the phone. "I'm not making you wait in there to be mean."

The phone makes no sound, nor does anything appear on the screen, yet I feel like it's almost pouting at me. A few seconds later, it gives off an 'okay fine' mood, then begins ringing.

Caller ID says Sam.

"Hey... got a minute?"

"Hi, Sare." My brother's voice is weird and echoey. He's also sorta whispering. "I'm still at school so I can't talk long."

He must have faked a bathroom request so he can call me. "Okay. What's he saying?"

"Blix says a demon got into Mom's computer. While you were fixing brains, he corrupted the data in the email. The person who received the data never noticed or opened it before Mom texted you." Sam laughs. "Blix said the guy's computer is totally busted right now. By the time they fix it, he probably won't even realize Mom sent him an email at all."

"Whew." I exhale and fall heavily into my computer desk chair. No wonder he brought me home. There's no reason for me to go to the recipient's place.

"Sweet. Thanks, Sam."

"No probs. Be home soon." He hangs up.

Ashley crawls over and sits cross-legged on the floor beside my chair. "So, what happened?"

"One sec. Let me reply to Mom and let her know she can stop freaking out, then I'll tell you." I open the text app and send Mom 'All clear. Like it never happened. You had a demon of a virus, but it's gone.'

Mom replies with five full lines of heart icons.

I toss the phone onto my desk.

"*Autsch. Bitte sei höflich,*" says the phone.

"Sorry," I mutter, then look at Ashley. "A demon's messing with us..."

CHAPTER 3
JUST ONE GLASS

E xpecting some issues, I make my way upstairs a few hours later before Mom gets home.

My timing is pretty on point. The Tahoe pulls into our driveway after only six minutes of watching Sierra shooting people in *Call of Duty*. Ever since Sophia enchanted her, she's been an absolute terror in the game. It's gotta count as cheating on a spiritual level. I mean, she's got the dexterity and reaction time of a baby vampire, which makes her really damned hard to kill in a video game.

Sierra, for her part, has zero qualms about exploiting that advantage.

I should probably have an issue with it, but I keep my mouth shut. The poor kid feels over her head and powerless in real life. Having that outlet, that one virtual reality where she's almost untouchable, is like therapy. And hey, it's educational. She knows how to call someone a 'mother effing cheater' in six languages now.

Sigh.

Sure enough, Mom looks fried when she comes in the front door. She smiles at me and Sierra, then proceeds directly to the kitchen without taking her coat—or shoes—off. Sierra gasps at this with the same level of shock usually reserved for someone going out in public naked.

Mom is wearing shoes in the house. The world hasn't seen an event this cataclysmic since that asteroid wiped out the dinosaurs.

All is *not* okay in Momworld.

It's not beyond saving though. She did close the door. If she'd left the front door open, I'd seriously be worried.

"Mom?" I ask, following her to the kitchen.

She opens the fridge, pulls out a bottle of red wine, and takes a glass down from the cabinet.

I stand there, Sierra peeking past me from the alcove to the hall, as Mom pours the glass to half full, sets the bottle on the counter, and takes a drink. It's more than a sip, less than a gulp. After swallowing, she closes her eyes and just stands there in silence. Her hands are shaking. It's near imperceptible except for that she's holding a glass of wine and the surface is wobbling.

"Mom?" I repeat.

"One moment." Mom exhales out her nose. "I'm having a nervous breakdown."

I pad over and stand next to her. "It's fixed. You don't have to stress out."

Mom swirls the wine around in the glass, giving me this wry half-smile. "This isn't me stressing out. This is me recovering from the stressing out."

"Something is still bothering you." I lean against her. "Look down."

Mom peers down. She seems confused for a moment until she notices her shoes, then sighs.

Sierra creeps in and stands on Mom's other side, trying to be silently supportive. The two of them have a lot in common, especially how much they hate being in situations where they feel vulnerable and powerless to stop whatever's going on they don't like. Mom's a bit too grown up to hide in her room and cry, so she stands in the kitchen staring into space. Both Sierra and Mom react to helplessness by wanting to be angry, but they have no good way to vent it. Sierra ends up crying, and it pisses her off even more when someone misinterprets her crying as weakness instead of impotent rage. Mom can't get emotional at work because guys cannot deal with a woman showing emotion in the workplace. They call us weak or think we can't handle the job.

"Drat." Mom steps out of her shoes, sighs, then takes another sip of wine. "You're right. Ever since you sent me the 'all clear' text, I've been fixated on how thin it all is."

"Thin?" I tilt my head. "What's thin?"

"The ice I'm on." Mom eyes the wine glass, then sets it on the counter. "Needs to breathe a bit. I mean, all the years I've worked there... and everything could go up in smoke in an instant. I'm rattled that my job, and even my freedom is on such a thin string. I could've been arrested for corporate espionage. It's not like anyone would believe a demon did it. If I even tried to say that, I'd get put in a mental hospital."

My turn to stare at the floor. "Sorry for bringing the weird stuff home."

"Sarah Leah Wright, don't make me go through this argument with you again." Mom tries to give me a serious stare. It's difficult for her to whip out the 'using the kid's middle name when she's really mad' thing on me ever since we found out about Sara Lee products. Yes, Dad picked my middle name on purpose for the pun.

Sierra covers her mouth to hold back a giggle. Her eyes are wide in an 'oh crap you're in trouble' stare that every younger sibling loves to give their older sister.

"Oops," I whisper.

Mom squeezes my arm. "I'm not saying it again. Do not feel guilty. I would much rather have you here, have all of this crazy nonsense going on than have lost you."

"Even if the nonsense is getting crazier?" Sierra grimace-smiles.

"Yeah. The four of you 'leveling up' is helping keep you safe, I suppose." Mom exhales. "I'll find a way to deal with it."

Sierra blinks. "Leveling up? Wow, Mom made a gamer reference. Nice."

I can't help but chuckle. "Okay. Deal. I'll stop feeling guilty for bringing the weird home. Can you do me one small favor?"

Mom raises one eyebrow at me. "Hmm?"

"Don't overdo it on the wine tonight. It really doesn't help."

She smirks. "I am not an alcoholic. Nor am I a 'wine mom' stereotype. Stop making it sound like I have a wine problem."

I cross my eyes and say in a goofy tone, "That's exactly what an alcoholic would say."

Mom laughs. "Alcoholics have more than one glass of wine a day."

"Some alcoholics only have one glass a day," says Sierra, "But it's a huuuuge glass."

Hah. I chuckle.

"Be fair." Mom nudges me. "I've gone whole weeks without even having a drop. One glass helps me calm down on the bad days."

"Yeah, I know. Just teasing."

Mom gives me a guilty look. "Your teasing is based on concern, though. Are you really worried about me?"

"Yeah. I don't want you to turn into a wine-mom stereotype because of the weird I brought to the family."

"Sarah..." Mom hugs me. "You didn't bring weird to us. The weird fell on your head too. Your dad and I are proud that you trusted us to help you with a crazy situation when you didn't know what else to do. We're here for you no matter what."

Sierra leans around Mom to look at me. "You know they're both going to haunt us for the rest of time, right?"

Mom snort laughs. "If it's within my power to do so, absolutely. Just..." She gives me side eye. "Hang something on your doorknob if you've got Hunter over. I don't want to walk through the wall and see that."

"Eww," says Sierra.

"The idea of you walking in on me and Hunter—or whoever I happen to be with a century from now—is making *me* want a glass of wine."

"Not advisable." Mom shakes her head. "It would probably burn on the way out."

I cringe. "Maybe I won't test that theory."

CHAPTER 4
RIGHT AT HOME - NOT

I shouldn't have expected the summer to officially end without at least one more reminder of how my reality has changed.

A text message from one of Wolent's mortal associates is waiting for me Friday when I wake up. Vampires, especially older ones, are almost as distrustful of technology as some conspiracy wingnuts. You know, those people who think the NSA are listening to every phone call we make. The text message didn't have much information other than a request for me to call in.

Not sure why they're paranoid about texts but have no issues about talking on the phone.

Still in bed beside a sleeping Ashley and Chloe, I call the number. A guy, obviously a mortal, named Mike tells me the boss wants me to head to Tacoma tonight. Specifically, my mission is to gain entry to a night club called Ephemeral. Once inside, I'm to locate a vampire named Natasha. Normally, I wouldn't say 'gain entry' like it's an actual quest objective from *Skyrim*, but for me... it's actually a task. There isn't a fake ID in the world good enough to convince anyone I'm twenty-one. I probably could've pulled it off as a mortal. Not so much after my Innocent makeover. Heck, I have a real driver's license that puts my age at nineteen. The picture—that's actually of me when I'd been alive—looks kinda like a slightly older sister. No one believes it's real.

Except cops when they run it and it checks out.

Pretty sure the door guy at a nightclub isn't plugged into the police database.

First world problems, right? If the most tragic thing about me becoming a vampire is I have to abandon my just-obtained ability to finally drive that I spent most of my early teenage years dying for, my unlife is pretty good.

Thankfully, this is a night job, so it's not going to be too big a deal to brute force my way past a club bouncer. Couple years ago, I played this video game on the PlayStation. I don't even remember the name of it, but it was set in feudal Japan. The character in the game had this hand grenade type item, basically a 'bowl of poisoned rice.' You'd throw it at a spot on the ground and one of the patrolling samurai from the enemy warlord's palace would spot it, eat it, and fall asleep.

I mean, if an evil warlord is dumb enough to hire guards who are dumb enough to instantly eat random rice they find on the ground, they deserve to be assassinated, right? Video games are cool and all, but sometimes, the writers for video games are astoundingly stupid.

Since I don't have chuckable rice bowls laced with sleepy time stuff to get past the club 'guards', I'll need to rely on charm power. Shouldn't be difficult. Even less so since I am sure Ashley will want to go with me. Her charm is stronger than mine thanks to her being Aurélie's progeny. But hey, I can open locked doors. Yay me.

Anyway, Mike explains this vampire called Natasha is potentially causing problems for the vampires in our area. None of our people know anything concrete yet, only rumors that she's trying to start a social movement among the undead to stop hiding from mortals and basically come out of the coffin, revealing ourselves to society.

I'm not seeing that ending well. Neither is Wolent. Stefano and Paolo probably suffered immediate cranial explosions when they heard that. Kinda makes me deciding to live with my mortal family seem tame by comparison.

Of course, it could all be rumor with nothing behind it.

That's my job. Find Natasha and feel her out. See if she's serious or just some vampire version of a pothead who's had way too much of the green stuff and is talking nonsense in the midst of a stupor. Not sure if it's a good thing or a bad thing our people have no idea what she looks like or much about her. She can't be making too many waves if she's so mysterious—especially since her goal is to be the opposite of mysterious.

Chloe wakes up soon after I'm off the phone. It's easy to forget she's a vampire as she acts so normal most of the time. Kiddo sits up, yawns, then gives me this sleepy hair-draped-over-her-face stare that says 'there isn't enough coffee in the world'. "Can I have cereal?"

I hesitate for a few seconds while my brain grinds on the question. Is she asking like that because her awful parents didn't feed her all the time and she's used to having to ask for food or because she knows she doesn't need to eat normal stuff now and simply had a random craving? Also, is she forgetting the inevitable aftereffect? What goes in must come out.

It's a small price to pay for the ability to enjoy actual food, to be honest. *Much* better than uncontrollable barfing fifteen to twenty minutes after eating. I hear Shadows have it the worst. Liquids (like beer) flow out on their own but anything solid they eat just stays in there and rots.

Ick.

And on that cheery note, I head upstairs with Chloe to pour her a bowl of cereal.

While I'm getting the Lucky Charms out of the cabinet, the kid bounces in her chair at the table, all eager and stuff, grinning. You'd think she just won the lottery or something. A moment of 'what am I doing' comes and goes. Like, I'm not ready for a kid. Mom had me when she was twenty-six. She'd have been thirty-three when I was Chloe's age. Did she have moments at that age where she felt too young and inexperienced to be responsible for a small person's life? Probably. I think my feelings are normal.

And hey, I'm getting off easy. I don't really have to be 'mom' here. The vast majority of things that give ordinary parents nightmares don't apply to Chloe. If she gets into cleaning chemicals, she'll probably get sick, but it can't kill her. If someone abducts her, I feel sorry for them. Playing with matches could still be an issue but I'm sure she knows better.

Still, she's seven—and will be forever. She's going to need adult supervision for the rest of eternity. Good thing I will be around that long. Well, hopefully. The longest-lived vampires are the ones who keep their heads down and don't get noticed, don't chase power, and don't do stupid things. Okay, so I've done a few stupid things but nothing on the order of starting a land war in Asia or bringing up politics at a family dinner.

Meh. Screw it.

I have a bowl of Lucky Charms with Chloe.

We're about halfway through the cereal when she pauses, peers down at the bowl, then looks up at me. "This is going to feel icky later, isn't it?"

"Chew thoroughly," I say. "Shouldn't be too bad. Not like that time I was a dumba—I mean an idiot and ate those super spicy chicken nuggets."

She squirms in her seat. "Aww. I like chicken nuggets."

"Nuggets are fine. It's the spicy sauce that's the problem."

"Ooh." She grimaces.

We talk about various stuff we can eat without too much problem while we munch on our 'breakfast.' After we're done, she scampers off back to the basement while I clean the bowls and put everything away. I stand there peering out the window over the kitchen sink at the backyard for a while, stuck at the silence. A pink bicycle, some balls, some dolls, and a whole mess of Sam's plastic spaceship type toys are scattered around the yard. The sunlight's taken on this autumnal late-afternoon quality that's saturating everything in a surreal sense of unreality. For a moment, I feel like I'm looking back at a moment frozen in time from a future where no one lives in this house anymore. It feels as though I'm gazing at some other property where some children I don't know used to live and the family just picked up and left one day without a trace.

Is that what I'm going to feel like thirty years from now when the Littles are grown up and moved off to their own homes? Or am I just being a maudlin idiot again for no reason? This is getting annoying. There's got to be something going on in my head causing these... well, I don't want to call them mood swings. It's merely a passing sense of inexplicable sorrow I can bat away easily. Before I died, I would've ignored the Littles leaving their stuff all over the place.

And wow. Our house is *super* quiet with Mom at work and the sibs at school. Dad's in the office today for some meeting type thing, so I get to be the adult in the room until either he or Mom return. Go me. Managing the house for a few hours is easy. My worst fear right now—other than Chloe accidentally doing something to expose the existence of vampires—is that she goes exploring and finds Ashley's stash of, umm... 'toys.'

Not like they're in a place the kid will never go, either. Ashley's massive collection of plushies is in that room, which is like a magnet for Chloe. I don't know exactly where Ash put the 'devices,' nor have I gone looking. I don't want to know. As long as the kid never finds them, it doesn't bother me what Ashley does in her private time.

Am I weird for not having at least one of those things? Like, are young ladies supposed to? Does—eww—Mom have one? Did she before she married Dad? Eww times two. I think I was about sixteen or so when I heard my mother make a joke about a guy named Bob, meaning 'battery operated boyfriend'. I wanted to implode like a dying star and disappear from existence. The big reason I don't have one is three siblings and a mother who all have the bad habit of walking right into my room unannounced whenever they cared to.

If any of them ever walked in on me while... yeah. I'd be living in a yurt somewhere in Kazakhstan now because I couldn't bear to show my face in the USA anymore.

Laughing at the imagined look on my mother's face if she found one of those things in my room, I head back downstairs, thanking nothing in particular that Chloe is only seven. That's like the perfect age. Old enough to have a sense of reason and ability to communicate. Too young for teen angst. I couldn't imagine having to deal with an eternal fourteen-year-old who's boy crazy, anxious over her looks, and, well, a teenager.

Eek. *Now* I understand why vampire society objects to turning children.

~

THE AFTERNOON IS fun and uneventful.

There's some shouting outside a few minutes past four when two boys chase an errant soccer ball into Niedermeyer's front yard. I really don't know what's wrong with that man. It's not like the kids are messing with him intentionally. They're playing soccer in the street. It's tempting to go out there and yell right back at him, like 'put up a fence if you don't want stuff bouncing into your yard.' Meh. No point. He's not reasonable or rational. Any opinion other than his is wrong and nothing anyone says will ever convince him otherwise.

I watch out the window to make sure he only rants at them. The two boys, who are about Sam's age, walk off making 'what's his problem' faces. They don't look scared or vengeful. Okay, no crisis there.

"He is *such* a butthead," mutters Sierra from behind me. She's taking another break from *Call of Duty* to play some sort of adventure type game with enormous giant monsters she's gotta climb while fighting.

"Yeah." I shrug and back away from the window. "Some people like to be angry for the sake of being angry."

Sierra pauses the game and jumps to her feet. "Hey, test me real quick?"

"On what? Algebra?"

She recoils. "Eek! No. I mean reflexes. Like light sparring."

"I'm not online. You're going to be way faster than me right now." I fold my arms.

"Yeah. I know. I'm not asking you to have a contest." She pads around the sofa, barefoot in her usual T-shirt and jeans ensemble. Today's shirt is almost the same shade of dark blue as her pants, with the word SMOL on it in white letters. "I just wanna make sure Soph's spell isn't going to wear off."

"Okay." I gather up all six mini pillows from the couch and proceed to hurl them at her like fat, puffy ninja stars.

Sierra blurs a little as she dodges all of them with moves straight out of *The Matrix.*

"You still got it." I smile.

"Awesome." She grins. "Thanks. So, is there anything trying to kick your ass lately I should watch out for?"

I fidget. "Just the demon from the barbecue."

"Are we sure Dad didn't summon something evil with his black arts?" Sierra jogs around to pick up the pillows.

"Hah!" I chuckle. "Yeah, I'm pretty sure being super mediocre at grilling isn't evil enough to attract the attention of the old ones. It's the demon from the sefil."

Sierra cringes. "Oof. Some guys just don't take no for an answer."

"Right..." I roll my eyes, then stop to give her a look. "Are you having an issue with a boy at school?"

She sighs at the ceiling in this 'oh gawd' mixture of annoyance and embarrassment. "No. They mostly don't even look at me. I'm not one of the hot girls. Just this one kid Kyle who sometimes teases me, but I ignore him. If any boy at school ever really did something serious, I'd kick his balls into his throat."

"Oof." I cringe. "You know that's supposed to be a metaphor. If you literally lodge some kid's testicle in his esophagus, there will be... problems."

"Yeah. Chill. I'm not gonna kill anyone, especially someone at my school." She drops into an almost-taekwondo stance. "Been practicing strength control. I'm pretty good at pretending to be normal."

I nod. "Good. Vulgar displays of supernatural power are not well-received by the norms. Also, what could he possibly tease you about?"

Sierra frowns. "Stupid shit like saying I have to be careful when taking a shower, so I don't fall down the drain."

"Ahh." I cringe. "Yeah. I got jabs like that at your age, too."

We stare at each other for a few seconds, then say, "Thanks, Dad" in unison.

"You're sure you're good?" I ask. "Had a little tone to your voice when you said that thing about not taking no for an answer."

"Just a creep at Safeway." Sierra smirks. "Not so Safe-way."

I squeeze my hands into fists.

"Relax." Sierra sighs, swiping some of her mouse-brown hair off her face. "This creepy dude said something like 'hey sweetie, cute butt' to me when we walked by him."

My jaw drops open. "What?"

Sierra grinds her big toe into the rug. "Yeah. I almost feel bad for him."

"That's not the response I was expecting." I blink. "Why would you possibly feel bad for a guy who says 'nice ass' to a child?"

She grins. "Because Mom heard him."

"Oof." I fake cringe. "Yeah. Good point. What did she do?"

"Tore his head off right there. Kept yelling at him until he scurried out of the store with like fifty people staring at him." She laughs. "I was ready to kick his ass when we left, but the dude disappeared."

I pat her on the shoulder. "You have my permission, for whatever that's worth, to break bones if some creeper touches you. Just... try not to make it look like a gargoyle ripped them in half."

"Pff." She rolls her eyes and flops back on the floor by the game controller. "I'm not *that* strong."

I'M FORTUNATE.

I have a fairly robust list of babysitters available to watch Chloe whenever I need to do something out of the house when bringing her along would be problematic. My parents have tons of experience taking care of children. If they're not available, I can bring her to Aurélie's place. Chloe loves it there since she's a big fan of dolls. You'd think most kids her age would be freaked the hell out by legit haunted dolls. Somehow, she's totally cool with them. On some level, the kid must understand she's a vampire and doesn't have to be afraid of much anymore. Or maybe her horrible bio dad was just so scary, monsters and ghouls are no big deal.

Grr. I really need to stop thinking about that.

Anyway, Mom and Dad are watching her while Ashley and I fly to Tacoma. Neither one of us knows much about the night club, Ephemeral. Their website didn't help us figure out the vibe of the place. Ashley's wearing this turquoise off-the-shoulder dress and matching heels somewhere between prom outfit and like she's going to a company Christmas party.

I don't have much in the way of 'trendy' fashion. Sierra and I are pretty much aligned when it comes to wardrobe: lots of jeans and T-shirts. I am, however, a bit more amenable to skirts and dresses (meaning I have some and will wear them sometimes by myself, not only when ordered to by the parents). No one in my family has ever cared about what 'the cool kids' are wearing or designer names. Lots of Marshall's, Walmart, and random online stores. We're not even at the Macy's level of 'pretending to be fancy but not really.'

Figured it was probably a good idea to be a little less casual than my trip to Mom's office the other day. Not going to dress up for this, though. Anything could happen tonight and I don't want to have any of my nice clothing shredded. While pretty, dresses aren't the greatest attire for fights. Instead, I go for some generic black tights with a baggy long-sleeved top that hangs down past my waist enough to impersonate a short skirt. If I were smarter, I'd make a belt out of some sort of flexible ninja weapon like that creepy schoolgirl character from *Kill Bill*. Unfortunately, I do not own such a weapon or even know what they're called. There's also the small problem of me not actually being a ninja or knowing how to use martial arts weapons.

So, I end up dressed a bit like the weirdo goth girl from *Breakfast Club* and Ashley's a prom queen. Either way, we don't look like an obvious threat to wary vampires. We don't really look like a threat to much of anyone, really. This is good. Some of the vampires around here think Wolent's being hard on me for making me do so much so soon. Others think he's a fool for trusting such a new vampire with stuff. The guy knows what he's doing. I'm the surprise no one sees coming. Our adversaries won't think of me as a danger until it's too late.

Adversaries. Wow. It feels so strange to say that.

Anyway, we fly to Tacoma. Gee, I really hope there's no one at Apple who gets data from phones and starts asking questions like why is this random girl's iPhone frequently traveling at speeds over a hundred miles an hour in straight lines where roads don't go? Smartphones really would make it easy for the government to find vampires if they thought to use that information... which makes me wonder if they do. I mean... the PIBs are a thing, right?

How crazy would it be if vampires have infiltrated the government, and it's so secretive even other vampires don't know about it? Makes sense, though. I mean... the CIA and whatnot is mostly mortals and mortals don't really know much about what they do. Stands to reason a vampire version of the CIA would keep its activities hidden from other vampires.

Ashley and I talk about this on the flight down. By the time we're cruising over downtown Tacoma, she's humming the *X-Files* theme.

The place is on Center Street, south of the Target. It's an industrial type area surrounded by warehouse style buildings. Not exactly the main drag where all the social butterflies would go. Hmm. Either the owners wanted some privacy or they took the only real estate they could afford. It's definitely an odd place for a nightclub. Then again, I'm clueless when it comes to that scene. Maybe it's normal to put these places out of the way. Guess it keeps the church ladies from complaining.

No, it's not an adult club. At least, nothing I've seen yet or been told indicated it's *that* sort of place.

Surprisingly, there's a short line of people waiting to get in the door. The wait doesn't look too bad. It's not exactly 'IHOP at noon on Sunday' long.

The building itself is incredibly plain on the outside. It still looks like the small warehouse it used to be with the addition of purple neon signs spelling out 'Ephemeral'. Doesn't look like there's an easy way in via the roof. It's got a couple of skylights, though they're blacked out. The HVAC units seem newer than the building.

"It's kinda mysterious and cryptic from the outside," says Ashley, hovering beside me.

I shake my head. "Yeah. Pretty plain. No windows, though."

"This is a good thing, right?" She nibbles on her lip. "It'll make it easier to escape."

"Oof." I give her a playful shove. "I do not want a repeat of what happened at Abaddon. You're not really expecting we're going to end up kidnapped, are you?"

Ashley giggles. "No. Just making a joke. Sorry if that's a bad memory."

"Nah." I flick a bit of lint off my sleeve. "I wasn't really that scared. The worst part was the boredom of being stuck there until the sun went down. Seriously. What kind of creep owns a night club with jail cells in the basement?"

"A vampire who wants to keep snacks on hand." She makes a goofy face, then points off to the side. "Let's get down before someone looks up and spots us hanging out."

I groan at her little pun, then follow her to a shadowed spot by the corner of the club building. We land out of sight from the door, do a final re-check on our outfits, then walk out into view pretending to be confident and ordinary. No point in making waves yet, so I add us to the back of the line.

The couple—a man and woman in their early thirties—in front of us, peer back upon sensing more people showing up. I can't help but think they remind me of the snooty rich couple from *National Lampoon's Christmas Vacation*. The woman kinda scoffs at me, then smiles in a 'good luck getting in, kid' manner. Her date has the same sort of 'yeah right' attitude as him at first, then he seems to zone out staring at Ashley. I peek into his head. He's somewhat entranced by her, thinking she's too pretty to be real while simultaneously having thoughts like 'ack, why am I thinking this way. She's too young.'

I lightly elbow Ashley and whisper, "Dial it back a little."

"Oops." She stifles a laugh.

The man's eyes flutter. He appears confused momentarily, then turns his back to us again. He and the woman on his arm get into a conversation about some relatives they find insufferable yet will be forced to deal with soon. Something about her older brother getting married for the third time. I tune them out. Don't care.

It takes about eighteen minutes for Ash and I to reach the front of the line. By then, another ten or so people are behind us, a mix of couples and friends hanging out.

Game time.

I step up to the guy checking ID. He's huge, with a square jaw and flat-topped afro. My head's only up to his chest. Dude looks like he probably plays college football and works nights for extra spending money. He's wearing a dark blue blazer over a burgundy-colored turtleneck. No nametag. He looks like a Curtis to me. Okay, I don't feel underdressed. This place isn't formal.

'Curtis' looks at me, then Ashley, then back at me, shaking his head. "There's no fake ID in the world good enough to convince me either one of you are twenty-one. You might want to get your money back, by the way. This fake ID only puts you at nineteen, which still isn't believable."

The guys right behind us chuckle, trying to keep quiet about it. Someone whispers 'five bucks' like he's trying to collect on a bet.

Don't pay so fast, pal.

I stare up at Curtis, projecting a compulsion into his mind to let us in... and I smack face-first into a metaphorical stone wall. Oh, wow. The guy's a vampire. Hmm. Can't charm my way past him. I don't think he's trying to read my mind since he doesn't look confused or amused.

"Take a closer look. You read it wrong." I hold up my driver's license and smile big. "That's really my picture."

Curtis examines the license, then looks back up at me. When he makes eye contact, I add fangs to my smile only long enough for him to notice them. Don't want someone in the background seeing too much. He blinks, stares at me for a silent moment, then focuses his gaze on Ashley. The subsequent combination of WTF and 'aww' on his face tells me he tried to read her mind and realized she's one of us, too.

"Let me see that again?" Curtis takes my license and pretends to examine it more closely under the light. He blows air past his lips, then shrugs. "Well damn. You look a lot younger than you are. Be careful in there."

A guy a few places behind us mutters 'shit' when Curtis hands me back my license and waves us in. A skinny blond dude in a blue sweater starts laughing. He's probably the guy who won the bet now.

"Thanks," chirps Ashley.

We go past the fuzzy rope barrier and up a short sidewalk to the front doors. They're steel-framed glass, but the glass is tinted black. 'Ephemeral' is spelled out on both doors in purple painted letters. Gah. I really hope this is not a nudie bar or something like that. All this blackout and lack of windows has gotta be from the vampires. Also, ack! Vampires. The door guy is a vamp. Could this entire club be run by vampires? Quite possible, even if it's just one or two pulling the strings of mortal proxies.

On guard, Sarah. You're not here to have fun.

Then again, the vamps running the nightclub aren't necessarily part of Natasha's group. This could simply be her favorite hangout spot.

Ashley pulls the door open. Music spills out and washes over us. It's something techno I don't recognize. Not too loud, though. People inside can talk over it without screaming. Ambiance rather than punishing.

We make our way into a foyer, then past a heavy black curtain to a room that's basically what would happen if Luc Besson and Tim Burton collaborated to design a cyberpunk Applebee's. Glowing blue LED strips create a circuit board effect on the walls around a mixture of ghoulish images and unidentifiable technology. Skeletons covered in implanted devices emerge partially from the milieu as if they're trapped and trying to escape from the devouring electronics. It's techno-creepy from hell.

The area around us seems more like a restaurant than a bar, divided into various tables and such like any TGIF or Applebee's. In the distance, there appears to be a dance area, concert stage, lounge, and a proper bar—which is in the rear left corner from the door. There is nothing X-rated going on here. Whew. The lack of windows is totally for the vampires, not because it's an adult club.

"Weird place." Ashley gazes around. "All these flickering blue lights are making my eyes wig out."

"Right?" I exhale. Someone's going to have a seizure in here eventually. "Not exactly sure where to go now. I'm not really into the whole bar thing."

"Yeah, I know." Ashley sets her hands on her hips. "We're geeks. We don't belong in a place like this. We're out of our *Fifth Element*."

"Hah." She picked up on the Luc Besson vibe of the décor, too.

The girl's not wrong. Neither one of us belong in a nightclub. It's totally not our scene. We're too shy, too naïve, too uninterested in that sort of thing. Like, I used to be terrified of guns. Being in the same house where someone had a gun stored somewhere would've freaked me out—as if the gun would magically float around on its own and hurt someone. Mom thinks anyone who has a gun—and isn't a cop or an active-duty military person—must be a bad person.

I laugh at myself now. Mom's still not too happy knowing I've used guns and shot people... well, shot vampires. No permanent damage. I rationalize it away as being no worse than a high-speed version of paintball. It would probably mess me up mentally if I had to shoot a mortal. Here's hoping fate never puts me in that position. My plan to keep my head down and avoid chaos is solid.

Problem being, Wolent sending me on jobs is the opposite of keeping my head down.

At least this one is supposedly tame.

And yeah, being in a night club is definitely being out of my element. I'm not chickening out though. I've been out of my element ever since I became a vampire. Tonight is merely one more situation I'd never have sought out before it landed in my lap. I can deal with this. No problem... even if I have to pretend I'm an actress playing a character at the moment.

"So, what do people do in these places?" asks Ashley.

"No idea what the normals do in night clubs." I gaze around at the crowd, looking for someone who appears to be a 'Natasha'. Easier said than done. No one's wearing name tags.

Ashley swipes her hair away from her eyes. "Hmm. I think we can skip the people having snacks and drinks. She's probably going to be in the back, hanging out. Maybe over by the dance floor."

"Yeah." I nod at her in a 'follow me' manner, then start walking to the right like I'm going somewhere specific even though I'm not. "Guess we just act casual."

CHAPTER 5
POPCORN

N ightclubs, or maybe just this one in particular, differ from restaurants in one big way: the seemingly endless stream of strange guys walking over and hitting on us. I get that in a restaurant people go there to eat and be with their friends or dates. Here, people go to socialize. So, it doesn't bother me too much. I'm not used to getting male attention like this, though. Lately, however, guys tend not to hit on me because they mistake me for a high school freshman. Being inside this place must be convincing them I have to be twenty-one despite my looks since I got past the door guy.

Kinda awkward to be honest, but mostly because it gets in the way of my mission.

It must suck to be a female CIA agent or whatever... sneak into a place to take pictures of spy stuff or plant a bomb and you can't take three steps without some random guy showing up and trying to get in your pants.

The attention is weird because I'm not used to having it. In school, I tended to either be the invisible plain girl no one really noticed or thought of as a geek. Hunter aside, none of the boys paid much attention to me. Come to think of it, Scott only approached me after I'd randomly decided to 'girl up' one day and wear a dress to school with some (my first attempt at) makeup on. His 'wow, I didn't realize you were pretty' remark wasn't the best pickup line. Still not sure how it worked.

Oh, wait. One of the football players, one of the *hot* football players noticed *me*. One of the guys the majority of the girls in the school had daydreams about spoke directly to *me*. My brain probably just shut off.

Yeah, I had stars in my eyes like a moron.

For the first two-ish years of high school, boys ignored Ashley. Go figure, when she stopped dressing like a giant six-year-old covered in rainbow unicorn stuff or pastel colors, they started checking her out. No one at our school wanted to date the 'weird anime-loving geek girl,' but when she normaled it up a bit, she got attention.

She's getting a lot of attention tonight.

I swear, her charm abilities have basically turned her into a bug-zapper that attracts penis.

The realization's clear on her face. Perpetually unlucky-in-love Ashely who never managed to date anyone for more than a few weeks at a time is soon to have a change in her luck with romance. Or maybe not. As rapidly as the 'ooh, I can do this' glinted in her eyes, it melted to disappointment. Anyone she can charm would be a mortal. She doesn't want anything long term with a mortal for obvious good sense reasons. Her becoming a vampire means she now has to search for love from another vampire if she wants it to last.

And, well, to be plain, it's a lot harder to socialize with vampires than find random mortals out in the world.

She gives this faint sigh, the same sort of resigned squeak she usually lets out while we're playing video games or board games and she does something arguably stupid then decides to just deal with the consequences. Perhaps her going vamp was a rash decision. However, she's fully committed. For one thing, it's not like she can go back now. For another, she chose our eternal friendship over what-ever sort of romantic future mortality might have offered her. A 'sisters before misters' type thing, only with fangs. Though it's equally possible she'd have ended up marrying a woman if she'd stayed mortal. Or maybe not. She definitely wanted to have kids someday, actual kids of her own, which kinda requires a man. Meh. No point theorizing about it now.

"Wow," whispers Ashley once we finally don't have guys hanging over us. "It's like we went to the lake and a swarm of piranha penis-fish are leaping out and flinging themselves at us."

Her comment is so WTF I burst out laughing. Now that I've got that image in my head—with associated sound effects—I'm not going to be able to take anything else that happens tonight too seriously.

She loses control of herself and laughs right along with me.

It takes us a few minutes to regain our composure. Finally able to breathe (or fake breathing I suppose), I rasp, "Seriously. It's crazy in here."

The guys are reasonably nice. No one's being a jerk or a creep. They are, however, impeding our mission. So, I don't waste too much time talking to them. Slight mental prods send them on their way without damage.

After almost twenty minutes of near nonstop guys approaching us—it abruptly stops.

Takes me a few seconds to realize Ashley's doing the 'don't see us' charm thing. It's the same ability I used the night I got stranded outside with no clothes. Only, for her, it's a bit more potent. She has two advantages over me there. One, Aurélie is way older than Dalton, so more powerful. Two: Aurélie's a charm monster.

We could probably walk right up to someone and take food off their plate and they wouldn't notice us. As long as we didn't have any intention to hurt them, they'd remain oblivious to our presence. Not sure why intent-to-harm messes with the power. Maybe our supernatural nature throws off fear that overpowers the charm when we're in a murderous mood. Folklore has tons of stories about peasants being morbidly terrified of vampires.

I mean... if I get truly angry, my eyes glow red and my fangs come out. Not too much of a stretch to think I'm also giving off psychic fear at that point, too.

Right, back to the job.

There are a few ways to identify vampires in a crowded public place. Looking dead is not really one of them since only an idiot vampire would show themselves in public without 'warming up.' Except for Shadows, any vampire can make themselves look alive with a little concentration and effort. Aurélie generally doesn't, preferring the porcelain white look of French nobility from the 1600s. As long as she's wearing period gowns, the paper-white skin thing works for her without looking ghoulish.

So, coloration aside. Vampires would not be eating or drinking. They might have snack mortals nearby. Also, I wouldn't be able to read their minds. That's probably my best bet for finding my quarry.

"Scan minds," I whisper to Ashley. "Look for someone we can't read."

"Ooh. Good idea." She grins.

We make our way around the nightclub, trying to act casual while staring at everyone for a few seconds. Ash is quite a bit slower than me at it since she's still concentrating on making people ignore us. This helps since no one freaks out when I stare at them for twenty seconds without blinking.

I brace for awfulness in people's minds. Ever since that one guy who was on his way home to assault his little stepdaughter, I'm a little nervous at what I might see every time I scan thoughts. Fortunately, the worst thing going across the minds of people in this club is cheating on their wives or husbands, and that's only like two dudes and one woman. Seems the place is full of sane, ordinary people.

Wow, what a shock.

Mind reading scans prove to be the best idea I've had in the last twenty-four hours. Not quite fifteen minutes after starting, I find the vamps. Two women and two guys, all vampires, are sitting together in the corner of the lounge area. An elongated C-shaped red cushioned seat wraps around an oval table. It's big enough for about twelve people, fifteen if three more pulled chairs up to the exposed part of the table where the padded seat isn't.

Except for the dude tending bar, who is clearly not Natasha, and the doorman, they're the only vampires in the room. One of those women has to be my target... assuming she's here at all tonight like Wolent's people think.

The woman at the center of the C-shaped bench has bright (super fake) red hair. She looks like a maraschino cherry with eyes. There has been zero effort to make that shade of red anything even approaching natural. Though, it does fit the vibe of this place. She looks older than me, but not too much so. Guessing about twenty-five. Other than her wild hair color, the rest of her wardrobe is fairly tame. She's in some sort of sweater top with a denim skirt and almost knee-high black boots. The man she's semi-cuddling with is about the same age. He looks like a guy who aged out of a boy band group and had to get a real job. Cute in a boyish sort of way despite likely being in his later twenties. His hair is normal, ordinary light brown with almost no effort put into styling it. Guessing he's a roll out of bed and walk right out the door type.

To her right is a slightly older woman who looks like a new suburban mom trying to dress like she's still a teenager from the Eighties. Big hair. Major floof, even. This is two cans of hairspray a week type fluff. Wow. She's gotta be a year or two shy of thirty but her looks, her posture, and what I can tell of her attitude is still trying to be my age.

A young guy sits to the left of the dude clinging to the fake redhead. He appears to be the baby of their team. My guess is he got the Transference somewhere between seventeen and nineteen. Unlike the other dude, this one's still in the boy band. He's got a bit of Hispanic in his blood. Since he looks hot rather than cute, he's most likely not an Innocent. Unfortunately for him—at least to me —he's so pretty my brain immediately rejects even trying to talk to him. For people in our age range at the time they go vampire, if they don't end up Innocent, the Transference turns them into the kind of guy armies of teenage girls would put posters of on their bedroom walls... or the kind of girl other teenage girls put posters of on their walls. Huh. That's weird. Super-hot teen girls usually get famous for singing or something and end up on other girls' bedroom walls. Boys put posters of older women on their walls.

That's kinda weird now that I think about it. Maybe I'll ask Dad later why that is. He mentioned having a Cindy Crawford poster when he was like twelve. Anyway, this younger guy came out the other end of vampirism super-hot gorgeous. So, he can't be an innocent.

At least, this is my guess. It made me and Ashley adorbs. This dude got the heartthrob makeover.

No, I'm not jealous. Just saying we have differences.

The last vampire at the big table is the oldest, at least in appearances. For all I know, he could only have been a vampire for a year. I want to say he's my dad's age, but I think he's probably a few years younger than Dad. The guy's about forty give or take a few years in either direction. He's also strikingly gorgeous. I don't mean in like a Fabio sort of way or even a Magic Mike situation. This man is not 'Hollywood hot.' In fact, his looks are initially kind of unremarkable, but the longer I look at him, the hotter he gets. He reminds me a bit of a Middle Eastern version of the dude from the movie *Three Hundred* crossed with Geralt from *Witcher:* chiseled features, slightly unruly hair, and a weathered look.

He's too old for me and I'm not seriously thinking of anything here, but damn. I can't even put my finger on *why* he's having that effect on me. Why do I want to picture him wearing like ancient Roman armor and wading into battle? Everything about the guy radiates strength, confidence, power... and yet he's just kind of hanging out on the end of the bench seat almost like a college professor quietly observing his students having a discussion.

"Ash?" I whisper.

"Yo."

"Yo?" I glance at her. "Since when do you say 'yo'?"

She shrugs. "Since now? What's up?"

"The man on the right side... is he doing any charm stuff?"

Ashley stares at him. "I don't think... wait. Maybe. It doesn't feel like he's trying to turn you on deliberately though."

"Where'd that come from?" I stammer, certainly blushing.

"Oh, come on." She nudges me. "I saw the look on your face when you were gawking at him. Doesn't take mind reading to know what you were thinking. Don't feel bad. He's having the same effect on me, too. He's a bit old for us, though. And what about Hunter?"

I bonk my head against her back a few times. "Idle fantasies. The same way you daydreamed about Legolas."

"Right." She makes this dreamy face. "The things we did in my dreams…"

It takes all my willpower not to laugh. We were like twelve when we saw that movie for the first time. Neither one of us had any clue what sex even was back then. I can't even imagine what Ashley dreamed about doing with him in the woods, but it was probably something super tame and embarrassingly adorable.

"He's doing something, but it feels like hiding." Ashley scratches behind her ear. "He's obviously there though. No idea what's going on. Is that them?"

"Probably." I look around us. "Everyone else here is still alive. Let's eavesdrop a bit."

She grins like a mischievous kid.

We creep closer to their table, not looking at them and trying to seem casual, even though we're relying on Ashley's power to stay out of sight. Without her charm, we're obviously being weird, just kinda standing there in the aisle between tables.

It's not long before their conversation makes it abundantly clear we've found the correct group of vampires. They're obliging enough to refer to each other by name a few times as they talk about the best way to make their dreams a reality. That dream, of course, being vampires going mainstream in the public eye.

Natasha's got the super red hair. Seth is the guy with his arm around her. The other girl is Laurie. The too-hot-to-be real guy our age is Robbie Vasquez. I know his full name because Seth refers to him as Vasquez while the other three vamps call him Robbie. Apparently, Robbie *really* wants to be able to show his face in public and get famous as a musician. Laurie feels 'persecuted' by having to stay hidden and wants freedom.

Seth is giving off the 'whatever you want, love' vibes. Like, the dude has no real opinion on it either way but he's in love with Natasha so supporting whatever she wants.

The smoldering hot man is apparently named Cassian. Strange name, but wow... it totally vibes with me wanting to see him wearing Roman armor. Something about him, he just feels like he's been through some serious stuff. He totally looks as though he *did* fight in wars when swords were still a thing, except, he's not giving off elder vibes. Pretty sure there haven't been any invasions of the Roman Empire within the past hundred years.

We stand there listening to them talk for a little while. It doesn't seem like they're the leadership of any sort of organized group. I'm pretty sure Natasha got the idea and found two other vampires—Laurie and Robbie—who agreed with her. Seth's along for the ride. Cassian... hasn't said much. When he does speak, he asks complicated cause-effect type questions about the plan that cause Natasha to make a whole bunch of faces like she took a bite of mystery food and isn't sure if she likes it. His last question was a real zinger. 'How are you prepared to deal with things if mortals decide we are monsters and commit themselves to wiping us out?'

"This is nothing," whispers Ashley. "It's only them right here, not a whole army of anarchists."

I nod.

"Mortals are reactionary," says Cassian after waiting a moment and not getting an answer. "You cannot guarantee enough of them won't react with panic."

"Umm." Natasha waves dismissively. "That's like medieval or stuff. Modern people aren't so superstitious. Look at all the movies about vampires they make. People would love us."

"Why don't we ask the newcomers what they think." Cassian turns his head to glance straight at the two of us.

"Eep!" squeaks Ashley.

Natasha, Seth, Laurie, and Robbie appear confused for a few seconds then jump as if we appeared out of thin air five steps away from their table. They give us wary looks as if they aren't sure it safe to speak around us... at least until they try to read our minds. They still look confused, though no longer wary. Vampires can recognize each other just by looking... except for Innocents. We fake being alive so well, other vamps have to try to read our minds to realize we're part of the club.

"Oh, hey," says Natasha, acting like we only now arrived. "You two must be pretty new. I haven't seen you around before."

"Relatively new," I say.

"Have a seat." Robbie slides in toward Seth a bit.

Ashley darts over to sit on the left end of the C-shaped bench, then gives me this 'now you have to sit by the hot Roman gladiator' smirk. Ooh. You little she-devil. And yeah, she wants to be closer to Robbie. Ashley is exactly the kind of girl who'd have put his poster up on her bedroom wall.

Cassian doesn't react outwardly when I sit. I'm not exactly 'next' to him given how big this table is. He is simply the next nearest person. Could probably fit two more people between us. However, 'next' is subjective. My heartbeat is picking up speed being near the guy. It's totally not me wanting to rip his clothes off right here. His vibe isn't like that. I'm just picturing him dressed like a pirate sweeping me into his arms and carrying me onto a boat away from an onrushing swarm of bad guy soldiers... or something like that. Epic romance. Totally unrealistic Hollywood stuff.

The guy gives a subtle lift of the eyebrow almost in response to my thinking.

Wait, what? Nah. Can't be. He doesn't feel old enough to read my mind. A vampire's gotta be like 150 years older than another vampire to do that.

"So, what brings you to Ephemeral?" asks Natasha.

I'm not a great liar, even if the lie is trivial. I'm also super distracted by Cassian being so close. If I try to speak now, I'm going to sound like a complete idiot. Ashley knows me so well, she doesn't give me the chance to make a fool of myself.

"Happened to be nearby," says Ashley while obviously checking Robbie out. "Noticed the guy at the door was one of us. Decided to look around."

I'm ninety percent sure she's being so obvious with Robbie as a distraction. As in, if they think she's some airhead girl chasing a quick hook-up they'll be less likely to think we're a potential threat to their 'movement.' Robbie's falling for it entirely. The guy's so vain he's got this 'of course you couldn't resist me, I know' attitude.

Natasha gives her a cautious nod, then starts into the small talk, trying to get a read on where we're from, how long we've been vamps, and so on. For the most part, I'm honest. Seattle isn't so far away it would be weird we're in Tacoma. Curiously, she doesn't ask us if we're anarchists or traditionalists. Nor does she even bring up who made us vampires. Given her lack of organization—this is no vampire Che Guevara about to murder the proletariat and seize power—I don't feel a super strong urge to be evasive about who I am or why we're here. Not going to blurt it. I will, however, be honest if directly asked. Maybe hearing that Arthur Wolent is concerned will change her mind.

"What is your opinion, my dear?" asks Cassian while looking at me.

"Of what?" Natasha blinks at him. "You haven't asked her anything."

Cassian flashes her a knowing smile. "She heard the question earlier."

"Well..." I shrug. "I'm thinking of two most likely outcomes if we went public. One, as soon as society recognized another exploitable market demographic, there'd be a capitalist explosion with all sorts of vampire-themed services and products. Two—and the far more likely option, in my opinion—mass panic and violence."

Natasha regards me for a long quiet moment, processing that Ashley and I probably had been listening in on their conversation for a while or at least know who she is and what her ideas are. "You look fairly young, and you feel fairly new."

"I am." I smile. "Was eighteen when it happened. But, being new to this life and young doesn't mean I'm reckless or foolish."

"What about you?" Robbie glances at Ashley. "Don't you want to be able to be who you are without having to hide?"

Ashley grins at him. "I am who I am. Doesn't feel like I have to hide at all."

"Sure, it doesn't... now. You're both young." Robbie folds his arms. "What are you going to do fifty years from now when people start noticing you don't look any older?"

"Easy." I shrug. "We don't really go out much. If no one even knows we exist, they can't realize we're not aging."

Robbie slaps the table. "I am not spending the rest of eternity staying home by myself."

"Chill out." Ashley pokes him in the side. "Some of us are hundreds of years old and doing just fine."

Natasha huffs, then shoots me this glare like a mother whose kid just said 'no' to an order to clean their room. "You really think they will get violent and wipe us out?"

"Yeah. People are stupid and reactionary. Especially in large groups." I frown. "It wasn't too long ago that society genuinely believed in witchcraft and burned people alive for it. Some people are morbidly terrified of ordinary humans who have a slightly different skin color. There are still people in the world in this age who would happily kill any gay person they run into. How do you think those people would react to vampires?"

Ashley wags her eyebrows. "Yeah, I mean, if they're so freaked out by ordinary people who are just a tiny bit different from them, they're going to go absolutely bonkers over super powered monsters with fangs and mind control."

"And," I add, "it might get even worse. You'll have groups of mortals who advocate for us and then the mortals will kill each other. Kinda like how some white people used to fight for black civil rights and ended up being murdered by other white people."

"Are you comparing Nat's struggle to make us part of society to racial equality?" asks Seth.

"No." I sigh. "I'm just saying. Mortals can be so fearful and hateful, if they're willing to murder people over something as trivial as a difference in ethnicity, they're absolutely going to lose their minds over vampires."

Natasha grumbles. It's pretty obvious by the look on her face she's well aware of the potential violence.

"The most likely outcome, I think..." Ashley takes a breath and lets it out slow. "Is the first group of vampires who tries to go public are going to disappear... and no one will remember it ever happening."

Natasha's face turns pale. "Are you threatening us? You're not anarchists, are you?"

"No, to both," I say.

"What?" Natasha blinks at me.

"We are not anarchists, but we're also not threatening you." Ashley smiles innocently. "I'm just saying. There are elders out there who like their privacy. If we were ever to reveal ourselves to society as a whole, it would have to start with the oldest among us. As long as the elders want us to stay secret, we're going to stay secret."

Natasha leans back, arms crossed. "So, you're not threatening me, but bringing a warning? Who sent you?"

"Arthur Wolent," I say. "He also didn't send us to do anything more than check you out. The elders don't know much about you. I'm not here to officially tell you anything. Personally, though, I think it's not a great idea. Someone way more powerful than me, and probably way more powerful than Wolent, is going to react poorly to any attempt to take us mainstream. Also, the government is aware of us already."

"They are?" Natasha gawks.

Laurie covers her mouth, staring at me. A flash of gold from her neck catches my eye. She's got a gold necklace on in the shape of 'Lorri.' Mom had one of those when she was a kid. I think it was a fad or something back then.

"You guys didn't have a meeting with the PIBs?" I ask.

"What's a PIB?" Seth chuckles. "Isn't that a soda?"

"Persons In Black," I say.

"Someone's a bit too PC," mutters Robbie.

I shrug. "One of them was a woman. Not going to call her a 'Man in Black.' Would you like to be referred to as she?"

He scowls at me.

"If two dudes showed up, I'd probably be calling them Men in Black." I twirl some hair around my finger.

"Basically, trying to go public is going to get a whole lot of people killed." Ashley sighs. "It's a nice idea to be able to exist freely, but the world isn't ready for us yet. Maybe if like a *Star Trek* future ever happens, society would be enlightened enough to accept us."

We get into a surprisingly intellectual conversation—well, except for Robbie. He's a total dudebro. Natasha doesn't seem unreasonable, merely sheltered. I get the feeling she's spent most of her twelve-some-odd years as a vampire isolated from the world at large. She doesn't know that much about organized vampires.

Eventually, it sounds like Natasha is going to think about her ideas for a few more decades before acting on them. It's not like any of us are in a rush to do stuff before we get too old to have fun. Ashley seems to have lost interest in Robbie. He's pretty... but yeah. Dudebro.

Once the topic of vampire publicity wanes, we end up talking randomly about unlife and comparing our experiences thus far. All of them knew their sires before they were turned and wanted it. I admit to being an accident, not even being aware of vampires existing at all until after joining them.

Due to my proximity to Cassian, I end up mostly talking to him about random stuff.

"I'm sorry it happened to you at such a young age." Cassian gives me this pitying look.

"Meh. I'm fine with it. There are worse fates than being eighteen forever."

He raises both eyebrows.

"Yes, I'm eighteen. Or was. I know I look younger." I lean back into the thick cushions and sigh. "I'm okay, really."

"Something bothers you," says Cassian. "I feel it on you like a miasma."

I give him side eye. This guy's older than he looks.

He smiles.

Oh, son of a... he *is* reading my mind. Why doesn't he feel like an elder?

Cassian flicks his gaze briefly to Ashley.

I almost slap myself in the forehead. Duh. Ashley said he's doing some sort of hiding charm thing. Wow. The dude *is* an elder... but he's hiding it. Holy crap! Is that why I keep thinking of him dressed like a Roman soldier? Cripes. The name 'Cassian' even sounds like a Roman Legionnaire.

"It has been a while since I used a blade." Cassian examines his fingers. "I believe I still might remember how."

I gawk at him. Okay, I've been around a handful of elders so far in my unlife, but this guy is, by far, the most laid back. He's like the vampire version of a celebrity who still shops for their own groceries, lives in a normal house, and drives a Honda.

Cassian laughs. "What about your existence bothers you?"

"Mostly, worry about my family. But there is something that's been bugging me."

"Oh?" He tilts his head.

"Every now and then—way more often than I like—I'll see something that makes me get fixated on my childhood. I'll stand there feeling maudlin. Makes no sense. I'm not that old. Not like I'm forty, stressed out with a dead-end job and too much responsibility and wishing I could just be a kid again. I'll get stuck thinking about like six years ago as if my child self died and I'm mourning her."

"Ahh. I understand." Cassian half smiles. "It is the vampire in your mind. There is a part of our psyche that struggles to process our escape from mortality. Because you were so young at the time of your change, your consciousness doesn't have much life experience to work with. Your mind is struggling to comprehend immortality and this mental struggle manifests as a sense of poignant nostalgia about events only a few years old as if they occurred a long, long time ago. What you are feeling is not sadness, but confusion and insecurity. Eventually, your subconscious will adjust to immortality and those thoughts will cease."

"Oh, wow..." I stare into space. "No other vampire's been able to explain it so well before."

"I've been studying our kind for many years. I find vampires fascinating."

Hmm. Humans have doctors, so why not a vampire who studies vampires? Makes sense. "Mind if I ask how old you are?"

"Old enough." He grins, then his voice speaks directly into my head. *A touch over 300. Alas, I am not the Centurion you picture in your thoughts. Though I have met one. The man is over 1,600 years old. Resides in Greece now, I believe.*

I go wide eyed like a kid seeing a magic trick for the first time at his voice in my thoughts. Dalton can speak to me telepathically, but he's also my sire. Aurélie has done it once or twice, but she's really old. This guy is older than Wolent, a little younger than Aurélie.

Ack. Ashley's right. Elders are already sniffing Natasha out and she has no clue.

I glance at her then Cassian. Guessing you're listening to my thoughts right now. Are you going to kill her if she goes too far with her idea?

No, child. I am merely curious to see how this plays out.

"Do you think it will lead to violence?"

"Most likely." He purses his lips, seeming displeased.

I nibble on my lower lip. And you're not going to do anything if she tries?

That is not in my plans. Consider me here to observe with a proverbial bowl of popcorn. He chuckles. *As your friend said so plainly, I will not need to act. Some others invariably will.*

He's studying vampire behavior out of curiosity... without intervening.

"Exactly." Cassian pats me on the hand. "The wisest thing any of us can do is enjoy the time we are given, even if that time ends up being infinite."

Not awful advice. He might be the sort of person who could react to any tragedy with a 'well, that happened...' attitude. I'm not. Then again, he's 300 years old. Maybe when I'm that old, and my family is gone, I'll stop obsessing so much over what happens around me.

Or maybe I won't. Professor Heath said our personalities tend to stay the same.

Ooh, boy. I'm in for one heck of a ride, aren't I?

CHAPTER 6

TRADITIONS

Eavesdropping on the vampire version of a clueless idealist is my kind of mission.

No one gets hurt. No one walks away with a nemesis for life. And maybe, just maybe, no one's going to do anything dumb. In an extremely long-game scenario, the idea of vampires revealing ourselves to society isn't necessarily a bad one. Right now? It's a horrible idea. Like I told Natasha, people are stupid, hateful, and reactionary. Humanity has a long history of trying to destroy whatever they don't understand or can't control.

Can't say I really enjoyed going to a night club, but hanging out and talking for a couple hours is much closer to my normal routine than firebombing a vampire nest or getting into Quentin Tarantino-esque sword fights. Making direct contact and talking to her probably wasn't what Wolent had in mind, though I don't think he'll be upset.

Ashley and I leave the Ephemeral club a little past one in the morning.

And crap!

The 'rents are watching Chloe. Neither Mom nor Dad has stayed awake past midnight since Sam was an infant. Gotta hurry this up and get home fast. Dad's more flexible when it comes to time since he works from home. He's probably staying up with the kid while Mom's sleeping. It doesn't matter exactly when my father gets his work done as long as he gets a reasonable amount of it done in a day.

We fly to Wolent's manor as fast as we can make ourselves go. Ashley's got her shoes in her hands, arms clamped tight holding her dress so it doesn't fly off. She's not so skinny an off-the-shoulder dress could slip easily over her hips, but 120 MPH winds do strange things.

Weird thing about flying for me is my arms. I'm not sure what I do with them when it's not on my mind. They might be at my side or stretched one or both forward like a superhero. When I *do* think about what I'm doing with my hands while flying, I get all self-conscious and feel a bit silly.

Great. Now I'm thinking about it.

Do I feel stupid for 'playing superhero' sticking my arms forward? Can't stuff my hands in my pockets for two reasons, not the least of which being these tights don't have them. Also, I like having my hands available and ready to catch any stray pigeons zooming for my face. Anyone who says birds are soft has never kissed one at over a hundred miles an hour. Also, having my hair full of bird guts isn't appropriate attire for meeting Mr. Wolent.

We swoop in and land near the front porch. As ever, Aziz 'the Moroccan Hulk' is standing guard. He smiles at us like a big brother as we walk up the stairs to the porch.

"Sarah, Ashley. Good to see you. I hope you are well." His lip twitches a little like he's fighting not to laugh.

I'm confused for a second until I notice Ashley out of the corner of my eye. Her thick red hair usually hangs down to just above her butt. At the moment, it's more or less sticking straight out behind her like a hairspray tragedy.

My self-control is not as powerful as Aziz. The instant I see the column of hair sticking straight out behind her, I laugh. This makes her turn her head toward me, swinging the hair log... which makes me laugh more.

"What?" Ashley stares at me, but I'm laughing too hard to

speak. She frowns, fishes her phone out and uses the selfie-cam as a mirror. "Oh, ha ha. Stupid ice. Sare, yours is doing the same thing."

That doesn't make it any less funny. We flew fast and high late at night in September over Seattle. It's humid and cold up there. Water vapor got into our hair and froze. I'm kinda disappointed it won't last long. The part of my brain still very much a child wants to see Wolent's face if we walk in there with our hair like that.

The larger part of my brain that's a tad bit more mature thinks it's a bad idea. So... I spend a moment fussing at my hair to get it back to a natural state.

Our whimsy is contagious. I think Aziz will be grinning for the rest of the night. He opens the door for us, then closes it once we're inside. It only takes a minute or two of inside warmth to get rid of the ice job on our hair.

We make our way through the lavish foyer, past the huge staircase, and down the hall toward Mr. Wolent's study. Coming here totally feels like we're back in like the 1930s visiting the home of some oil tycoon or Wall Street king.

The feeling only gets stronger when we enter the study. Wolent's seated at his huge desk. Stefano Bianchi's reclining in a wingback chair against the wall on the left. Paolo Cabrini's in the adjacent wingback chair with a little round table between them. All three have tumbler glasses nearby, undoubtedly containing treated blood. The dark suits, the perfect slick hair, yeah I *totally* feel like I've just walked into the set of a *Godfather* movie.

"Ahh, Sarah." Wolent nods at me. "Miss Ashley." He nods at her. "I hope it went well tonight? Learn anything?"

"Hi," chirps Ashley. The queen of anti-formality.

She pays no attention to Stefano or Paolo. Not sure if it's due to politeness or trying not to be hated, but I pause long enough to offer a slight nod of greeting/acknowledgement in their direction before approaching the big desk.

"It's a non-issue," I say. "Natasha has zero clue. She's got basically two supporters and a boyfriend who's just there to keep her happy."

"And an elder." Ashley holds up one finger. "But he's only there to watch the show. He's not on her side."

"An elder?" asks Paolo.

I explain everything we learned. Ash bringing up the elder is a good excuse for why our mission to eavesdrop unnoticed turned into a direct conversation. Cassian undoubtedly became aware of us there the instant we got close enough to overhear their conversation. Wolent and Stefano both react in an 'oh... him' manner when I mention the name Cassian. There's a slight hint of an eye roll from Stefano. Wolent appears to file the entire issue aside as nothing to worry about.

"You seem almost pleased," says Stefano.

"Yeah." I look over at him. "It's a bad idea. The world is not ready."

Stefano's attention shifts from me to Wolent. "Don't be so confident Cassian is going to intervene if this Natasha person does something foolish. The man would happily sit back and watch society rise up and wipe ninety percent of us out."

Wolent waves somewhat dismissively at Stefano. "True. Though, from what Sarah learned tonight, it does not sound likely Natasha will present a problem. If Cassian's aware of her, then others are watching as well."

I blink. "Wow, he'd really just watch? What's wrong with him?"

"The man has no passion nor care," says Wolent. "Whatever happens, happens as far as he is concerned."

Speaking of passion... my weird infatuation for Cassian stopped the moment we stepped outside the club. I blame vampire stuff. He must have been radiating a charm of sorts similar to how Aurélie does. I'm not going to throw myself at him, though I might have a dream or two. Totally not my fault. I mean I'm a healthy, normal, permanently-eighteen-year-old girl. You can't expect me to see a guy like that and *not* have... thoughts. Okay, well, maybe I'm not healthy (I am undead after all) and I'm not normal either. I'm kinda quirky and geeky. Then again, what is normal? Certainly not standing in a room at almost two in the morning talking to the vampire godfather of Seattle and his two lieutenants.

Wolent's lip twitches. He's better at hiding the urge to laugh than Aziz.

Okay, now I'm blushing. He heard that.

"I must say..." Stefano rises from his chair and walks over to me. "It surprises me you disagree with her ideals. I'd expect the... younger generation to freely cast aside the burdensomeness of tradition without care to the ramifications."

It's obvious where he's going with this, and it doesn't even upset me anymore. Yeah, I know I did a weird thing according to vampires.

"I stayed home for my family's benefit, not so much mine." I briefly forget these leggings have no pockets and look like an idiot trying to stuff my hands into nonexistent hidey holes to kill the urge to fidget. "Sure, okay, at first I might've been a bit of a homesick child, but I *stayed* with my family because they absolutely could not have handled me dying."

Ashley leans against me. "I couldn't have handled you dying, either."

"Hmm." Stefano studies me for a moment. "Curious."

"I'm okay with traditions." I end up fidgeting my fingers together in front of myself. "Just think that some traditions are pointless and cruel. Not everything that people—or vampires—have always done are good ideas. Just because something's been done a particular way for as long as anyone remembers doesn't always mean it's the best way to do things. I understand that revealing myself to my family seems like no big deal to me, but it could potentially lead to problems. I'm managing that risk. I'm not saying all new vampires should go home to their families, either. Pretty sure there aren't too many like me who are mostly content to stay home all the time."

Wolent and Paolo chuckle softly.

"Our tragic lameness and social ineptitude protects the secrecy of vampire kind." Ashley thrusts her arms out to either side in triumph.

"Are you prepared to take steps if things spiral out of control?" asks Stefano.

"I'll do whatever I have to do to protect my family, even if it means making them forget I exist." I look down. "But... things have kind of evolved. We're all a bit weird now. The kind of weird that requires secrecy. My siblings aren't vampires, though each one of them has stuff going on they can't talk about openly. I trust them to keep secrets."

Stefano pauses, still trying to peel me apart with his eyes. I don't think he was prepared for me siding with him on the Natasha thing. Considering I threw tradition to the wind and outed myself to my mortal family, he definitely expected me to roll in here and start trying to convince Wolent that going public would be a good idea. There's a big difference between one new vampire telling the truth to her family and the entire vampire population jumping into the public eye. Does that make me a little selfish? Maybe. Like, I can do it but no one else does. Granted, I'm not telling *everyone*, not even extended family. My grandparents don't know, nor will they. If the Littles have kids of their own someday, they'll remain in the dark, too. Not really sure how much contact I'll have with my siblings once they're grown up and look older than me.

Then again, at least two of them might not grow up... any time soon.

Sophia said she didn't want to freeze herself at eleven years old but if her heart really does desire that, she might've done it by accident. Not that she wants to remain a child, she's just scared of change. She wants our family to stay as it is right now. The near miss of me almost dying and being gone left a mark on her psyche. It doesn't help that Dad agrees with her. His idle joke about 'if you have the ability to stay a kid forever, do it. Adulting stinks' did *not* help. Even Sierra's kind of on that boat. Faced with the choice of being able to sit around all day playing video games or having to get a job with responsibilities, she's going to choose laziness. Of course, she is still a kid so she's not thinking rationally.

Right... my unlife. It's weird and getting weirder.

And the newest 'weird' is Stefano seems to be chilling out in regard to me.

Dunno if I can handle that.

CHAPTER 7

LAME IS IN THE EYE OF THE BEHOLDER

D
ad is still watching Chloe, and it's way too late for him to be awake.

Ashley and I politely excuse ourselves from Wolent's office after our post-mission debrief is over. This vampire thing is so odd. I feel like a bizarre combination of CIA agent, mobster, and one of those unrealistically capable teenage protagonists from action movies.

Right, back to the real world for me. Or at least as real as it can get now.

"How weird was that?" Ashley whistles.

She's flying beside me, almost shoulder-to-shoulder. We're not rushing now, so it's possible to talk without screaming.

"Plenty weird. Which particular weird are you referring to?"

"Stefano basically admitting to being proud of you." Ashley makes a goofy face at me.

"He did not admit to being proud of me. He said he was surprised I wasn't a dumbass."

Ashley laughs. "He did not."

"That's what he meant." I grin into the wind, swerving a little to make my hair swoosh back and forth.

"His thing isn't even that you went home," says Ashley. "He's mostly annoyed at you for not being afraid of him."

I stare at her. "I'm plenty afraid of him. He's an elder. He could end me easily if he wanted to."

"Not what I mean." She waves dismissively. "You don't act like a servant girl tiptoeing around the king."

The laugh that bursts out of me sounds like someone drop-kicked a chicken. "He's really that old to think girls should be timid all the time?"

"Yeah." Ashley gently swerves away to the right, rolls over, then swings back close to me. "But he's at least trying to accept women aren't required to be subservient anymore. Some guys just can't change easily. Look at how Dad's stuck in the Eighties. Take that and stretch the idea out over centuries."

"Heh. Sure, but Dad's love of Eighties' movies is harmless. Treating women like servants isn't."

"Fair." She nods. "But he's not acting on it. The guy's at least trying to modernize. I think you scored some points with him tonight by not agreeing with Natasha."

I blow a raspberry. "If there's anything I'm ever *not* trying to do on purpose, it's score points with Stefano Bianchi."

She giggles.

"Umm. I mean, I don't want the guy to hate me, but I refuse to suck up to him."

"Right..."

Since home is in sight, our conversation gets put on pause. Random voices coming from the sky might make people look up... not that there's anyone awake at this hour around here. Except maybe Mr. Niedermeyer decked out in full Special Forces night vision gear and a ghillie suit sitting in his yard in case nocturnal children stray onto his lawn.

We land on the back deck, let ourselves in, and go straight across the kitchen to the hall.

"Dad?" I ask in a whisper as I pass through the archway separating the living room from the hall.

Chloe's sitting on the sofa watching *Frozen*. The volume is down so low only a vampire could follow the movie. No sign of Dad. Even weirder, a small army of dolls has gathered around the kid. They're all the sort of old-timey dolls in big fluffy dresses like Aurélie collects. I count eight. Problem is, we do not own eight of these types of doll. Even if Chloe managed to talk Dad into buying her dolls, Amazon doesn't work that fast. Worse, these dolls are giving off crazy heavy vibes, almost like they're alive... or at least aware. Things make sense as soon as I recognize the doll she's holding: Rebecca, the one that sorta transported me back in time, even if it had been more of a vision thing in my mind than really going places.

Eek. These must be Aurélie's dolls. What are they doing here?

Umm. Okay. I can't believe my father went to sleep and left Chloe on her own. Well, she's not totally on her own. In addition to the dolls, Blix is on the sofa next to her.

"Hi." Chloe smiles at us.

"Where's Dad?" I ask.

"He fell asleep, so I put him to bed," replies Chloe in a nonchalant tone as if discussing one of her dolls.

Ashley purses her lips. We stare at each other in a moment of mutual 'oops, we messed up.'

Nothing is on fire. No one's screaming. Nothing is glowing. Well, the TV is glowing, but that's okay. It's supposed to do that. I think fate gave us a pass this time. Also, Blix stepped in to keep Chloe company. It's not like she was left entirely on her own. The imp definitely counts as an adult because he's gotta be a few hundred years old. Alas, his effectiveness as a babysitter is somewhat limited due to the language barrier.

There's a certain quality to Chloe's posture and voice right now. She's quiet and tense, like she thinks she might be in trouble. The kid isn't afraid of anyone here hitting her, though she is a bit flinchy around strange adults making fast hand motions. No, it's kinda worse to be honest. She's worried if she does something wrong, we won't want her anymore. I don't think this is the kind of thing where any amount of telling her we'll never abandon her will help. We have to live it. A few decades of stability will hopefully ease her fear. I really hope it does, and she isn't frozen in this thought process the way we're frozen at whatever mental age we are upon the Transference.

Right. Act casual. Nothing went wrong, no reason to be upset or even complain. She didn't do anything wrong. I shouldn't even feel guilty here. I left her in the care of a responsible adult... though we did stay out a bit longer than expected.

"Oh, okay." I gently pick up the two dolls on the sofa to her left, sit, and place the dolls seated in my lap.

Yes, touching them feels weird. There's definitely some sort of energy infused in them. I'm not reading any sense of malice though, merely creepiness. Soon after I start holding them, their mood shifts to happiness. They're probably so used to people freaking out around them, my nonchalance is a welcome shock.

"Where did your friends come from?" I peer down at the dolls, then over at Chloe.

"Aunt Aurélie brought them over." Chloe smiles. "She's gotta go somewhere for couple days, and the dolls didn't wanna be alone. I'm keeping them company. They get sad when they're lonely."

Ashley flops down on her other side. She seems to zone out for a moment, then her expression gives off a sense of 'oh, okay.' The same way Dalton and I can speak telepathically over vast distances, she can do with Aurélie. "She's going to some sort of fancy thing in Louisiana... be out of town for a week or two."

Great. We have eight creepy haunted dolls in the house for a week or two. What could go wrong? Almost as soon as I think that, Rebecca turns her head toward me. I smile and wave to her. Personally, I don't have a problem with the dolls. My worry is purely coming from adding this much more supernatural oddness to this household.

We proceed to watch the movie with Chloe like nothing strange happened.

It doesn't take her long to stop being tense. She knows I'm not the type of person who won't react to something she does wrong right away and ambush her with it hours later. If she doesn't get in trouble immediately, she's safe. Not that she gets in trouble, really. I know every parent says this, but Chloe is a perfect angel even if she does have fangs. And by 'perfect angel,' I mean about as good as a seven-year-old can be. She still has her moments of stubbornness, moodiness, and anxiety, but I'd be more worried if she didn't.

Soon, Chloe's enthralled in the movie again.

"Still feels strange," says Ashley.

"A talking snowman *is* strange." I chuckle.

"No, not the movie. I mean how we're up at this hour and I'm not even a little bit tired." Ashley looks down at herself. "Ugh. I want to change. Why am I sitting around in a nice dress?"

I shrug. "Because you are. For the time thing, you'll eventually get used to it."

"Are you?" Ashley raises an eyebrow at me.

"Sorta. It doesn't feel as weird as it used to but it's still kinda odd to think about."

Ashley lets her head drape backward over the sofa. "Ugh. What are we going to do with ourselves for eternity? Everyone else is sleeping when we're awake."

I mute a laugh. "The same thing we always used to do, just time shifted from day to night. Not like we went out much. Why does it matter that everyone else is asleep? It's not like we constantly hung out with a huge army of friends from school."

"True." She sighs. "We are pretty lame, aren't we?"

"You guys aren't lame." Chloe snuggles against my side.

Ooh, there's win. If I'm going to be responsible for an eternal child for the rest of my existence, I'm really glad it's one young enough not to think I'm 'lame.' Not sure I could handle an older tween constantly telling how uncool I am.

"Nah," I say. "We're only lame to the Bree Swanson crowd. You know, the kind of girls who think their life's worth is measured by how many people they don't know from school show up at their house parties."

Ashley snort laughs. "Yanno, I had a little crush on her. It didn't last long though. Pretty much imploded the first time I heard her speak. The girl's so conceited and obnoxious."

"Not surprising. Anyone even remotely attracted to girls had a crush on Bree... and she knew it. Exactly why she is the way she is."

"Right." Ashley stands. "Back in a moment. Gonna get comfy."

I continue watching this movie I've seen a dozen times already. Chloe reacts to it like she's never seen it before. This is not a by-product of vampire mental issues. It's just how kids are.

Ashley returns a few minutes later, having traded her 'prom dress' for a nightgown.

We have a fairly normal almost-hour before the movie ends.

Chloe peers up at me. "I'm hungry. Can we go eat someone?"

She's so creepdorable.

I'm also impressed she didn't bite Dad or sneak off to a neighbor's house around here after he passed out.

"Sure, we have about an hour before sunrise." I get up and gently set the two dolls I'm holding back on the sofa. "Might not be the widest selection out there this close to sunrise, but I'm sure we can find someone." I take her hand.

She knows the drill. It's a bit risky to take her out of the house at this hour. Most people would think it bizarre for a kid her size to be out and about after four in the morning. We don't usually feed this late. But kids, right? They need that glass of water right before bedtime. Or glass of blood as the case may be here. Hmm. Maybe I should ask someone to teach me how to do that 'treated blood' thing so we can keep some in a bottle for times like this.

Chloe apologizes to Rebecca for not being able to bring her outside while we go eat, then stands, and places her on the sofa. "We'll be back quick." The child takes my hand and gives me an 'I'm ready to go' look.

I head for the sliding glass door in the kitchen out to the deck.

Ash follows us, barefoot in her nightgown.

"You're not going to get dressed?" I ask.

"Nah. I'm pretending to be a ghost from an old vampire movie." She tugs at the fabric.

"I didn't bite anyone here," says Chloe as we leap into the sky off the back deck.

"Good." I give her hand a little squeeze.

We definitely need to keep the supernatural stuff away from home. Can't let the neighbors see too much weird. We've gotten last-minute feedings down to a practiced science. Chloe feeds first. Either Ashley or I will hide somewhere with the kid while the other one of us goes out to lure someone into the dark alley or wherever. Then we repeat the process twice: once for me, once for Ash.

Two guys at a gas station with a pickup truck pulling a boat on a trailer make for a convenient one-stop feeding. I have no idea what it is about fishing that makes people want to wake up so damn early. Despite being a vampire, something about setting an alarm clock to 4:00 a.m. still makes me cringe.

The three of us make it home with twenty minutes to spare before sunrise.

Oh, yeah. I do check on Dad. He's still fully dressed and more 'on bed' than *in* it. Looks like Chloe physically dragged him up the stairs and threw him onto the bed next to Mom. I push past the awkwardness and take his shoes off before stuffing him under the comforter. It shouldn't feel awkward. After all, he tucked me in plenty when I was a kid.

I'm only returning the favor.

CHAPTER 8
BOY PROBLEMS

Yay weekend.

Not-Yay: Saturday is mostly over already.

What is the opposite of 'yay'? Ugh? Hmm. There's a thought to bring to my next philosophy class. Other than my phone pestering me in German every twenty minutes for an update on spectral freedom, my Saturday was pretty normal. I spent most of it with Hunter.

At the moment, I'm in the basement shower letting warm water fall on my head, replaying my afternoon in my mind. Hunter and I made a 'date' of helping his mother clean out a portion of their massive house. Three families could live in the place. Two-thirds of it is pretty much empty except for junk. Whoever she and her ex-husband bought the place from did *not* take care of it. Probably how Hunter's parents got it so cheap. One of these days, she's hoping to be able to bring in some renters. Unfortunately, the house is still nowhere near in shape to get a certificate of occupancy. She can't rent legally until it's been fixed and cleaned up.

After a few hours of that when it started to get dark, Hunter and I went to Olympia, had dinner at a bistro type place specializing in burritos, then went on this little paranormal hotel tour. Not sure what impressed me more between the size of the burritos the restaurant makes or that the supposedly haunted hotel really did have three ghosts in it.

No, I didn't get guilted into helping any of them do anything resulting in me being at war with the Forces of Evil™. One's a crotchety old man who had a heart attack while staying the night at the hotel seventy years ago. He's really possessive of his room and objects to people being there the way Mr. Niedermeyer objects to children walking on his front lawn. The other two spirits are both Native American. I couldn't talk to them due to a language issue. Got the feeling they're not terribly happy a hotel was built where it was. They didn't seem dangerous or overtly hostile, just sorta glowered at us like disapproving parents watching their kid go to college and major in philosophy.

Ghost/paranormal tours ring differently to vampires. At least ones like me who can see ghosts.

Rather than going to a place to be creeped out and scared, it's like I'm visiting a history museum where the reenactors are super good at their jobs.

When the tour ended, Hunter and I went for a walk in the woods... which turned into us having sex in the forest by a stream. Mortal me never would've dared do something like that. Having the ability to make people forget things certainly has lowered my inhibitions.

We ended the day back at Hunter's place, hanging out in his bedroom half-watching a movie and talking until he had to go to sleep because he's working tomorrow. I chickened out and didn't bring up anything about my worries concerning his being mortal. As soon as I stared into his bright hazel eyes and saw how much he is truly and completely in love with me, I caved. Even if it didn't make me super guilty to think about doing, I don't believe my vampire powers are strong enough to make him forget me. I'd need to ask Aurélie to do it. He's so into me that even *her* mind powers might not fully work. While he'd probably forget me specifically, he'd be aware of a hole in his life and stuff would happen. Bad stuff.

I suppose it's fair to say he loves me more than I love him. Not that I don't love him. I do. Just... he would choose to die rather than lose me. I could cope with erasing myself from his mind for his own protection. Sure, I'd be an emotional mess for a while. However, I wouldn't be ready to fling myself into the sun over not having him. Does that mean I don't really love him? Is this whole thing with us mercy on my part? Or have I simply come to terms with our inevitable separation at some point?

I'm a vampire. He is not.

Our relationship is going to end in one of three ways: we break up, he dies, or he goes vampire.

Oh, wait. Maybe there's an option four. Could Sophia enchant him to stop getting older? I could ask. Then again, her magic isn't exactly predictable. She could turn him into a life-sized Energizer rabbit as easily as make him immortal... and she'd have to get more soul goop. Owing demons favors isn't a thing to be taken lightly.

Nah. Can't burden her with that. My family's thumbed our collective noses at the natural order of things enough already. Don't want to keep tempting fate. There's only so long a person will put up with a fly buzzing around their head before they swat it. The Universe can't be that different. I'm a vampire. Ashley went vampire, too. Sophia's got magic. Sierra's... something. Sam cavorts with demons, plus we have an imp and a hellhound living with us. Feels like it wouldn't take much more to open the gates of catastrophe.

So, bleh. Can't ask Sophia to do anything here.

I start to dread the idea Hunter's going to seek out some other vampire to turn him. We only have a few years before it'll start to get strange. If my psyche is stuck in place, it won't matter that Hunter is Hunter twenty years from now. He'll seem old to me. Does it make me a coward to keep falling back on the 'let's just wait and see what happens' option?

Yeah, I think it does.

I don't want to hurt him. I don't want to lose him. But... losing him and hurting him feel inevitable. The more time passes, the greater the chances someone else is going to solve this problem for me, and not in a way we like. It's on me to do something. Just gotta figure out what.

And... not yet. I'm gonna give it some more time.

Ashley found her way back to the vet clinic today while I was out with Hunter. Nothing like vampire mind powers to smooth over her unexplained absence. I think she said something about making them think she had a death in the family and had to take a long trip. Pretty sure she didn't tell them the death in her family happened to be her. Speaking of which, it's super crazy Mrs. Carter isn't a mess. I suppose having Ashley around still, seemingly alive and normal, makes the idea that she technically died so abstract it doesn't set off any emotional fireworks.

Whatever desire Mrs. Carter had for grandkids, Chloe is helping with.

Yeah, we told her. I mean, the woman already knows Ashley and I are vampires. It's not like telling her widened our risk factor. Besides, having someone else around who can help us keep Chloe secret is a good thing.

Speaking of Chloe, Mom watched her today. I smile into the shower stream thinking about how happy Mom was when eleven-year-old me first helped her clean windows. No. I'm not getting maudlin even if the image of that sunny backyard through the dirty glass burns itself into my mind. I'm not really maudlin. It's my vampire brain experiencing a program code error. It's got insufficient information to run the routine it wants to run.

My good mood remains. Thinking of making Mom happy distracts me from worrying about what to do regarding Hunter. It would be easier, I think, to handle the situation if not for Ronin and Sam. Our families are connected now in more ways than just Hunter and I being a couple. Sam and Ro are thick as thieves. Sam's got three sisters and there's a big age gap between Hunter and Ronan. The two of them adore basically having a 'brother' close in age.

Okay. Enough showering and bathroom philosophy.

I cut the water, dry off, and hurry back to the bedroom. Chloe's still upstairs keeping Mom and Dad company. After throwing on a long T-shirt, I unbundle my hair from the towel and sit on the edge of my bed, bent forward, working the blow dryer.

The bed shifts a few minutes later, scaring the ever-loving hell out of me. I jump up, half yelping, half snarling. Ashley's sitting next to me, leaning back, wide eyed and raising her arms to defend her face from my claws.

Crap. I turn off the blow dryer. "Sorry. You startled me."

"Apparently..." She whistles. "Guess you didn't hear me walk in with that thing running."

"Nope." I sigh out my nose. When using a blow-dryer—or any sort of machine like that—a vampire has to turn down our hearing or we'll cause damage. I also didn't see her with my hair draped around my face. "Sorry."

"It's okay. My fault."

Thankfully, neither one of us ever got into the habit of prank scaring each other. She didn't try to 'get' me.

"How'd it go at the vet place?" I ask.

"Fine. Gonna pretend to work there sometimes." She grins.

She's not doing it for the money, though she'll totally take it. She's doing it to help animals.

I notice an odd scent on her. An unfamiliar person. "Who do I smell?"

"Benjamin."

"Who is that?"

"Met him at the clinic. He brought in a sick ferret. We hooked up after I left the clinic." Ashley examines her fingernails. A little more pink than usual in her cheeks tells me they went all the way.

"Wow. On the first date?" I whistle. "Naughty."

Ashley laughs. "We didn't date. Just a hook up."

"Umm. Really?" I bite my lip. "That's a bit unusual for you."

"Yes. It is. But..." She extends her fangs. "I'm a bit more unusual now. It's not a great idea to get involved with a mortal."

I sigh, hard.

"Oops." She winces. "Sorry."

"No, you're right." I let my hair dryer thud to the carpet, then flop back across the bed, staring at the ceiling. "I just don't know what to do about Hunter."

"If you really love him, give him the Transference." Ashley

pounces on me and pretend-bites my neck, then hovers up to look me in the eye. "Or let him go."

"I dunno... Ro and Sam are like brothers. Be kinda weird if I broke up with Hunter." I cringe. "It would be equally weird to give him the Transference. I think that would make me feel more like his mom than his girlfriend."

Ashley rolls off me and sits up. "You're over him?"

"No. That's not what I mean." I grumble. "Just, it feels like every choice I make is the wrong one. I'm just being a chicken and putting off committing to anything for now. Wait, I take that back. I'm committing to being a chicken."

She laughs.

"So..." I roll onto my side, facing her. "How'd it go with Benjamin? Is his ferret okay?"

"It wasn't bad. Surprisingly large. Not what I expec—" She blinks. "Oh, you meant the actual ferret."

I stare at her.

Ashley giggle-snorts. She totally said that on purpose. She knew exactly what I meant. "Yeah, the little fuzzy guy basically has a cold. Doc gave him some meds."

"Cool. So, you had fun on your hook up?" I smile.

"Yeah. He's nice. Really mellow. Kind of a sensitive type guy. Has three ferrets, a guinea pig, and two cats. Maybe he's a bit too into smoking weed for me. Talking to him is like being on a Zoom call with someone in Australia. There's almost a three second delay."

I laugh.

She overacts pouting. "I'd have wanted to keep dating him if I was still normal. Figures I find a decent guy after I die."

"Hah. Ash, you were never normal." I stick my tongue out at her. "Neither was I."

"Can't argue that." She goes cross-eyed. "What kind of dork shows up to school in her new unicorn PJs thinking they're cool and amazing."

Oh wow. I remember that. We were in sixth grade. Most of the other kids laughed at her. Honestly, it was funny. She didn't take it too badly, though. Not like it left mental scars, though she never went that over the top again. Pajama pants, sure. Lots of us did that. Full on unicorn hooded top? Not so much.

The remainder of our Saturday night goes by in a flash of talking about crazy stuff that happened at school, crazy stuff that happened in vampire society, watching anime, and being general goofballs. For a few wonderful hours, I feel completely normal... like we're still in the midst of our senior year.

Okay, maybe freshman year. The giggling is a bit epic.

CHAPTER 9
A SERIOUS DOWNGRADE IN ACCOMMODATIONS

I wake up. It's Sunday... and it's raining like hell.

This is one of those cold September rainy days where if it happened to be Monday, the temptation to call out of work and stay in bed for an extra four hours would've been near impossible to resist. Good thing for me I don't have a job. I don't bother moving for a while, surrendering to the warm coziness of my bed.

Can't really enjoy it while I'm sleeping. Then again, mortals don't enjoy their beds while asleep either, so I'm not so different from normal.

At some point, I become aware of a tiny voice. Curiosity needles at me until I open my eyes.

Chloe's sitting over in her corner of the room by the dollhouse, having a tea party with the eight haunted dolls, two Barbies, a teddy bear, and one of Ashley's plush unicorns. It's totally unintentional, but the big-eyed expression on the unicorn stuffie is giving off a 'get me out of here' vibe.

Yanno, it's totally normal for a vampire to have haunted dolls in her room. We're like a rainbow pink version of the Addams Family or something. A moment later, Ashley pushes herself up off the bed, lifting her face out of the pillow. Her hair is a wild tangle. One of her eyes is closed, the other half lidded. Her mouth's stuck partially open. She looks like she just got hit over the head with a shovel and doesn't realize what happened.

"Girl, you sleep *hard*," I say.

She stares vacantly at me for a few seconds before closing her mouth, then trying to dry swallow a few times. "Ugh. Need water."

"You okay?" I ask.

She crawls off the bed making zombie noises and continues crawling out of the room into the basement.

Yes, she's totally overacting.

Sophia breezes in without knocking. She's in mid-stride toward me when she stops abruptly and peers to her left at Chloe. "Oh, that explains it."

"Explains what?" I ask.

My kid sister hurries the rest of the way over, sits on the edge of the bed, swipes her hair off her face, then clasps her hands in her lap. "Super crazy dream. I was having a tea party with dolls in the back-yard. Lots of wind, falling leaves. October vibes. And the dolls were alive."

"They wanted to say hello," chimes Chloe. "Mary says you host excellent tea parties."

Sophia makes this face like she really wants to scream but holds it in.

"Do you need a hug because of a scary dream?" I ask in as serious a tone as possible, so she knows I'm not trying to make fun of her.

"I don't, but I'll never say no to a hug." She pounces. After the squeeze, she sits back and grins at me. "Anyway, I figured out how to set that ghost in your phone free."

"*Wunderbar!*" shouts my iPhone.

Whoa. I raise both eyebrows. "Really? How dangerous is it going to be?"

"Not too bad." She holds up two fingers. "We need two things: a cheap electronic device we can destroy without guilt and either a bucket of lava or super strong acid."

"*Sie müssen scherzen*," moans my phone.

"Umm. I don't think they're going to have that on Amazon, even with Prime."

Sophia laughs. "Right. That's the hard part. I didn't say it would be easy. Just not dangerous."

I feel her forehead for a fever. "Handling a 'bucket of lava' is dangerous."

"Only if we're not careful." She twirls some of her blonde hair around her fingers, unwinds it, then re-twirls. "I consider danger when someone else is trying to hurt us."

"Right." I exhale. "I don't even know where to begin looking for lava. Or acid. Why do we need those?"

Sophia makes a dunking gesture. "The ghost is trapped being attached to an electronic device. It's just a ghost thing. Sometimes they get attached to stuff like that. He's so convinced he's stuck there, he's stuck there. No amount of talking will change his mind. It's too programmed into his mind. I'm guessing you don't want to melt down your iPhone, so we'll need some old electronic thing I can transfer him to that no one will care about. Once the ghost is in it, we toss it in the lava, and I throw a little magic at it. When the device is entirely destroyed, he'll be free."

"*Mein Gott!*" yells my phone. "*Das kann nicht dein Ernst sein. Bitte sprechen Sie dieses kleine Mädchen zur Vernunft.*"

"Hmm. Why electronics?" I reach over and grab the phone off my nightstand. The screen is already open to the translation app. He thinks she's crazy and wants me to talk some sense into her.

Sophia keeps twisting her hair around her finger. "I'm not really sure why it's his thing, but it's his thing. Maybe because when he died, he collapsed over a desk lamp. Ghosts kinda feed on electricity though."

"Hmm." I examine my phone's battery indicator. "Is that why it's draining so fast?"

"No, you have an iPhone," says Sophia. "The older they get, the faster the batteries go down to make you have to buy a new phone."

I laugh. "Someone's been talking to Dad about phones."

She beams. "Is it true? Or does Dad just like to poop on Apple products?"

"Well, he certainly prefers PC to Mac." I rub my chin. "Not sure if it's true."

"*Schau auf den Bildschirm*," says the phone.

"What?" I glance down to see the translation app reading 'look at the screen.' "Okay, I'm looking."

The text deletes and retypes to 'will it hurt?'

I show the screen to Sophia.

"No. You are a ghost." She glances to her left at the dolls, shivering ever so slightly. "You only feel pain if you want to."

"Dad's got a whole bunch of ancient cell phones in a box." I tap my foot on air. "Every cell phone he ever used in his life, he still has. Don't think he's going to let us destroy one though. He's sentimentally attached."

Sophia holds her hand out like a surgeon waiting for an assistant to hand her a scalpel. Seconds later, Klepto appears in a violet flash standing on her arm. The kitten drops an old, grey, Motorola flip phone in her hand, then scurries back as if repelled by the device. I'm about to make a comment about the cat being a technology elitist but it's not the age of the phone she's recoiling from. It stinks of garbage, like it had been soaking in the nasty water that dribbles out of a garbage truck.

The look on my sister's face is priceless. She clearly was not expecting to touch something that's been buried in a landfill. This is the same building expression of disgust as she got the time she stepped barefoot in dog poop at Nicole's house.

"Eww," deadpans Sophia, frozen statue still.

"Mew." Klepto snorts.

"I know I asked you to grab something no one would miss, but I did not tell you to raid a garbage dump. This is not my fault." Sophia gags.

I chuckle. "Well, that is definitely a phone no one will miss."

"Does it still work?" asks Sophia.

The kitten makes a noise halfway between purr and meow. I imagine her saying 'how should I know? I'm a cat.'

"Eww." Sophia gingerly picks up the phone and opens the bottom flip part to expose the well-worn plastic buttons. She makes a face of determination at it... and the screen lights up green. It's a tiny screen, only one strip of backlit LED similar to an old calculator. "Okay, it works. Just needed some power."

I stare at her. "Did you just charge a cell phone with magic?"

"I did. It's an easy spell. I use it all the time on my phone." She beams. "I don't even remember the last time I plugged it in."

"Okay, so now what?"

"We transfer the ghost into this, then figure out where we can find lava or something like it." Sophia nods once. "We can't just smash the phone. It has to be destroyed completely. Like melted into nothing."

"That's going to be a challenge." I rub my chin. "I think there's a steel mill in Seattle somewhere. Could we drop the phone into molten steel?"

"Yeah, that should work." Sophia jumps, staring to the left. "Umm. Eep. Are they mad at me?"

I notice most of the dolls have turned their heads to look at Sophia.

"No." Chloe looks over at us. "They're just listening. Not mad at you. They like having company."

Sophia grits her teeth at me. She's clearly pretending not to be scared so the dolls don't get mad. "Umm. Okay. Let me do this..."

I hold my iPhone out. Sophia lets the old Motorola sit atop her left palm while hovering her right hand over my phone. Tension climbs up the muscles in my back. She's nervous because of the dolls and trying to use magic. Calamity is about to occur. With luck, she won't turn our home upside down—literally. The walls of my room sway and wobble like I'm living inside an inflatable bounce house that's rapidly losing air. Chloe, the dolls, the dollhouse, and a few random items from my computer desk float into the air.

"Umm. Is this supposed to be happening?" asks Chloe.

"I don't know."

For a brief moment, my computer screen shows the image of a desolate grey landscape full of scorched trees, like a forest after a bad fire swept through. A huge mass of black fur appears close, as if my monitor was a window to another world. Eep. It's Fuzzydoom. He's about ten times the size of the 'opening' so can't fit through, but he's looking at us. Since he's an entirely featureless puffball without eyes, it's impossible to tell if he's like 'oh, hi guys, what's up' or trying to give us a sense of 'I'm coming for you.'

Sophia's expression falters, like she's having a scary dream.

The computer monitor goes back to normal. An unintelligible stream of German muttering comes from somewhere between the two phones. Can't tell which device is making the sound. Maybe both.

After a bright flash, we're floating somewhere outside, surrounded by a vast swath of rolling plains grass. Me, Sophia, Chloe, and all eight dolls are hovering in midair, three feet off the ground in a sunny meadow. A duck the size of a garbage truck walks by in the distance. He's completely unimpressed with our existence. Whoa... this is tweaked.

Flash.

We're back in the bedroom. Chloe sucks in a breath to scream, but doesn't make a sound upon realizing we're home again. She glares at us with a 'don't do that again' sort of face, then goes back to her tea party.

Sophia keeps concentrating. A few seconds after our reappearance in the room, an intangible 'snap' happens. It's neither a sound nor a flash, more of a feeling like something broke loose. A sense of power bursting outward follows, then quiet.

A muted scream, like the German ghost is really far away, starts on my right side and rapidly yanks to the left. For another minute, Sophia remains still and silent, eyes closed. Finally, she lets a breath out and opens her eyes. She seems tired.

"Did it work?" I whisper.

"Yeah."

I look around. "What was up with the meadow thing?"

She grumbles. "There's a demon messing with us."

"Right. Almost forgot." I blink. "Explain the giant duck."

Sophia smirks. "Autocorrect. I'm working with cell phones."

It takes me a second to do the math. "You thought a dirty word?"

"Don't tell Mom. That demon tried to mess up my concentration." She frowns. "I think I won. And thinking it isn't as bad as saying it."

"Ghost?" I glance between the phones. "Are you still here?"

"*Ja*," says the old phone. "*Hier drin riecht es wie auf einer Müllhalde. Bitte beeilen Sie sich und werfen Sie dieses Ding in die Lava.*"

"What did he say?" Sophia cringes away from the old phone. "Wow, it smells."

"He's probably saying the same thing. As bad as it stinks to us, imagine being inside it."

She gags.

"Right." I look around for a disposable baggie or something to put the contaminated Motorola in. "Now all I have to do is come up with a way to destroy this phone completely and you'll be free."

"Yep." Sophia nods once, then grimaces. "We may have a slight problem."

"Uh oh. Figured." I grasp her clean hand. "What happened?"

"A bit of magic went stray at the end there. I'm not sure what it did or where it went." She bites her lower lip, guilt wafting from her.

"Oh..." I wince internally. "I'm sure we'll find out."

CHAPTER 10
BEING NORMAL... SORTA

Monday.

Yay... not.

So, I decided to do it. I'm back in class... because why not. Year two at Seattle Central College. It helps the 'rents feel normal. Guess it helps me feel normal, too. Also, due to my age when I became a vampire, it just kinda feels natural to be in school. Ugh. This is *really* going to suck if I spend the rest of eternity with a compulsion to feel like I'm doing something wrong if I am not attending classes of some kind.

Least I can do is put in the four years to make Mom and Dad happy, then I'll get my lazy on. I did, however, swap majors. Since I couldn't decide on anything, I ended up going liberal arts. Also, it's not like any degree I may get is ever going to help me with legitimate career prospects. I'm never going to work a normal job, at least nothing more involved than delivering pizzas or slinging coffee if I get bored. I don't need to work. Thanks to the leprechaun—yes, I said leprechaun—I've got enough money in the bank to live on for a long, long time as long as I continue to lead a sane, ordinary life, never go out, and don't pee it away on bullcrap like needlessly expensive televisions.

Lucky for me, I am just the kind of geeky introvert to have no problem with that lifestyle.

Yep. Liberal arts. Go ahead and laugh. I know it's useless for getting a real job. Jokes on the haters, though. I'm not trying to get a real job. The two best ways to light money on fire are to buy Twitter or get a liberal arts degree, and option two is much cheaper.

I'm being adventurous this year, too. Two of my classes start at 3:00 p.m. Thanks to those morons chaining me to a tree and trying to kill me with sunrise, my Innocent ability to tolerate sunlight experienced the equivalent of a training montage in one of Dad's Eighties movies. In five minutes, I went from a useless newbie to the second coming of Neo. Well, something like that. It was more than five minutes. Felt like fifty days of agony. Also, being able to withstand some sun is hardly going to kick anyone's ass or make me a powerful force of nature.

The worst part about signing up for classes that start at three in the afternoon is, on the best days, I'll have approximately thirty minutes to get to campus after I wake up. Seems 2:30 p.m. is the absolute earliest my body will regain consciousness in the absence of provocation. Going from my bed to a classroom at SCC in thirty minutes is not exactly reasonable. It's not that physically far away from home, but traffic can seriously suck. Obviously, there's not going to be any flying for me in the afternoon.

Time for cheating.

Blix has agreed to help me out twice a week, pulling me through the mirrorverse. I figure despite the potential risks of being on the other side, a two-minute walk is going to be significantly safer than trying to drive to SCC fast enough to avoid being late for class. That, and whatever dangers may lurk behind the mirror would only hurt me. Driving like an idiot can hurt other people. Heck, Ronan's been going back and forth through the mirror for over a year now without too many problems. Okay, so he almost ended up paralyzed by demonic poison for several decades, but he got better.

Also, I'm not a curious nine-year-old boy. If I see a giant, glistening slug covered in needles, I am running the other way.

Danger and inconvenience aside, I'm going to try the afternoon class thing this year. My two early classes are art history on Tuesdays from three to six and chemistry on Thursdays. This year's schedule has no classes on Friday. Yes, I did that on purpose. Since I'm coasting with the liberal arts thing, I might as well go full slacker with permanent three-day weekends. Not sure what's worse... that some people who aren't vampires with no need to prepare for a career actually pursue a liberal arts major—or that society thinks less of them for it. How much different would things be in the world if people could learn about stuff without the pressure to study something *useful* to a career?

Like, from the moment kids first set foot in school, we're basically a lump of clay the educational machinery is processing into a member of the workforce. We're not encouraged to study what we love or what we find interesting; we're force-fed a generic one-size-fits-all learning plan that tries to get us ready for the next fifty years of nine-to-five. And then, once we're all washed up and too dried out to work anymore, the government tries to take away our benefits.

Ugh. I've been talking to Dad too much. He's a big fan of George Carlin.

Maybe I should major in philosophy... not like I need a job.

So, anyway. Here I am back at Seattle Central College. I'm even wearing an SCC sweatshirt. No reason other than it's three sizes too big for me and looked comfortable. Never been one of those 'school spirit' people. Not one of the kids who hated school either, but it just never clicked with me to be thrilled about a place we're required to go. Like sports. I do not understand how some people get so wound up in a particular pro sports team.

Tonight, my journey into the liberal arts begins.

Monday night is reasonably tame. The class is plainly titled 'Writing.' It's more or less focused on professional writing, nothing creative. I figure by the end of the semester I'll know how to send an email and not sound like an idiot. Most of the other people in this night class are much older than me. One downside to night school is being the youngest in the room. All the normal kids my age—who are going to college—take morning classes. Not that big a deal. I didn't come to school to socialize, make friends, or anything like that.

The teacher, Vivian Black, looks like a character from a movie. She's older, at least fifty, with wild Einstein white hair, huge glasses, and a fondness for oversized denim button-down shirts she wears like jackets over her normal clothes. Vivian is on the shorter side, a little heavyset, and full of energy. This is the perfect person to teach a class on how to write business emails... not. Why do I feel like I forgot to pick my wand up before arriving here? She could totally be a teacher at Hogwarts.

We're treated to a twenty-ish minute presentation on how writing is cool and not as boring as everyone in here thinks it will be. Her enthusiasm is entertaining at least, even if the subject matter is going to be dry.

My mind wanders, tuning out the useless motivational pep talk type stuff. This isn't course material I need to pay attention to; she's just trying to reassure us we won't hate the class. On the subject of school, Ashley—likely following my example—has decided to keep going to school as well. She spent the remainder of her post-vampire summer talking about being lazy and not bothering. Mrs. Carter isn't exactly loaded with cash. I mean, my parents aren't rich with disposable income either, but I have two of them and they both work. I suspect Mrs. C earns less than either my Dad or Mom individually, so paying for college isn't a triviality to her.

Enter the leprechaun.

Ooh, now there's a title for a crazy movie. Imagine a kung-fu movie that tries to take itself totally seriously, but the main character is a leprechaun instead of Bruce Lee. Anyway, we talked to Mrs. C about it and I'm covering the tuition for Ashley right now. It's not like she's going to Harvard or anything. Still, she may or may not end up finishing. Even if she does, she is now in the same boat I am. Vampires don't need jobs. The ones—like Professor Heath—who have them do it for fun. Of course, in his case, he happened to be a college professor before joining the ranks of the undead.

Ashley modified her goal slightly. She no longer wants to be a veterinarian. I mean, she kinda does in a way. Unfortunately, being an actual doctor-veterinarian tends to put you in the spotlight at the clinic. People notice you more. It would make it difficult for her to come and go, disappear, and so on. Now, her focus is on becoming a vet tech since it will let her help animals without becoming the focus of everyone's attention. She can spend a few years at a clinic before extricating herself and going to a different clinic. If she's going to be out in public, she can't stay at the same place too long or it'll get weird.

I'd say Innocent vampires have that one downside of looking younger than we are, which makes our agelessness more obvious. However, it's not entirely the fault of our vampire type. It's a combination of it plus being actual teenagers when the Transference happened. Like if we were thirty when it happened, we wouldn't have ended up looking like high school freshmen... just I guess, 'cute.' Like some women are hot. Vampire women tend to fall into that category. Other women are really pretty but no one calls them 'hot.' They get called things like 'adorable' or 'cute' or 'girl next door'.

Meh. Either way, as young as we look, it's not so easy to keep showing up at a workplace year after year before the normals there start asking questions. Though, with her charm ability, she can probably make the other people at the clinic disregard her eternal youth. Maybe she'll do that.

Eep! Professor Black's left the motivational speech behind and is now talking about real class stuff. Better pay attention... if I can hear her over the war going on in the gut of the dude sitting in the row next to me on my left.

Tonight, we learn about the fundamentals of professional writing. Did you know that the purpose of writing was to communicate ideas? Gee. I had no idea. Glad I'm taking this class.

Sounds thrilling... not.

CHAPTER II

A NORMAL KIND OF WEIRD

I

t never occurred to me that magic was real until Sophia started using it.

Thinking back on last year, I almost wonder if people who seem normal might be doing magic even if they aren't intending to. Example: Dr. Chelsea Mercer, the calculus teacher. She seemingly had the power to make time slow down.

Vivian Black must have magic, too... in the other direction. Despite the subject matter being relatively boring, the three-hour-long class period shot by fast. The woman also teaches classes here on creative writing, literature analysis, advanced English, and some other things. I get the feeling this basic writing course is her 'gotta teach it because I'm required to' type class. Still, she somehow brings passion to the driest of dry topics.

Then again, some people are passionate about the mating habits of the common Pacific Northwest wood louse. People can be weird, all right.

Speaking of weird, time to go home.

These seven-to-ten classes are great. I can fly in and fly home. Don't have to muck around with annoying trivialities like roads, cars, speed limits, and traffic. It's so crazy to think about how badly I wanted the ability to drive when I was a little younger. Now that I have it, it's kinda meh. The only time driving is preferable is in a heavy rain. Though, considering where I live, it's not an uncommon situation.

You'd think what with me being immortal, there wouldn't be a desire to rush home as fast as possible. Or rush anywhere, really. I've got all the time in the world, so why hurry? Well, for one thing, going from SCC to home doesn't offer any new scenery worth appreciating. Also, I'm still in that mode where I want to have as much time as possible with my family while I can. Yeah, I know, tragically lame. Modern teenagers aren't supposed to want to spend time at home with their parents and siblings. If I wasn't a vampire, I'd be well on the path to growing old by myself with forty-three cats.

Then again, if I wasn't a vampire, I don't think I'd be quite so clingy with the fam. There's nothing like death to make a girl rearrange her priorities.

Yeah, Ashley's right. One semester at USC probably would've broken my limit for homesickness, but I'd still be fairly normal otherwise... looking to move out, get my own place, proverbial gaze toward the future and so on.

Can't complain though. I'm still looking toward my future, even if it is kind of *Groundhog Day*. Well, I think it would be more accurate to say I'm not *dreading* my distant future rather than looking forward to my future. As a vampire, my 'future' is more of the same. I'm already in the future. Little about my existence is going to change. I do not have to dread getting old, getting sick, ending up unemployed, or suffering any of the million different ways life can stink for mortals.

Unlife has plenty of ways to stink for vampires, too... but at least they're more manageable than the unstoppable march of time.

I've gotten into the habit of looking around the area when arriving home, just to make sure nothing crazy is going on... or any suspicious people are casing my house. Could be vampire hunters, rival vampires, demons, or overly motivated Jehovah Witnesses who *really* want to give me that damned literature. Would it be unethical of me to give those door-to-door people a mental compulsion to leave that cult? Does it count as saving them or coercing them?

Anyway... things look normal, except for a strange mood.

Know that opening scene in a haunted house movie where the camera pans over a normal neighborhood and everything seems fine... until they reach the house where the movie is set? Just *looking* at it, there's a creepy 'something is definitely wrong here' vibe. Yeah... my house is *that* house tonight.

I haven't been a vampire long enough to know for sure if the creepiness is my imagination or if I'm really picking up on some supernatural vibes. Hmm. Sophia's magic kinda got away from her a little the other night. Maybe she enchanted the house by accident. Am I going to walk in the door to find a bunch of ghosts having a party?

One way to find out.

As usual, I circle around and come in for a landing on the back deck. The kitchen is dark. Flickering light leaks down the hall from the living room. My ears tell me the parents are watching TV... or at least they have the television on to fill sound space while they do other things.

I head inside, leave my backpack on the table, and meander down the hall to the living room.

Sure enough, the 'rents are on the sofa. Both have their laptops going, not paying too much attention to the news on the screen. Can't help but get the feeling they're both a bit tense. Nervous even.

"Hey, I'm back," I say.

"Hope you flew safely," says Dad.

"How was class?" asks Mom.

"Yes, and fine. Strangely engaging." I fold my arms.

Dad peers away from his laptop screen to look at me. "Strange?"

"Yeah. It's a class on professional writing... like how to write emails and stuff. I figured it would be pretty boring, but the teacher's eccentric."

Mom chuckles. "Writing and-or English teachers usually are a bit eccentric. You'd almost have to be."

"What makes you say that, hon?" Dad glances over at her. "Perfectly sane people can teach English."

My mother spends a moment tapping at her laptop keyboard, then, as if reading from the page, says, "Buffalo buffalo Buffalo buffalo buffalo buffalo Buffalo buffalo."

Dad simply stares.

"Uhh, what?" I ask.

Mom gestures at the screen. "The word buffalo eight times is a grammatically correct sentence in English. Some of them are nouns for the animal. Some are adjectival proper nouns referring to the city of Buffalo—as in a buffalo from Buffalo. And some are verbs, as in 'to buffalo' meaning to harass or confuse."

A moment passes in awkward silence, then Dad nods once. "I concede. Anyone who immediately makes sense of that, and in fact enjoys discussing such things, has got to be eccentric."

"Guys?" I ask.

The 'rents look at me.

"I get the feeling you're both nervous or anxious about something. Can I help?"

They shift their gazes to each other, make pensive faces, then seem confused.

"I'm not sure." Mom fidgets. "I thought it was just leftover anxiety from what happened at work. Honestly, I have no idea why I feel anxious."

Dad twists to his right, peering down the corridor to the kitchen. "Did we leave the stove on?"

"Nope." I shake my head. "It's off."

He sighs. "Good question. Feels like I'm sitting in a conference room with the rest of the technology team wondering which three of us are getting laid off when the manager walks in."

"So, 'this is going to suck' fear mixed with a heap of anxiety about the future, not mortal terror," I say.

"Yeah. Something like that." Dad rubs his chin while gazing around the living room. "Is it the thing in the grill? Or are the hairs on the back of my neck standing up purely because your siblings have been so quiet for the past few hours?"

Considering there is a demon threatening my family, I bend my promise a little and peek at the tip of my parent's brains. If something is messing with them, they might not be able to tell me. Looks like both are suffering generalized anxiety without an apparent cause, like some sort of primordial holdover from the days when humans lived in the wild and had to be on guard for danger. Mom and Dad are both feeling like a couple of caribou who know a lion's nearby but not exactly where it is or if it will strike.

Considering I felt something weird on the house from the air, it's probably that.

"Got a weird vibe from the house just now when I flew in." I set my hands on my hips like a cleaning lady determined to go hunt down a mess. "There's a definite mood in the air from something."

"Can you fix it?" asks Mom.

"Not sure what *it* is yet." I smirk.

"Isn't that a Stephen King book?" Dad tilts his head.

"Hah." I grab a small pillow and ninja-star toss it at him. "Technically correct to what I said but not what I meant."

"English is confusing." Mom holds up one finger. "Sometimes, I think the people who invented the language made it purposefully ambiguous."

Dad reclines, smiling. "I dunno. People who get too wrapped up in the finer points of language miss the point. Language evolves. No one today says 'groovy' or 'gnarly.' In fifteen or twenty years, no one will say 'yeet' or 'cringe.'"

I roll my eyes. "Dad, 'yeet' and 'cringe' are already dead."

He blinks. "Really? That didn't take long. The speed of evolution is increasing. Soon we'll just be communicating in chat emojis."

Mom laughs, though it's a nervous sort of laugh like her boss told a lame joke she has to laugh at for office politics reasons. It's not Dad's lameness. It's the weird energy.

"Right. Let me figure out what's going on here..." I head for the stairs.

"Sarah, shoes in the house?" calls Mom.

"It's fine. I'm levitating." I glide up to the second floor.

Mom doesn't object to the existence of shoes as much as she

doesn't want people tracking 'outside germs' all over the carpet. Sophia's the one who thinks shoes are a crime against humanity. She must get that from Mom's older sister Jody. The woman's basically a modern-day hippie: pyramid power, healing crystals, copious amounts of weed, and of course, she goes barefoot everywhere.

The sense of creepy otherness doesn't get stronger when I go upstairs. Good sign.

One by one, I peek into my siblings' rooms, trying to be stealthy and unnoticed. Sophia's sitting on her bed reading a Kindle. All seems fine here. I move farther down the hall and peek into Sierra's room. She's sitting at her desk staring at the computer screen. It's on the desktop, not a paused video game. Something's not right here.

I lightly knock, then step in.

Sierra glances back at me. For an instant, the panic of 'crap, need an excuse' flickers across her eyes until she realizes it's me walking in and not Mom or Dad. Her expression and posture shift; she's obviously relieved I'm here but too proud to outwardly act like something scared her. Not sure when I got so good at reading body language. Must be a vampire thing. Comes in handy to analyze prey, right?

"What's wrong?" I ask, not giving her the chance to deny anything is.

"Umm." Sierra hesitates a moment, then waves for me to come closer so she can whisper.

I glide over and sit on the corner of her desk, still keeping my shoes off the carpet.

"All day at school, I kept seeing a man with a gun out of the corner of my eye." She pulls her legs up, heels on the front edge of the chair, half hiding her face behind her jean-covered knees. "Whenever I looked directly at him, he'd disappear. I dunno if I've finally cracked, if the dude was real, or what."

I bite my lower lip. Our family doesn't have any history of mental problems on the order of hallucinations, at least. While anyone would be worried about school shootings nowadays, Sierra is, for some reason, extra sensitive to it. Something about the drills her school ran left mental scars not significantly weaker than if an actual shooter attacked her school. I'm not sure those drills do more good than harm to be honest. I can't think of any reason for her to be so affected by the idea of a school shooter so much more so than any other kid. Not like she lived through a shooting or anything even remotely scary happened at the middle school.

Then again, Sophia's terrified of a giant black pom-pom. Logic isn't a requirement for a kid to be scared of something.

"Can you look?" whispers Sierra. "I wanna know if I'm going crazy or maybe having a psychic thing."

"A psychic thing?" I raise an eyebrow.

"Yeah. Like I'm seeing something that's going to happen before it does." She shivers.

I slip down from the desk, kneel beside her chair, and stare into her eyes. Sierra is wondering how to handle seeing a future event. Like, would she get in trouble or thought of as crazy if she tried to warn people? Or, if she kept quiet so she didn't get thought of as a crazy kid, how guilty would she feel over anyone who got hurt because she didn't warn them. It's not like anyone would believe her claim of having a precognitive vision. They might even misinterpret her as threatening to do the shooting herself.

Digging a bit deeper, I grab for recent memories from earlier today.

Looks like she had a reasonably normal day at school. However, an apparition appears in her periphery here and there. It's human shaped but indistinct, like one of those shadow people you see on ghost hunter videos. Yeah, it does kinda look like a guy with a handgun and a baseball cap on, at least in terms of silhouette. There are no facial features to recognize. No suggestion of ethnicity or age beyond 'definitely not a child' based on his height.

It is difficult for me to tell the difference between hallucinations and things people saw for real. That's the problem with hallucinations. The person really believes they saw the thing. Seems this shadow gunman followed Sierra around the school all day long. She first noticed him in the parking lot while walking from the bus to the front door. The more I see of it, the more concerned I become of her imagination running away with itself and blossoming into a legitimate mental concern... until I notice another girl react to the shadow.

The moment happens during lunch. Sierra's in the cafeteria, trying to eat food she's not interested in touching due to her anxiety. Poor kid's been on edge all day, expecting the shooting to start at any second. A shadowy gunman figure appears in the darkened doorway leading to an atrium just outside the cafeteria. I remember the room, since I went to the same school at her age. It's where the administration puts all the trophy cases for the sports teams, sorta like a central hub between all three hallways of the main school building.

A younger girl—who's probably in fifth grade—two tables away from where Sierra's sitting startles visibly, gawking at the apparition. The kid seems about ready to scream when the 'man' disappears. She looks around, realizes no one else is reacting to what she thought she saw, then nervously resumes eating her lunch while remaining fixated on the doorway.

Sierra did not consciously notice the other kid's reaction. She'd been too focused on the 'shooter.'

Memory editing isn't always about content. I can shift contrast too. It's like tweaking the settings on a TV so the picture gets brighter or darker but the image (memory) doesn't change. A few mental tweaks allow Sierra to realize someone else saw the guy. That done, I drop my connection to her brain.

"You're not nuts." I give her hand a squeeze. "That other kid saw it too. What you saw is definitely not a real guy, though."

Sierra's fear implodes to rage. The last time she had this look on her face, she got grounded off the PlayStation for two whole weeks because she screamed an F-bomb until her lungs ran out of air. It would have been a month, but Dad sympathized with her. Something about he knows how it feels to have tried to do something in a video game like a hundred times, failing over and over again, then come really super close to doing it only for something 'cheap' to happen at the last second and make it fail again.

At the moment, she does not request another grounding.

By that, I mean she doesn't yell bad words.

"Was it the barbecue demon?" she grumbles.

I almost laugh. It's pretty damn difficult to find humor anywhere after being saturated in the topic of school shootings. However, the idea of the former sefil being forever known as 'the barbecue demon' is almost worth a chuckle. Such a silly title would surely piss him off.

"Can't say for sure beyond guessing, but probably." I let a long, slow breath leak out of my nostrils. "Unless you ended up getting on the bad side of some other demon recently."

"Just my math teacher." She frowns.

"Your math teacher is not a demon."

Sierra folds her arms. "I'm not so sure of that. Who, other than a demon, would take such great delight in tormenting children?"

"Not every demon is bad." I pat her hand.

"Hashtag 'not all demons'" She rolls her eyes, then ends up almost smiling.

"Seriously though, how is she tormenting kids?"

Sierra gives me this flat look. "She makes us do math."

"Oh, the horror." I sit back on the floor, relieved she's not having a mental issue. "Do you struggle with math or just not like it?"

"Doesn't matter." Sierra rolls her eyes. "I don't care if I struggle with it because I don't like it or if I don't like it because I struggle with it. I'm not going to start liking it."

I point a thumb at her computer. "If you want to get into a career making video games, you're going to need to love math."

Sierra makes a face at me like I just suggested she eat raw broccoli.

"This might be playing with fire to suggest. However, if you're more afraid of the demon than what might happen, you could always ask Sophia for a protective ward."

Sierra leans her head to the left, then the right, then the left again. "Mmm. Maybe. She's getting better at stuff like that. Things only get out of control when she's trying to actively *do* something. Defensive magic is easier... or so she says."

"Cool." I smile. "And hey, back to the math thing, you don't necessarily have to be a programmer." I point at one of the sketch pads on her desk. "There's always making the artwork used in video games. Someone's gotta create the backgrounds, the levels, and the character models. I don't *think* the digital artists need to be math geniuses. That's really for the people who develop the game engines."

"Ooh." She perks up, like she totally just forgot all about her scary day at school. "That's an idea!"

I keep her company for a bit, talking about video game stuff and art. Up until now, she's doodled here and there. She likes artistic stuff, though hasn't really taken it seriously. Her desire to be a video game designer kept smashing face first into her fear and hatred of math. Now that I've blasted a hole in that brick wall with the idea she could be part of video game creation in a way that wouldn't require her to be a math geek, she might pour herself into practicing art some more.

Or... she could get bored with it within a week. Who knows?

Doesn't matter, really. As long as she's happy and not constantly stressing out.

Once she decides it's time to get ready for bed—before Mom comes up here to pester her about it—I pop over to Sam's room. My brother, Ronan, and Blix are totally absorbed in the PlayStation, unaware of any unnatural creepiness in the house—or the time. I don't feel like being TimeCop or Mom right now, so I leave unnoticed and head downstairs, stopping in the kitchen long enough to remove my shoes and leave them on the shelf by the door.

Yes, I've migrated my shoes mostly to the kitchen shelf since I tend to go out via the backyard more often than the front door lately. Light's coming from Ashley's bedroom, so she must be in there. Also, since light is visible, the door must be open, which means she's doing something innocent like reading or playing a game on the computer.

I walk into my room. Everything looks fine. Chloe's sitting on the floor in the back left corner by the dollhouse and Barbie stuff. She's got the eight visiting dolls plus a teddy bear arranged around a pink plastic table, yet again doing the tea party thing. Five of those dolls turn their heads to look at me.

Oh. Duh. I almost forgot about them being here. That explains the unearthly vibe saturating the house. Sophia's doing her best to ignore it despite being frightened, because she knows what it is and isn't worried they will cause harm. Sierra had another issue to be anxious about. She might not have even noticed the paranormal energy, though I'm sure it made her anxiety worse. Sam probably knows—thanks to being around Blix all the time—exactly why the house feels weird. That leaves Mom and Dad to experience unexplained nerves. They must be picking up on the energy of the dolls being here and since they don't know how to process or explain it, they're on edge.

Hmm. I should tell them we have guests. Probably isn't going to make them feel any less anxious. Though, knowing why they feel strange might stop it from getting worse.

"Sarah!" chirps Chloe, patting the rug. "Come have tea with us."

I'd make a comment about how can this kid 'play tea party' so often and not get bored with it, then I remember I still play *Skyrim*. "Sure. Give me a moment. Need to tell Mom and Dad something, then I'd like to get out of these jeans and I'll be right there."

"Okay." She grins.

CHAPTER 12
GETTING UNREAL

T oday's the test.

It's Tuesday. My first class starts at 3:00 p.m. As a mortal, I hated alarm clocks. In fact, I hated whoever decided that school *had* to start so damn early. Someone did a study not too long ago stating that teenage brains aren't equipped to function at seven or eight in the morning and students performed better if they were allowed to sleep later. Unfortunately, society ignored it.

I don't have any science degrees and I could've told them that years ago.

Gone are my days of being a sluggish morning person. Vampires sleep like cats. We go from fully awake to out cold in an instant, and we wake up just as fast. As soon as I realize I'm up, I scramble out of bed, leaving Chloe and Ashley to their rest. Eventually, we'll all wake up at the same time. It took me a little over a year to settle in on regaining consciousness consistently at about 2:30 in the afternoon. Chloe gets up only about ten to twenty minutes after me. Not sure if the actual innocence of her being a child has anything to do with it or if it's more a case of how children learn faster than adults.

No clue. Maybe I could ask Cassian about it. If he's a professional studier of vampires, he might know. Then again, he also might regard Chloe as an irresistible curiosity. I don't want to turn her into a science project even if the worst thing he does is ask her questions and follow us around for a few days observing. Good chance he won't 'microwave' her like St. Ives did. Not saying that chamber was a literal microwave oven, but it had a similar effect.

So glad that bullcrap is done with.

Why do the smart people always seem so stupid? St. Ives having to do tests to see if Chloe's vampirism was still reversible strikes me about as dumb as a scientist walking into a concrete wall to confirm that solid matter is still solid.

I'm not planning to take the Sentra to school, so there's no need to break my neck rushing. Regardless, I haul ass across the basement and hurry through a shower. Probably don't need to. It's merely a habit. I'm still a vampire no matter how lifelike I appear. It takes considerably longer for me to get funky than a living person. Also, that I *do* still get funky makes me feel better. Old Guard and so on don't. They can go months without showering and a person would never smell the difference. For them, no biological processes are going on to create any of the stuff that makes people stink.

Guess I still have half a foot in the door of being alive... in a manner of speaking.

Right, so... quick shower, then I sprint to my room to get dressed. Blix is waiting for me on my computer desk. Chloe's flopped on the floor coloring in a book. Ashley's awake but still in bed, peering at me lazily through a curtain of hair.

I'm not self-conscious changing in front of the imp. No more so than I'd be getting dressed with a dog or cat in the room. Sure, he's not a pet, nor an animal. But he's Blix. I dunno why it feels like no big deal; it just does.

Once I'm dressed, I nod at him, grab my backpack, and return to the basement bathroom.

We jump through the mirror into an industrial hallway full of bare cinder blocks and huge purposeless metal pipes. It's somewhere between the space in a mall running behind the stores and Freddy Kreuger's steel mill.

Thankfully, it only takes me about three minutes of jogging after

Blix (without paying attention to the scary stuff moving in the shadows) before he's found a good mirror to leave through. The rectangle is small enough to be a little annoying but not so tiny I have to float like Supergirl and go through horizontally.

I emerge in one of the ladies' rooms at SCC.

Eep. I pause standing on the sink with one leg still going into the mirror behind me, frozen in the sudden worry someone might walk in at any second and catch me. Relax. Not a big deal. Bathrooms here don't have windows. I'm online even though it's only afternoon. If some woman sees me emerge from the mirror, it should be really easy to make her forget. People would want to reject that sight anyway. Human instinct is to disbelieve something like that could possibly be real.

Anyway, the coast is clear.

I jump down off the sink and turn around to face the mirror.

Blix peeks back at me from the other side. He waves.

"Thanks! You are amazing." I high-five the mirror glass above his tiny hand.

He grasps the lapels of a jacket he's not wearing, flashing a 'yes, I know' face before making a 'money' gesture rubbing his fingers together.

"Sure, no problem. Just let me know what game you want." I pause. "Make it two as a thanks for getting me to Mom's work so fast."

He grins, then nods so fast his leathery ears flap.

Yes, I am bribing my demonic travel associate with video games. Or, less a bribe and more payment for a service. Either way. I'm sure he'd help me without the promise of payment if it was important, like going to help Mom. A quick ride to school, though... that's me being lazy so I don't mind paying for it.

Whew. I'm on campus at 2:49 p.m.

A year ago, I would never have imagined it possible. There's still no way in hell I'd ever be able to attend morning classes like an ordinary person. However, an afternoon class that starts roughly thirty minutes after I wake up is giving me the same experience as rolling out of bed and scrambling to make it to class by eight.

I head out into the hall. It takes me a moment to figure out where on campus I am. Blix is good. He took me to the same building my first class is in. Since today is the first day of having this class at all, I almost get lost trying to find the room. It's on the ground floor toward the back, down this little corridor that's kind of easy to miss. This is definitely the art department. The smells of paint and various other chemicals is overwhelming, even when I am offline. Oof. It's a good thing I decided to take Art History in the afternoon. These smells would blast the crap out of my vampire nose.

Not that anything particularly stinks or smells bad. The aromas are merely strong.

A few other students give me weird looks as I rush into the designated classroom. The afternoon crowd is noticeably younger than the night school group. For most of the students around me, this is their last class of the day before they go home. I'm among a majority of nineteen-to-twenty-year-olds now. The looks I'm getting are pretty much 'what's that kid doing here' type stares.

Hmm. I might start wearing tighter-fitting tops to this class. Not that I'm the sort of girl who likes to show off her figure (trust me, I don't have the boobs for that) but... I *do* have boobs. I look much less like a fourteen-year-old if I'm not wearing baggy clothes. I didn't get shorter or legit become childlike. The Innocent thing is almost entirely in my face. It's kind of neat in a way, at least if I want to be a master of disguises. Depending on how I carry myself and what I wear, I can pretend to be anywhere from like twelve to twenty.

I ignore the stares and look around for a seat.

This classroom is full of art stuff. Paintings, statues, pottery, posters, and so on. It's arranged like a normal classroom rather than a studio. It is, after all, art history. We're not going to be creating art in this class, merely studying it and making up crap about what the artist was thinking when they created whatever piece.

My butt isn't in the seat for more than two minutes before a skinny guy with a thick black moustache strides in. He's brimming with energy. Kinda reminds me of a Hispanic Freddie Mercury in a way, only shorter.

"Hello everyone," says the man. His voice has a mild accent I can't quite place. "Welcome to Art History. My name is Pedro Guillermo, and we'll be spending the next several weeks together talking about the artistic endeavors of people who died long before any of our great, great, great, great grandparents were kids."

Faint chuckling comes from the students.

Pedro walks back and forth, nearly bouncing on his toes. Wow, did this guy eat a whole bag of gummi bears before class? "Let me start off by saying I am well aware that the majority of you are only here because this is considered an easy class to satisfy your elective credit requirements. To those of you who are here only to pick up a few credits, I get this subject can be kinda boring."

Students laugh a little more sincerely.

"For you, I will try to make this as interesting as possible." Pedro claps his hands together and half bows. "Some of you are here because you adore art. You understand why people still care what someone did four hundred years ago with a brush and some paints. You are my people. If you've come here to broaden your appreciation of how humanity has been able to capture the beauty of reality, you're in for a treat. By the time we're done, you'll be able to tell a Caravaggio from a Van Eyck, or a Reubens from a Raphael just by looking at them."

The students are quiet.

"I am sure this ability will serve you greatly in life during those corporate meetings." Pedro wags his eyebrows. "Why, yes, Marcia, the art on this coffee cup is definitely Botticelli. Oh, Brad, it's amazing you realized that. I'm promoting you immediately."

People laugh again.

Pedro continues zipping around in the front of the classroom like a hamster who ate half a bag of espresso beans while telling us various nonsensical ways being good at art history could (not really) help us out in life. Some of his ludicrous examples are pretty amusing. At one point, he says unlike most people, when we get stranded at an airport on a long layover, we'll have the skills to stare deeply into some random painting and question what might have been on the artist's mind at the time, so we won't be bored. Even I laugh at that one.

"I'd like all of you to approach this class not with the mindset of 'this is not going to help me' or 'I'm only taking it because I want a few easy credits.' Instead, think of it in the abstract. Learning about art history is learning about history, about humanity, about how people see and relate to the world around them. I apologize, but there will be some boring memorization and tests—the school makes me do that or I get in trouble." He pauses while the laughter rises and falls. "In all seriousness, this class is as much about learning *how* to think and feel and less about what to think. Keep that in mind, and you'll have fun... or at least not want to run screaming out the door after a month."

I get the oddest feeling someone's staring at me. A subtle look around fails to reveal the source of the odd sensation.

Pedro goes over a rough summary of the course syllabus, telling us about how we'll be starting off with the Baroque period before going into Renaissance artists and then to more modern artistic movements.

"Later in the semester, we'll be doing a little bit of field trip work, visiting a museum or two." Pedro grins like a small boy who just can't wait for that day trip to escape the school building. "As you are all adults, we won't be using school buses. I'll post the schedule at least a week ahead of time, and you'll be expected to meet up at the venue. If anyone has transportation challenges, reach out to me and I'll figure something out. Also, any admission fees to wherever we end up visiting are included with the tuition, so you won't need to worry about that."

He keeps going on with the introductory stuff. It would be damn near impossible to fall asleep in this guy's class. That's two for two thus far. My writing class teacher is quirky and fun. This guy's on a permanent sugar high.

The sense of being stared at builds to near intolerable. I'm half an inch away from yelling 'who the hell is staring at me?' when I notice the culprit. It's not a person at all, but a statue. Among the many bits of random art in the room is a life-sized statue of a nude man. Well, he's mostly life-sized. Poor guy's hung like a chipmunk. Looks like the artist just stuck an acorn on there. It's probably a reproduction of a famous statue or some such thing. Pretty odd to have a nude statue in a classroom to begin with. Even odder is how the *statue* feels like it's watching me.

I'm quite offline at the moment and yet the statue's smacking me with a strong paranormal vibe. The feeling reminds me of Aurélie's dolls, spirits trapped inside artificial objects that sorta look like humans.

This is like that thing where it's hard to have sex while a dog is in the room watching. It's going to be difficult to study with a naked dude watching me. A simple statue is no big deal. This isn't a normal statue. There may as well be a live naked man staring at me. Talk about awkward.

I can't leave this alone, nor can I do anything right this second.

So, I decide to wait until dark. Once I'm online, that statue's getting checked out. If the spirit or whatever else is inside it doesn't want to talk and doesn't need help, I'm going to turn it so he's not staring at me anymore. It's the only way I'll ever be able to pay attention in this class.

I'm abnormally preoccupied with the statue for the remainder of the class period. Alas, it's a once-a-week class from three to six. Gah. Dude. Chill out. Stop throwing anxiety at me. Like some sort of minor celebrity trying to avoid paparazzi, I shrink down in my seat and fluff my oversized sweatshirt up to conceal my face.

At least Pedro is high energy. If I concentrate on him, it's almost possible to disregard the staring statue. Some teachers go easy on day one of a class. Not this guy. He dives right into the material like we're midway through our second month. It's only a shock because it's the first night. He isn't hammering us with a ton of work.

As soon as it's socially acceptable to do so, I leave the room. Problem being, so is every other student. Sun's still out. My phone's predicting sunset at 7:40 p.m. Almost two hours to go. Meh. Probably better off. Suppose shoving people out of my way with inhuman strength would be a violation of that whole 'keep vampires secret' thing. Bleh.

I take my time putting my books away, letting the majority of the students jam themselves into the doorway. I'm not in a hurry.

My next class isn't for an hour. Yeah... Tuesdays are my 'heavy' days with two classes. Art History from three to six and 'life science' from seven to ten. Might as well go scout out the location of my second classroom so I don't get caught in a last-minute scramble.

Once the bulk of the students are gone, I get up and head out the door. Old habits are hard to break. I've always felt reasonably safe in school. So, unlike being outside, I tend to walk with my head down, not paying too much attention to what's going on around me. It's less about shyness and more of an 'I just want to be done with this and go home' sort of attitude. At the moment, I'm not simply trying to ignore the other students, I'm studying a small map of the campus layout and trying to figure out which way to go in order to be in the correct building and classroom.

Looks like I've gotta go outside, cross the street, and go two buildings north. The life science class is in the 'Science and Math' building, just north of the little section where East Howell Street is more of a courtyard for people and not a street for cars. Okay, I am sorta familiar with the building. My calculus class happened there.

It occurs to me the hallway's gone abnormally quiet. As soon as I process the unusual lack of commotion, my senses become aware of an otherworldly wrongness. Uh oh.

I lift my gaze off the drab floor to find the hallway empty. No students anywhere in sight. Doors to other classrooms hang open, no sign of anyone there. It's as if I'm the only person in the entire building.

Whoa. That's odd. I turn in place, looking around... and spot a guy watching me from around a corner about fifty feet back. He's huge. Super tall. Broad shoulders. Blue janitor type jumpsuit. Oh, did I mention his face looks like a slice of overcooked pizza glued to his skull? The skin's more like scorched cheese than flesh. No eyes. No mouth. Not even a nose.

Yanno, there's logic. Like I should really be thinking 'no way this Michael Meyers/Jason Voorhees knock off is real'. Operative word being 'should.' It's considerably more difficult to think clinically and objectively when a giant monster is staring at you. It's even less easy to stay rational when said giant monster starts walking toward me, raising a massive knife.

Maybe I've got some PTSD issues with knives considering how I lost my mortal life. Maybe this guy is just paranormally terrifying.

I'm honestly not thinking much of anything, really. A scream echoes in the distance. Might've been me. Next thing I know, I'm running down the corridor. Classrooms rush by me on both sides. Reality does that warp effect where the middle of the hallway ahead of me seems to be pushing itself farther away while the scenery nearer me is zooming by.

I don't look back. I'm not *that* much of a horror movie bimbo cliché. Mostly, the reason I don't look back is I don't have to. Thudding footsteps are coming up behind me, getting closer. Sounds like the dude is trudging but still somehow keeping up with me. Yeah, if I look back, I know exactly what I'm going to see and I do not like it.

Running faster, I aim for a hallway up ahead on the left, rounding the corner into another seemingly infinite hallway full of classrooms and open doors. I'm probably still screaming. Not really sure. A sense of presence looms up behind me. I'm still too terrified to risk looking back. Feels like the guy's almost close enough to grab me. I pour everything I can into speed, leaning into my stride. This hallway goes on forever.

Even though I don't expect anything to change, I try a right turn at the next opportunity... and dammit!

It's a dead-end alcove only fifteen feet long with one classroom door on either side.

I barely have time to think 'oh shit' before the huge man grabs me from behind and throws me against the wall on the left. One second, my forehead's making contact with the cinder blocks, the next thing I know, the guy's got me off the ground in a one-handed chokehold around my neck. The size comparison between us is like some enormous WWE wrestler has grabbed my little brother. This dude's fingertips almost meet behind my neck. If there's anyone I never wanted to be nose-to-nose with, it's this guy. Wait, he doesn't have a nose, merely blank flesh stretched drum-tight around a skull. Stuff's moving under the surface of the skin. Looks like bugs. Oh, please just break my neck and end it. Don't have your face burst open to shower me with creepy crawlies.

I brace for something vile—or painful—or both.

He raises the knife, ready to plunge it into my heart... and then disappears.

Weird. I don't drop back to my feet. He had me held way up off the ground, but I'm already standing on the floor. A small crowd of students surround me. A guy in a dark red sweater's the closest. He's staring at me like he's asked a question I totally didn't hear and he's waiting for an answer. Dude's got thick but short black hair and kinda looks like a more realistic Christopher Reeves. By 'more realistic' I mean not quite so unbelievably handsome. Someone to my left asks no one in particular if they need to call 911.

"You okay?" asks red sweater guy.

I gaze around. I'm only like twenty feet from Pedro's classroom. Shit. That whole running and screaming thing happened in my head in the space of a few seconds. Well, maybe some screams happened in reality. Ugh. How embarrassing. I'd almost rather have another naked morgue experience than freak out in a crowded place and have everyone stare at me. Probably shouldn't say that out loud. If I keep doing jobs for Mr. W., sooner or later I will find myself waking up in a morgue again if something goes wildly wrong.

"Uhh. Yeah. I'm okay." I wipe a hand down my face. "Didn't get enough sleep."

"Are you sure?" asks an Asian girl who I realize is holding my arm. She's a little older than me and appears concerned. "That looked like you had a panic attack."

Dammit. I glance over at her. "What happened?"

"You shrieked, then started flailing like someone was attacking you... then just stopped," says red sweater guy.

"Wow." I try to act calm like I wasn't almost stabbed to death by an inhuman monster. "That's never happened before. I must've passed out on my feet and had a mini nightmare. Weird."

"You might want to see someone," says the girl holding my arm. "Anxiety attacks can be serious."

"Yeah." I smile at her. "Thanks. I feel okay now."

Red sweater guy hands me my backpack, which I evidently dropped. "Here, this is yours. Want me to walk with you?"

This is another unfortunate side effect of appearing young. Everyone wants to take care of me.

"Oh, thanks. I'll be fine. Just going to another class. Won't be alone." I sling the pack over my shoulder. "Eek. How embarrassing. I really need to get more sleep."

The girl lets go of my arm. "If that happens again, please go get checked out."

"Sure. I will."

It takes me a few minutes of random excuses and small talk to gracefully elude the good Samaritans. They eventually seem to think I'm okay and acting normal enough, so they let me walk off unescorted without insisting anyone accompanies me to make sure I get to my next class okay.

Ugh, great… I grumble to myself as I walk down the hall, this time keeping my attention firmly on the world and people around me. Everyone in the hallway thinks I'm either crazy or on something. This has to be the barbecue demon. Yes, asshole, I'm calling you that now. You're not a sefil anymore. You're the bane of overcooked hamburger, the prince of excessive lighter fluid usage.

He's trying to draw attention to me. Maybe he hoped to scare me so much I freaked out. No, that concerned woman wasn't right. I did not have a panic attack. If a vampire has a panic attack, it would be damn obvious… and there'd likely be two or three random people dead. Thankfully, it takes a *lot* to give us a legit panic attack: like a sudden face-full of sunlight.

Yeah… if this demon exposes me publicly as a vampire… problems.

Shit's getting real.

Demons, vampires, magic… hah. Maybe I should say shit's getting unreal.

CHAPTER 13
UNLIFE SCIENCE

N ightmares suck.

At least, I'm fairly sure what happened to me was some form of a nightmare. It couldn't have really happened. Men don't get as big as that guy. Nine-foot-tall humans are like one in ten billion and they usually have health issues that would make it challenging to catch a girl my size running at the speed of scared out of her mind. That dude pulled the horror movie cliché of being right behind me no matter how fast I moved.

There's also the whole disappearing into thin air thing.

So, yeah. Nightmare. Or hallucination-slash-vision. Hmm. I'd say it's not possible for me to fall asleep, but I'm not sure. The sun is still up. I probably could still sleep if I wanted to. The two most likely situations here are hallucination... or me getting pulled into an alternate dimension that couldn't quite hold on to me tight enough and I slipped back to where I belong at the last minute.

None of the students who witnessed me make a fool of myself said anything about me appearing out of thin air. Yeah, guess I just had a hallucination. It felt like I ran away from the monster for a long time, but only seconds had passed.

I don't remember the last time I had a serious nightmare. Probably a good thing I can't remember the nightmare. Think it happened when I was like nine or so, and probably because Dad let me watch a scary movie I shouldn't have seen so young. Up until the night Scott stabbed me, my life had been pretty cushy, normal, and tame. Not a whole lot of trauma fuel in there.

And no, Universe, that is not permission to dump it all on me now.

Despite knowing it didn't happen, I can't quite get my hands to stop shaking. Even though I'd never had a bad experience myself, being chased down and attacked by some big, strong guy has always been one of my fears. Pretty sure a lot of girls have that in the list of their top five anxieties. I try to think about being angry instead of scared, since it happened while I was offline. Hate feeling weak like a mortal. Dammit. I'm a vampire now. I'm not supposed to be afraid of being alone.

Anger only helps a little.

The nightmarish vision was too realistic, or maybe... the demon is manipulating my emotions more directly than making me see things. He's pretty pissed off at me for destroying the physical body he managed to inhabit, ruining his plans for running amok in the mortal world. Which, by the way, is totally unfair. That guy kicked my ass. *I* did not destroy him. Mel did. If he's going to have an attitude with someone, why not pick on her? Oh, right. Guys like that don't pick fights with anyone who can whip their butts.

At least he's going after me and not Sam. Though, to be fair, he's probably got it in for my whole family. The only good part is how weak he is right now. Blix said something about how if a demon is in the mortal world and 'killed,' it's soul or essence returns to its home plane in a weakened state. For several decades, it's stuck there with limited ability to exert influence outside of its home realm. Apparently, there are certain ways to kill demons in the mortal world that send them back for longer and weaken them even more. Alas, that requires magic type stuff that humanity has largely forgotten how to do.

Right, so. For the time being, I have school to deal with and try to calm down. It will be dark soon. Once the sun sets, I can stop feeling like a helpless little kid hiding in a break room from the monster I think is waiting for me out in the hallway.

A handful of other students in here busy themselves with the old-style arcade games or the pinball machine... or just sit at the tables having snacks from one of the vending machines. Guess it's pretty lame of me to just sit here by myself doing nothing, wasting most of the hour before my next class. Then again, it's not like there's really anything to do here. I'm not a social butterfly. Randomly approaching people and trying to make friends with total strangers has never been part of my personality. That's a good trait to have for a vampire. The fewer people who remember/know me, the easier it will be to manage the passing of time.

Also, I am a not perfect angel. Every now and then when I see a woman over forty go by with some sag, or extra baby pounds or age droop in places, I have a little feeling of 'whew that's never going to be me'. I'm not mean about it. Nothing wrong with those older women. Not laughing at them at all. I'm just happy time isn't going to do that to me.

Oh, Sophia, what did you do to yourself?

My sister thinks she enchanted herself to stop growing up when she hits around my age. She's almost as clingy as Ashley. She didn't want me to be sad someday in the future when she got old and died. Problem is, Sophia is kind of brittle emotionally. She's afraid of losing her innocence. I don't mean that in a 'grow up and have sex' way. Right now, she's pretty innocent. She doesn't really understand how cruel and awful the world can be. Growing up into an adult means she will come to realize people can be horrible to each other. She wants to stay blissfully ignorant of that and continue believing the world is like one of her cartoons where the good guys always win and everyone's happy at the end.

Good guys always winning and happy endings only happens in books and movies. Some people look down their noses at happy endings, but I don't mind them. The real world has enough bad endings. People need the escape of a good story having a nice ending so they can feel good for a while, even vicariously.

Ugh. I wish my life was a book or a movie.

Anyway...

The clock finally pokes me in the backside to get moving. I sling my backpack over one shoulder and hurry out of the break room. Once again, I hate feeling like a mortal girl having to keep her head on a swivel. It's even worse at the moment, really. Not supposed to feel this on edge inside a school building. I've got the level of anxiety reserved for parking garages at one in the morning where only half of the lights work.

I should not be scared inside the school with people all around me.

Damn that demon.

This is only going to keep getting worse. We're going to need to get proactive here before he drives us insane. I'm not sure how to go about doing that. Hmm. I'm taking Sophia to visit the mystics soon for her monthly 'class.' Maybe I could ask them about this issue. Probably a safer bet to hope they can help than writing to Dear Abby about how to deal with an angry demon trying to sabotage your family from the depths of Hell.

Or whatever they call the plane he lives on.

Anyway, class.

Life Science indeed. The instructor, Dr. Calvin Reed, seems friendly. He's a young-looking forty something black guy in a suit and tie. The man's got a presence somewhere between a motivational speaker and a guy who owns the tech company responsible for making the *Terminator* robots. Everything about him is neat and professional—as opposed to my art history professor who's trying to be super casual. I'm not exactly the most formal person in the world. Still, something about this dude makes me want to address him as 'sir' if I ever need to talk to him in person.

This classroom is huge. It's one of those auditorium style rooms where the seats are on an ascending grade facing down at a central 'pit' where the professor stands. Reminds me of an old theater where live actors did shows in bygone days. It doesn't have much in the way of thematic decorations like some of the other classrooms. My guess is that's due to it serving shared duty for multiple different subjects and instructors. It isn't one particular professor's 'domain' to make home.

I'm one of about seventy students in this class. Again, most are on the older side: thirty, forty or so.

Hey, older to me. I'm only eighteen.

Mom hates it when I refer to a thirty-four-year-old person as 'being older.' To her, 'older' means seventy plus. Time is relative, I guess. Chloe thinks people my age are 'old'.

Dr. Reed, as most of my teachers thus far this semester have done, begins with an introductory/summary type speech. This course examines the theme of evolution as a concept throughout history as it pertains to things like genetics, cell biology, cancer, biochemistry, ethics, and so on, focusing on humans and how we interact with the planet.

Ugh. Dammit. I switched to liberal arts so I could be lazy. How was I supposed to know I'd end up in a class where I'd really need to pay attention?

My iPhone vibrates.

The sheer size of this classroom, the elevated angle of the seating rows, and my position kind of in the middle on the right side affords me the ability to check the screen without the professor noticing. Normally, Follows Rules Girl wouldn't play with her cell phone during class. But my life has gone to plaid. This could be an emergency. Then again, I'm not a child anymore even if I am the youngest student in the room. College teachers don't have a 'collect everyone's phone' policy. Some of the people here might be like firefighters or medics or some such thing and need to be able to receive important notifications.

My screen's showing a text message from 'Mike.' One of Wolent's mortal associates. It's a reminder of a soiree coming up this Friday night. They know Aurélie is out of town and were wondering if Ashley and I planned to be there. I say 'wondering,' but the tone of the text is totally 'you're going to be there, right?'

I hurriedly reply with 'Sure, we'll be there, but won't be fanci.'

Yes, I spell it with an i. No idea why.

That done, I tuck the phone away and lean back in the seat,

listening to Dr. Reed talk. Something tells me despite the relatively interesting subject matter, this class is going to be the one that feels the most tedious and long. Most of my time here is going to be just listening to this guy talk and do a presentation, then take tests about what he said. There are too many students in this room for any sort of interaction to be feasible. Maybe he'll sometimes ask questions to see who's awake, but it's not going to be the sort of dynamic interactions we had in Professor Heath's class.

I can't help but think of some old movie Dad put on... one of those Eighties college comedy movies. Damn but I can't remember the title. They had this recurring throwaway gag where a room like this increasingly changed from being full of students to just full of boom boxes recording the guy as the movie progressed. The last shot of the room was a big tape recorder of the professor 'talking' to an audience of tape recorders.

We've only been in here for twenty minutes and I already understand the joke.

Almost tempted to go back into the hallway and get chased again since it's less dry.

CHAPTER 14
A CAREFUL DIET

T wo bits of good news.

One: class is over.

Two: no more demonic interference.

The sun went down roughly a third the way through my Life Sciences class. As soon as I came online, my fear disappeared... or changed. Rather than terror at becoming a victim of some monster, anxiety manifested as worry what the demon might trick *me* into doing to some innocent person. I'm really thankful I have no memory of the time I blacked out and shredded those drug dealers. It makes me feel lousy enough not remembering it. Don't want to imagine how bad I'd feel if I watched it happen.

Guilt is a strange animal. Like, I *should* feel much worse than I do about that. I mean, several people dead deserves more than an 'ugh, that sucked' reaction. Does that make me psychotic, in denial, or have I simply accepted it was entirely out of my control? Bright sun unexpectedly slapping me in the face equals deadly panic attack.

As much as Hollywood and my own romantic notions paints vampires as amazing, we are still something inhuman. Or are we? I mean, if you take a mortal human and try to push them underwater to drown them, they're going to freak out and fight. Once a person believes they are genuinely about to die, they snap. The mind takes over on a subconscious level and goes haywire, desperately fighting to survive. Vampires aren't any different... we're simply much stronger than mortals and have claws. Well, some of us do.

I sneak across campus and break into the art history classroom. The statue seems normal now. No sense of presence at all. Huh. Okay. Guess it wasn't a trapped spirit after all. That demon who tried to scare me must have been in here watching me. Cool. Saves me the trouble of dealing with a ghost.

My flight home is uneventful. I land on the deck, step into the kitchen, then slip my sneakers off while sliding the big glass door closed. A faint glimmer catches my eye. There appears to be some sort of faint writing on the door and the giant window next to it. Looks mystical, like something straight out of that movie *Thirteen Ghosts*. Uh oh. Mom's going to be upset if Sophia enchanted the deck door without permission. Hopefully, mortals can't see this writing.

Still not sure what Sophia's runaway magic did. Definitely not this. This takes much more focus and deliberateness. One does not accidentally erect protective wards. Not going to make an issue of it. She's only trying to help.

Ahh, home at last. I get to veg out for the rest of the night. Didn't get too much homework, so I don't have to jump right on it now. I am hungry, though. Gotta be from the stress. Might not be a bad idea to go out for a bite. It's not quite 10:30 p.m. yet. We have plenty of time. Yeah, it's a little bit late to take Chloe out of the house, but not totally unheard of. No one's going to freak out seeing a seven-year-old outside at this hour. At least, they wouldn't flip out as badly as they would at two in the morning.

Ashley and Chloe are in my bedroom, the kid playing with dolls —I mean Chloe—and Ashley's reading some anime graphic novel. Also, Ash isn't on my bed like a loyal dog missing her human. She's in here because Chloe is in here. You know, we're being responsible and mom-like and stuff.

"Welcome back," says Ashley without looking up. "What happened?"

"Class happened."

She shifts her gaze up to peer over the book at me. "I can smell your fear."

"Creepy," whispers Chloe.

Ashley's serious face breaks apart into a fit of laughter. "Seriously, though. Something scared the hell out of you. Seems a little more severe than almost taking a pigeon up the nose on your way home. What happened?"

I glance at my wrist. "We've got about forty minutes before it's eleven. You guys hungry?"

"Yeah!" Chloe jumps to her feet, grins at me, then faces the visiting dolls. "Excuse me. I need to go for a little while. I'll be back soon."

"You're dodging." Ashley tucks a bookmark into her graphic novel, sets it on the bed, and stands. "And what's with staring at your wrist."

"It means we're running late," I say.

Ashley blinks. "What?"

"Umm." I shrug. "Dad always looks at his wrist when he complains about running out of time. I have no idea why he does it."

She tilts her head at me. "Weird. What's your wrist have to do with time?"

"Clueless." I flap my arms. "I'll ask Dad next time he's awake."

"Okay." Ashley pokes me in the stomach. "You're dodging my question. What scared you?"

"I'll explain in the air." I tug at her oversized T-shirt. "Get dressed. Don't wanna take the kid outside *too* late."

"Okay, okay..." Ashley scurries out and goes to her room to change.

"It's fine." Chloe walks over to me, grinning. She looks like a big doll thanks to her frilly dress, one of the ones Aurélie gave her. The purple polish on her finger and toenails has to be Sophia's doing.

I rub my chin. "You look adorable. Might be better if you changed into something a little less memorable."

She peers down at herself. The child's facial expression is blank. Not sure if she's about to erupt in a 'but I wanna wear this' argument or not.

"It's fine," repeats the child. "We have a system."

The kid is, of course, referring to how either Ash or I will hide with her somewhere while the other goes out and finds someone to bring back to the hiding place. True. If we play things right, no one who won't be mind-erased will see her.

"Okay." I take her hand. "You're right. I'm trusting you to be careful."

She nods, all seriousness.

Ashley returns in a baggy sweater and jeans. The two of us are the epitome of unassuming Pacific Northwest teenagers. Perfect. Dressing to be functionally invisible—as in no one pays attention to or remembers us—is a skill. Thankfully, it's one I practiced all throughout high school. Again, not from shyness. I just didn't want drama. Guess the joke's on me now, huh?

We make our way upstairs to the kitchen and outside onto the deck. Neither Ashley nor Chloe bother taking the time to grab shoes. Since I still have socks on—and wet socks suck—I step back into my sneakers and follow them. Seriously, in the realm of non-life-threatening trivial annoyances, there isn't too much in the world that feels more uncomfortable than being stuck in a wet sock. I'd rather go barefoot in snow. Maybe that's not entirely fair since I cannot suffer frostbite. Whatever.

We fly almost straight up to a safe—as in hard to see from the ground—altitude, then head toward Seattle downtown. No sooner are we at cruising altitude than Ashley breaks into snickering giggles.

"What?" I give her side eye. "Did you see something down there?"

"Nah." She takes a moment to collect herself, then looks at me, then bursts out laughing again.

I blink.

Chloe looks at me. "I dunno what Ash is laughing at. You aren't funny."

"Thanks." I smirk. The kid isn't criticizing my sense of humor. She means there's nothing about me right now that would make someone laugh. "Ash? You okay?"

"Yeah." She snickers into a long sigh. "So, tonight's my art class."

"You're taking an art class?" I raise both eyebrows. "Why?"

She shrugs. "Why not? I have to fill some elective credits. Anyway, it's the very first night and the instructor's like"—she over-acts like a pirate boat captain, thrusting one hand upward—"'let's dive right in, shall we!' and all of a sudden, this man walks out from a closet in only a bathrobe... and he takes it off."

"Seriously?" I whistle. "That sounds a lot more exciting than my art history class."

"Umm, I kinda made a mistake. I thought it was just 'art'." Ashley laughs. "It's a life drawing class. Live nude models come in every so often."

Not that anyone would know from looking at us, but between Ashley and me, she's the sex kitten. She did it before me and has done it more than I have—with both guys and girls. Not saying she's an epic slut or anything. Having had more sex than me isn't saying a whole lot. Anyway, it's kinda weirdly juvenile for her to be giggling at the idea of a naked man.

"How is that funny? Did the dude look strange?" I ask.

She makes this slightly-scrunched-nose face. "Nah. Too old for me. It's funny because it was right in a classroom with people around. Just seemed so weird. Some dude getting naked in a class-room is as awkward as farting in the middle of a funeral."

Yeah, okay. I can see that. "Crazy coincidence."

"What's that?" Ashley glances at me. "Does you coming home scared have something to do with a nude model?"

I chuckle. "No. But I did have a naked dude in my art history class today."

She gawks. "Seriously?"

"Yeah." I pause for effect. "Though, he was a statue."

Ashley rolls her eyes at me.

Chloe shakes her head. "I'm glad I won't ever be old enough to go to college. It sounds like a silly place."

"It is." I offer a solemn nod. "A very silly place."

"So, what scared you?" Ashley nudges me.

I explain what happened. My story creeps her out a bit but Chloe doesn't bat an eyelash. Here's hoping this won't give Ashley a nightmare. She's more prone to bad dreams than I am, but nowhere near as bad as Sophia.

"You don't have to worry about me." Chloe gives me a hug once we land in a dark street somewhere in the southern end of downtown. "My friends won't let anything hurt me."

It takes me a few seconds to realize what she means by 'friends.' She wouldn't use that term to refer to me or Ash, or the Littles, or the 'rents. The only thing left to make sense is the dolls. Hmm. Now I'm wondering if Aurélie sent them over for reasons beyond not wanting the dolls to be lonely.

Anyway, feeding time. I go out of our hiding spot in a small alley between a Vietnamese place called 'Pho Sure' and a Subway. Dad would love the Vietnamese place simply for the punny name. Not sure he's ever had Vietnamese food. Don't think I have either. Hmm. Should try it. Place is closed, or I'd totally impulse order right now.

I wander around for a few minutes before locating a group of three guys coming out of the Subway. They seem to be about my age or a year older. I'm guessing they're college students out for a late snack or maybe high school seniors. Kinda hard to tell. Doesn't matter. Perfect targets, really. Young and healthy. The guy in the green beanie hat looks high, though. Gotta make sure Chloe doesn't touch him. None are carrying food, so I'm guessing they ate inside. Even better. I don't have to feel guilty their food's getting warm and soggy while we delay them.

It's a simple matter to walk up to them like I'm looking for directions, then whack them with the Derp Hammer. I lead them back to our hiding place and the biting commences. Chloe's gotta fly to reach the guy's neck. She latches onto him like a little remora cleaning a shark. Her weight's supported by flight power, though it totally looks like she's just hanging there by her mouth alone, arms slack at her sides. It's kinda hilarious in a creepy, twisted way.

Guess what my guy's blood tastes like.

Yep. Subway. Gee, I wonder what put that thought in my mind.

Noise from the building behind me warns of approaching people. The three of us rapidly disengage from feeding and try to act casual.

A plain steel door opens, revealing an older guy in a filthy tank top shirt and white pants. He's kind of like a gritty version of Mario. Thick black hair, mustache, and an expression like he's just ready to stomp the ever-loving crap out of some turtles. I'm guessing he works in a kitchen and does most of the dirty jobs. He carries a pair of massive trash bags outside. Two younger men follow him, also carrying trash.

The trio looks over at us in passing. No big deal. Just a bunch of kids hanging out in an alley. Nothing suspicious here. All three kitchen workers give Chloe weird looks. Dammit. Yeah, they're concerned at a little kid being outside past eleven at night. That she's barefoot in a doll dress, rather pale, and has black hair is setting off their 'this is a kid from a horror movie' vibe to a point. Mostly, they're giving the dudes I grabbed to feed on dirty looks. They look older than me and Ashley, so those guys are obviously the ones responsible for 'three young girls' being outside so late.

"Uh oh," whispers Ashley.

"I got it," I mutter.

It doesn't take me much effort to make the kitchen workers forget seeing us. Their worry hadn't escalated to the point of doing anything more than thinking it's weird for a little girl to be outside so late. Not like they planned to call the police or even walk over to challenge us. I send them on their way back inside. 'Mario' owns the bar and grill type place they came out of. It stays open until midnight. The foremost thought on their minds is going home soon.

Works for me.

I head back over to the others. We finish feeding quickly, leave the college guys in a mental fog, and zip into the air. Life (or unlife) provides experience. With experience comes wisdom. Seems like I can't let myself start taking feeding too casually. Unless we're out in the middle of nowhere, every time we go out to eat, we need to pay attention to our surroundings so no one observes things they shouldn't see. This is a world where everyone—well almost everyone—carries video cameras in the form of cell phones. A little careless-ness is all it would take to cause big problems.

On that note, I start to wonder about Chloe. Maybe I should try to teach her how to stay unnoticed. Yeah. She might be a little girl, but she's also a vampire. Any little thing I can do to protect her, I have to do it, even if it's empowering her to protect herself sometimes.

Just... not tonight.

CHAPTER 15

PROPER DEMONIC PREPAREDNESS

O h, Wednesday, how you torment me with your longness.
I wake up and realize it's Wednesday. This is only annoying because Wednesday is not Friday. It's even more annoying because I'm too young to be 'working for the weekend,' not to mention a vampire. Weekends are only precious to those who have obligations during the week like students and anyone with a day job. That the pressure of school is a needless drain on my time caused entirely by me only makes me grumble more.

Yeah, yeah, I know. I did it to myself. I can quit anytime I want without major consequences beyond feeling a bit guilty for disappointing my parents. Though, honestly, I think they are both still overjoyed to still have me around (as opposed to dead for good) they might not really care too much if I gave up on college. Mom's getting more and more comfortable with the supernatural stuff. I mean, I've pulled her bacon out of the fire twice now. However, to be fair here, her bacon wouldn't have been in the fire this time (with the email thing) if not for the paranormal stuff.

The heavens split asunder with the cacophony of a dozen semi-truck sized boulders bouncing down the mountainside. I'm kidding. It's only Sam coming down the stairs to the basement. I think that's a paradox more bizarre than Sophia being able to use magic. How on Earth does a scrawny ten-year-old boy make so much noise on stairs?

My little brother walks into my room without knocking. He's wearing an expression of mission as well as a dark blue T-shirt with grey sweatpants. The boy's also carrying a clipboard and pen. I feel like I'm about to be surveyed. Wonder what he's trying to get the 'rents to do this time. He pauses by the door only long enough to determine it's me, Ash, and Chloe in bed—and not me plus Hunter.

Yeah, that's happened once or twice since Ashley moved in. She and Chloe go to her room whenever I have Hunter over.

"Sare, you awake?" asks Sam.

"Yep." I sit up.

The boy walks up to the bedside, glancing down at his clipboard. "What's your worst fear?"

"Hmm." I tap a finger to my chin. "I'm not sure it's terribly wise to answer that question when asked by someone who's known to associate with demons."

Sam smiles, totally aware that I'm joking. "Your worries are not irrational. Though, my association with demons isn't bad. I assure you any information shared will be kept in confidence."

"Gee, Sam, you sound like a website trying to get me to accept cookies."

He holds up one finger. "I will gladly accept any cookies you want to give me."

"Heh. Dammit. Now I'm hungry."

Sam taps the pen on the clipboard. "Seriously, though. What are you afraid of most? The sefil is going to attack us."

"Ack!" I yank the covers off and swing my legs over the side of the mattress so I'm sitting on the edge. "It's back already?"

"No," replies Sam in a calm tone. "He's only a demon now, not a sefil. He's stuck in the bad place."

"The waiting area at the DMV office?" I ask.

He winces. "No, not *that* bad."

"Hell?"

"It's not hell. Just his home realm. Hell is something humans made up to scare people." Sam sighs.

I glance at the enormous textbook on my desk from the 'Life Science' class. There's an entire college course about humanity's tendency to fill in knowledge gaps with made up stories. "Guess that means there's no such thing as Heaven either?"

"Well..." Sam rhythmically clicks his pen. "The ideas of a Heaven or Hell are hyper-simplified explanations of imagined demi-planes. I'm not saying they're imaginary, just demi-planes humans imagined to be certain ways. Kind of like how people imagined what Antarctica was like before anyone actually went there."

"Riiight."

"Reality is like a giant Mandelbrot fractal," says Sam. "Planes and planes knit together in an endless repeating pattern in four dimensions. You can 'zoom in' infinitely and it just keeps repeating itself forever. The plane we call the normal world is one of millions. Some are parallel dimensions, some are physically elsewhere. Others exist in a fourth-dimensional relationship to our world. It is quite possible that one such demi-plane resembles the 'heaven' described by ancient philosophers."

I stare at him. "Where did that come from?"

"Olmaz, mostly." Sam shrugs one shoulder. "He likes to talk about stuff like that."

"Oof. Well. Okay. Just don't go running off to another plane of existence without asking Mom if it's okay first."

He nods. "Promise. I'm not really interested in leaving this plane... except the mirror sometimes because it's handy."

"Wait, is the mirrorverse another plane?"

"Not exactly." Sam keeps fidgeting at his pen. "Olmaz described it like... picture our reality like a giant dollhouse that's made entirely of glass. The mirrorverse is the shadow cast on the space outside our reality."

"Made of glass?" I scrunch my nose. "What's that supposed to mean?"

"See-through. The shadow it casts—the mirrorverse—reflects everything, inside and outside. It's flipped around like a reflection in a mirror but it's more than just the image that's reversed. Moods, reality, and fate are inverted." Sam stops robo-clicking the pen. "The mirrorverse is a four-dimensional space wrapped around ours. That's how we can walk for only a few minutes there and cover the same amount of distance it would take hours to walk here."

"Ugh." I rub my face. "I'm not awake enough for this esoteric a conversation."

"Sorry." He clicks the pen once. "Worst fear?"

"Why are you asking?"

"Because the demon formerly known as sefil is going to attack us." Sam places the pen against the paper on his clipboard, ready to write my answer down. "He can't act directly but he can influence the world around us. I'm trying to work on protections."

I hang my head. "Great. More random acts of seeming bad luck trying to kill me."

"I need to know what to watch out for and guard against." Sam smiles. "I promise I won't tell anyone, no matter how embarrassing it is. But I need you to be honest if the protection's going to work."

Hmm. I peer through my fingers at the carpet between my feet. "Not too long ago, I might've said my worst fear was confrontation, especially with a boy I wanted to break up with."

He cringes, then rests a hand on my arm. "Oof."

"Thanks." I pat his hand. "I'm over Scott. Really. Not sure that aversion to conflict and arguing is a 'real' fear though. It's not the sort of thing people have nightmares about. I can't really say for sure what my *worst* fear is now. It's a toss-up between losing my family or that I'm going to be responsible for bad stuff happening to you guys."

Sam scribbles some stuff down on his paper. "About what I guessed."

"What did the others say?" I ask.

He finishes writing, then looks over the clipboard. "Sierra's is school shooting. Sophia's is implausible."

"Fuzzydoom?" I chuckle.

"No. She said her worst fear is suddenly finding herself naked in class at school." Sam frowns. "Like that's going to happen."

I chuckle, thinking of the London mystics trying to teleport-nap her. "It almost did. Thankfully, she happened to be in a bathroom at the time."

"Oh, yeah." Sam bites his lower lip. "But, she was afraid of getting caught in school with no clothes before they did that. Honestly, she's not specifically afraid of a spontaneous wardrobe malfunction. She's really afraid of being humiliated, made fun of, and laughed at. If she tripped in the cafeteria and threw her lunch all over the place, or someone at her dance class dropped her, or she fell off the stage at a recital, any of that would bother her just as much as her clothes vanishing."

"Hmm. Does she have nightmares about it?"

He shrugs. "You're the mind reader. I don't know."

"Should we be concerned she's still got such a childish fear?" I scratch at my right eyebrow. "I mean, being suddenly naked in class and having everyone laugh at her is really tame compared to being afraid our entire family's going to be killed."

"Nah. I'm kinda jealous." Sam exhales. "Her fear is easy to mitigate. And, if I fail, no one is going to get hurt."

"True."

"Also." Sam holds up one finger. "Fear of public embarrassment isn't *that* childish. Dad said his greatest fear is public speaking."

"Wow, really?"

Sam nods. "Yeah, but he's fibbing. He's really afraid of us getting hurt."

Oof. My brother's not wrong. We're all in trouble now. It's manageable trouble, though. Not like we are facing inevitable doom —merely danger. Can't help myself, so I pull Sam into a squish hug. He doesn't mind. Pretty sure he and Dad are on the same page for worst fear. Grr. I hate that my ten-year-old brother's worst fear is losing his family and not something silly like Sophia's, or closet monsters.

I know without a doubt that my brother being aware that losing his family is a thing that can happen is my fault. It wouldn't even be on his mind if I hadn't died and become a vampire. Okay, maybe that's Scott's fault more than mine.

Whatever. Point is, there's a demon out there gunning for us, and he's really angry. He's not going to want to simply kill us all. That would be over too fast. If I had to guess, he's going for the Petra tactic: mentally destroy us to the point we beg for death, then keep on torturing us for a while more.

While that's horrifying to think about, it also gives me time. I don't have to worry about anyone in my family being blown up or killed in a sudden freak accident. The demon's not going to let us off the hook that easily.

CHAPTER 16

THE MICROSCOPIC LINE BETWEEN LAZINESS AND PRAGMATISM

Yep. Still Wednesday.

It's only been like five hours since I woke up. Feels like two days.

I have one class Wednesday nights from seven to ten. This class is titled 'Rise of Modernity.' It's about how society evolved from religion and magic to science and technology. Our teacher's a woman about Mom's age named Meredith Ross. If 'normal white suburban human' had an entry in Wikipedia, this woman would be the photo used for it. She's ever so slightly 'science nerdy' but not to the point of having a pocket protector. Honestly, just by looking at her, she could be middle management at any big company in the area.

She does have two Christopher Hitchens quotes as well as a James Randi on posters, so it's pretty obvious to me where she stands on the whole 'religion and magic' thing. I do have to respect Randi to a point, though. He thought magic and psychics were complete bull; however, he was willing to examine any evidence presented to him. That's the sign of an open mind. A reasonable person changes their opinion if given sufficient proof of being wrong. Unreasonable people continue to insist they're right while ignoring any evidence to the contrary.

Unfortunately—or perhaps fortunately for us—no one showed up to give him compelling evidence. He only got the charlatans and the con artists. Obviously, magic is real. I wonder if the mystics have the same sort of secrecy thing as vampires. I'm not sure if there are mortal psychics, like legit ones. I'm not talking about the Miss Cleos or tarot card readers. I mean, *I* can read minds and change memories, but I'm also a vampire. Psychic phenomena are a thing for a fact. Question is, do people have to become undead to take advantage of them?

Professor Ross welcomes us to her class. By the way, this is happening in a normal-sized more traditional classroom, not an auditorium. She goes through a brief summary of the class subject matter, then dives right into the material.

Oh, boy. Looks like the crux of this class is talking about how humanity invented gods to explain stuff they couldn't figure out... and the more science explained, the less humans needed to make up spirits and gods. We'll apparently be starting with ancient stuff like sun worship and Mayan human sacrifice and moving forward through history from there, going over stuff like when people thought magic was real and burned witches, all the way to humans setting foot on the moon.

Sounds interesting if not particularly useful from a career stand-point. Lucky me, I don't care about becoming employable. This curriculum is taking a modernist viewpoint, talking about magic like it was never real and entirely something primitive people made up. Imagine the exploding heads I could cause if I brought Sophia in for 'show and tell.' I'd like to see science explain a teleporting kitten.

Speaking of science... I'm not sure any science could explain what happened to me in the hallway yesterday.

Hmm. Weird thought. I should already get credit for this course since Dad's a tenured professor of common sense. All my life, he's been teaching me to think critically and ask questions. Okay, to be fair, he let me have Santa Claus for a while. I grew out of that on my own around age ten. Yeah, this class looks like a deep dive into stuff like 'what's more likely, the crops didn't do well because rain was scarce or you didn't kill enough children to appease the gods.'

Ugh. Humanity can be evil sometimes. They blame vampires for being monsters, but good grief. Mortal humans have done way worse things than pickpocketing blood from total strangers a few times a week.

Professor Ross isn't the most exhilarating speaker. She's not too bad, though she's nowhere near the energy level of Professor Guillermo from my Art History class. Then again, not many people are.

I metaphorically melt into my seat, lulled into a mental haze by her hypnotically toneless voice and various bodily noises going on around me. In a way, I sorta miss my teachers from last semester. It's probably only because I got used to them. Except for Professor Heath, it's not like I really miss their company as people. That's a bit of Dad in me. He likes routine. Dislikes change. As soon as I get used to this semester's teachers, I'll have a new set. Next year, I'll wind up missing them.

One thing thus far... my teachers are all pretty normal. Haven't met Dr. Markov yet... her class is tomorrow night. Though, the others are sane. No vampires. None of them are trying to be stand-up comedians like Professor Connolly. None are intolerably slow like Dr. Mercer. I'm taking a high dose of normalium this year.

Not the most exciting experience, but at least it's easy work. No calculus. Crazy thing... last year, I thought a computer science degree would be a good idea. Only reason I picked it is Dad's a programmer. Not a great reason. I don't have a personal love of computer stuff or coding. I mean, I *could* have tolerated it if need be. But it doesn't need to be. Right, the crazy part—when searching for an easy major that would let me cruise through another three years of school, I did a search for 'most useless college degrees.' You know what surprised me? Computer science was on that list. Apparently, it's considered too general. Employers still need to provide training for more specific computer-related things to make someone employable. Like a CS degree doesn't make you into a programmer, or a network administrator, or one of those super freaky nerdy people who design new microchips.

Yeah, I made a good change. If I'm going to earn a useless degree, it's not going to be one requiring heavy math and a lot of hard work. Bleh. I guess that means I'm just lazy. Or is it pragmatic? Why work hard when I don't have to?

I sit there trying to listen to Professor Ross, though my brain is going anywhere but her. Random body function noises come from all over the room. Between half-digested food, upset intestines, saliva swishing around, and chairs creaking, I may as well be in the middle of the Amazon rain forest listening to wildlife. It's near deafening. This one dude's gut microbes are cooing at each other like lovesick toucans.

Hmm. Maybe taking an easy class load isn't a better idea. Boredom sucks every bit as much as hard work.

Bubbling noises from close behind me cause my brain to imagine gas bubbles navigating the back-and-forth bends of an intestinal tract like a really disgusting cartoon. A chair squeaks. That amount of gas moving through someone has only one end result. Whoever it is has the decorum to shift their weight enough so the fart-splosion is silent. Or at least, silent to mortals. To me, it sounds like the Tasmanian Devil trying to blow out a birthday candle.

Oh, no. Please no. That was close. Too close.

I stop breathing.

Even though I'm no longer moving air in and out of my body, the smell hits me anyway seconds later. Acute vampire senses can be a curse. This stinks so much I can taste it. It stinks so acutely bad I can tell the person had some sort of Italian food with mussels, tomato sauce, and a ton of garlic.

So glad I didn't eat any normal food recently, or I'd be throwing up all over the hair of the woman in front of me. Did this fart-from-hell literally originate from Hell? Is this the sefil demon trying to make me act weird in public? Gah! My eyes are watering.

A few other people around me cough or make subtle 'I smell that, you're a jerk for doing it in class' gestures. I'm glad no one is looking at me like it's my fault. They probably take one look at me gasping for breath, eyes watering, nearly about to faint and figure I'm a victim, too.

I cover my nose, close my eyes, and just wait for the thermonuclear flame wave to be over with.

After a moment, the room falls quiet. A lull in Professor Moss's presentation lines up with a coincidental lack of body function symphony. The putrid gas cloud shifts tone from mostly digested Italian seafood to rotting eggs. Not sure, but that might qualify as an improvement.

An anxiety spike hits me.

It's not natural. It's the sort of 'you are in deep shit' subconscious warning thing vampires have. A squish comes from ahead of me, slightly to the left, like someone easing their weight onto a bloated ketchup packet.

I snap my eyes open.

The classroom's changed. It still mostly looks the same, but similarity ends with the layout of desks and walls. The other students and the professor are gone. Rather than posters and books, the room's decorated in bloody chains, spiky things, and five tall, cylindrical cages with domed tops. Each cage contains a skinless, writhing body... too mutilated to tell if they're men or women. Wails of agony come from faces embedded in the walls. Blood dribbles off the ceiling, spattering on the desks around me. A directionless jingle of heavy chains comes from seemingly everywhere at once.

Another skinless person, not in a cage, shambles toward me from six desks away. He (or she, can't tell) has this barbed meathook thing in their right hand. Got a good feeling they're planning to attempt inserting the pointy end of the hook into some part of my anatomy.

Now this is what I figured an advanced calculus classroom would be like, maybe with a bit more agonized wailing.

Nice try, demon. This is too over the top. It's not as scary as the big guy chasing me with a knife. Throwing me into a scene straight out of a Clive Barker movie immediately makes me disbelieve what I'm seeing.

At least it does for two seconds. Then I remember my vampire instinct felt danger. It's the same mental reflex that can kick me awake in the middle of the morning if someone's about to try ramming a stake through my heart. That shouldn't work for a nightmare, should it? Also, it's after dark and I'm online. I'm not capable of falling asleep now. This can't be a nightmare. Something weird is going on.

Shit.

I spring out of my seat, leaping up to hover a few inches off the ground. A brief 'fight or flight' debate races across my brain. The shambling corpse coming at me seems pretty slow. Also, I don't feel like doing another 'running for my life' thing two days in a row. Stupid screwed up by deciding to make his move at night. I am not helpless now.

The... whatever it is... swings the meat hook at me. I zip to the side, swing myself around, and plant an axe kick into the side of the flayed person's skull, smashing it into a pulp. Gooey red stuff goes flying like I punted a bowl of strawberry pudding. It seems this skinless abomination works in advertising. Not having a brain isn't slowing it down. Evidently undeterred by no longer having much of a head, the thing rakes the meat hook at me again.

This time, I glide backward to dodge, then sprout claws and lunge in, shredding at the fiend's chest a few times as fast as I can. Brittle skin with the texture of overcooked fried chicken bursts apart with a parchment like crackle. Thousands of cockroaches—big suckers, too—spill out from the chest cavity and rain down to the floor.

Eww. Gross.

Yes, they're hissing at me.

No, I am not touching the floor. Those bugs can be as angry as they want; they can't reach me.

Right as I make this 'hah, you can't get me' face at them, the roaches' shells split open, revealing wings.

Okay, I don't care how tough or brave you are. When 2,000 four-inch-long cockroaches all sprout wings and buzz into the air at you, you will scream. The next several minutes pass in a blur of flying in circles, shrieking, and flailing. I *think* the bugs are trying to bite me. Maybe sting, I dunno. Do cockroaches have stingers?

I'm so caught up in fending off the buzzing swarm that I don't notice the other flayed body coming for me until after he grabs me from behind. I say 'he' because he's significantly taller and broader than me. It's a guess. Let's just say his mostly skinless body is so mutilated you couldn't say for sure if he was really a he before. Yes. It is missing. Entirely.

Poor guy.

Dude collects me and tries to pin my arms so he can drag me over to the now-empty cage he came from.

Uhh, no thanks.

I do the same thing any reasonable, ordinary girl would do if a strange man grabbed her from behind: I rip his arms off. To be fair, I hadn't been trying to do that, just break out of his grip... but his shoulders are brittle.

The torso-on-legs ambles after me, moaning like a zombie. More huge cockroaches start to crawl out of his mouth like they really can't wait to join the fight and bite off a piece of me. Eek! I backpedal from him, each of my hands around the wrist of his disembodied limbs. They're not exactly swords, but I suppose this counts as me being *armed*.

Since I'm already holding them, I attack. Ripped-off arms don't make for terribly effective weapons. They break apart after only a few hits at vampire levels of strength without doing too much damage to the skinless thing.

Seemingly frustrated by his inability to grab me, the guy bends over backward so severely his chest tears open across the middle of his stomach, sending another mass of roaches spilling to the floor.

I have never in my life wanted a flamethrower as bad as I do right now.

Something hot and slimy grabs me around the left ankle. Oh, no. I do not like the way that feels. Not at all.

Said slimy thing coils around like a snake and starts going up under the leg of my jeans.

Screaming, I jump into the air, feeling like a pixie with a ball and chain attached to one leg. The slime-covered bloody tentacle struggles to hold on to my leg. Right as it begins to slip loose, another tentacle breaks up from the floor and seizes my right leg.

Eek! This stops now. I'm not sure what I'm more afraid of: ending up as the lead character in a crazy tentacle hentai cartoon or being immobilized while those demonic cockroaches devour all my skin. Those flayed people coming after me kinda make sense now. The damn bugs ate their skin off.

I lurch downward, raking my claws at the demonic tendrils. They cut as easily as noodles; painfully hot blood sprays everywhere. Like an overinflated helium balloon having its string cut, I zoom straight up the instant the tentacles succumb to my bladed fingertips. I don't even care that my back slams into the ceiling. The other six tentacles reaching for me can't get me up here. They flail and wave, trying to stretch, but keep falling short.

"Sorry, looks like you're not long enough. Hear they have pills that might help," I snap.

Right, this is going to be endless. Bugs. Why did it have to be bugs? So, what if I squirm at the idea of cockroaches? They're nasty. I grew up in a clean environment. Never saw a roach this close before. I'm allowed to find them disgusting right? Not like I'm the kind of girl who screamed when a boy put a beetle on my arm. Did I mention they're *four freakin' inches long*?

Ten thousand giant cockroaches with wings... though? *Aggressive* cockroaches trying to eat me? That's different. I am totally justified in screaming. Oh, this bastard of a demon. What would a strong, fast vampire have trouble fighting? A billion bugs.

Staying in this room is not helping. It's endless. I swerve around in midair and fly for the exit. My sneakers smash into the door at the same time, nearly breaking it off the hinges and knocking it wide open.

I drop through the open doorway... and land seated in my desk.

Three realizations dawn on me simultaneously.

One: that probably didn't happen for real.

Two: my claws are out.

Three: my fangs are out.

Wait, there's a fourth realization: no one's noticed me yet. I close my mouth and stuff my hands under the little desk attached to this chair. Hiding my hands takes less time than retracting the claws. I sit there, paralyzed with dread that someone saw evidence of my vampiric nature. Any second now, a roach is going to walk onto my desk or something. Every damn horror movie does that, so the viewer isn't sure if the terrifying event was real or imaginary.

One... two...

Six seconds later, and no roach showing itself, I relax a bit.

I'm nowhere near as freaked out as I was when the guy chased me. Knife-wielding big guy hits a tender nerve of mine. Over-the-top horror movie gore is droll by comparison. The bugs got me, though. That's not terror as much as it's an *eww eww eww* situation. Even if I only hallucinated that, I'm hopping right in the shower the instant I get home.

Yeah, the demon wasn't trying to scare me there. He wanted to cause a public vampire freakout. Guess I'm a bit more stoic than I give myself credit for. Either that or Professor Moss is so captivatingly dull she's hypnotized the class into a trance so deep no one realized what I did. Maybe whatever Sam's planning to do helped out. This demonic attack definitely didn't hit me as hard as the last one.

My hands aren't even shaking. I just feel... unclean.

Eww. Roaches.

Bleh.

CHAPTER 17
SCHRODINGER'S DREAM

As soon as I get home, I barge in on Sam in his room. Like any other given night, he and Ronan are on the PlayStation.

"Did you do anything yet?" I ask.

Sam continues playing, staring at the screen. "I've done lots of things. Can you be a little more specific?"

"Anything about anti-demon protection." I swipe my hair out of my face.

"Oh." He pauses the game and looks up at me from where he's sitting cross-legged on the floor, his back against his bed. "Did something happen and are you okay?"

I exhale, nodding. His response makes me think he hasn't quite done anything yet. "Not sure if I had a second hallucination, daydream, or what."

"Uh oh." Ronan goes wide-eyed. "Are we in trouble?"

"No. We're in danger." Sam yawns. "Trouble's like when Mom's upset at us. We're handling it, though. Don't freak out."

Blix crawls out from under the pillow and babbles in my direction.

"He says it's both a dream and real." Sam fidgets at the PlayStation controller. "The demon can slip into your thoughts if you're really tired, drunk, high, or in some sort of altered state of consciousness."

Blix points at me and chatters away.

"Since you can't be drunk, or high, and weren't able to sleep after dark," says Sam, "Blix thinks something else must've happened."

I fold my arms. "Being hypnotized into a near trance by a monotone teacher while the Fart of Ultimate Doom scorches my sinuses out? I swear that stank so bad I got light-headed."

"Ooba noba." Blix snaps his fingers.

"He says that would do it." Sam laughs. "The fart of ultimate doom. Epic."

Ronan laughs.

"Yes. It was fartmageddon. The buttpocalypse," I say. "Total ass-nihilation."

The boys crack up laughing so hard they're in tears. Not impressive. Fart jokes and preteen boys go together like PB and J. Or should I say fart jokes and males. Dad's still totally a twelve-year-old when it comes to toilet humor. He laughs at the dumbest, grossest things.

I tell my brother about what happened, though I avoid making any hentai tentacle remarks. I don't think he understands what that is and I'm not going to be the one to explain it to him. Kinda wish *I* didn't understand what that meant. Thanks, Ash. Not. He nods, taking it in. According to Blix, the events were simultaneously real and all in my head. The demon pulled a tiny portion of my consciousness into a demi-plane. It's why the events had a simultaneous real and dream quality, why my vampire sense felt danger. Evidently, if I died in the middle of that experience, I'd really have died.

Or at least, I would if I was mortal. Blix has no idea what would happen to a vampire that 'dies' in one of those weird demonic dream-not-dream things. Probably about the same existential torture as having to sit through a six-hour marathon of Dr. Phil episodes. It won't kill me, but I'd probably rather be dead.

Anyway... talking about a swarm of enormous cockroaches has me feeling all sorts of squirmy again. Time for a shower.

∽

I CUT THE WATER—RELUCTANTLY—AND step out of the basement bathroom's shower stall.

Unlike the main bathroom upstairs, this one is cozy. 'Cozy' is a way to call a place cramped and tiny while making it sound nice. However, a welcome side effect of the smallness of our basement bathroom is it tends to end up as warm as the shower—especially if one takes their time. This allows me not to rush drying off. While I am a vampire and cold doesn't really bother me, it takes a minute or two for my brain to process the adjustment. I suppose a few minutes of being paralyzed with cold is hardly the same as being mortal and stuck suffering until I find warmth. Still, no one likes a sudden blast of coldness when they're all comfy and warm.

Speaking of...

I'm like midway through drying off when Mom screams upstairs. The tone of her scream is way too severe for her to have found a mouse, unexplained animal, or simple mess. It's even a bit beyond the rage-horror of finding a muddy footprint on the carpet. This sounds genuine. Her scream is close to the sound she made the first time she saw an imp.

Mom is in trouble. Ack!

About three quarters of the way across the basement, heading for the stairs, I realize I'm damp and naked. Vampire reflexes and speed make up for a lot of sin. I swerve around to go the other way back to my room, then realize I'm still holding a towel. Okay, that works. I keep spinning until I'm facing the stairs again and zoom up to the kitchen. Somehow, by the time I make it to the living room (where the scream came from) I've got the towel wrapped around my body. If any sort of paranormal battle is about to happen, I have no hope of keeping it. Maybe I shouldn't even try to. Mom would be upset if something ripped her nice towels.

Dad's in his usual recliner catty corner to the sofa. Mom's on the sofa. My father looks like he's trying not to laugh though is also visibly unsettled. My mother's more or less paralyzed with dread. It takes me a few seconds to discover the source of her unease.

One of Aurélie's dolls is on the sofa sitting next to Mom.

"You guys okay?" I ask.

Mom stares at me. "Sarah! What's going on?"

"Lots of stuff." I clamp my arms across my chest to keep the towel in place. "Can you please be a little less vague?"

She side-eyes the doll. "This doll just appeared out of nowhere. One minute it's not there. The next, it's there. And I swear it moved."

The doll turns its head toward her.

Mom lets out an uneasy whimper.

"Relax, Mom. She's not going to hurt anyone. Well, maybe she will if people keep referring to her as an it." I squish my toes into the carpet repetitively. "Aurélie had to go out of state for a week or so. A few of her dolls wanted to come keep Chloe company so they aren't lonely."

Apparently convinced the creepy doll is, in fact, not a threat to us, Dad covers his mouth and does his best not to laugh out loud. Mom kinda glares at him in that way where if the doll had spooked anyone else but her, she'd be laughing, too.

"I guess she wanted to check out what television was." I glance at the screen. Looks like they're watching some old movie. Like late Seventies old by the looks of it. "Okay, no crisis here. I'm going back downstairs..."

We—that's Chloe and I—did warn Sierra the dolls were in the house. Nothing quite freaks a tween girl out as bad as being half awake and watching a doll crawl into your bed to snuggle. At least two of the dolls hate sleeping alone. While they don't mind being around vampires, they much prefer to snuggle with living people at night. I'm honestly surprised. Both of my sisters are okay with the dolls. Even Sophia got over her initial fear. Now, she thinks of them as ghosts possessing dolls. She's okay being around ghosts who aren't trying to hurt people. Sierra's unfazed by them. She rationalizes it as having a tiny bodyguard watching out for danger all night while she sleeps.

No, she's not become paranoid something's going to get us at night in our beds. But, there is a demon issue going on now. A pair of unblinking glass eyes couldn't hurt. And, I do suspect Aurélie sent them here as much to help watch out for us as for their benefit.

I plod back to my room, slightly annoyed at being abruptly chased out of the nice, warm bathroom. Oh well. At least I'm no longer in a constant state of squirming over giant roaches.

CHAPTER 18
TEASING THE RULES

The remainder of my Wednesday is fairly tame.

Guessing when the highlight of the evening is watching my two sisters and Chloe have a tea party with eight haunted dolls, a teddy bear, and two unicorn plushies, my life has reached an epic state of lameness. Yeah, my sisters are a bit too old for doll tea parties, even though Sophia sometimes doesn't act like it. She didn't have the least bit of embarrassment flinging herself wholly into it. Sierra threatened revenge if any cell phone cameras appeared during the event.

Of course, she wasn't there to pretend tea party. She's curious about the paranormal stuff.

Sophia, as it turns out, can talk to the dolls like they're people. I really hope she doesn't tell the wrong person that the dolls talk back to her. All eight do indeed have spirits in them. None of them are anyone notable in a sense of being historically significant or famous, though they're all quite old. Rebecca's the youngest, having died somewhen in the 1800s. I think one of the Maries (there are two) lost her life in 1749. All eight died tragic deaths. Five murders and three diseases. All had been between nineteen and twenty-five at the time of their deaths and ended up being stuck in the dolls as some sort of side effect of their not wanting to die yet.

Sigh. So sad.

None of them have any weird powers or insight into the future like Coralie, though they would be able to see a demonic presence if one happened to be around.

Right, so... the world's creepiest tea party later, it ends up being Thursday afternoon.

Argh. One more class until the weekend. Yanno, part of me is annoyed at the whole looking forward to the weekend thing. I'm a vampire, dammit. I shouldn't exist beholden to the oppressive work-life balance forced on us by the corporate masters. Oof. There I go channeling Dad again. He does kind of have a point though. Most people spend the vast majority of their able years, and the vast majority of daylight during those years, serving some employer rather than living. By the time they have the free time to do what they enjoy, they're too old to really enjoy it. Corporatism sucks the life out of humans as effectively and insidiously as any monster from a horror movie. Perhaps even worse since most people don't even see it as a monster draining them.

Being a vampire is weird. I never had thoughts like this before. What person my age would? Then again, how many eighteen-year-olds get pied in the face by mortality? I got a super close-up look at the thin membrane separating life and death. That tends to leave a mark.

Speaking of leaving marks, I should probably do some homework.

I kill most of the afternoon mopping up the assignments from my other classes. All is well until I notice several things. One: children's voices come from the backyard, seemingly having fun. Okay, no problem there. Two: Chloe is not in the bedroom with me. Hmm. That is not necessarily a problem. She could be with Ashley in her room or upstairs with the 'rents or hanging with Sophia. Three: one of the happy voices coming from outside is Chloe's.

Frap.

That's a mixture of an f-bomb and crap. It's stronger than saying 'crap!' but less strong than dropping an unfiltered f-bomb. Eep. Okay, it's not the end of the world if some neighborhood kids see Chloe. Might get dicey if they make friends with her to the point we can't say she's some niece of ours visiting from out of state.

Oh well. Looks like I'm using mental powers on children tonight. I'd better go take inventory so I know which houses the 'truth faerie' needs to visit. Or should I say the anti-truth faerie.

I head upstairs to the kitchen and peer out the sliding glass door. Kids zoom around the yard. Okay, not a huge deal. It's just Nicole, Megan, Priya, and my sisters plus Chloe. They're running back and forth playing Frisbee.

No 'strange' kids from nearby houses I've never seen before. My sisters' friends are around often enough to where I don't need to worry about finding a good opportunity to give them a mental compulsion to ignore Chloe's unchanging age. There's no need to make them forget her. All the problems caused by a vampire child come from people finding a little kid not growing up to be strange. If I program a person not to think it's strange she's permanently seven, they won't cause problems.

I also intend to add a little side command not to talk about Chloe to anyone outside my family.

Anyway, it should be heartwarming to watch her playing and acting like a child, finally getting to have fun and do the sorts of things she'd been too scared to do in her old life. Other kids refused to go near her house since her father was such a jerk. Chloe hadn't been allowed to go over friends' houses either. Weird. Her parents didn't really want a kid, and they punished Chloe for existing every chance they got.

Grr. I'm going to dive into the forbidden bookshelves at the mystic place next time I'm there so I can find a way to raise them from the dead—so I can kill them a second time.

I watch the girls play for a few minutes. Somewhere in the back of the yard, Max the hellhound rests peacefully watching them as well. Sounds so crazy to think about him there with children, but he's a big teddy demon. I'd almost feel sorry for anyone who ran into our yard intending to hurt the girls.

Almost.

~

I HAVE A CHILD PROBLEM.

A confluence of events has come together to complicate my unlife tonight. To be fair, the complication is 100% my fault. If I wasn't trying to be normal and go to college, there wouldn't be an issue at all. So, what's wrong? Well... the 'rents went to some social thing at Boeing tonight. I can't fault them that. They don't get out much. As boring as an office party sounds to me, they've been looking forward to it. And hey, I go to those vampire soirees and don't hate them. Both Mom's office party and those soirees are really just a bunch of people wearing needlessly formal clothing standing around in a room having snacks and talking.

Since I don't hate the soirees, I guess that means I've matured.

Or something.

Anyway... the 'rents are occupied. Oh, speaking of my parents... Dad's birthday is tomorrow. September 8th. I got him one of those miniature 8-bit Nintendo things with like 300 games in it. He's going to flip.

Ashley's got a class tonight, too.

Michelle is so damn busy I barely get to see her anymore.

Aurélie is in Louisiana.

Mom and Dad are trusting the Littles to babysit themselves for a few hours. Some people might think it dodgy to leave a twelve, eleven, and ten-year-old on their own even for like three hours. However, my siblings are unusually responsible for their ages. Plus, we have a bunch of paranormal stuff going on, an imp, a hellhound, and a ghost (probably) in the house. None of my siblings are going to get themselves in trouble if unsupervised. They are not the 'play with matches' type of kids. The worst thing that might happen in terms of them doing something bad is Sophia being paralyzed with fear and indecision and just standing there crying if something goes wrong (like a fire on the stove).

They know how to call 911 and they have my cell phone number, knowing I can fly home in mere minutes if need be.

As mature as they are for their ages, taking on the responsibility of watching a vampire child is a bit much. I wouldn't feel right asking them to look after an ordinary seven-year-old.

I've got nothing else to do with Chloe. It's either miss my first class to babysit or... bring her with me. I mean, people in SCC have brought their kids to school with them here and there in the past when they couldn't get a babysitter. Granted, those kids were like two years old or smaller. I don't think the school has an official ban on bringing kids in emergencies. Not like a small child is going to earn college credits without paying simply for being in the room.

Also, I cheat.

Oh, dammit! I still need to teach her how to hide herself in the open. Haven't really had the time to do it yet... and there's still a bit of hesitation. I mean, teaching a child how to basically become invisible couldn't possibly go wrong in any way, right? At least it doesn't work on other vampires without a serious age gap or specialization —like Ashley. Chloe wouldn't be able to use it to hide from me or Ash. Also, I don't expect her to misbehave. When considering all possible benefits and all possible problems, the net result feels like it's ending on the side of good.

Allowing for some small amount of mischief is a mild price to pay if she can keep herself from being noticed by mortals.

Anyway... so Chloe is coming to school with me tonight. She's excited, though she keeps asking me if there are going to be naked men in the classroom. I really hope she doesn't blurt that out loud when we're not alone. With any luck, going to my chemistry class tonight—where there's no good reason for nudity beyond an unexpected catastrophic mishap with corrosive substances—will convince her 'college' doesn't always involve naked dudes.

I guess it depends on what sorority one joins, but still.

The sun is still being a pain in my butt, not going down until after seven at night. Can't fly in. Grr. Driving it is. I leave home with enough time to spare so there's no need to drive like an idiot. I'm on high alert for demonic interference. Either the demon's tired or it's difficult to possess people moving at the speed of highway traffic. We make it to SCC without a scratch or even a mildly harrowing experience.

Chloe looks like a smaller version of me with paler skin and black (instead of brown) hair. We're dressed almost in uniform: purple T-shirt, jeans, sneakers, hoodie. The only difference really is my shirt's plain while hers has a chibi unicorn on it. She's not particularly into unicorns. Ashley bought the shirt for her.

Hey, it's cute.

She's even carrying a small backpack. Rather than schoolbooks, hers is packed with Barbie stuff and a Gameboy (Sam's old one he hasn't really touched since getting a PSP). Gotta give her something to do for three hours, right?

I park in the usual garage on the second floor. Chloe's twisting around to look at everything—this is her first time downtown. I take her hand and try to act like a normal person escorting a normal kid. The day's super cloudy, almost dark enough for me to have risked flying. Alas, I know my luck. Since the sun is still out there behind the clouds, if a freak wind made an opening, the two of us would've had a Wile E. Coyote moment where the flying just stops working at a really inconvenient time and we fall out of the air to make a little puff of dust on impact.

Guessing that probably hurts a lot more than they make it seem in the cartoons.

Anyway, we make our way into the science building. As soon as we're around people, I start giving off the negative charm effect... encouraging people not to pay attention to us. No nefarious plans in mind. I simply would rather not have anyone see me with a kid, remember that, and then see me again six years from now and she's still the same size.

Maybe I'm being overly cautious. Better that than the vampiric powers that be decide it's too much of a risk to allow Chloe to keep existing.

The teacher is waiting in the classroom, rather earlier than most professors show up. She's a rather unassuming looking woman in her later forties. Her navy skirt suit makes her seem more like a lawyer than a teacher. She's totally got curly 'grandma hair' despite not being *that* old. The hair's brown, not grey. Just from looking at her, she seems really approachable and friendly.

I slip in the door, guiding Chloe with me toward the back of the room. Sitting in the back isn't usually my thing. I'm more of a 'middle of the room' kid. Front row is for the nerds and the teacher's pets. Back row is for slackers and troublemakers. Next time I'm here, I'll move to the middle.

Unlike the other classrooms, this one is more of a lab. The left half of the room is full of those black-topped chemistry tables just like my high school had in the chem lab. On the right, a collection of combination chair-desks is crammed into the 'spare floor space.' Looks like we'll be sitting there for lectures and book work, then getting up to do stuff practically at the tables.

Oh boy.

This is, of course, the first night of the class. Gonna go out on a limb here and guess we won't be trying to synthesize a new form of carbon fiber tonight. Safe bet we'll be doing stuff more complicated than high school chemistry.

"The desks are so big," whispers Chloe.

"That's because the students are." I grin.

She gazes around, then bites her lip at me. "Am I going to get in trouble?"

"For what?"

"Being here. I think I'm too little."

I shake my head. "Nah. Lots of people who go to school here have kids and can't always find a babysitter."

Chloe crawls into my lap as soon as I sit down.

Since we have a few minutes before class starts, I take the Gameboy out of her pack and show her how it works. Chloe seems content to play with it for now. I sit there watching the little screen. When it gets close to seven, I ease off the charm. It would be kinda stupid to get noted as absent while being here, right?

The teacher, Dr. Tatiana Markov according to my syllabus, eventually notices us sitting there. She smiles at us—mostly Chloe—before giving me a slightly odd look. Yeah, no way in hell would anyone believe the kid is mine. I was what, eleven years old when her mother had her? Worse, I look younger than I am. So, yeah. Not even going to try claiming she's mine or even that I adopted her. No one in their right mind allows an unemployed eighteen-year-old to adopt a kid.

Kinda crazy though... if said unemployed eighteen-year-old gets pregnant, society doesn't seem too concerned about how she's going to care for the baby. But adopt? No way kid, you're not responsible enough.

Sigh.

Right, so... our official public story is that she's my little cousin. We don't look related. Claiming her as my little sister might not be believable. Cousin is an easier sell. Of course, wherever possible, I'm steamrolling over any questions with vampire power. No need to tapdance around the bush when I can flamethrower it to a cinder.

On that note, I poke Dr. Markov in the brain as soon as we make eye contact. She's going to remember asking me about the kid already. She's my little cousin I 'got stuck' having to watch tonight. Oh wow. This woman apparently teaches science in high school during the day while also occasionally filling in at middle schools. Wow. And I thought Mom had a crazy work ethic. Dr. Markov only seems to go home long enough to sleep, shower, and eat. Then again, she *adores* educating people about science, especially kids. I suppose if your job is the same thing you do for fun it doesn't matter if you have no leisure time. All day is leisure time.

It would be like Sierra making her living playing video games.

A few minutes after seven, Dr. Markov gets up from her chair and officially starts the class. She goes through a quick introductory speech summarizing the curriculum. Her voice has a fairly heavy accent, though her speaking pace makes it easy to understand. She's an animated lecturer, moving around a lot and using various props. She's totally into this, radiating the enthusiasm of a kid. I imagine this is what Sophia would be like when she's getting close to fifty if someone asked her to talk about faeries.

Unsurprisingly, Chloe is not interested in college level chemistry. She tunes out the professor. A half hour or so later, she's had enough of the Gameboy—which she can play any time at home—and decides to wander around the classroom checking out the various pieces of equipment and display items. Dr. Markov has a number of cases full of 'shiny rocks.' Guessing they're samples of various elements.

I keep one eye on the kid, the other on the teacher, trying my best to divide attention between the subject matter and the child. Even though I know Chloe, I'm kinda surprised at how well-behaved she is. The girl doesn't touch anything, merely looks.

Some whispers come from my right, a woman asking the guy sitting next to her if he 'just saw that.'

"Saw what?" whispers the man.

"That cabinet just opened itself."

I glance in their direction. A late-thirties redhead in office worker attire points at one of the storage cabinets near the door out of the room. Can't see into it from all the way back here. No sign of ghosts in the area, though. The door is not presently moving by itself, and Chloe is on the opposite side of the room—in the back left corner. Ironically, she's also opening cabinet doors to peer inside at a whole mess of little white plastic jars.

Uh oh. Is the demon planning to mess with me? Three days in a row, it's given me crazy not-dreams at school. Damn. Maybe bringing Chloe here was a mistake. I should've stayed home and made the bad impression of missing the first class. Not like I couldn't 'fix' it later, even if it would've made me feel a bit guilty. Grr. Why did I have to be cursed with such an overdeveloped conscience?

On edge now, I wave at Chloe to come back to me. She shuts the cabinet doors and scurries over to sit on the floor next to my desk. The storage cabinet in the front of the room doesn't move. I'd like to dismiss it as the office woman seeing things. Alas, I know better. People sitting in a classroom only hallucinate things like that when the instructor is boring or the day after an all-night study session. Dr. Markov is not boring, and it's unlikely anyone's pulled a ramen-and-coffee fueled bender during the first week of a semester.

I'm ready for weird shit.

In hindsight, I should have asked Sam for more details about these demonic-induced daymares. Like, is it possible to break out of them? What's the best way to handle being trapped in a nonreality that can kill me? If it tries the big dude chasing me with a knife thing again, should I run in a panic or fight him? Feels like the 'scenario' wants me to run. Does doing the unexpected weaken the demon's influence or put me in more danger.

These are questions I need answers to.

Luckily, the material tonight isn't too heavy, not things I have to pay strict attention to since my mind is wandering down demon-infested hiking trails. Honestly, I'm getting a little angry. They say no good deed goes unpunished. This thing wants revenge on my family for destroying it. But what the heck did it think we should do, let it run amok murdering everything it sees? Apparently, the sefil are super, super dangerous to vampire kind. The more of us it eats, the stronger it gets, until it reaches an apocalyptic point. One sefil left unchecked could bring about the end of us all. And once there are no more vampires to devour, it'll erase mortal society.

Yeah, that's a hellscape even worse than the idea of Kanye West ending up in the White House—but not by much. At least the sefil would kill us relatively quickly.

Chloe is an absolute angel all night. Well, as much as three hours counts as 'all night.' Bringing a kid her age to a class like this is not fun for them. Three hours to me had to feel like nine hours to her. I almost feel guilty. How much of her good behavior is because she's afraid of being destroyed? The kid isn't afraid of me. She's afraid of causing trouble that gets Wolent angry. Dammit. I really hate that she's aware of the fact her right of existence could be revoked.

It would probably take more than I think for Mr. Wolent to change his mind. Like, he'd have to think she deliberately tried to cause trouble. Accidents shouldn't bring down his wrath—though they might get the Stefanos and Paolos of the vampire world grumbling.

Dr. Markov lets us go at 9:40 p.m., twenty minutes early. She said all she needed to say on night one. "Next week, we're going to dive right in up to our elbows. Bring gloves."

Hesitant chuckling comes from the students since most of us

aren't sure if she's being literal or metaphorical. I cheat and peek into her mind. Oh, she's being literal. We'll be doing practical chemistry next week. Crap! There's a 'chemistry supply kit' I needed to buy from the bookstore here and totally forgot about. It includes gloves.

Damn. Store's closed now. I'll have to grab that kit Tuesday between classes.

Chloe collects her Barbies and the Gameboy into her backpack. We get up and shuffle toward the door in the crowd of students all trying to squeeze out the same opening in the wall. It's only slightly faster than everyone trying to disembark from a 747 at the same time.

I'm about seven feet away from the door when my 'oh shit' sense goes off. For no conscious reason, I whip my head to the right and stare at the mysterious self-opening storage cabinet. My vampire reflexes are on full blast, making time around me seem to crawl. The white steel cabinet contains jars of various sizes, some plastic, some glass. The glass ones either contain powders, liquids, or small nuggets of metal submerged in liquid.

Within half a second of me looking at the cabinet, one of the small jars spontaneously shatters, spilling clear fluid. In addition to the fluid, a glass ampoule of silver liquid falls to the shelf. The ampoule rolls to the edge, falls to the floor, and shatters. For an instant, there's a splat mark of silver like spilled mercury metal— then it explodes into an amazingly intense fireball that throws tiny meteoric comets through the air, each one trailing smoke. A rain of fine glass shrapnel sprays over us, not that I really notice it too much. I'm blinded in the flash and freaking out at the heat wave.

The whole thing is over in a second, like an old Wild West camera flashpan blowing up, just with much less smoke.

I'm hissing, fangs bared, claws out.

So is Chloe... except her little claws are embedded in my leg, as she's clinging to me for dear unlife.

Uh oh!

With as much speed as inhumanly possible, I collect myself and put the claws away. Hiding fangs is a little easier since I only need to close my mouth. Dammit. That bastard demon. He's trying to expose me... and Chloe.

Dr. Markov yells in alarm and comes running over. After a brief glance at the cabinet to make sure nothing else is about to explode, she begins checking on students. I'm checking on other students, too, but not for cuts, scrapes, or burns. I gotta know if anyone saw us. The eight or nine closest people around us were fortunately too busy screaming, panicking, and freaking out at the explosion to notice the kid and I getting our vamp on.

I hurry jumping from brain to brain, peeking into their thoughts. Yeah. We got lucky. A hunk of reactive metal blowing up grabbed everyone's attention. No one noticed us. Whew. Dr. Markov's going nuts apologizing. She's not sure what caused the explosion. Thinks the jar might've had a crack she failed to notice, and it just happened to pick this moment to finally fail. I sense a note of skepticism in her voice, which gets me looking at her mind, too. Apparently, the silver liquid was cesium metal. That it promptly exploded into a fireball on contact with air is normal. Eep! No wonder she had it inside a glass capsule submerged in oil.

She's also highly concerned at how the cabinet opened. It should have been locked.

Ugh. I hope she doesn't get in trouble for this.

Damn. So much for an early night. Stupid demon. I can't just walk away and let things happen from here. Human curiosity works in my favor. The students who'd only just gone out the door stopped and came back to these what made the loud bang. I rush over there and start playing parking garage attendant. No one gets out until I'm done with them.

People are not going to remember the explosion.

Dr. Markov isn't going to get fired for failing to secure dangerous substances. No one will complain to the school. Yeah, mind controlling people is a bit pushy and wrong. However, it doesn't bother Follows Rules Girl. This is a supernatural zero-sum game. When crazy supernatural stuff causes problems, I have no qualms using crazy supernatural stuff to balance it out.

Eventually, I make my way through all the students and

approach Dr. Markov. She's content that no one got seriously hurt and is trying to figure out what the hell happened. Five minutes of staring into her eyes later, she's missing one jar of cesium and has no idea where it went. The scorch mark on the floor is kind of a clue, though I hope she won't connect those dots.

I leave her on mental pause long enough to do my best to clean up the broken glass and spilled oil.

All things considered, this counts as a win. The demon tried to fire-scare me into exposing myself as a vampire. He succeeded only in making me fifteen minutes late leaving campus. Instead of getting to go home at 9:40, it's already 10:16 p.m. and I'm still in the class-room. Bleh. I'll take it. Beats having two dozen cell phones posting pictures of a vampire online. Losing half an hour is a small price to pay.

After all, I'm off tomorrow.

CHAPTER 19

THIS COULD BACKFIRE

I awake Friday afternoon at my usual time to find a transparent man in his middle twenties standing near my bed. His clothing is antiquated like a background extra from a World War II film.

"Hello, Sarah," he says in perfect English.

"Umm." I blink at the guy. "Do I know you?"

"In a manner of speaking." He smiles. "You'd recognize my voice if I spoke German."

"Oh!" I sit up. "You got out of the phone?"

"Yes. Your sister's cat..." He shivers. "Brought the phone to a steel mill and dropped it into the glowing slag. There is an experience I hope never to repeat."

I shiver at the thought of being thrown into molten metal. That would probably end a vampire for good. I mean, it killed the Terminator, so it's gotta be deadly to vampires, right? Yeah, I know murderous androids from the future don't really exist. While that silly thought leaves my brain, I notice the ghost has a tiny clock on his wrist.

And I am an idiot. It's not a tiny clock. It's a watch. Duh. No wonder Dad looks at his arm whenever he's worried about being late. When he was my age, people wore watches. Now that I think about it, Dad used to wear one when I was little. He stopped bothering once he had a smartphone. Hey, it's not that stupid for me to forget what a watch is. Who even uses them anymore? They're not needed. Okay, except for rich jerks who want to advertise they have more money than sense, so they strap on a ten-thousand-dollar Rolex or something like that.

"Anyway, I am here to thank you." The ghost bows. "You and your sister—and her cat—have finally freed me from decades of imprisonment in that damnable lamp."

"It's almost weird hearing you speak English." I chuckle.

He gives a resigned sigh. "Well, I was a spy. That part is true. Wouldn't make a very good spy if I couldn't pass myself off as a British person."

"Yeah, true."

"I did not assassinate nor attempt to assassinate anyone," says the ghost. "By the way, my name is Tobias Krüger. As far as I am aware, I do not have any living relatives. No need to trouble you with any request to contact them. It's been so long since my death... However, I would like *you* to know that I did not support the Nazi party. Back in those days, we didn't really have much choice, you see. It's why I arranged myself into the role of a spy in Britain. I could send them random bits of useless information and keep myself safe while not helping them."

"You got found out, though." I cringe.

"No... well, I did but not by the Germans. British intelligence was about to contact me in regard to serving as a double agent. I choked on my lunch. My death wasn't so exciting as an assassination." He lets out this long suffering sigh—like he'd been holding it for decades. "All that stuff about British food being boiled beyond recognition and mushy is exaggerated. Or, I suppose, my luck is that bad to have found the one bit of solid material and choke on it."

"Oof." I cringe. "So, what's next for you now that you're free of the desk lamp? On the hunt for a nice floor model to move into? Perhaps a ceiling fan?"

Tobias laughs. "No, my dear. I am quite finished with this place. Your sister said once I've done all I needed to here, I'll go somewhere else... and probably reincarnate into a new person some years from now."

I nod. "Cool. What do you have left to do here?"

He bows to me. "Only wanting to thank you for your part in helping me."

"You're welcome."

With that, Tobias Krüger smiles one last time before simply fading away. At the instant before there's no visible sign of him, his expression gives off a mild sense of surprise, an 'oh, that was easy.' Huh. I guess he expected the process of going elsewhere to be more involved than simply happening immediately once he felt ready.

Right. So... interesting start to my day.

For the most part, my Friday afternoon is consumed by school-work. Unlike me, Ashley has a class today. However, it's an 'early' class running from five to six-thirty. I get distracted by a brief wave of guilt thinking about her driving to school in the same car she'd been so thrilled to get soon after obtaining a license. Between saving up every penny she ever earned working summer jobs throughout high school and her mom helping out, she got a used VW Jetta. They took a chance buying it directly from the owner instead of going through a lot. Worked out, though. A private seller ended up being far more vulnerable to her cute, eager face. That car probably would've cost a lot more at a dealership.

Anyway... it gets me thinking about how she kept saying she'd keep that car until it literally fell apart, talking about driving it to wherever she ended up going to college, then to the job she got after. Ashley expected to drive that Jetta until she turned forty.

Okay, the sads are gone.

We get to be eighteen forever. That's awesome.

The Littles are quiet today. Sophia and Sierra went to Nicole's place. Sam's out with his friends Darryl and Jordan, which means Ronan is with them, too. As far as my ears tell me, it's just me and Dad in the house.

Problem... Chloe's being too quiet.

A brief storm of panic comes to a nice end when I find her upstairs in the living room. She and the eight dolls are on the sofa watching *Ice Age*. Or one of the *Ice Age* movies. Not sure which sequel it is. Looks like Dad set her up with video. Chloe is adoring having the big screen all to herself, rather than Sierra monopolizing it.

Hmm. I wonder how the 'rents would react to me buying Sierra her own huge TV. The only reason she's in the living room all the time is the size of the screen. One might consider getting a twelve-year-old her own sixty-inch screen spoiling her. Then again, I'd be doing it to liberate our living room from constant virtual gunfire.

Meh. Something to think about. Hardly an emergency.

Since the kid is safe, I go back downstairs to finish off my assignments from the writing class. I have to write fake emails as if I'm giving 'a customer' good news, bad news, awful news, and ludicrous news—as in, we're sorry your order cannot be completed. The mushrooms came to life and ate it. Or something silly. I knew Vivian Black really prefers to teach creative writing. She's doing the professional writing course only because the school demanded it, I bet.

I have plans tonight.

Well, two plans. There's a vampire soiree going on, but not until later. It starts at eleven. Before it happens, I'm finally going to teach Chloe how to make mortals not notice her. If I don't do it tonight, the excuses will keep piling up and she won't be prepared if ever she needs to hide herself. She will undoubtedly use it for a bit of mischief here and there, but she's not the type of kid to do something really bad with it.

Ashley gets home from her class, sorta grumbling about having so much homework from it on the first week. Her exact words are more like the professor Trimble screwed her so hard she ought to have bought dinner first. Yes, she's got a teacher named Professor Trimble. Helen or Hannah… something with an H. Sounds like the woman should be teaching at Hogwarts, right? It's a biology class with a focus on mammalian animals likely to show up at a vet's office.

She huffs into my room and spikes her backpack down on the bed, then pauses, realizing she autopiloted to my room instead of hers. Easy error to make since we co-sleep all the time now. It's not creepy, weird, or clingy. Vampires just kinda do that when living in the same place. Okay, sure, so whenever we had sleepovers as kids, we usually shared the bed. Now we have an excuse other than being clingy. We're vampires. That whole nesting thing.

She swishes back and forth, trying to avoid picking the books back up since that would be admitting to an error.

I chuckle. "Ack. If you're busy, I can take Chloe by myself."

"Oh right!" Ash's grumpiness disappears. "So, you're sure you want to do it?"

"Yeah. Any additional layer of protection we can give her is good." I lean back, making my desk chair creak. "It's almost guaranteed that we'll end up in a situation where we're forced to bring her outside at an hour considered 'too late' for a kid her age to be awake. If she can blank herself out of people's minds so they don't realize she's there, it saves everyone a headache."

Ashley grins. "Except maybe the mortal being brain zapped."

"Hah. It doesn't give people headaches."

"I know. Just being a goof." She plucks her backpack up off the bed. "Speaking of goofs..."

"No worries. *Mi casa es su casa.*"

She grins and heads for the door. "Be right back."

So, there's the flipside to the dynamic of our friendship. Ashley's almost always the passive one, going along with whatever I decide to do. Sometimes that makes me feel guilty. However, she's the one with truly private space. My bedroom has always sorta been a shared area between us. Her bedroom is truly her bedroom. I don't go there much. Wonder what that means? Does it mean anything?

Meh.

I don't care. Got too much to get done tonight and not enough time for idle thoughts.

Since tonight is Dad's birthday, we go out for dinner.

My family is nothing if not creatures of routine. We hit Shogun West—which is ironically owned by Arthur Wolent via a few layers of proxies. Fancy clothing time, which includes Sierra wearing a dress. It's black, which makes it more tolerable for her. Sophia's wearing a dress, too—shocking, right? Only, hers is bright pink. Predictably, the hibachi chef goes to scare Chloe with the fake soy sauce squirt, but hesitates at her 'don't you do it' glare... then retargets the prank at Sophia, who jumps and screams. Hibachi chefs don't typically lose staredowns with children, so I'm assuming mental prodding has occurred.

Sophia has been here often enough to know about it. Yes, she *still* freaks out like he's going to spray her with actual soy sauce. Once it's obvious the bottle is a prop for a joke, Chloe bites her lip in an 'oops' manner. Hah! Seems she thought the guy was really about to squirt soy sauce all over her. Seeing the length of black yarn hanging from the bottle seems to be making her feel a bit guilty for smacking him in the brain. Can't fault her for that. It's kinda cute.

After dinner, we go home for cake. Dad's absolutely thrilled with my gift. Just about every game he played as a child is on that thing, all in one device without the need for cartridges. It's like a grey plastic block of solidified nostalgia for him. Sophia gave him a red headband... that she enchanted somehow. She says it'll 'keep him safe if things get weird.' Sierra gives him a lump of porcelain she made at school. I'm not sure whether it's supposed to be a birdhouse or a diorama of little houses. It does, however, have 'best dad' painted on it. Sam gives Dad a $20 gift card to Best Buy so he can get more old movies on DVD. And Mom? I'm not going to mention what her gift is. I don't want to think about what they do upstairs in their room later. Not at all. Out of my brain.

Since it's his birthday, Dad gets to set the activity for the remainder of our Friday night. Take a wild guess what he wants to do. Yep. Family movie night.

I still need to take Chloe out for a quick training session. We've got a little time before the movie. The excuse of needing to grab a bite is enough to get us out of the house without interrogation. No, I didn't lie to my parents. We're going to feed while we're out. It's just not the only objective of this trip.

The three of us dress reasonably normal for the Pacific Northwest in September. Chloe and I are doing the jeans and long-sleeved sweatshirt thing. Ashley's rocking denim too, but in the form of a skirt. We have matching Uggs. Yes, Chloe's tiny Uggs are adorable. No, we're not doing the pumpkin spice latte thing. First, because we're not *that* basic. Second because it's out of season. Starbucks has peppermint now. That's not a stereotype, so we indulge.

If anyone at the Starbucks thinks it's weird to give a young girl a latte at almost 8:00 p.m., they don't say anything. Guess they figure it's me who will have to deal with the kid being unable to sleep in an hour. Little do they know. It's hardly going to be an Uncle Ricky situation. Oh, what's that? Well... when I was around three years old, my parents had to do something and needed a babysitter. Mom asked her little brother, my Uncle Ricky, to watch me.

Whatever the 'rents ended up doing, they stayed out much later than they told Ricky they would. To get revenge, he gave me a bottle of Jolt cola. Imagine Pepsi or Coke with *extra* caffeine. I'm pretty sure I didn't sleep for two days, and neither did my parents. Dunno if it's a side effect of over caffeination or just being so young at the time, but I don't remember it personally. The story gets told at least once every other Thanksgiving or Christmas.

We don't have to worry about that with Chloe. No amount of caffeine will keep her awake when the sun comes up.

Back in the air with our peppermint lattes, we cruise around looking for a good place to do this.

"Where are we going?" Chloe tries to take a sip of her drink. "Can we land somewhere and sit?"

I tap my foot on nothing. "Yeah. Soon as I think of a..."

"Westfield Southcenter?" asks Ashley. "They're open a little later. Think they close at nine. Not a lot of time, but it should be enough to try."

"Good call. Yeah. Should be enough people there for a test but not enough to be overwhelming." I swing around in a wide, sweeping turn and head for Ash's favorite mall.

Maybe we'll have to hand in our girl cards if anyone ever finds out, but neither she nor I have ever been mall rats. Of course, we're not boys either. Whenever Dad goes to the mall, he already knows exactly what he wants, from which store. He goes straight to his target and leaves. Mom or Sophia could spend all day at the mall wandering around and looking at stuff. Soph's a bit too nerdy to have the sorts of friends who like hanging out at the malls just to be seen. Oh, what am I saying, people don't do that anymore. We're not actually in the Eighties. Dad just loves to think we are.

A short flight later, we cruise in and land in the dark under Southcenter Parkway on the western edge of the mall parking lot. Some trees help keep us hidden from view of anyone at the mall until we're on the ground and walking like normal people.

"Okay," I say as we make our way across the parking lot to the enormous shopping center. "So, the reason we brought you here tonight is it's time to teach you some stuff."

Chloe peers up at me, equal parts eager and nervous.

"We can hide ourselves from people even if they're almost right in front of us," I whisper. "It's not honestly difficult. I did it the very first night after I turned."

Ashley stifles laughter.

I give her side eye. Honestly, I don't know why she finds the thought of me stranded outside naked so funny. She didn't find it funny when *she* ended up kidnapped by Tilloa's sire. Not only did she get stuck outside the house with nothing but handcuffs on, she had to deal with being stuck naked throughout an entire car chase and roving gunfight, too. I mean, that didn't exactly traumatize her. She called it 'an adventure.' Then again, the events of that night cemented her desire to go vampire. She'd been toying with the idea for months before that. Being used as a pawn-slash-bait to lure me into a trap was the last straw for her.

"How does it work?" asks Chloe.

"It's surprisingly simple." I look around at people entering and leaving, pausing my conversation while we're squished in close proximity with strangers passing through the doorway. Once we're in the mall concourse a few minutes later, I head toward a group of benches around a small fountain with some small trees-in-giant-flowerpots for shade. "All you have to do is concentrate really hard on not wanting to be seen. Build that idea that no one can see you, and believe that you're making people not see you, and they won't."

"Being a vampire is kinda like using a Mac." Ashley sits on a bench. "You just kinda try to do something and the software figures it out and does it."

Chloe hops up beside her.

I sit next to the kid. "What kind of Macs have you been using? I can't make sense of them."

"They're intuitive." Ashley shrugs. "Everything looks like what it's supposed to do. You like stuff that's more complicated. That's Dad's fault though. He's trained you to think if something can be done in one step instead of six, there must be something wrong with it."

"Heh. Maybe." I shrug. My father definitely is a PC guy. "It's not the complexity, I think. More the proprietary nature of Macs. You have to get everything from Apple."

Chloe tugs on my arm. "Can we hurry up and do the thing? Movie tonight. You can have your boring computer argument later."

Ash nearly sprays peppermint latte when she laughs in mid-sip.

I laugh too, but my coffee happened to be at a safe distance from my mouth.

The kid folds her arms and taps her Uggs together, making this hollow, leathery thumping noise as she waits for us to stop being idiots.

Once I can speak without laughing, I take a few deep breaths to further collect my composure. "Okay. All you have to do is believe no one can see you. Think about using your abilities on everyone in sight and be sure they can't see you. The farther away from you someone is, the easier they are to hide from. If you touch someone, it stops working on them. Try not to get too close. Making too much noise can ruin the effect and get people to notice you, so try to be quiet while doing it. Finally, if you become suddenly determined to hurt someone, the anti-charm stops working on them. Watch. I'll demonstrate."

Chloe smirks at me. "If I'm gonna kick someone's ass, I won't be trying to hide from them."

I hand my coffee to Ash to hold, then focus on radiating the negative charm. Once I'm sure it's on, I proceed to walk around the mall while making goofy faces at random people. No one pays me any attention, continuing to walk along like I'm not even there. After a few minutes of this, I circle back to Ashley and Chloe on the bench.

"See?" I hold my arms out to either side. "No one noticed me."

"Nice." Ashley grins. "There's only one magic stronger than vampires for making people in public refuse to see you exist."

"What is that?" Chloe tilts her head.

"Putting on an orange vest and trying to collect money for your kid's sports team," mutters Ashley.

The kid's expression falls. She gawks, open mouthed at Ashley. Not sure if she missed the joke or thinks it's dumb. Either way, she evidently decides to ignore it and looks at me. "Are you sure it worked? Maybe people were just ignoring you because they're looking at their phones."

Only a few of the people I 'buzzed' with stupid facial expressions had their phones out. Still, a teenager making silly faces *is* something most adults would probably ignore even if they realized they saw me. They might have assumed I was doing a dare or a silly TikTok.

"Yeah, it's way easier to stay unnoticed with smartphones being a thing." Ashley puffs a strand of hair away from her eyes. "It had to be a pain in the butt back in the day when people walking down the street actually paid attention to what went on around them." She pauses, then gives me a confused stare. "Or did everyone stare at like newspapers before phones existed?"

I shrug. "I dunno. We could ask Aurélie when she gets back."

"Like she'd know." Chloe rolls her eyes. "Aunt Aurélie spent all her time sitting in fancy places doing fancy things. She didn't go to town."

I shrug. "Oh, I'm sure she did on occasion... but only to fancy parties."

Chloe grins. "Are you sure the people didn't just ignore you?"

Sigh. "Okay. Fine. I'll prove it to you."

Ashley tilts her head. "Why do you feel the need to prove yourself to a seven-year-old?"

"Because." I concentrate on the 'don't see me' charm. "She has to believe it will work. The more confident she is it's really going to work, the better it works. I'm going to do something that should definitely get me noticed. Watch."

Ashley and Chloe sip their peppermint lattes in unison at me.

I can't believe what I'm about to do, but this is for the kid's benefit. So... I pull off my sweatshirt and tee, revealing to the entire mall my hatred of bras. As in, I seldom wear one. They suck. Uncomfortable, awkward, expensive, and—depending on which articles you read—not good for my health. Well, it's probably a bit late for me to worry about 'health' concerns.

Chloe finds it hilarious to watch me free-boobing it at the mall. She buries her mouth in the crook of her sweatshirt to avoid making too much noise.

Ashley raises both eyebrows. "That'll do it."

A supermodel I'm not, but boobs are boobs. They don't have to be huge or perfect spheres to get people staring. Entirely confident I'm as private as if I'm standing at home in the bathroom by myself, I walk the same circuit around the concourse, mentally projecting my desire not to be noticed. I'm also tapping into whatever bit of Lost One Dalton gave me and trying to blot myself off any security cameras. Since I can, evidently, open locks with my mind, figure I can do that, too. Here's hoping. Oh well. Worst thing that will happen is a security guard comes running over to me and I make up a fib about being dared. Innocent fun. I'm not hurting anyone.

Sure enough, no one looks at me. No way in heck does a girl wander around topless without at least one person staring, one person complaining, and several dozen cell phone cameras going nuts. Something paranormal definitely happened here.

I return to the bench. Ashley hands me my shirt and sweatshirt. I pull them on, fluff my hair out, and sit beside Chloe.

"There. See?" I ask. "No one reacted because I didn't let anyone realize they saw me."

"Wow." Chloe stands. "My turn now?"

I bite my lip. "Umm. Not sure we should have you streaking the mall in case it doesn't work for you the first try."

Ashley shrugs one shoulder. "She's small enough to get away with being mischievous if we pretend to yell at her."

"Will I be in trouble?" asks Chloe.

"Of course not. We'd be acting." Ashley grins.

"Okay. I'm Captain Underpants!" Chloe puts her empty Starbucks cup on the bench and grabs her jeans like she's about to shove them down.

I grab her hand. "Wait. Hang on. I have a better idea that won't get us investigated by CPS."

Ashley rolls her eyes.

"Heh. I'm kidding. But, really... I've got an even better idea to absolutely prove to Chloe she can hide herself." I gesture absentmindedly at the mall. "People here are busy. They might not pay too much attention to a little kid zooming by in her underwear."

"What is it?" Chloe blinks at me. "Wait. Let me try something else here first? I don't wanna take a real test without at least *some* practice."

I squirm.

"I won't do Captain Underpants." Chloe grins. "Okay. No one can see me..." She wanders off. "No one can see me..."

Ashley and I watch her go. After a few minutes of seeming normal, she starts flipping people off. There's something about the sight of a seven-year-old girl giving the finger that's just... hilarious and so, so wrong. The first few people do double-takes like they thought they saw her but aren't sure. Each successive person she gives the finger to reacts less and less. By victim number eleven, they don't bat an eyelash at her.

"Wow, she's doing it," whispers Ashley.

"I told you it's not hard." I frown. "I'd been a vampire for less than two hours and I got it to work."

"Extreme emotional distress," deadpans Ashley. "You were embarrassed as hell being outside bare-assed. Chloe, on the other hand, is not the least bit embarrassed flipping people off."

"Nope." I shake my head, then take a sip of peppermint-infused coffee. "Not at all. She's loving every minute of this."

"So, what's your better idea?" Ashley leans against me.

"It is a way we will know, without a doubt, that she's mastered the arts of vampire stealth." I nod once. "Follow me."

"Okay, but you're not going anywhere."

"I can't. You're leaning into me like a lonely cat."

"An affectionate cat." Ashley meows. "It bothers you?"

"Not at all. But it does make it a bit difficult to stand."

She grins. "Aww. Okay. We should probably get home soon, anyway. Dad's really excited about the movie."

"Eek." I whistle. "That can't be good. Probably has a wicked pun."

"Oof. Maybe we can take a little longer..." Ashley pauses a second, then un-leans. "Nah. Don't wanna disappoint him. It *is* his birthday."

~

"Seriously?" says Ashley when I fly home. "I thought you had some big kahuna test for her?"

"I do." Instead of going into the house through the sliding glass door, I head down the steps to the backyard.

Chloe and Ashley exchange an 'okay, let's see where this goes' type look before following me.

I go through the gate in the fence to the 'slightly messier than it should be' space on the left side of our house. The weeds could use some attention. Not now, though. The three of us make our way out onto the cul-de-sac, almost to the street, and stop.

"Umm, what?" Ashley blinks at me. "This isn't epic."

"Trust me." I squat down to eye level with Chloe. "Okay, kiddo. If you can pull this off, you are a master of vampire stealth."

She continues looking at me, expressionless.

I gently grasp her shoulders and spin her around to face Mr. Niedermeyer's front lawn. "Summon every ounce of your power and concentration not to be seen. Then go walk on that grass."

"Ooh!" Ashley squeaks. "Are you sure you want to do that? She only just started trying to use her powers tonight. Shouldn't we start off with something easier, like going to a Seahawks home game wearing a bunch of 49ers gear?"

"Ack!" I shiver. "I'm trying to test her, not get her killed if she fails."

"You guys are dorks." Chloe sighs. "Just walk on the grass? That's it?"

"Trust me. It's enough." I pat her on the head. "An older guy lives there. He does *not* like children. I swear he's got supernatural Spidey Sense that goes off if a child even comes within two inches of his lawn."

Ashley's giggling into her hands too hard to say anything.

"What?" I peer back at her. "I'm serious. A kid remaining undetected on that lawn is ten times more difficult than her doing a Captain Underpants at the mall and not being noticed."

"Okay, okay." Ashley cough-chuckles. "I believe you. You're not wrong. Go forth, young padawan."

"Dorks." Chloe laughs, then puts on her game face.

A moment later, she marches forward across the cul-de-sac, onto the sidewalk, and directly onto Mr. Niedermeyer's lawn. I brace for the overdone special effects. A child has set foot on the forbidden grass. Cue the searchlights, sirens, and tower guards. The living room windows flicker in the glow of a television, so I'm sure he's home.

Yet... no reaction.

Chloe's pacing back and forth on the grass and he's not flying out the door to chase her away.

"Stompin' on your grass," says the child. "Here I am. Come get me, mean old man!"

She jumps up and down in place, spins, then jumps again.

Nothing from the house.

"Wow. Is she doing it or is he dead?" asks Ashley.

"Good question." I smirk.

Ash floats up into the air and glides faster than walking speed over to the window. She hovers there for a few seconds before zipping back to stand beside me. "He looks fine. Watching TV. Chloe, try giggling. He can't resist the sounds of a happy kid."

It's difficult to make a child laugh convincingly on cue. Chloe tries, but her giggles sound fake. They have no effect on Niedermeyer.

Ashley rambles off some lines from *Frozen* in a goofy voice.

It only takes three quotes before Chloe giggles for real. Like the 'scent vapor' wafting up from a pie in a *Tom & Jerry* cartoon to tickle the cat's nose, 'happy child noises' seem to set off some manner of paranormal nerve in the old man. Four seconds after she giggles, Niedermeyer's face appears in the front window. He's part Popeye, part creepy groundskeeper from *Harry Potter*. Chloe's standing there right in the middle of his precious lawn, but he doesn't come flying out the door screaming at her to get off his property. He doesn't even glare at her. It's like she isn't even there.

"Amazing," whispers Ashley.

Niedermeyer looks at us. His expression remains suspicious. We are neither small children nor on his property. We're quite safely on the road in the middle of the cul-de-sac, not even on 'his' sidewalk. He seems to think we're up to something, but isn't sure what. I mean to be fair, the two of us *are* staring at his house while standing there strangely still like the Children of the Corn.

Nice. When I peek into his thoughts, he's got no conscious memory of seeing Chloe on his lawn. She's doing it. She's really doing it.

"Great job, kiddo," I whisper. "Keep concentrating on it until we get inside. He's watching me and Ash. Don't want him seeing you appear out of thin air."

"Okay." Rather than run to us, Chloe sprints to the sidewalk and follows the circle of the cul-de-sac to our house.

"Well, she did it." Ashley nods once. "We now have a fully-functional stealth-enabled vampire child."

"Yep."

"Did we mess up?" Ashley glances sideways at me.

"Nah. She'll be okay with it." I chuckle. "Not like we taught your cousin Frankie how to do that when he was little."

Ashley shivers.

She's got this cousin named Frankie on her father's side who's like two years younger than us. We haven't seen him in forever. I think he was like eight the last time his parents came to visit Ashley's place. The boy was a handful. If he could effectively turn himself invisible, he'd get into *all kinds* of trouble. Total *Dennis the Menace* type stuff. Wonder if he's mellowed out or if he's still a selfish brat.

Anyway... we're done for the night.

I hurry over to the house where Chloe's waiting for us, beaming with pride.

"Great work, kiddo." I scoop her up into a hug. "Please be responsible with that, okay?"

"I will." She hugs me back.

"Don't tease Mom and Dad with it." Ashley boops her on the nose.

Chloe shakes her head. "I promise." Her joy melts to a serious expression. "I love having good parents. I'm never ever gonna be mean to them."

Ugh. Now I'm going to have to explain to the 'rents why it looks like I've been crying when we walk in.

CHAPTER 20

A GIANT MISTAKE OF THE DAD KIND

T hankfully, I didn't choke up enough for either Mom or Dad to notice and ask what got me upset.

Is it weird for Chloe to have thoughts like that? Yeah, she's seven, but at times, a precocious maturity comes out. Not sure if it's vampirism or her life experience doing it. Then again, I've had inexplicably 'adult' thoughts ever since becoming an undead, too. Like, what eighteen-year-old cares about twenty years in the future type stuff? Sure, I'm an odd duck but I'm not *that* weird. Gotta be vampire stuff.

Dad's got this cat-who-ate-the-canary smile. Whoo boy. What's up that sleeve tonight?

After a few minutes to get comfy, Ash, Chloe, and I join the family in the living room. Ash put on pajamas. I'm in my usual 'not going anywhere' attire of a long T-shirt. Sierra's doing the long T-shirt thing too, now. No idea if she's doing it for the same reason I am (just in our psyche) or she's emulating me. Chloe and Sophia both love nightgowns. Sam and Ronan are doing the PJ thing. My brother's got plaid pants and a Batman T-shirt. Ronan's gone commercial with a Pokémon print pajama set, the sort of 'little kid' pajamas

Sam's decided he's now too old for (unless they're Minecraft related). Ro's sleeping over for movie night.

Grr. I wish Hunter was sleeping over tonight. But... we have that soiree later and he's gotta work tomorrow morning.

All of Dad's anticipatory glee makes sense when the movie starts. He's put on *Hotel Transylvania*.

"This isn't an Eighties movie," says Sierra.

"Dad might be getting old." Sam smiles. "Losing track of time."

"Ha. Ha." Dad waves them off. "I know this isn't a classic from the greatest time cinema has ever known,"—Mom rolls her eyes—"but I thought you'd like it."

So, yeah. No big pun waiting to drop on our heads. It's a movie about vampires where one of the characters is briefly shown as a vampire child. This is undoubtedly for Chloe's amusement... and she's glued to the screen. Well, her attention is glued to the screen. *She* is not. My unlife is so crazy now, I should probably be careful with metaphor. All it would take is one bad run-in with a demonic slug in the mirrorverse and she could literally be glued to the TV.

"Fear not." Dad holds up a finger. "I have a proper Eighties classic ready for the weekend."

"It *is* the weekend." Sam tilts his head. "Friday night counts as weekend."

Dad pauses, realizing he's been caught. "Well. Good point. I'll say it's ready for Saturday night then."

Yes. My family is out of control. The highlight of our partying week is a movie from the Eighties on a Saturday night. We better be careful. Someone might get hurt.

Not long after the movie starts, Mom jumps with a yelp. A doll's appeared on the sofa right next to her.

"She wants to watch the movie, too," I say trying to be casual.

"Creepy," mutters Sierra.

"Don't be mean." Sophia nudges her. "She didn't ask to be trapped in a doll for eternity."

Mom eyes Soph. "Wait, you're saying this doll is alive?"

"Didn't I explain that already?" I wave at Mom like 'hi, I exist.'

"No." Sophia shakes her head. "Not technically alive, but she's aware."

The doll turns her head to look at Mom, who tenses up.

"She's nice as long as people aren't mean to her," says Sophia.

I swear. My kid sister isn't even trying but she could totally play the 'creepy little girl in a horror movie' with ease. After a few awkward minutes, Mom repositions the doll on her lap to give her a better view of the screen. Wow. She's not freaking out. Impressive. I guess my mother's starting to adjust to our new reality after all. Not a wine glass in sight, too.

Well, Chloe *adored* the movie. She wants to watch it again immediately.

"It's bedtime," says Mom.

Sophia makes an 'aww okay' face. Sam looks disappointed but unwilling to argue.

Sierra sighs. "We're not little kids anymore, and the only little kid here *can't* sleep yet."

"You embark upon an argument where the cost will far outweigh the benefit." Sam rests his hand on her arm. "Sare had a bedtime until she was sixteen."

"To be fair, I kinda cheated it around fifteen. Bedtime became more of a suggestion then."

Mom makes a shooing gesture at the Littles. "We can renegotiate terms when you're getting closer to fifteen."

Chloe's making faces at me like she *really* wants to watch the movie again while simultaneously feeling guilty the others have to go to bed.

The usual bedtime scramble occurs. Three tweens competing for bathroom time to brush teeth, pee, and do whatever before lights out.

Once they're out of earshot, Chloe tugs on my arm. "Can we watch the movie again after they're asleep?"

"You don't want to wait for them?" Ashley raises an eyebrow.

"I can watch it again and again. I won't get tired of it." Chloe grins.

"There are two more movies in the series," says Dad. "That's only the first one."

"Ooh!" Chloe squeals in delight before bouncing into my lap. "We need to invite the zombie and the fish monsters and the mummies and stuff to the house so we can play."

Sierra pokes her head out of the downstairs bathroom. "Umm, if we're gonna start inviting monsters over to hang out, can we please leave Uncle Hank off the list?"

Dad barks a laugh, then tries with minimal success to hide his amusement.

Mom smirks. It's not a bad smirk. She's also trying not to laugh and doing a better job. "Sweetie, it's mean to call him a monster."

"If he doesn't want me to call him a monster, he can stop acting like one." Sierra vanishes into the bathroom. "He's like the beast that devours happiness and joy. If he's not dead by Christmas, and he shows up here, I'm gonna wear a Handmaid's Tale robe the whole time."

"Sierra!" yells Mom. "The man may have unsavory, outdated opinions, but I am appalled that you're wishing him dead."

"Unsavory, outdated opinions," I whisper to no one in particular. "That's one way to describe it."

"I'm not wishing him dead. I *wish* he wasn't such an asshole. The guy's older than heck. I'm just being practical." Sierra pokes her head out the doorway again. "I'm not saying I *want* him to die. Just... the odds of him making it to December aren't in his favor." She blinks. "Whoops."

Mom sighs. "Swear jar or extra chore?"

"Yanno, the subject of Uncle Hank came up," I say. "You should let that one slide. The guy really is an asshole. It's not undeserved."

"If we keep making exceptions, there's little point to having a rule about swearing." Mom looks over at Dad.

"I'm okay with suspending that rule." Sierra grins. "It's a dumb rule."

Dad overacts rubbing his chin. "I'll suggest a compromise. Old swear rules still apply if anyone under the age of eighteen in this house hurls language like that in a mean-spirited or aggressive way. Simple declarative statements of demonstrably ass-holic conduct will be tolerated if frowned at."

Mom throws a small pillow at him.

Dad laughs.

"Sierra…" Mom twists around to look at her over the sofa back. "I'll go along with what your father suggests with one modification."

Sierra tilts her head in curiosity.

"Screaming obscenities at the PlayStation is still off limits. If you get *that* angry, you should take a break before those words go flying."

Dad nods at Mom. "Ranting at the PlayStation falls under the 'using language in an aggressive manner' clause."

"Ugh." Sierra hangs her head.

"She doesn't scream that much at the TV anymore." Ashley smiles.

"No, because she's kinda cheating now." I snicker. "Her reflexes are… good."

"Question." Sierra walks a few steps out into the hall. "What if I like drop something on my foot and scream an F-bomb before I think about it?"

Dad nods. "Excited utterance. Allowable, though not encouraged."

Mom gives him epic side eye for trying to sound like a lawyer. "I'll set the minimum age at twelve for that."

"Yes!" Sierra does a fist pump.

It's not much of a win. Neither Sophia nor Sam—who are not yet twelve—curse too much.

"Is there an undeath exception?" asks Chloe. "Sometimes, a girl just needs to say f—."

I cover her mouth, then kiss her gently on top of the head.

Mom twitches as if slapped. Even if the child didn't finish, there's just something about such a tiny, innocent voice dropping words like that. Makes me and Ashley want to laugh. It has a different effect on my mother.

Apparently caught off guard by the question, the word, and

exactly how to handle an immortal child who will never reach the age of twelve—and thus be permitted to curse in moments of unexpected pain—Mom stares at us in silence for a little while. "Umm. I'll process it on a swear-by-swear basis for her."

"Are you sure, hon?" Dad grins. "She's from New Jersey. If you're going to examine each swearing utterance individually, you won't have time to do anything else. A blanket policy might be easier to manage."

Mom rubs her face. "All right. Fine. Same as Sierra. Tolerated if not used aggressively but with disapproval."

"What's that mean?" Chloe tilts her head.

"It means, don't be mean to people." I smile. "Retaliation is fine."

"Okay." Chloe grins. "Movie?"

"We have to go out for a bit." I relocate the child out of my lap to the sofa next to me, then stand.

Mom blinks. "At this hour? I thought you were staying in since the three of you changed clothes."

"Can't watch a movie for family night in 'outside clothes.'" I tug at my long tee. "It wouldn't be right."

Chloe flies up from the sofa, orbits the room once, then sticks her face right up to Dad, almost nose to nose. "Bla-bla-bla!"

Dad, without missing a beat, attempts to do an impression of Adam Sandler doing a Transylvanian accent. "I do not say 'bla-bla-bla.'"

Chloe giggles, cheers, and flies around in a circle again.

Oh, no. I stare at him. "Dad, what have you done? She's going to be obsessed with that... forever."

My father gives me this wicked little smile. It's kind of the way the grandparents grin at the parents who have to deal with the kid for the rest of the night after picking them up. Only, in this case, I'll be dealing with the 'bla-bla-bla' thing for eternity long after he's moved on. Much to my surprise, rather than getting maudlin at the idea my father is making fun of his mortality, I find myself laughing —and throwing a small pillow at him.

It's just like he got my kid hopped up on caffeine after babysitting her.

Ooh. Now I have to plot some appropriately whimsical revenge.

CHAPTER 21
POWER IS STRANGE

Ashley, Chloe, and I are standing in my bedroom staring into my huge walk-in closet.

To be fair, it's not really a bedroom nor is it a walk-in closet. My room is, or was, a large basement room of undetermined purpose. It used to be storage. The 'walk in closet' is, well, I suppose it's more storage space. Or maybe another place where a water heater might've been installed. Point being, the builder of this house hadn't intended this to be a bedroom.

Works for me. The maker of vampires never intended us to go live with our mortal families, either.

Sophia 'niced it up' for me a few weeks ago with magic. So, it feels more like a bedroom and less like I'm a basement-dwelling troll. I mean, our house's basement was pretty nice already, finished and all. Not like the basement at Hunter's place which looks like they could film another *Nightmare on Elm Street* movie in it. I am not surprised Ronan is terrified of the basement at his house. No, there's nothing supernatural down there at all. It's just seriously creepy, dark, and scary to a child.

Anyway... Ashley, Chloe, and I are between outfits, in underpants. We're like a bunch of actresses or fashion models in the changing room. Only, those models have someone else making decisions for them about what to wear. They get the easy way out. Us? An assortment of stuff we put on, had second thoughts about, and tossed to the floor in exasperation is strewn around us. Chloe thinks we're playing dress up, and she's totally into that. The kid is not suffering our indecision. She's absolutely confident in her decision to wear one of her fluffy 'doll' dresses, but she hasn't put it on yet. Since we are playing dress up, she changes into a new outfit every time Ashley and I do.

I'm stuck trying to figure out what to do for the soiree we're dangerously close to being late for. A dress is tempting simply because every other time I've been to one, I've been wearing a dress... if the elaborate things Aurélie puts me in count as 'dresses.' On the other hand, all the dresses in my closet are kinda lame. I'd end up looking like I'm going to a prom or a funeral or a wedding. For all I know, the dresses are just fine and the problem is me.

Nah. They're... not right. Aurélie's gowns are way, way, way too formal and ostentatious for the event, not to mention super anachronistic. The other vampires have come to expect that from her, so they don't care. They don't think less of me or Ashley for wearing them either since what are we going to do, say no to Aurélie? Well, they do think less of us to a point. We're like her pets or something. At least I have some respectability in not having sought her out and begged for her protection. She just adopted me at first sight. So, the other vampires don't blame me for anything.

Ugh. My dresses aren't right for this. Everyone else at these things wears fashion appropriate for adults attending a cocktail party. My dresses look too, uhh... juvenile. They're not sophisticated enough. The most adult-looking one I have is the one I wore to my prom. Not happening. It'll remind me of Scott all night. As a matter of fact, I think I'm going to donate that one to charity, so I never have to look at it again. We're also running out of time.

Screw it. I'm not going to even try to be fancy.

Once I commit to just doing the jeans-and-a-T-shirt thing, Ashley decides to be low-key, too and skip the frilly dress. She's got more of a wardrobe than me in terms of cute dresses. She does the oversized plum-colored sweater over a basic shirt with yoga pants thing. Me? I look like a background extra from a Nirvana video. Yes, I'm even doing the big flannel shirt as a jacket deal, too.

Chloe mostly gets into her dress by herself, but she needs a little help with the zipper. She loves these fluffy, gossamer white mini-gowns that make her look like a ghost from a hundred years ago. I don't bother even insisting she put on the matching ballet flat style shoes since I know she'll 'lose' them somewhere at the hotel.

"Gotta pee!" yells Chloe out of the blue before running for the door.

Huh? Oh, duh. Must be the Starbucks.

Ashley nudges me with her elbow. "Did we do something bad teaching her how to hide?"

"Nah. Not like she's going to school where she could abuse the heck out of it."

"Oof. True." Ashley flashes a playful grin. "Wow. We could seriously do some crap, huh?"

"What do you mean?" I pick through my collection of socks looking for a pair of suitable fuzziness.

Ashley wobbles her head side to side. "Like we could go anywhere and do anything we want. Sneak into movies without paying, prank people, and stuff."

"Hah!" I laugh at that since I know she's totally kidding.

Chloe walks in, her face grim. She gives me this 'you wouldn't believe what I just saw' stare.

"Something wrong?" I ask.

"It still smells just like peppermint coffee," whispers Chloe. "Weird."

"Don't try to drink it again," says Ashley.

"Eww!" wails Chloe.

I kinda gag at the idea.

Anyway, it's kinda funny Ashley's mind went to such childish uses for our power and not stuff like shoplifting, bank robbery, or worse. It's good the two of us have an overactive sense of guilt. Though, maybe guilt isn't the right word. It's not like we'd do bad things and don't purely because we'd feel bad or get caught. We just don't have the motivation to do bad things. Yeah, I know. We're lame.

"It's a good thing we're so tragically uncool and sweet." I fake roll my eyes. "Or we could get into deep trouble."

"Right?" Ashley exhales. "Maybe that's why fate trusted us with it."

I wag my eyebrows. "Infinite cosmic power."

Chloe scampers into her dollhouse and peeks at us through one of the windows. "Itty bitty living space."

CHAPTER 22
CHAOS AT THE FAIRMOUNT OLYMPIC

For the first time, I arrive at the Fairmount Olympic Hotel without riding in a limo.

No big deal. I can honestly do without the extravagance. We fly downtown, find a nice, secluded alley in which to land, and walk a block or two over to the hotel. Chloe's practicing her 'don't see me' power. This is a prime example of when she needs to use it. Under normal circumstances, I wouldn't take her out of the house at ten minutes before eleven at night. However, like it or not, she's part of vampire society now. The more we can demonstrate she's safe and responsible, the better it will be for us.

I'm under no illusions. We got lucky being in a relatively progressive part of the country in terms of vampires. I mean, they tolerated me going home. It wouldn't surprise me if in some places, the vampire community is a bunch of asshats who'd have destroyed her without hesitation.

It's an unusual feeling to walk into this big hotel and not be stared at. Kinda odd now that I think about it. The way Aurélie dresses us for these events is the opposite of subtle. People stare at us like they're wondering if a movie's being filmed here or something. Tonight, we look ordinary. Except Chloe. She's a creepdorable little haunted doll. Not that she's *trying* to act weird. It's the dress.

I'm so glad she's not like Ashley's cousin Frankie. If she had his personality, she'd totally run off away from me and start trying to scare the hell out of hotel guests by pretending to be that kid from the *Ring* movies. Thankfully, she knows doing stuff like that attracts attention. Her continued existence relies on the absence of attention. And yeah, I guess there might be some overstatement there. It's not like the local vampires are on our asses 24/7 just looking for an excuse to light the kid on fire. That's my fear, albeit exaggerated. Honestly, the vibes I've been getting from the elders around here is hesitant acceptance tinged with pity. She's so small and cute, even guys like Stefano would feel like a monster giving the order to get rid of her. Also, it's not like she asked for undeath.

Finding the right conference room isn't difficult. It's the one where an event is obviously going on but no signs announce exactly who's hosting the thing. Like, other rooms have signs about pharmaceutical sales conventions or motivational speaker seminars. Our room? Nothing. It wouldn't shock me if the collective presence of vampires here is repelling mortals so they see the room as empty/idle.

One of Wolent's enforcers—I kinda remember the dude's name being Virgil—stands outside the door to the conference area. He raises an eyebrow at us, then smiles a little before opening the door.

As usual, the soiree's going on inside a massive, windowless room. They've got tables set up along the interior wall full of snacks for the mortals as well as the few vampires willing to endure later discomfort to enjoy the flavor of food in the moment. Around thirty or so vampires mingle while a dozen or so snack mortals wander around like zombies... or college students who woke up before ten in the morning.

And wow. I think the three of us could've walked in here bare-ass naked and gotten stared at less. Well, two of us. Chloe's not getting stared at. The other vampires are used to seeing her in a creepy white dress. For at least two-thirds of the vampires present, this is the first time they've seen me not all dolled up as a Disney princess.

Right as I start to think I should've worn something more formal, their curiosity shifts away. Hmm. Okay. They processed an unusual sight and went back to what they were doing. Maybe I didn't screw up. My ordinary attire does feel a little *too* casual for this event. Next time I attend one of these things without Aurélie, I'll try to dress nicer. How about that? I never thought I'd feel more awkward *not* wearing one of those super elaborate gowns.

We're not really social friends with anyone here. Everyone is older than us both in undead terms as well as life terms. The youngest other 'society' vamps look mid-to-late twenties. Ash and I are kids to them. However, we are used to this. Most of the time throughout school whenever we attended parties, the two of us would just kinda hang out together off to the side and watch.

Same thing happens tonight. Hey, we're here. That counts, right?

A few people come by to dispense with the social pleasantries. Vanessa Prentice is the alpha in the room tonight since Aurélie is not here. Alpha, that is, in terms of believing herself the prettiest woman around. The elegant redhead carries herself like a queen much more obviously, prancing about like an A-list Hollywood celebrity who deigned to drop by at an event full of B-listers and no-name wannabees.

I don't intend to sound mean or catty. Vanessa has been nice to me the few times we've interacted. She gave me something to wear and showed me where I could clean up the time I returned to Wolent's manor post-claw-shredding.

She pauses by us for a few minutes for a more-than-superficial 'hi, how are you' type chat. By that, I mean it kinda appears like she's merely going through the motions, but her tone is more genuine. Before long, she excuses herself to resume talking to people more at her level—meaning older and interested in things teenagers find boring.

Ashton James swoops by soon after to greet us. He's a lovely man, the picture of tall, dark, and handsome. He's had his hair changed around, trading the Wesley Snipes flattop for some more contemporary looking dreads. He, and his pseudo-husband Henry Arnold, are dolled up in the Victorian equivalent of tuxedos, complete with top hats. Ashton's is a pale shade of lavender. Henry opted for a more traditional black and white color scheme.

They're both considerably older than us. Both look about twenty-five or so, though Ashton's over eighty. He likes to quip that he became a vampire in an age when two men kissing would've been gasped at less than had he been seen kissing a white woman. He's trying to be funny but ugh. Sometimes humans can be horrible.

Their conversation lasts longer than Vanessa gave us, since both guys are less worried about making sure they talk enough to 'the right people' for political reasons. Before they meander off to chat up other people, they spend a few minutes complimenting Chloe on her dress. Henry suggests adding a light touch of violet eyeshadow with glitter. Ashton doesn't think a girl her age should wear makeup at all. Chloe's all about the glitter and loves the idea.

Over the course of the next hour, various people drop by for the obligatory chat. Jennifer Ruiz is the youngest one here other than us, having been turned at the age of twenty-two almost forty years ago. At least she's into movies, so we have something to talk about. We're in the midst of discussing the evolution of the zombie film when a scream echoes across the conference room.

Vanessa's flailing her arms for balance—and standing there in only some racy black lace lingerie. Her expensive designer dress is on the floor mostly behind her—and Chloe's right there. It looks like the kid stomped on the train of her dress so she walked/ripped out of it.

Except, I know better. Chloe wouldn't do that unless Vanessa started a fight. Also, the kid looks genuinely startled. For like six seconds, Vanessa stands there paralyzed in shock. Either that, or she's trying to decide what would be more advantageous to her socially: pretending to be mortified or giving the guys a show. Of course, it's not like someone got pantsed in gym class. No one here is going to laugh at her. It's also not like we're in Hollywood. No one's taking photos. The mortals are too out of it in mental fog to react and the vampires have seen far worse than a wardrobe malfunction. Someone would need to lose body parts to get any eyebrows raised in this room.

"I didn't touch it!" says Chloe. "I swear."

Vanessa gasps, drops into a crouch, and hastily gathers her dress around herself. She glares at Chloe. Alas, she's not quite old enough to read the minds of other vampires... so she shoots Paolo a look.

Speaking of Paolo, he's still wearing the same suit he always does. His hair's slicked back in that 1940s mobster style he loves so much. Someone could edit him into a photograph beside Al Capone and it wouldn't look like an altered image. He shifts his gaze to Chloe for a second or two, then makes a dismissive sort of face at Vanessa.

The annoyance she'd been radiating at the child evaporates to confusion.

"I believe you." Vanessa examines the dress, evidently decides it's ripped beyond saving—at least saving right now—and sighs.

Chloe's expression is dangerous. I imagine a cartoon speech bubble over her head with words like 'Bitch, you only believe me because you had him read my mind!' She doesn't say that. After taking a moment to calm down, she offers a weak, "Sorry your dress got ruined. It's nice. I hope you can fix it."

It takes a certain kind of woman to stand up and walk around a crowded room confidently while in nothing but her Victoria's Secret, stockings, and heels. I'm not exactly sure what kind of woman it is, but Vanessa is that kind of woman. She's not moving in a flaunting manner, simply attempting to pretend nothing happened. And she's heading right for me.

Uh oh.

A few of the guys pay her a bit more attention than they might have otherwise. A fact I am sure she's aware of and not upset by.

"Dear," says Vanessa, handing me the bundle of fabric. "Might I ask you a small favor?"

Right. This is my problem to fix because 'my child' didn't do it. Whatever. I'm not annoyed. It isn't like I'm deeply involved in this party, anyway. Besides, she took care of me when I had a wardrobe malfunction here a while ago. "Sure. What do you need?"

"Would you be a sweetie and take that to my room upstairs, and grab a suitable replacement?" She tugs at my oversized flannel. "And if it isn't too much of an imposition, might I borrow this?"

"Yeah, no problem." I pull the flannel off. Really, I'd been wearing it as a jacket-slash-accessory over a T-shirt. "Wait. You have a room at this hotel?"

"I do. For the night. It's much easier than trying to rush back home after the party." She puts my flannel on. It's long enough to cover her like a micromini skirt. As long as she doesn't bend at all, she's 'decent.'

"Okay. Which room?" I hold out my hand expectantly. "I'll need the key."

"311." Vanessa gestures at the bundle of dress. "The key is in my purse, which is in there."

I peer down at the wad of fabric I'm holding. "Wow. Small purse."

"It is. I don't need much." Vanessa huffs. "Please hurry dear. No offense to your wardrobe, but this doesn't match my shoes."

Heh. "Okay. Be right back."

"I'll keep an eye on Chloe," says Ashley.

I nod at her and hurry for the door. It doesn't take me long to fly (literally) up the stairwell to the third floor and find room 311. Sure enough, there's a tiny purse in the dress. Must've been on her shoulder and got caught up in the material when it pulled off her. It contains a hotel room keycard, two lipsticks, and a really, really small handgun. Eep. Wow. I'm glad undeath has helped me get past the overdeveloped fear of guns I inherited from my mother. I can even be in the same room with them now without feeling like a cop is going to materialize out of thin air and throw me in jail.

I've even shot people.

Well, vampires. Not quite the same.

The keycard works, letting me into a needlessly large room. And... holy shit. Vanessa's got a full closet of stuff here, in a room she rented for one night. Who brings twenty some odd dresses to one party at all much less takes the time to unpack and hang them in the closet? Is she expecting catastrophe or suffering massive indecision?

Hmm. I'm not the right girl to task with picking an appropriate gown. Hmm. Which one of these will go with her shoe color. Oh, never mind. She's brought a dozen pairs of shoes as well. Amazing.

Bleh. I pick a turquoise gown and grab the matching shoes, then hurry back down to the party.

Everything's more or less normal. Vanessa, in my flannel shirt, is huddled against the wall by Ashley. Looks like someone is making a movie about my life and they woefully miscast some drop-dead gorgeous supermodel in my part. Ugh, Dad. Really? Your genes did this to me. I had to refer to a vampire as 'drop *dead*' gorgeous.

Chloe's amusing herself by flying around in lazy circles pretending to be a faerie. Normally, someone who flies around inside during one of these events is regarded pretty much the same way normal mortals think of that one distant cousin who shows up uninvited at weddings, gets drunk, starts a brawl, and ends up peeing in a flowerpot in full view of everyone. However, Chloe's a child. She can get away with things adults cannot. I think part of it is due to the cuteness factor, though most of it is coming from the 'it keeps her busy and out of my way' attitude.

While no one here seems antagonistic toward her existence, being interested in her and wanting to directly interact are another thing entirely. Vampires don't know how to process the concept of a vampiric child. Everyone's pretty much ignoring her the way people tend to do when someone brings their seven-year-old to a wedding where the invitations said 'adults only,' so she's the only child in the room.

I slip back into my flannel shirt after Vanessa changes.

"Thank you, dear." She flashes a smile that looks superficial but isn't, then flits off to resume socializing as if nothing happened.

Ashley and I hold up the wall, talking about whatever leaps into our heads. Our conversation bounces from school to demon stuff to random things like 'I wonder whatever happened to (insert name here)' in regard to people we knew from high school.

It would be kinda interesting in a National Geographic sort of way to keep tabs on our graduating class through the coming years to see how they all end up. It's a lot of work, not to mention more than a touch creepy/stalkery. Sounds like the kind of thing a hardcore Old Guard—who feels removed from and superior to mortals— would do.

Wham!

No, not George Michael. I mean there's a freakin' loud-ass crash from the left side of the room.

It's so loud and sudden, Ashley and I both yelp at the same time. To be fair, about three-quarters of the vampires in here also yell. My attention darts to a whole bunch of stuff flying in the air. Thanks to my supernatural reflexes going into 'combat mode,' time seems to be slowed to an almost crawl.

Chloe's in mid faceplant, cheek mushed into the end of one of the long cafeteria type tables. Her body's bent forward, feet almost touching her head. Her arms jut out to either side like she'd been flailing in a panic in the split second before she crashed down on the table. In stupefied horror, I gawk at a bunch of snacks and drinks flying off the opposite end of the table, catapulted into the air by the force of the child coming down.

The cloud of hors d'oeurves, beer cups, little fruit salads, and cheese bits falls like a hailstorm on Paolo and Stefano, plus a trio of their hangers-on. A slender black-haired woman in a super-low-cut evening gown beside Paolo gets a gooey chocolate-covered strawberry right in the cleavage. A small bowl of onion-and-chive dip nails Stefano in the face like a cream pie from the *Three Stooges*.

Chloe hit the table so hard, it flips up into the air and comes crashing down on top of her. Or would have if Jennifer Ruiz hadn't been close enough to intercept it. The woman unsticks from slowed time, running at a seemingly normal speed, catches the table before it lands on top of Chloe, and shoves it sideways to empty floor.

Time returns to normal.

Paolo and Stefano stand statue still as the pelting of foodstuffs falls on them. Both men are scarily calm, staring at no one in particular with facial expressions that suggest they are trying to alter the very fabric of reality by simply refusing to believe what just happened.

I spare only six-tenths of a second to look at them before sprinting over to Chloe.

Shock wears off her soon after I scoop her up off the floor; she starts wailing like a kid who fell off a bike and skinned her knee...

except her jaw and neck are both broken, probably collarbone as well. Ashley helps me gather the kid up and straighten her out.

For almost a full minute, her crying is the only sound in the entire room. Everyone's staring at us. Paolo and Stefano haven't moved an inch. Onion and chive dip dribbles. He is unamused.

A one-inch cube of Swiss cheese loses its traction on Paolo's shoulder and falls to the floor.

"I'm sorry!" Chloe sniffles, then whispers, "I'm crying 'cause I'm scared. Not 'cause this hurts."

Ashley gawks. "That doesn't hurt?"

Chloe shifts her gaze off to one side, radiating shame. "I've had bigger ouches than this."

Grr. I clench my jaw and gently hug her tighter.

The room remains tomb silent except for the scuffing footsteps of the snack mortals wandering about in Derptown. Yeah... everyone's waiting to see who's getting lit on fire for this. Three minutes later, the silence is becoming burdensome. I'm about to jump up and start defending her, if not for the fear of making it worse.

An audible crackling snap comes from Chloe's neck.

"Eek," says Ashley.

"I'm okay." Chloe rolls her feet around. "I can move again."

Someone walks into my peripheral vision. Black suit legs. Super expensive shoes. They're clean, so it's neither Paolo nor Stefano.

Chloe shifts her gaze off me to peer up at the man. "Someone grabbed me and threw me at the table."

Might as well get this over with. Here's hoping punishment isn't too severe. I gradually lift my head to make eye contact—with Mr. Wolent. This could be good or bad. Good, because he's a reasonable man who is generally nice to those he trusts. Bad because he's the most politically powerful vampire in the area. If he's upset, bad things happen.

His eyes aren't giving away much of a mood beyond analytical.

"Are you all right, girl?" asks Wolent.

Chloe rubs her face. "My mouth hurts. It'll be okay."

"What did we learn?" asks Stefano in a forced-calm tone. Like, if it had been anyone other than Chloe, he'd probably be screaming in a rage.

The girl hangs her head.

"Easy, Stefano." Wolent raises a hand at him while giving a super slight head shake. "Something seized her and threw her into the table. She did not do it on purpose."

Guilt and shame evaporate from her expression. Wide-eyed, she looks up at him adoringly, the words 'wow he believes me!' practically tattooed on her forehead. Yeah, kiddo. When you tell the truth to someone who can read your mind, they are extremely likely to believe you.

Wait, what? Some*thing* grabbed her?

"Mr. Wolent?" I ask. "Some*thing*? Not someone?"

He crouches in front of her, tracing a finger across her bruised jaw. "The child was moving too fast and too high for anyone to have reached her. She didn't see what grabbed her. I suspect you have an idea of who, or should I say *what* to blame."

Stefano approaches, holding his arms slightly aloft in the universal body language of 'I just stepped in something foul'. "There is still a lesson here for her, even if the mess was unintentional. If the girl had not been flying around..."

"I'm sorry." Chloe grinds her big toe into the carpet.

Wolent takes her hand, pats it, then lets go. "It's nothing to be sorry for, my dear. You were attacked by an outside force."

"Yes, sir." I gaze at the ceiling. "I've got a bit of a demon problem."

"A demon problem," repeats Stefano, eyebrow raised a tick.

Paolo's anger and frustration grows. He's not the sort of man who takes being made to look foolish in stride. He *really* wants to vent his frustrations on someone. I don't understand guys like this. If someone spills coffee on your shirt, beating the stuffing out of them doesn't make you look any less foolish. In fact, it makes you look a hundred times worse.

The woman who took the strawberry directly to the boobs is still standing there motionless, gawking down at the offending chocolate-covered fruit missile. You'd think from the look on her face, a lump of dog poo hit her and not a candied snack.

Suppose I should be thankful Paolo isn't about to fly off the handle and go after Chloe. Doesn't look like he's particularly angry at her, beyond generally irritated at the presence of a child at this event.

"Yes." I lower my voice for some stupid reason. Not like every vampire in this room couldn't hear a flea fart. "Remember the incident with the sefil?"

Wolent nods once, his face going grim.

"Apparently, the demon who embodied it is super mad at me—and my family—for ruining his chance to rule, destroy, or whatever he wanted to do to the world. He's trying to mess with me from whatever plane of existence he's stuck in."

Wolent stands up, lips shifted to one side in a 'this is a problem, but what the hell can we do about it' sort of expression.

Chloe floats up to eye level with him, grins, and says, "Bla-bla-bla!"

Some vampires close to us wince, gasp, or stare in shock.

Mr. Wolent's eyebrows inch upward, then he chuckles.

Stefano gives me a sideways look. "This is what you're teaching her? We're not all from Eastern Europe."

"It's from a kid's movie," says Ashley. "Dad let her watch *Hotel Transylvania*."

"What?" Stefano flicks a small pretzel from his sleeve. "They made a children's film about *vampires?*"

I nod. "Yeah. It's kinda cute."

"You've never seen bats so adorbs." Ashley gives off a faint 'squee' noise through her nose.

"How... demeaning." Stefano sighs. "There is nothing *cute* about vampires."

Chloe flashes a fanged smile, hands clasped together in front of her while twisting her toes into the carpet.

Wolent smiles, gesturing at her. "The small one begs to differ."

CHAPTER 23
SHOWDOWN AT THE OK CUL-DE-SAC

I t's Saturday.

I think. At least for a few minutes, the only fact my brain is capable of processing is that I'm conscious. We made it through the remainder of the soiree without serious catastrophe. The demon trying to make my family's life difficult is either an idiot, or he's so enraged he's not thinking clearly. Or, he's got a low opinion of vampires. Trying to make it look like Chloe caused a scene to get us in trouble doesn't work terribly well when every elder in the room can read her mind and be certain she didn't do it.

Then again, it's not like Paolo and Stefano need logic on their side to carry a grudge. Even if they don't insist on her being punished for something 'she did,' they're going to remember the great snack-storm for decades. Every time they think of it, they'll think of Chloe, and me. The demon is trying to make things hard for me. He must know those two guys aren't exactly cheerleaders for Team Sarah.

And can I say I just about dropped dead—well dead*er*—when she bla-bla-bla'ed at Wolent? It's like being invited to meet the President of the United States while having a three-year-old boy in tow who blurts 'I have a penis' to the president on national television.

Okay, maybe not *quite* that embarrassing. Wolent handled it well, though. He almost seemed amused.

Yeah, I'm pretty sure it's Saturday.

From the sounds in the house, everyone else is well underway in enjoying the weekend. By that, I mean it's silent. No one is here. Mom used to reserve Saturdays—at least the Saturdays where she didn't have to work—cleaning the house. Hmm. That makes it sound like Dad's lazy. He's not. Both of my parents used to clean the house. My father only did it during the week. With me—and now Ashley—taking on the bulk of the housekeeping since we're up all damn night, my parents get to relax. More or less. Mom still does some vacuuming and whatnot on Saturday. It would be super inconsiderate of me to run the vacuum at three in the morning. Ashley and I are basically the ninja cleaning service—silent.

We have more time than house, so we've been hitting her place, too.

Anyway, I should get up.

Except for being on high alert in case of demonic interference, my day is pretty normal. Maybe abnormal. Not too many people my age get to sit around at home doing nothing on a Saturday. It's not like I have a job or a pack of friends interested in 'going out and doing stuff.' Michelle's been kind of absent lately. She's quite busy with school and work... and I think she's a tiny bit freaked out over Ashley going vamp. Not that she's afraid of Ashley personally, more like she's concerned if she spends too much time around us it'll be her joining Club Undeath.

At least my parents aren't giving me a hard time about being a bum without a job. I joke. They know exactly why I appear lazy. Besides, I've got leprechaun gold. Ugh. That's going to sound ridiculous every time I think about it. The money isn't even gold anymore. Aurélie turned it into a bank account for me. Go figure that by not caring about the little guy's gold, I 'earned' more money in thirty seconds than most people make over the course of an entire working life.

Almost feels like cheating.

Not going to complain, really. I don't feel rich. For one thing, it isn't *that* much money, and for another, I'll have to make that money last a lot longer than a mortal would. Random thoughts about working ordinary jobs hit me on and off, causing me to laugh for no apparent reason. I'd be the worst nightmare for a 'Karen' if I worked retail. Wonder what a vampire compulsion to 'stop abusing people, be quiet, go home, and reexamine your life choices' would do to someone.

The Littles plus Ronan return home shortly before dark, having been out all day with the 'rents. Not sure where exactly they ended up going, either one of those interactive science museum type places, then the mall, or something else mostly fun but that could pretend to be at least somewhat educational.

Mrs. Lawrence lucked out with free babysitting. I think Ro is here more often than he's at home these days. If this keeps up, we might as well adopt her, too. And... chaos ensues. The instant they're back in the house, the Littles swarm all over me, trying to talk at the same time. They did, in fact, go to the science museum. Crazy stuff happened to them all day. Some of the interactive exhibits they tried to play with malfunctioned. Sam went headfirst into a giant water tank when 'something' pushed him from behind. He got tangled up in the mechanism and couldn't get out—but Sophia panic blurted some magic to pull him out.

My little brother nearly drowning was the worst of the attacks. The remainder all seemed more like pranks. Sierra is convinced a giant metal statue really wanted to fall on and kill Dad, but it didn't move. Blix, perched on Sam's shoulder, flaps his arms and chatters away. My brother translates. Basically, the imp spent the day with them fending off an apparition trying to do harm. He's not sure what, exactly the being is other than 'demonic energy.' It's not the sefil demon, though. That bastard is stuck wherever he is. The thing that followed my family around today is merely a minion. Blix is not bragging when he takes credit for stopping over thirty attacks. He's only trying to explain the scope of our problem. This dark presence tried everything from making heavy things fall from high places onto my parents or ripping Sophia's dress off in public or making guns carried by nearby cops go off when Sierra was close. Seems like it's going after our worst fears list after all.

Weird that Sophia's not as red faced as I'd expect when it gets brought up that the demon nearly embarrassed the crap out of her at the mall they went to after the museum. I'm tempted to look into her head to see why she's not blushing. But I promised. She doesn't look guilty. I know for a fact she's still dreadfully afraid—irrationally so— of being caught somewhere naked. The London mystics aren't going to try to teleport nap her again. The odds of her clothes spontaneously disappearing are even worse than an American politician admitting they were wrong about something. Why is she so focused on that fear? Is she having body image issues? It's not like her to care much about being pretty. I mean, she *is* pretty. Of the three of us, she's by far the most photogenic. In my opinion, she could totally do modeling or be an actress—at least if only looks mattered. She's far too shy to be an actress.

Okay, now I'm concerned. Does she feel like she's *too* thin? Some of the girls in her class are already starting to look mature. Not Sophia. Even Sierra, who's twelve, still has all the shape of a broom handle. Takes us Wright girls a while to fill out. They both had me as an example. The boob faerie didn't visit me until... geez, I think I was well into fourteen. The hips faerie started hanging out more recently, though she decided to stop returning my calls once I died.

Honestly, I'm okay with my looks. Neither the hottest girl in the room nor the most plain. Average is my spirit animal. I know Sierra couldn't care less about appealing to boys. That's a combination of her age plus being preoccupied with the idea of school shooters. She doesn't have time to think about anything else. Sophia's a girly girl but she's not a Bree Swanson. She also doesn't spend all her time doing beauty stuff and talking about boys.

Quick peek into Sophia's mind, justified by me being concerned for her health.

Whew. Okay. She's not hating on herself. However, it's weird. The idea of how super awful it would be if something embarrassed her like that is repeating at the tip of her brain almost like a mantra. It's as if she's daring the demon to rip her dress off in a public place.

Hmm. The girl is up to something. She definitely does not *want* that to happen... yet she's goading the thing into doing it to her by thinking about how much it would ruin her life.

Drama, right? It's not really going to ruin her life to be laughed at.

I try to dig a little deeper... and get stuck. Oh, drat. That's right. She enchanted herself to resist vampire mental stuff, mostly so she couldn't be mind-controlled and made to attack us, like what happened to Sierra at the hangar outside the private jet. Right. Dumbass me. What was I thinking bringing her along on a mission, even one so tame?

Dad interrupts our discussion about demons, snapping me out of my wobbly mind link with Sophia. "You guys ready for the movie?"

Before my 'death,' Sierra would've made some sarcastic comment about how she didn't have a choice. Now, she offers a genuine 'yeah.' Sophia, of course, is super excited about movie night, even if it happens every week. Sam acts nonchalant, but he's the first one on the couch.

"What manner of cheese are you going to inflict on us this week?" asks Sierra in an uncharacteristically bright tone.

"It's an adventure movie." Dad holds up a DVD case. "One of my favorites when I was your age."

Looks like the movie is called *Explorers*. Oh, I remember this one. It's about some boys who build a spaceship out of an old amusement park thing and go into space. Dad showed it to me years ago. Don't remember exactly, though I was probably younger than Sam at the time. This is one of the 'core movies' Dad loved so much as a kid he had on something called VHS.

He pops the disc in the player, then hurries over to his recliner.

"Wait!" Sophia jumps up. "Popcorn!"

Dad waits on hitting play while Sophia runs to the kitchen. Four-ish minutes of Dad telling us how cool he thought this movie was when he was little ends with Sophia running back into the living room carrying a big bowl of popcorn. She intends to run by, behind the couch, then circle around the end where I'm sitting... but she doesn't make it. Sophia's half a step into the living room from the hall when she trips and goes down hard. The popcorn rockets upward, setting off a small snowstorm of freshly-popped buttery goodness all over us, the couch, and the rug between couch and television.

Mom screams.

It's the sort of scream that can only be produced when her powerful concern for the wellbeing of her children crashes headfirst into her overprotectiveness toward the carpet. Sophia, still on the floor behind the couch, bursts into tears.

Dad jumps to his feet, peering over at her. Sierra, Sam, Ronan, Ashley, and I all twist around to look down at her.

"Are you all right, sweetie?" asks Dad.

Sophia rolls around to sit up and continues wailing. "I'm sorry. I wasted all the popcorn."

"Forget the popcorn. Are you hurt?" Dad waves at her in a 'come here' gesture.

Sophia, sniveling like a much smaller child, scurries around the sofa and cling-hugs him, crying into his chest like she just burned the house down.

Sierra stares at me and mouths WTF.

Sam's ignoring her for the moment, instead staring at the hallway to the kitchen like a Vietnam War era machine gun operator waiting for the enemy to show themselves.

"But I wasted it," wails Sophia. "It's all over the rug."

Mom gets up and fast walks into the hall. "Nothing a vacuum can't solve."

"But the butter!" Sophia sniffles.

"Dork." Sierra bonks her with a pillow. "Magic it out of the rug."

Sophia wipes at her face, still sniffling. Her 'oh, yeah, duh' expression is adorable. She's still too upset to concentrate on magic, though. Ugh. Poor kid. She must be wound up so much over the demonic attacks something small like this becomes a tragedy.

Ronan's keeping quiet, though he's staring at her making this 'what the hell is wrong with you' face.

"What tripped her?" asks Sierra.

Sophia sniffs again. "You think something tripped me and I'm not just a popcorn-wasting klutz?"

Blix holds his hands up, shaking his head. "Neem Noba!"

"Yeah, we know you didn't do it," mutters Sam.

"It's still my fault. Mom always says not to run in the house." Sophia hangs her head.

I lightly bonk her on the head with a pillow. "Good grief. Stop beating yourself up. It's only popcorn."

Sophia thrusts her arms out to the sides. "But it's our last bag! And it's buttery. Now it's on the carpet."

"Soph..." Sierra gives a faint sigh. "Stop panicking and start magic-ing. You can save the popcorn. You are the chosen one. You can make the kernels clean again." She puts her hands together, fist to palm, like a monk. "Embrace the meditative order of Redenbacher. Be the kernel."

Dad stifles a chuckle.

Rattling and clattering comes from my right as Mom fights with something in the hall closet.

"You okay over there, Allie?" calls Dad.

"Yeah. Fine. Having a little trouble getting the vacuum out of the closet," grumbles Mom.

"Maybe it's not ready to let the world know who it really is?" Sierra wags her eyebrows.

Sophia, Sam, Ronan, Ashley, and Mom all groan.

Dad makes this face at Sierra like it's the proudest dad moment of his life. The progeny has punned.

"Ack!" yells Mom, then she gurgles.

That's not a normal Mom sound.

I grab the top of the sofa and pull myself up, leaning out far enough to peer down the hall to my left.

Our vacuum is attacking Mom. The power cord's wrapped around her neck like an angry—but really thin—snake. The hose thrashes around ineffectually whomping on her legs.

"Uh oh. The vac is trying to strangle Mom." I leap over the sofa back and jog up to her.

She's mostly got the cord off her neck by the time I get my hands on the wire and help. The force isn't too strong. Sophia might not have been able to overpower it but Mom's good.

"Saaaam!" yells Mom, while we're trying to unwind the cord from her throat. "I need you get over here and exorcise this vacuum right now."

"Why?" asks Sierra. "Is it gaining weight?"

Ronan voicelessly screams, "Why!" at the ceiling. Ashley throws a small pillow at her. Sam jumps over the sofa doing his best Batman leap. Sierra accepts the buffeting pillow as an appropriate response to the lameness of her pun. Dad's so proud of her he's about to faint.

Sam stares at the vacuum. "Mom, can I swear a little?"

Mom grunts from the effort she's putting into fighting the power cord. "Fine. Just not too bad."

Ashley rushes up beside me. She's all wide-eyed curious though her claws are out like she's ready for things to escalate.

My brother raises his arms as if he's going to throw a fireball like Ryu from *Street Fighter*. "Get away from my mom, you piece of shit!"

Nothing weird appears around his hands or flies toward the vacuum. However, the appliance abruptly slides away from us as if kicked, sliding several feet down the hall toward the kitchen. A shadowy black mass peels out from the plastic housing and collects into a humanoid shape roughly the same size as my kid brother. It's featureless, entirely made of vapor, and does not give off a sense of being a malevolent child despite its size. It's a huge imp—or something like that.

"Nice," says Dad. "*Aliens* reference."

"Huh?" Sam blinks.

Dad tilts his head. "Ripley confronts the queen at the end—get away from her you bitch?"

"Oh. Right." Sam shrugs. "Not intentional."

Dad snaps his fingers in mock disappointment.

Ashley gives me side eye. "Can we kill it?"

"I dunno. Is it bleeding?" asks Sierra. "If it bleeds, we can kill it."

A single tear of pride forms in Dad's eye. My sister's quoting *Predator*.

"Don't think so. Sam can though." I gesture at it in a 'what are you waiting for?' manner.

The shadow apparition zooms away from us, through the kitchen, and out the sliding glass door.

"Crap!" yells Ashley. "After it!"

Not really thinking too much about what I'm doing, I grab Sam like he's a giant football with eyes and charge for the door. Ashley, unburdened by the—admittedly slight—weight of my kid brother, beats me there and opens it for me. Demonic shadow things are pretty damn fast, being all immaterial and whatnot. This is one of the few times since I've become a vampire where I feel slow. It's almost like I'm a mere mortal trying to chase Ashley's old cat. I swear he was psychic. Knew a vet visit was coming. Always a project to get a hold of him.

The demonic mass zips across our backyard and goes through the fence like a ghost. Since I am made of solid matter, I fly over it. Sam's making weird noises, part gurgle part scream. Oops. I may have accelerated a little too fast. We chase the shadow among the trees for barely two seconds—though it feels more like eight or nine —before it goes into Mr. Niedermeyer's house.

Aww, hell.

I land on his back porch, set Sam on his feet, and grab the door handle, opening it and barging right into his kitchen. Ashley zips in to set down beside me. Sam seems almost afraid to set foot in this house. It's nothing about demons. Every kid in the area dreads this place and the man who lives here. Pure childish stuff, though. Niedermeyer isn't a serial killer or anything. No one over the age of thirteen is afraid of him. Teens just think he's a jerk.

Gasping comes from the doorway out of the kitchen.

I follow the sounds of someone having a heart attack down a short corridor to a plainly decorated living room. Mr. Niedermeyer's in a pea-soup-green recliner, wearing striped pajamas and fake leather slippers. If 'mean old man' had an entry on Wikipedia, he'd be the picture.

Only, I feel bad for him now. He's pale as heck and looks to be in the middle of a massive coronary event. Before I can decide if it would be appropriate to call 911, he stops convulsing and clutching at his chest.

"Ack! Did he die?" whispers Ashley.

He turns his head to look at us.

"Nope." I shake my head. "Mr. Niedermeyer's okay."

"No, he isn't." Sam takes a step back. "That's not Mr. Niedermeyer."

The old guy gets up from his big, ugly recliner and faces us. He looks calm. Too calm. No way would he be this calm if people—especially a kid—broke into his house. He can't handle people on his lawn.

"What do we do?" whispers Ashley.

Mr. Niedermeyer walks past us to the kitchen.

"Are you sure he's possessed?" I ask.

"Positive." Sam leads the way down the hall, following the old guy. "And I'm gonna do the same thing I did to the vacuum."

Ashley tilts her head. "Heh. Why'd you request to swear?"

"So, I didn't get in trouble." Sam stops three half-steps into the kitchen.

"I mean, why'd you need to swear at all?" Ashley smirks.

"Because it helps." Sam raises his arms.

"I know... saying 'oh fiddlesticks' when you drop a battery on your toe just doesn't cut it." I chuckle.

Sam peers back at me. "It's more than that. Swear words are called curses for a reason, right? It adds power. The words are like a wide conduit for emotions to go into magic."

"Umm. What are you doing using words like conduit at nine?" Ashley snickers.

"I'm ten, not illiterate." Sam faces Mr. Niedermeyer again.

"Oof. Burn," I mutter.

The old guy pulls a huge carving knife from a block on the counter. "This is a nice little town. Only thing wrong with it is... too many children."

Ashley leans back, gasping.

"That's not Mr. Niedermeyer," I say. "The demon's trying to make me kill this guy."

"Not gonna work." Sam waves his hands around doing an impression of Emperor Palpatine throwing evil lightning. "Leave that poor guy alone, shithead!" After shouting, Sam grabs nothing and pulls as if tearing a poster off the wall.

Mr. Niedermeyer seems to lose consciousness. The shadow apparition exudes from his back; the knife tumbles from the old guy's hand and clatters to the floor. Ashley and I both rush to catch him before he falls and cracks his teeth on the counter edge. Sam scrambles to recover the dropped knife, then lunges to his feet into a Captain Jack Sparrow maneuver, slashing at the apparition. In his hand, that enormous carving knife is basically a sword. The apparition's too fast for him, swerving out of the way before rushing down the hall to the front of the house. Sam tosses the knife to Ashley, then braces for me to grab him again. No, my brother isn't careless with sharp objects. He knows Ashley is a vampire. He'd never 'throw' a knife like that to anyone who wasn't already dead.

Ash snags the huge carving knife out of the air with the grace of a circus performer. Hey, it's not that difficult to do with reflexes like ours. I leave Mr. Niedermeyer to her care, grab Sam again, and give chase.

The demon shadow goes out through the wall of the house to the front yard and off down the street. Mr. Niedermeyer is a jerk, but he doesn't deserve property damage, so I slow down enough to use the front door rather than smashing my way out his window. Gee, I really hope the neighbors aren't looking outside right now to see me pulling a Supergirl maneuver. If someone did catch me flying, would they believe their eyes or dismiss it as not getting enough sleep?

Dad, Sierra, Sophia, Chloe, and Blix add themselves to the chase. They'd been coming across the cul-de-sac already toward Mr. Niedermeyer's place. When Blix points out the entity going down the street, they change course.

I follow the entity down the street past several houses until it decides to go into one.

Crap. I don't know who lives here or what to expect, so I land on the sidewalk where the walkway to their front porch intersects it. Ooh, this thing is infuriating.

Chloe catches up to me first, then Ashley, then Sierra. I put Sam down on his feet.

Dad and Sophia run up to us.

"Where'd it go?" asks Dad.

"The demonic vapor went in there." I point at the house.

Sierra blinks. "Demonic vapor? Did Sam fart?"

"This thing isn't as deadly," says Sophia in a completely serious tone.

"Why are we just standing here?" Ashley glances over at me as if I'm the one in command.

I can't help myself and look to Dad. He might be a normal mortal but he's still my dad and the adult here. "Should we just barge into someone's house?"

"We just barged into Mr. Niedermeyer's place," says Sam in a flat tone.

"Yeah, but we kinda know him." I shrug. "Or at least who he is. No clue who lives here."

"That doesn't change anything." Sierra points. "There's a demon loose and it's gonna hurt someone."

"But..." I flap my arms. "It's a fart shadow. What are we going to do to it? I can't claw vapor... can I? Do vampire claws hurt ghosts?"

"It's not a ghost." Chloe shrugs.

Sophia steps up beside Sam. "I think we can send it back. This would be a lot easier if I had an empty soul jar."

Dad goes for his phone. "Let me check Amazon."

"I don't think they have two-minute shipping." Sierra folds her arms.

"They could... with Klepto helping." Sophia smiles.

"Mew!" comes from under her hair.

"Dad?" I ask.

He doesn't take his phone out of the holder. "I think it's justifiable in these circumstances. Go ahead and kick down the door."

Sigh. "I don't have to. I can just open it."

Blix mutters something to Sam. Can't understand demonic, though the phrase had the unmistakable sense of 'no problem' to it.

The front door flies open as if punted from inside, revealing a small blonde girl in *Little Mermaid* PJs and pink dinosaur slippers. She's like eight or nine years old—and she's got a big knife. The kid flashes a psycho killer grin.

"I'm not hitting a little girl." Dad nudges Sierra forward. "This is all you."

Sierra gasps. "Dad! Why do you think I'd beat up a little kid?"

The distant-neighbor child stalks down her porch steps, walking toward my family. She's grinning in a super, super creepy way. Ack! Her eyes have turned completely black. Oh, this can't be good. This is exactly what can happen if parents leave their kids unattended for too long in front of the *Teletubbies.*

"Guys!" I say, trying to give off a sense of yelling without actually making too much noise. "No one is going to beat her up."

Sophia glares into space. A second later, she shoves her arms out to either side and stomps, her bare foot making a faint clapping sound on the sidewalk. Then, she nods at Sam. A purple light flash and a 'Mew!' happens behind my little brother. Hmm. He's got his right arm tucked back as if hiding something.

"Leave her alone!" Sam swings his left hand in a 'begone with you' wave, like Stefano Bianchi dismissing a peon.

The kid stops marching at us. She stops in place, swaying on her feet for a second or two before the shadow being melts out of her, coalescing into a small humanoid shape standing a few paces behind her.

Sam whips his right hand out from behind his back, takes aim with his big, orange Nerf pistol, and shoots three darts into the black vaporous being—which promptly explodes into a scattering of inky, slimy fragments.

Dad does that whistling 'wah wah wah' thing from *The Good, The Bad, and The Ugly.*

Sam holds his Nerf gun up and blows over the barrel. His 'cool gunslinger' act lasts only as long as he realizes he's got pajama pants on—and no holster to put the toy gun in.

The little girl looks around, clearly baffled at how she ended up outside.

I hurry up to her. "Hey, kiddo. Are you okay?"

"What happened?" She looks up at me.

"Nothing." I smile—and dive into her head. "Nothing happened at all. You're still in bed."

The kid stares into the Eighth Dimension.

I glance over at my family. "Be home in a minute. Just gotta reverse kidnap this girl and make sure no one in the house saw anything. Go ahead and start the movie. I've seen it already, and I won't be long."

"Reverse kidnap?" Sierra scrunches up her nose. "What does that mean?"

"It means breaking into a stranger's house to put their child back where they belong without notification, permission, or anyone remembering I was there."

Dad pats me on the shoulder. "Justifiable. You're only undoing supernatural weirdness. How long do you think it'll be? We can wait on starting the movie."

Sierra gawks at him. "Dad, are we seriously going to just go home and watch a movie like normal after this?"

"Why not?" He smiles. "The demon's dead."

"Just a minion." Sam frowns. "There will be more. We should be safe for at least the rest of tonight, though. Movie time!"

CHAPTER 24

THE OTHER SIDE OF THE SLAB

The movie's cute.

Unrealistic as all heck, but cute. By the way, Sophia managed to clean the rug and save the popcorn, even returning it to a nice edible warmth. Magic doesn't always save the world. Sometimes, it only prevents the last packet of popcorn from being wasted.

As the Littles are getting up to go to bed, Mom points at her. "Soph, I don't want you getting any ideas. You are not allowed to attempt making a force bubble and sending your siblings, friends, or anyone under the age of ninety-five into space."

Sophia holds up a hand in a swearing-in gesture. "I won't send anyone into space."

"Are you giving her permission to exile old folks to the outer reaches of the solar system?" asks Dad. "Seventy-five seems kind of arbitrary."

"Of course not, Jonathan." Mom pokes him.

"Oh." Sierra shrugs. "I thought she was talking about Uncle Hank."

"Do not banish your Uncle Hank to distant galaxies." Mom holds up the Finger of Authority.

Wow. I can't tell if she's being serious or joking.

The Littles head off to bed. Dad and I undertake the challenging project of convincing Chloe we can't watch *Hotel Transylvania 2* now because it would be unfair to the Littles who haven't seen it yet. She's disappointed but we bribe her by re-watching the first movie.

My phone rings at 11:58 p.m.

Not even telemarketers call this late, so it's gotta be important. Probably going to be annoying. Oof. I hope it's not punishment for what happened at the soiree.

Nervous, I take my phone off the coffee table and answer.

"Sarah?" asks an unfamiliar man.

"I've been called worse names." I chuckle. "Yeah, umm. Who is this?"

"Mike," says the guy. Oh. It's one of Wolent's people. Not the same guy who called me about the Natasha job. They always use the name Mike for some reason. "Are you available to deal with a minor matter of some urgency?"

Ashley is usually the more accommodating of the two of us. If someone asks her for help with something, she's not wired to be able to say no. I have the ability to say no, even if I don't use it too often. Alas, when dealing with Wolent's people, I turn right back into some child stuck in the 'pleasing others' stage of development. As long as they don't ask me to do anything diabolical, I'll pretty much do whatever job they send my way hoping they'll like and trust me.

"Yeah. I can help. What's the situation?"

"An associate ended up losing control of himself and was, unfortunately, picked up by the authorities," says Mike.

Associate is code speak for another vampire. Losing control could mean he freaked out and went on a rampage. However, 'picked up by authorities' tells me the loss of control is referring to being knocked out by a wound that would've been fatal to a mortal.

"Ahh. So, he's... chilling somewhere."

"Precisely." Mike chuckles. "He needs a ride home before morning."

"Can do. Where?"

"Pierce County Medical Examiner."

I nod even though 'Mike' can't see me. "Okay. I'll go right now."

"Great. Much appreciated. Oh, his name is Theo."

"Got it."

We hang up.

"What's that about?" Dad peers over at me, yawns, then tries not to look tired.

I exhale hard. "Some vampire named Theo got himself shot and mistaken for a dead guy. I need to get him out of the morgue before they do more damage."

"Sounds simple enough." Ashley grins. "Want a hand?"

"Sure. Bodies are kinda awkward to carry by myself, especially if they're stiff."

"Eww," says Chloe.

Dad looks at his wrist. No, he's not wearing a watch. "How long will you be out?"

"I dunno. Anywhere from half an hour to two depending on how crazy this gets." I fidget with my phone. It's almost weird it no longer says things randomly in German. "It sounds simple, which means it's probably going to end up being a near miss with sunrise."

Chloe perks up. "You can't bring me for good luck. Someone might see me outside and it's too dark for me."

'Too dark' is her way of saying it's much too late for her to be seen outside.

"It's Saturday night." Dad offers a sleepy smile. "I'll keep her company."

"Don't worry." Chloe grins at me. "If he falls asleep before you get back, I'll be good."

It's cute and funny, but... also true. I really shouldn't be inclined to trust a seven-year-old to be home alone—well, not alone but with no conscious adults watching her. Yet, the idea doesn't make me immediately consider myself an awful person. Chloe is no normal child. She's even worse than me in terms of being Follows Rules Girl. She's stuck with some level of fear that if she gets in trouble, my parents or I might not want her anymore... or the other vampires will call for her destruction.

Yeah, that's a bit more motivation than I had as a kid to behave.

I wish I could change that. It's not fair she understands the position she's in so well. I hate even more that she feared death as a punishment for messing up bad enough even before she became a vampire. Grr. She didn't even do anything wrong the night the bastard killed her. Whatever set him off had nothing to do with her. She just happened to be there as a target for his impotent frustration.

Chloe gurgles when I squish hug her. She doesn't protest. One: she doesn't need to breathe anymore. Two: she knows exactly what it means when I spontaneously do this. I get overcome with emotion every time I think about what happened to her. Maybe that's why she trusts me so much. Either that or she instantly decided to trust me when I demanded Eleanor St. Ives let her out of the cat carrier. How warped is it that I was the only vampire in the entire room who thought it shocking and wrong to stuff a little girl into a portable kennel?

Bleh. I can hold her like a doll all night long after I get back. We have to get Theo out of the morgue before some doctor cuts him open and starts asking unanswerable questions.

Ashley and I hurry down to my room and change into ninja mode: black leggings, black shirt, black hoodie. I finally ordered a pair of black sneakers. Ashley already had some from the summer she worked as a hostess for this little steakhouse place.

Once we're in stealth gear, I run upstairs and appropriate one of Dad's old shirts and a pair of khaki pants that look older than me. Can't really say borrow as I don't expect to get them back. After checking with him to make sure neither item has any sentimental value—they don't—we head out via the back door.

STUFF LIKE THIS IS WEIRD, thrilling, and scary.

I land in a darkened spot on the opposite side of Pacific Ave from the morgue. Behind me is an imposing two-story brick building with strange windows. Thin strips of brick turn the huge windows into rows of narrow ones, almost making them look like giant bars on a giant prison cell. A blue sign labels the place as 'Tacoma-Pierce

County Health Department.' Maybe because it's a rainy night, but that building looks like the physical embodiment of 'dreary.'

My target, across the street from us, is a perfectly rectangular white building. It's like the being who built our reality couldn't be bothered to design anything and left it as the 'basic white cuboid' model. Black lettering above the entrance reads 'Office of the Pierce County Medical Examiner.' The blue-painted steel double doors into the building stand recessed a little back from the wall. At least we'll be out of the rain while breaking in. Also, this place is seriously charged with weird energy. I don't see any ghosts right now... but so much death touches this building, it's marked. The hairs on the back of my neck are already on end and we're still across the street from it.

Yeah. Stuff like this is certainly weird, thrilling, and scary. Whenever I think about how sneaking around at night breaking into places is so totally not who I am, it helps to consider that I'm Sarah Wright 2.0. The timid, rule-following, normal version of me died like two years ago. While I am mostly the same person inside, certain truths of my new reality demand evolution.

I want to stay with my family. I want them to be safe. Keeping them safe requires playing nice with the society vampires. Playing nice with the society vampires requires doing things that give Follows Rules Girl heart palpitations.

It's okay. I've given her a whole box of rocky road ice cream as copium.

Or I *plan to* give her ice cream in the near future. No, I'm not going to eat the whole thing at once. Gotta make it last, even if it won't go straight to my ass. Okay, well I suppose in a strictly technical sense, it really will go directly to my butt... just not in a 'gaining weight' sort of way.

"Ready?" whispers Ashley.

"Not yet. Gotta do the thing."

She nods once.

I spend a moment chasing Zen, telling myself what I'm doing is not wrong. This will not hurt anyone. I will not get in trouble. I am helping someone. I belong here. I am a vampire, and the world is my playground. Mortal laws don't apply to me anymore. I am beholden to basic decency and kindness, not what judges or cops think. Getting a vampire out of a morgue before someone cuts him open and their entire worldview shatters is a good deed.

Hmm. He's not a Shadow. Would a vampire's guts look obviously different from a living person's? Didn't seem to be that odd when I've cut some open with a sword. Maybe it's less what the doctor would see and more worrying about Theo waking up in the middle of the autopsy. Still, there's gotta be *something* about vampires a doctor might find and think weird, or they wouldn't need him out of here in such a hurry.

Or maybe an autopsy process can kill us permanently? I don't see how. It can do some damage, but that'll only make it take longer for us to wake up. Now, being buried in a coffin would absolutely suck. Nightmare fuel right there. What would embalming do to us? I really don't want to know.

It would feel like we're on fire and can't put it out, says Dalton's voice in my mind.

Grr. I said I didn't want to know.

But you did want to know. He chuckles.

Sigh. Okay, he's got me there. And ouch. Really? Is it fatal?

No. Being embalmed won't destroy us... however the pain is so excruciating, oblivion seems welcome.

Oof. So, right up there with being forced to listen to ICP.

What is ICP?

Be glad you don't know. So, since you're tuned into my brain right now... I'm about to do that thing where I try to hide from security cameras. Any tips?

It is the same as how you compel mortals not to notice you. The only difference is you think about not wanting to exist to electronic devices.

Sounds easy enough.

Honestly, it is. We got lucky. Our stuff's not too challenging to learn.

Okay. Here goes. Also, how are you? Been a while.

Fine, luv. Relaxing, staying out of trouble. Having a blast.

You? Staying out of trouble? Hah. Blast indeed. Wonder who the target is.

His laughter fills my thoughts.

I concentrate on nonexistence. I'm not really here. I am a glitch in the matrix. After a moment, it doesn't seem like it's possible to concentrate any harder or convince myself any more thoroughly that it's working. I nod to Ashley and we make our way across the street to the morgue.

The door opens as soon as I tug on it. I knew it would. I wanted it to, and it did.

"That's so cool," whispers Ashley.

We step inside.

A guy in a security guard uniform darts out of a doorway, having heard the door squeak. I'm moving slow and deliberate since my concentration is heavily focused on hiding from security cameras... and people. The guard doesn't react to us being there at first, though he squints as if he's kinda seeing something but isn't sure what.

"I got him," whispers Ashley before staring at the guy.

The man blinks again, then exhales past fluttering lips, shaking his head while making a face like he thinks he needs to stop drinking or get more sleep. Yes, he really did hear the door open. Maybe the guy saw the two of us for an instant before Ashley charmed him. Curious, I take a shallow peek into his mind. Yeah, he did see 'two young ladies' standing here in the lobby. My charm kept us indistinct enough for him not to be able to recognize faces. Heck, he didn't even realize Ash is a redhead. Oh, interesting. He saw through my 'don't notice me' charm because he's specifically on alert for people being here when they shouldn't be. Outside in the world, he wouldn't have even registered us.

Thankfully, Ashley's charm is a touch more potent than mine. Only problem is, she can't sweet-talk security cameras. Between her stronger charm on mortals and my ability to mask us from electronic security systems, we are basically like something right out of an anime: superpowered teenage girls kicking ass. Though the only ass kicking we're up to is making good time and feeling almost competent at breaking into a place. With the precision of a SWAT team—okay, a rookie SWAT team—we make our way through the building in search of the cooler. One more security guard and two medical workers end up under Ashley's spell, carrying on with their nightly routine like we aren't even there.

Getting past the living is easy. The dead, not so much. This place has ghosts coming out of the walls—and I'm not being metaphorical. They're actually emerging from walls to stare at us. Most have an expression of WTF like they died very recently and aren't sure what happened. A few glare at us with obvious jealousy, or is it anger? Like, 'how dare you cheat death while I'm stuck like this' type vibes. I count at least forty spirits already and we're not even through one sixth of this building.

Can I just say... eek!

What kind of person would want to work around dead people late at night? There's gotta be something not quite right with them. I'm a freakin' vampire and the idea of being alone in a room full of corpses in a creepy institutional setting like this makes my skin crawl. Even if I couldn't see the ghosts everywhere, it would be *so* so creepy. Huh... I wonder if it's creepier because I am a supernatural being and able to pick up on all this energy? Mortals might be oblivious to it.

"This has to be familiar, huh?" asks Ashley.

"Heh. Right?" I sigh. "This place is a lot bigger than the one I ended up in. Also, totally different situation. This dude isn't a baby vamp who's going to wake up not even knowing he's become a vampire. He got shot."

"By who? What happened?" Ashley blinks at me.

"No clue. Mike didn't say." I peer back down the hall where we came from, slightly nervous about being followed. We are being followed, but it's only ghosts. "Hoping he didn't mention it because it's not a continuing problem."

"Right. Here's hoping." Ashley holds up crossed fingers.

We go from room to room looking for the coolers. Many of the doors have magnetic locks worked by ID card scanners. Not that they stop us. As long as my concentration holds, I open them as easily as if they were left unlocked. So neat. I believe they'll open for me, and they do. Every time my abilities give physical security the finger,

Ashley makes this faint squeal of delight. It's like I'm pulling rabbits out of a hat for a little kid at her birthday party.

"The two of us make the perfect team." She nudges me in the side. "You whammy all the locks. I whammy all the people... and guard dogs."

I glance at her. "Guard dogs? Where?"

"Just saying. If there were guard dogs... I'd charm the heck out of their cute widdle faces."

"Wow. This is why criminals don't hire ten-year-old girls to break into places."

She rolls her eyes. "I'm not ten."

"Not physically." I grin. "When Sophia's spell hit you, I think it reverted your outward form to match your true self."

"No way. I'm not still a little kid. I can be adult and still embrace the cuteness." She examines her fingernails. "That's what's wrong with society. People are expected to stop being happy when they get old. Why is it considered weird or lame for a grown woman to love fluffy plush unicorns?"

"I don't know. But it is."

She raspberries off to the side. "Well, poop on that."

Finally, I spot a sign on the wall indicating a direction to the coolers. Figures it's in the damn basement. I should've gone down there first. Ashley keeps working her magic on the handful of employees. I have no idea if they're doctors, clerks, medical students, or what. They've got white lab coats or scrubs on. None react to our presence at all. It's kinda neat but also unsettling. Is this how it feels to be a ghost? Within seconds of Ash staring at them, they get this inspired 'oh, I really want to grab some coffee now' look on their faces and fast walk away from where we are heading.

The first cold storage room is a door on the right side of the hall about forty feet from the stairwell. It's got the same sort of badge-swipe magnetic lock as most of the doors in this place. I push it open with no resistance. The mechanism doesn't even beep. The computer it's connected to does not log that the door opened at whatever time it is now.

A blurry apparition of a man in his early sixties paces around to my right in the corner, continually muttering 'no' to himself. Poor guy. Nothing I can do for him, so I act like he's not visible and start opening cooler doors, starting from the left. If there's a body in there, I look at it long enough to determine if it's a corpse or a vampire. If it's under a sheet, I have to pull the tray out and peek. If there's no one in there, I simply shut the door and move to the next space.

Empty... empty... empty... old woman... old man... younger dude but he's not a vampire... empty... empty... I get to the last cooler door in the machine, which is also empty. Damn. Our guy is not in this room.

We head across the hall to the next nearest cooler storage. Gotta be this one. I hope.

Good sign: four guys who seem to be in their younger twenties, all with obvious bullet wounds, are having an argument in the middle of the room, calling each other dumbasses. Seems they understand they got killed and are reacting with anger. Upon noticing me and Ashley enter the room, they stop shouting, glare at us, and disappear. New ghosts can be shy I guess. Mike said the vamp we're looking for got picked up by the authorities who mistook him for a dead guy after a shootout. Seeing the ghosts of shooting victims in this room tells me they probably put all the John Does in the same place.

I start going through the coolers here. First two contain old people. Next three are empty. The one after that's got a body bag in it, only it doesn't appear to contain a body shape. My nose tells me there's a corpse in that bag. Dribbles on the sliding tray suggest the body is no longer considered 'solid matter.' Eek. Did someone get crushed by a steamroller? I don't want to know.

Slam.

Moving on!

The next two trays contain the remains of two of the guys I saw arguing. Ooh! I'm getting close. Cooler number nine contains a body under a sheet. It's *obviously* man since he's pitching a tent. I pull the tray out to full extension.

"Wow." Ashley unsubtly stares at the shape of his erection poking up at the sheet. "Talk about die hard... with a vengeance."

"Ugh. You had to go there, didn't you?" I peel back the sheet to check on the face.

"Yep. I did." She grins. "I guess they call dead bodies 'stiffs' for a reason, huh?"

The man's somewhere between twenty-five and thirty-five, a white dude trying to pull off puffy dreadlocks. His hair is probably supposed to be light brown, though it's tinged green. Cause of death is pretty obvious: a bullet hole in his forehead above the left eye. It's oddly small for a bullet hole and pretty much sealed up already. Yep. This must be Theo. His body is healing in sleep. Even more convincing, he feels like a vampire.

"He's our guy." I pat him on the shoulder and fling the sheet off.

Theo's got an above average amount of pale brown body hair, a couple tattoos, and an enormous boner. I'm not exactly a connoisseur de penis, having seen exactly two of them before tonight. Well, two in person: Scott's and Hunter's. Theo's got them both beat for size.

Yanno what's really uncomfortable?

Ashley—my best friend who I've known since we were small—is staring at it the way she usually stares at a giant ice cream sundae with hot fudge on it right before she digs in.

Gah. So awkward.

"Ash, you're drooling."

She laughs. "I am not. It's just... kinda magnificent."

"Is it?" I scrunch my nose. "Not like I've seen too many up close."

"Not the biggest one I've seen, but within the top three. Any bigger is just too much. This one is like... I dunno. Perfectly proportioned." Ashley gestures at it. "If someone made the ideal one, this would be it. Great size. Ideal ratio of length to width. No deformation, no bizarre shapes. It's just the ideal D, a medically perfect penis."

"Like something from a Greek God?" I whisper.

"No." She snickers. "The Greeks gave all their statues super tiny dinguses for some reason. Or was that the Romans?" She huffs. "Don't remember. Some culture somewhere thought tiny dicks were the best."

"Oh, that explains the statue in my art history class."

"Small?" asks Ashley, wincing.

"Hung like a squirrel."

"Oof."

"This man is definitely not hung like a squirrel." Ashley holds her hands out toward it like an artist 'framing' a scene before painting it. "I'm kinda tempted to take a picture of it to put on my wall. But that would be rude."

"Mom would faint."

Ashley clamps her hand over her mouth, trying not to laugh.

No, I am not staring at it. I'm trying to avert my gaze. One brief glance is enough for me. "Medically perfect? That's kind of a weird thing to say. Are you trying to say 'aesthetically perfect?'"

"Umm. Yeah, I guess. It's just beautiful." Ashley makes a face like she's admiring a bit of fine art at a museum.

"I can't believe we're discussing the aesthetic merits of his—"

The beam of a fairly powerful flashlight washes over us. I was trying not to look at Theo's, erm, 'monument,' but the flashlight beam has turned it into a giant shadow on the cooler above him. The Leaning Tower of Penis.

"What the hell?" mutters a man.

I shift my gaze to the right, looking past two autopsy tables at the only door out of the room where a guy in a security uniform stares at us in horrified shock.

Great. He caught Ashley and I standing on either side of a naked dead man like a pair of female Indiana Jones wannabees seconds before they attempt to steal the Great Golden Dong from the Incan temple. Hmm. If we set off *that* trap, would we have to run away from two boulders?

"Uh oh," whispers Ashley. "Busted."

"Oof. Could this possibly get any more awkward?" I whisper.

"I've been conscious for the past few minutes listening to you two talk about my dick," says Theo.

"Okay. Yeah." I cringe. "That's definitely more awkward. Sorry for asking."

Theo sits up.

If the security guard was shocked at the two of us checking out a dead guy's naughty bits, he's *super* shocked now. It's not every day a pale dude with a bullet wound in his forehead sits up and talks. The guard opens his mouth like he's going to scream. Only a little gurgling wheeze comes out of him before he crumples to the ground, out cold. Ashley starts to laugh, as does Theo.

Theo grins at us, absolutely zero shame on his face.

Ugh. Ground swallow me now. Theo heard everything we said, including me calling him a Greek God and Ashley claiming he's got an 'aesthetically perfect penis.' A bizarre compliment to be sure.

A blurry mass of light rises up out of the security guard then floats off to one side.

"Shit!" I fling Dad's old khaki pants at Theo, then rush over to the guard. "He didn't faint! He had a goddamned heart attack."

"Eek!" Ashley chucks the shirt at Theo before following me.

I start CPR on the guard. Ashley counts the timing while I do chest compressions.

Theo continues to snicker. He hops off the slab.

After a few minutes, it becomes painfully obvious the security guard is not coming back. I'm fairly sure I did the CPR thing correctly. Just... this guy's heart wasn't having it. Half of me wants to cry because some random dude died. The other half of me can't believe this guy literally dropped dead over a corpse sitting up. Like, it wasn't *that* scary. Come on, man. What's wrong with you?

The dead guard doesn't look old enough to have a sudden, massive heart attack. He can't be too far past thirty. According to the laminated ID hanging from his shirt pocket, his name is Joseph Burke.

"This isn't right," I blurt. "How's a guy this young drop dead so fast just because he thinks a dead guy woke up?"

Ashley grabs my left arm in both of hers, clinging for support. She's trying to make me feel better. "This place has a super weird energy. He was probably scared out of his mind already just from being here."

Theo's bare feet move into my field of view, the ends of khaki pant legs draped mostly over them. The guy's a little bit shorter than Dad. He's still chuckling at the guard.

"How can you laugh at this?" I gesture at the dead man.

"Because it's hilarious." Theo hooks his thumbs into the waistband of the pants. "You didn't see the face he made right before he went down."

Grr. "There's nothing 'hilarious' about a man dying."

"I beg to differ." Theo holds up one finger. "I've seen several unfortunate morons expire in the most hilarious of ways. Dude in California around 1942 or so tried strapping rockets to his plane to make it go faster."

Ashley scrunches her nose. "Why is that stupid?"

"Because this plane was made out of wood. Dude got up to altitude, ignited the rockets..." Theo thrusts his right hand forward, clapping it off his left. "And *bam*. Ripped both wings right off." He pantomimes his right hand into a nosedive to the floor. "Guy had about eighteen seconds to ponder how much of a dumbass he was before hitting the ground."

"Ugh." I rub my forehead. "What are we going to do with this guy?"

"Should we turn him?" asks Ashley.

"Nah." Theo shakes his head. "If we turned everyone we killed by accident, there'd be more vampires than mortals."

I give him side eye. "Remind me not to spend too much time around you if you're that accidentally dangerous."

"Oh, come on. You've never accidentally killed anyone?" Theo 'pffs' at me like I said something dumb.

"No. Well. Okay." I sigh. "This one time—"

"At band camp?" Ashley grins.

"Ugh. How can you make jokes right now?"

"I think of them and they slip out of my mouth before my brain gets involved." She offers an apologetic grimace smile. "Sorry, that line. Can't resist."

I'm approaching 'can't even.' "Can we be a little more serious please? A man just died." I wipe my hand down my face, trying to de-stress.

"Probably heroin." Theo sniffs at the dead guy. "Or cocaine. Something like that. His heart was pretty brittle. Dude looks healthy on the outside, but he wasn't."

"Whoa," whispers Ashley. "You can tell that by smelling him?"

"Yeah." Theo swipes one of his inch-thick dreadlocks away from his eyes. "So, how'd the little angel accidentally kill someone?"

"She killed a bunch of drug dealers," says Ashley. "Total accident."

Theo blinks. "How do you wipe out a whole *bunch* of drug dealers by *accident*? Did you sneeze while holding an Uzi?"

I bow my head. "Lost control of myself when I got smacked in the face by the sun."

"Oh, that'll do it." He winces. "Doesn't really count though. Not like you screwed up."

"Thanks, but... we have a problem right now." I gesture at Joseph. "What are we going to do about this? Can't just leave him on the floor here with a morgue tray hanging open. That'll get the PIBs upset."

Ashley makes a serious face for about two seconds, then breaks out in this hyper-eager, manic grin. "We could burn the whole building down?"

I stare at her.

"Whoa," says Theo.

"Kidding." Ashley rolls her eyes. "Geez, you guys are wound up tonight."

"Hmm. We could strip him and leave him on the slab?" Theo glances back at the tray we found him on.

"That's not any better." I shake my head. "People are going to question how the guard wound up in the cooler. *Especially* in a cooler that should be holding someone else's body. You disappearing is already going to raise eyebrows."

Ashley folds her arms, making 'thinking' faces for a moment. "The guy had a heart attack. We don't *have* to do anything but put him in a chair somewhere. Whoever finds him will think he just had a heart attack. If Theo's right about the drug abuse, it will probably show up when they autopsy him."

"Duh. Good point." I smack myself in the forehead.

Ashley stands. "They'll think he died naturally. I mean, he is kinda old."

"Old? He's like thirty-five." Theo chuckles.

"That's old." Ashley shrugs.

She's both wrong and not wrong. Yeah, thirty-five feels pretty old to me. But, my parents are older than that. They'd both throw pillows at me if I called them old. It's that whole relativity thing.

Anyway...

I grab Joseph's right arm. "Help me move him to a chair."

"You need help lifting a dead dude?" asks Theo.

"Need? No. I'm strong enough. But... I'm trying not to leave any suspicious bruises." I stare at him. "If we squeeze people too hard, they bruise."

"Like bananas." Ashley takes his other arm.

We drag the guy out of this room and take him down the hall a bit before finding a spot in the hallway with a bunch of decorative chairs. You know, those chairs that corporate offices put in strange places that no one's actually expected to sit in. They're only there for looks. Mom's office has them everywhere. Just random mini chairs and little tables tucked in corners, hallways, or dead ends.

Once we've got Joseph situated to look like he sat down and slumped over, another worry crosses my mind: security cameras. Sure, whatever bit of Lost One ability I inherited from Dalton's probably enough to keep me—and likely Ashley if she stays close—off camera, someone's going to notice Joseph walking into that room, dropping dead, and then magically sliding all by himself down the hall to this chair.

This is, of course, assuming my concentration didn't lapse at any point enough for me to stop hiding.

Crap. "Gotta do something about the security cameras."

"Aren't you doing that already?" Ashley peers over at me.

"Yeah, but they're going to see this guy drop dead and go sliding off." I look back and forth down the hall.

Ashley bursts into giggles.

"What now?" I sigh at her.

"Just picturing the reaction of the guard watching the video and seeing a dead guy body surfing the corridor." She covers her mouth.

"Where is Ashley and what have you done with her?" I playfully grab her by the shoulders and shake. "You shouldn't be giggling at a dead guy."

Her expression goes brittle for a second. "It's either this or fall to pieces and start crying. I'm freaking out and trying not to think about what happened until we're out of here."

"Oh." I let my hands drop from her arms. "Okay. Sorry. Got worried there."

"Worried?" She blinks. "About what? Going vampire turning me into a sociopath detached from humanity?"

"Something like that." I exhale hard out my nose.

"Nah. Our personalities don't change." She crosses her eyes. "I was already a bit psycho. You know, all redheads are crazy."

I chuckle.

"Security room is upstairs on the ground floor." Theo points down the hall at a stairwell. "Didn't know you were a computer hacker, too."

"I'm not." I frown. "Hoping to find someone to mind control."

I lead the way at a jog, rushing up the stairs. It takes us about eleven minutes of running around searching, Ashley forcing people not to realize we're here, and me ignoring the entire concept of locked doors before we find the security office.

Wow. No wonder people keep asking Dalton to do nefarious stuff. The man can probably go just about anywhere. I'm not even a Lost One and I'm breezing through this place. Wonder if reality is like a video game. Like... are there some locks that are 'too hard' for me since I'm watered down compared to him?

Bleh. No time to think about that now.

I have a serious problem: there are no guards in the room available for mind control. Just my luck the one who died is the guy who should be in this room watching cameras. Oh. Duh. I bet he came downstairs to check on why all those cooler doors opened by themselves. I might've been blanking myself from the security cameras—not the cooler hatches.

Argh. No guards here I can mind control into helping us, only a bunch of desks and computers. The only good thing is the camera control station is incredibly obvious. One desk—okay it's more of a big table—has eight enormous flat-panel monitors full of camera views. Each screen's divided into four separate video feeds. Ugh. Yeah. The room we found Theo in as well as the hallway outside it all have cameras on them. Joseph's body is plainly visible on one.

A hacker, I am not. I can't even get past the initial password prompt. I don't even know why I'm trying. The odds of me correctly guessing someone's password entirely out of the blue are so astronomically bad there's more chance the Chicago Bears will win the World Series. Wait, Bears are football? Super Bowl. Heh. Even though I messed that up, the way I said it first works even better. Yeah, the chance of me getting this password right on a blind guess are worse than a football team winning the World Series of baseball.

Though it would be kinda hilarious watching baseball players get tackled.

I search around the desk hoping whoever works here is an idiot and they've put the password on a Post-It note somewhere obvious. Under the keyboard, in a top drawer, somewhere... With each passing second of not finding anything, my anxiety grows. Someone's going to find that video. People will ask questions. If it's not one of Wolent's people who realizes I'm a total screw up and made a mess of this, it's gonna be the PIBs showing up at my house and telling me I'm too much of a risk and need to go into hiding.

No! It's gotta be somewhere. I can't mess this up!

Upon realizing I've picked up the middle keyboard six times and no Post-It note with a password on it has magically appeared, my panic and frustration build. I feel like the good girl who got pressured into doing something mildly illegal (like shoplifting) by 'friends' who promised nothing would go wrong. And now I'm staring at the cop who's caught me holding the stolen merchandise. In the blink of an eye, I imagine my entire unlife being upended and thrown away. Yeah, I know I'm not going to wind up in jail because I'm a vampire, but prison is the least of my worries. The giant spike of anxiety is the same in the moment of 'shit, I'm busted.

All because of security videos I can't delete. I have to kill those files or I'm screwed. For a seventh time, I discover there is no password hidden under the keyboard. My panic manifests as a scream and a small bit of violence.

I yell, "Argh!" and pound both fists down on the table, making the three keyboards jump.

All the camera feed images on the screens go blank. Seconds later, the grid separating the different feeds disappears, too. The monitors turn off, then back on. The center one pops up an error screen: operating system not found.

"Wow." Ashley whistles. "I think you nuked the entire computer."

Theo leans down, almost resting his chin on my left shoulder, to stare at the screen. "Yep. That's pretty borked. Neat trick. How'd you do that?"

I grab two handfuls of my hair and stare at the error message. "No idea. I was about to freak out."

"You probably did something Daltony," says Ashley.

I let go of my hair and poke at the keyboard. The error message isn't going away. "Duh. Banging the desk doesn't usually delete the operating system off a computer. But deleting the OS doesn't necessarily mean the video data is gone."

"Two things." Ashley holds up three fingers. No, she's not an idiot. She's trying to distract me with humor. "One: shy of lighting this place on fire, there's nothing more we're going to do at this computer right now. Two: I am pretty sure you deleted everything deletable."

"How can you say that?" I ask.

"With my mouth." She winks, then points over the screens. "But... look."

I sit up tall in the chair, gazing over the monitor in front of me. The other six computer workstations in this room are *all* showing 'operating system not found' errors. A sinking feeling grows heavy in the pit of my stomach. Whatever I did, it got away from me and out of control in a moment of absolute panic.

"I say we take off... nuke the entire site from orbit," says Ashley trying to mimic a man's voice.

"Fuckin' A," adds Theo.

Ashley looks at him, grins, and they high-five. *Aliens* is like her favorite movie. Go figure. The girl who can't stand horror. Then again, she loves science fiction. She also adores the story arc of Ripley and Newt finding each other and forming a family, filling in the holes in each other's hearts. Now that she's a vampire, I think she might actually make good on her threat to rip the head off whoever directed *Alien 3*—the movie that does not exist.

Anyway...

"Well, I certainly nuked this entire website from orbit." I drum my fingers on the desk. "Nothing more we can do here. Just hope I got everything and this wipe of their computer system isn't going to make more trouble for us than video of a hallway-surfing dead security guard."

Ashley snort laughs. "Oh, I'm pretty sure a blank computer system can be more easily explained by mundane reasons than a corpse power-gliding."

Theo rests a hand each on our shoulders. "Girls, thanks for the assist."

"We'd been ready to carry you out of here and hide the body until you recovered." I stand out of the chair and sigh. "Guess you didn't really need us to get you out of here."

"Oh, you helped." He nods. "Opening those cooler doors from the inside is a serious pain in the ass. Also, the two of you being nearby woke me up a bunch faster than if it had been quiet."

I blush, thinking back to what we happened to be talking about.

We hastily make our way to the exit. After a quick look around to make sure there isn't anyone close by outside to see us leaving, we're off down the street trying to act casual.

"So, uh, what happened to put you in there?" I ask.

"Bah." He scowls. "A bunch of anarchists saw me with a couple friends. Dunno why they had a bug up their ass, but they started shooting. Didn't say a word. Was I the only vamp in there?"

I wince. "Yeah."

"Damn. Bastards got away then." He grumbles. "Keep your eyes open if you go out. Seems like there's a cluster of anarchists looking to start shit with us."

Us being 'traditionalist' vampires.

Two blocks later, Ashley smiles up at Theo. "I couldn't help but admire your, umm, equipment. Wanna hook up?"

I stifle a cough. Good grief, Ash! Since when do you ask dudes you just met if they want to have sex?

Theo smiles in a somewhat awkward manner like he's proud but also a little uncomfortable. "Uhh, thanks... but geez, kid. You're too young for me."

Ashley grumbles. "Dammit. I'm eighteen."

"Uh huh," says Theo, sounding unconvinced. "Even if you are, you don't look it. I'd feel all kinds of wrong taking advantage of you."

Huh. Didn't expect that. What bit of respect for Theo I lost for him laughing at Joseph dropping dead, I gain back with extra.

Ashley grumbles again, louder.

I throw an arm around her, laughing. "Welcome to my world."

CHAPTER 25
MAGICAL STUDIES

There is no way I'd have made it as a Lost One.

At least, not without several decades to hammer the anxiety out of my psyche. So, in seventh grade, Ashley and I saw Tyler Olsen sneak into an empty classroom where he set off a stink bomb. We just happened to be on our way out of the bathroom at the time Tyler crept, snickering to himself, into the room with illicit firework in hand. He didn't see us. We had nothing to do with the prank.

Yet, we also didn't tell on him. We knew who did it, and we kept quiet.

I was convinced we were going to get in trouble as bad as if we'd done the bombing ourselves. It took me three days before I could sleep normally. Figured after that long, no one knew we 'helped' him. The events at the coroner's office last night would have done the same thing to me except for the beautiful fact of how vampires *cannot* lie awake in the morning. That sun comes up, we're done.

It does not, alas, suppress the anxiety crash in the afternoon when I wake up.

Dalton tried to help right before sunrise. He'd been a bit involved in something he declined to tell me about, so he hadn't been paying attention to me while we were in the morgue. He agrees with Ashley in that my desire to erase the video, empowered by panic, affected the computers. Being kind of old school, he hasn't done too much in terms of using his vampiric influences on high tech things. The same mechanism that lets me open locks reared up and sledgehammered the PCs in that room. He's pretty sure the computers gave an error about not having an operating system because I erased every ounce of data on their hard drives, which includes the video files.

I didn't quite set off an EMP blast. My iPhone survived without being wiped, evidence of at least some attempt to direct the force of my wrath. Dalton described what I did as 'precision surgery with a sledgehammer.' Instead of deleting a few files, I wiped everything. Really hope it only affected the security computers and not all the patient data.

Whatever my power did, it's too late to worry about now. Wolent's people are happy we got Theo out of there before they cut him open. Theo's happy to be out of there. Ashley's a bit disappointed she didn't get to play with his 'aesthetic perfection.' She spent the remainder of Saturday night playfully griping about 'looking like a kid.'

It's gotta be that relative age thing. She doesn't look like a kid to me. Then again, I'm not romantically interested in her. She's my sister, as much as a non-blood relative can be one's sibling.

Anyway, so I'm anxious for multiple reasons. The demon thing is still going on. Sophia has a bit of unaccounted for released magic, and I'm worrying something about my rescue mission to get Theo out of the morgue is going to bite me in the butt.

It's Sunday.

At least I've got something specific to do today. I'm taking Sophia to the Aurora Aurea lodge for, umm, magic class I guess. It's kinda like dance class, except she's the only student and things occasionally explode.

A couple hours after I get out of bed, Sophia pokes her head into my room. "Sare?"

Nothing weird is going on. I'm just playing *Skyrim* on the computer—after another wasted half hour scouring the Steam store for something new. Nothing caught my interest.

"Yeah. 'Mon in," I say, pausing the game and spinning my chair around.

Sophia walks in wearing an old timey beige dress, gloves, and black boots. She looks like a time traveler from 1800s London. Klepto's draped over the top of her head, seemingly sleeping. "What time did you want to go to the lodge?"

"Four or so, like usual. Right?"

"It's ten minutes to four."

"Eep." I scramble to my feet. "Sorry. Lost track of time."

"It's fine." She grins.

"Looks like you lost track of time, too." I chuckle. "As in, what century we're in."

Sophia swishes side to side, modeling the outfit. "I'm doing it on purpose. The mystics like wearing old clothes. And there's a lot of layers. It would be difficult for an annoying demon to rip this off me at a bad time."

I raise an eyebrow at her. She's being kinda weird. That tone. Again, it's like she's daring the demon to do it. There's no way she wants to be disrobed in public. Something's going on I'm not fully able to comprehend. She gives me this nervous sort of smile.

"It's fine." Sophia darts over and hugs me, causing the kitten to fall off her head. The little furball teleports back to her shoulder before hitting the carpet. "I'm not in a rush. Take your time. Thank you for bringing me to see the mystics. If you're busy, it's not really that super important. We don't have to go if you can't do it."

"Umm. Sure. No problem." This is strange. She's going clingy again. The overly adoring way she's looking at me is pretty much the same as right after I came home following my death. Oh, maybe she had a nightmare about me dying... or the whole vampire thing being a dream. "What's up?"

Klepto sits on her shoulder like a fuzzy version of a pirate's parrot.

She tilts her head to one side so far her long, blonde hair almost reaches her knee. "What do you mean?"

"You're acting kinda weird. Is everything okay?"

"Sorry. Am I being too needy?"

"Not at all." I hug her. "Just seem a bit scared and maybe a touch brittle. Did you have a nightmare?"

Her cheeks redden slightly, though her expression gives off hints of annoyance (at herself) rather than embarrassment. "No. I'm just worried about the demon trying to do stuff to us. Really glad you decided to stay here to protect us and keep us safe."

Yeah... well. At least some of this danger is my fault for existing. I'd say maybe the vampires have good reasons for distancing themselves from their mortal families... but it wouldn't be accurate. Ninety-nine percent of the reason that became tradition is preservation of secrecy. The vast majority of them don't really care that much about what their mortal relatives think. To them, dying and returning as a vampire literally is death and a new existence, so they wash their hands entirely of their old lives. Sure, there are a handful who regret not doing what I did, but we are a super-minority. Even fewer of us than there are people who openly admit to being Nickelback fans.

Sorry. Low-hanging fruit. It's too easy to make jokes at the band's expense.

I don't get why people rag on them. Their music isn't bad.

Crap. Did I just admit to being a Nickelback fan? Umm, I'm only saying I don't hate it.

Right... anyway...

I throw on some clothes—nothing fancy. Jeans and a Black Mage T-shirt. He's cute. Little 8-bit Final Fantasy video game wizard. Sophia's boots click on the sidewalk from our front porch to the Sentra.

When we reach the car, I stop to look across the roof at her. "Soph?"

"Yeah?" She blinks at me.

"Where did you get that outfit?"

She smiles, as if proud of it. "I hopped through a time gate in my closet and went shopping in London."

I blink.

Sophia giggles. "I'm teasing. Mom ordered it online."

"Wow." I open the door and get in. "Clothing you got online actually fit?"

"Uhh…" Sophia stares at me like I said the dumbest thing imaginable. "Of course not. Nothing was the size it should have been. I fixed it."

Klepto curls up in the cup holder.

"Ahh. Right." I start the engine, drop it in reverse, and back out of our driveway into a big loop in the cul-de-sac so the car's facing the street. "Couldn't you have just conjured it?"

"I haven't done much conjuring. Summoned objects are super unstable." Sophia smooths her gloved hand down her sleeve. "Magical alterations to make real clothing fit are permanent. Conjured clothes might destabilize and disappear after a while. Since there is a demon who is very likely going to steal all my clothes when I'm in a crowded place so everyone laughs at me, I didn't want to take the chance."

I shift into drive and step on the gas. "You're obsessed with that."

"It's my worst fear." She looks out the window on her side. "I simply couldn't handle it if a bunch of people saw me butt naked and laughed at me."

Now I'm confused. Sophia is a rotten liar, just like me. Right now, I can't tell if she's lying or not. It kinda sounds like she's lying; however, she's not giving away a sense of deceit when she says she'd absolutely dread being humiliated in public. I have no doubt she's irrationally terrified of that happening. The fear is irrational because it's so unlikely to be a real possibility. I mean people don't generally end up nude in public except for some really specific situations. Like, a cheating spouse ducking out the window to avoid being caught, a really bad night in Vegas, Hunter and me having sex in the woods and getting lost so we can't find where we left our clothes, a vampire waking up in a morgue and having to escape…

And I suppose, mystics from another country trying to kidnap you with magic and screwing up the spell.

Sophia's not going to sneak out of an adulterer's bedroom, nor will she be gambling in Vegas any time soon. Any sort of naughty escapades in the woods are at least seven years in the future for her —twenty years if Dad gets his way.

No, he's not really like that. He just cracks jokes about the over-protective father who doesn't want his daughters dating until we're forty.

Right... so any realistic odds of Sophia ending up in such an embarrassing situation would require paranormal interference. Given that we have an angry demon after us, I suppose that trans-lates to a non-zero chance her worst fear would manifest. A demon's ability to affect the physical world while trapped in their home demi-plane is somewhat limited. The more severe an interaction, the harder it is to pull off. Causing a catastrophic wardrobe malfunction is a lot easier than trying to inflict serious injury.

Maybe she's right to be so worried about it.

The rest of us are all anxious about the demon hurting or killing everyone. Her fear is the most trivial and also the most easily exploited. It also makes the least amount of sense. I mean, even if something did zap her out of her clothes in public, she could make illusions on herself to appear dressed... even back time up a few seconds so no one sees anything.

And no, it's not like she can casually play with time. It takes a serious emotional event to give her enough of a power boost. Some-thing like Mom about to tell her she can't keep Klepto—or being suddenly naked at school both qualify as 'emotionally powerful' to her.

It's really a nonissue. She could fix it easily.

Why the heck is she so fixated on it then?

This is a good opportunity to see if she's having body image issues. I bring up the idea of how in the US, it's considered socially unacceptable for girls to go topless at the beach but in Europe, it's not a big deal.

"No idea. It's silly." Sophia rolls her eyes. "Boys have boobs, too."

"What?" I chuckle.

"Murray's got bigger ones than Christina, and Christina's in eighth grade."

She says 'eighth grade' like it makes the other girl a grown woman already. That's only two grades ahead of her. I whistle. "I'm not sure what to find more strange... that a boy has boobs or that someone in the modern age named their son 'Murray.'"

"What's wrong with Murray?" Sophia scrunches her nose in confusion.

"It's just... I dunno. An *old* name. You don't see it much. Like girls named Esther or whatever."

At the next red light, I smile at her. "You're not feeling a bit... inadequate are you?"

"Nope." She laughs. "Doesn't bother me. I'm not worried about what boys think of me. Don't have time for boy drama. I've gotta learn magic."

Hah. That's totally her age speaking. Oh, how rapidly things will change for her in a year or two. My attempt to be subtle faceplants, so after another five or so minutes of conversation, I bluntly admit to worrying about her having some body positivity issues.

"I'm fine." Sophia holds her head up high. "Yeah, I sometimes get teased for being a twig. Doesn't bother me. I can't control that. Also, my feelings of self-worth aren't based even a tiny bit on what other people think of me. Okay, not kids at school or strange adults. If you, Sam, Sierra, or the 'rents started picking on me, it would give me a complex."

"That's rather mature of you."

"Pff. I have magic." She waves dismissively. "Vampires exist. What some boy in my class thinks of me, a boy I'll probably never see again after I'm done with school, doesn't even rate."

"Nice."

"Also." Sophia grins. "The boob faerie will eventually visit me. Maybe. I mean she visits our family eventually, right? Probably a few years after I turn eighteen."

"Ha. Ha." I smirk. "I'm no Bree Swanson, but they exist, thank you very much."

"If you ever want them bigger, I can try to come up with a spell..."
I clutch the girls defensively. "They're fine exactly as they are. I can't even imagine having ones Bree's size. The drag while flying would shave at least thirty MPH off my top speed."

Sophia cackles.

～

UNLIKE THE LAST time I drove her to the park to meet the mystics, I don't smoke.

My relationship with the sun is on better terms these days. It's not exactly comfortable to be outside during the day, but it no longer hurts. It's like being in the supermarket when a Frank Sinatra song comes on. I'd really rather not endure it but it's hardly intolerable.

I dunno what it is about his music. I know he's supposed to be amazing and beloved and all that but... nah. Can't stand it. I'm way too young for music like his I guess. There's just something about his voice that grates on my nerves.

Anyway... we're here.

We cross the park, navigating the hedges and whatnot to the shaded gazebo deep inside the place out of casual view from the street. Sophia's an old master at working the translocative magic here. One second we're in the park, the next... somewhere else. I still don't know for sure what this place is. Did we go to another physical location in the world or are we in a pocket dimension?

My brain would melt before I understood this stuff.

Most people looking at Sophia think she's the stereotypical airheaded blonde. She's crazy smart but doesn't like to show it. I mean, everyone in my family is smarter than average. She and Sam are the geniuses. In Sophia's case, it's like we're characters in a role-playing game and her player totally cheated on stat rolls. She's smart *and* pretty. Then again, she did use strength and willpower for her dump stats. Even at eleven, she struggles to open the door out to our deck by herself... and it doesn't take much to scare a scream out of her.

Guess no one can be completely perfect.

Except Cassian. He... argh. Dammit. Where did that come from? Now I feel unclean, like I'm having a crush on my teacher or something. He's way too old for me. Mind powers. Just lingering mind powers. Also, no. I'm not seriously thinking about trying to hit on the guy. This is no different from how I daydreamed about Aragorn or Kyle Reese from *Terminator*. Yes, I know the movie is old and the actor who played Kyle Reese is older than my father now. I should've been daydreaming about guys like Zac Efron or something, but nope. My father's into Eighties movies. Also, none of my daydreams were even past a PG-13 rating. I was a tween. Innocent infatuation.

And now that I've made myself blush, we go into the mystic's lodge.

Landon greets us by the arch leading to the grand hall. I call it a 'grand hall' but it's not really that big. We're basically inside an old English mansion. He's dolled up in a bluish suit with an overdone frilled thing down the front. Dude's totally ready to catch the latest Mozart concert.

"Welcome, Sophia." He bow/nods at me. "Sarah."

"Hi." I wave.

"Lovely outfit, dear." Landon smiles at her.

"Why thank you." She curtsies.

We go down the hall to the first set of double doors on the left. The room's part library, part medieval wizard's lab. There's a huge square table in the area right by the door. It's gotta be four inches thick, covered in an uncountable number of nicks, scratches, scorch marks, and stains. Some of the nicks appear to be sword strikes. Farther in past the table, the room's full of shelves, some of which contain books, the rest laden with various jars, containers, and artifacts. Dozens of animal skeletons hang from wires all over the place. Some are recognizable, others not so much. Everything here looks older than the United States.

Other than me being the only 'parent' here, it's a lot like taking her to dance class. I sit somewhere off to the side watching while she does her thing. This class involves a significantly higher amount of flashing stuff and flames. Something tells me it would be a bad idea for a dance class full of kids to hire a pyrotech for special effects.

Darren, Landon, and Callum gather around the table, each of them on one side of the square with Sophia by herself on the fourth plane. Klepto jumps down from her shoulder to the table, then sits by her hand.

They spend a while talking about sigils, elemental transformations, spirit warding, and all sorts of stuff that sounds like it belongs in a D&D game. It's surprising to me how similar real magic is to the stuff in the games and movies. The major difference is reality doesn't do the big-budget special effects type stuff. Fireballs, bolts of lightning, giant globs of acid thrown like meteors... that stuff is all made up.

Real magic doesn't throw fireballs, it causes flames to spontaneously erupt wherever Sophia wants. She hasn't quite managed to do it yet though, mostly because she's scared and feels bad about hurting things. Her magic is much more powerful when used defensively or for utilitarian purposes. I have no doubt that if someone was about to hurt me or anyone in the family, Sophia could probably light them on fire to save us. However, she'd feel awful about it later. No way could she casually scorch someone. She does, however, manage to light a candle from across the room.

The mystics are impressed by whatever it is she's doing. Callum keeps 'stepping things up' by asking her to try doing stuff the other two think she shouldn't be ready for... and she does them. More or less. She's not perfect—or even successful—with much of it, though the fact that she got something to happen instead of merely staring helplessly at whatever magical puzzle they put in front of her has them heaping praise on her.

"Impressive again, my dear," says Darren after Sophia transformed a big rock inside a jar into air and back into a somewhat-differently-shaped rock. "Your family line must have been quite powerful back in the day."

"Indeed." Landon bounces on his toes like an eager schoolboy. "The power wants to be used. It's like keeping soda under high pressure for too long. When there's a crack, it explodes."

Sophia gasps. "Eep! I'm not going to explode, am I?"

The guys chuckle.

"No, sweetie." Landon beams at her. "I'm simply trying to tell you that you have a significant amount of power."

"Not so much control yet, though." Callum rubs his chin. "It's a bit like putting a child in charge of a nuclear power plant. Try to be careful."

"I will." Sophia kneads her hands together.

I chuckle at a random thought, which gets all four of them staring at me. The guys look curious. My sister seems worried.

"What's funny?" whispers Sophia.

"Just thinking. Great... our life's turned into an anime. The cute little girl is the most powerful entity in the universe."

Sophia laughs, then bites her lip. "Eep. I hope not. Those powerful kids usually end up dying... or having something really tragic happen to them."

"Speaking of tragic..." I stand and approach the table. "Guys, maybe you can help us out with something. I'm not really sure who else to ask for advice about this."

The men all regard me with curious stares. Wow. It's so surreal being here in this room with three guys dressed in Victorian finery. The room says King Arthur and Merlin. Their clothes say Sherlock Holmes.

I glance from one guy to the next, then to Darren since he's basically the boss. Those little round glasses and the long, black hair kinda give him a bit of a Dracula-in-human-form vibe. "I'm trusting you with confidential information, but yeah. You guys are part of that world so no big deal. Just saying I could get in a little trouble if the wrong vampires learn I talked about stuff."

"What's bothering you, dear?" asks Callum.

"Do you guys know what a sefil is?"

Darren makes a face like he's heard the term somewhere before but can't remember. The other two look clueless.

"Guess not. Okay. I'll make it simple. It's a vampire version of apocalypse. If one of them exists, it could easily mean the end of everything. All vampires destroyed, all humans dead. They start off relatively weak but the longer they live, the more powerful they get.

It's basically a vampire, but instead of a human soul inside the body, it's a demon."

"That has bad idea written all over it." Landon cringes.

"Yeah. Totally." I shiver.

"Are you asking us how to fight one?" Darren fidgets, leaning back from the table.

"Not really. We already destroyed it." I exhale. "Problem is, the demon is pissed off. Destroying the sefil's physical existence in our world only sent the demon back to wherever it came from. It's stuck there for a while—decades probably—but it's doing stuff to attack me and my family from there. Do you guys know of any way to stop it?"

The guys get into a quick back and forth discussion about magic, throwing around terms like 'dimensional wards' or 'reverse feedback conduits' and a whole bunch of other things that go right over my head. Not sure what a 'witch's bottle' is. Landon seems to think that might help us, but only to keep the demon's influence out of our house. Sophia mentions that she already shielded every window in our house, so we're pretty much safe there. Witches' bottles are apparently another means to do the same thing she did by '*Thirteen Ghosting*' the windows. Ugh. It doesn't sound like they've got a single good answer, just a bunch of 'this might help a little bit' type things.

Eventually, the guys stop talking and stand there making pensive faces at each other.

"So, umm?" I ask.

"Some rituals may offer protection." Darren glances off at one of the distant bookshelves. "Alas, nothing is guaranteed... nor would it last very long. A few weeks at most."

"There are more permanent wards." Callum raises an eyebrow.

"Of course. Bear in mind who we are talking to." Darren smiles at me, then nods to Sophia. "Nothing that requires blood or souls to power is an option here."

"Umm." Sophia holds up her hand. "I might be able to do soul magic if we have to."

The guys gawk at her.

She rolls her eyes. "Oh, come on. No. I'm not going to murder anyone. I can get soul goo straight from the Abyss because my brother's got some demon friends. And yes, I purified it first."

Landon squirms.

"Erm... what did you do with the essence of rarefied evil?" whispers Darren.

"I think it coalesced into a Justin Bieber album," I mutter.

Sophia grimaces. "I wasn't sure what to do with it, so I flushed it down the toilet."

The mystics stare. Callum appears ready to burst out laughing. Darren seems genuinely worried. Landon's making a face like he just walked in on his grandparents making love.

"Oh dear." Darren taps his fingertips together. "I hope we don't have another devouring fatberg incident."

Sophia makes a strange noise. "A what?"

I tilt my head. "I am afraid to ask, but I gotta know. What the heck is a devouring fatberg?"

Callum gives a nervous laugh. "The London sewer system is notorious for buildups of grease and awfulness. Lots of people sending stuff down the drain they shouldn't. Grease, cooking lard, that sort of thing. It congeals in the sewers to form massive blockages of the absolute most foul-smelling miasma you can imagine."

"In the late Seventies, an associate of another lodge was even more careless than the everyday British citizen with what they put down the drain. Somehow, the essence of rarefied evil infused with a particularly enormous fatberg... and brought it to life."

"Oof." I cringe. "That's horrifying."

"It ate several sewer workers and a few constables before the lodge became aware of its existence." Landon shakes his head. "Most people believe a simple fatberg broke loose from the sewer walls and suffocated those poor bastards. I cannot think of a worse way to go than being crushed under a ton of sewage-infused rotting lard."

"Not terribly far from the truth of it." Darren grimaces. "History's just left out the part where the fatberg moved under its own power and chased its victims down rather than simply falling on them."

Sophia's got both hands pressed into her stomach. "Can we please stop? I can almost smell that."

"Trust me, child." Landon shivers. "Whatever you're imagining the smell to be, it's ten times worse."

She gurgles.

"Okay, guys. I'm undead and I'm about to throw up." I exhale. "So... topic change. You're saying there's not much we can do magically to protect ourselves from the demon?"

"There are plenty of rituals." Darren makes a 'come here' gesture with one hand. A book leaps off a shelf on the other side of the room, flying sixty feet through the air into his grip. "This book has most of the easier ones. None are guaranteed to help, nor will their protection remain effective for significant amounts of time."

"A few may even make the situation worse," adds Callum.

I rake my hands up through my hair, sighing in exasperation. "Is there any way to fix this problem permanently?"

"There is, though it's far from practical." Darren sets the book on the table by Sophia. "You may borrow that if you like."

"Thank you." Sophia briefly peeks inside the book—the pages are covered in handwriting and doodles that make no sense to me.

"What's impractical for most people isn't necessarily out of bounds for me." I smile, showing off fangs. "What, exactly, would I have to do?"

"Well..." Darren exhales. "Take this with a grain of salt. We are not experts on demonic magic. That being said, most of the literature about them states that they cannot truly be killed unless you are on their home plane."

Oof. I hang my head. "So, I'd have to literally go to hell."

"There's no such place," says Darren.

"Yes. I know. I am using 'hell' because it's much faster to say than 'the particular demi-plane this demon considers to be its home.'"

"Fair." Darren chuckles.

Great. Wonderful. All our worries about what this demon might do to my family could be solved quite simply. All I'd have to do is find a way to cross planar boundaries, then get into a swordfight with a demon who previously kicked my ass.

How much effect did being a sefil have on his power? Did it make him super effective at fighting vampires? Since, you know, sefil eat vampires to gain power. Would he be more or less dangerous in his true demon form, on his home plane? Going down there to take him on sounds like an idea almost as foolish as going to the mall two days before Christmas. Though, I think hell probably would have some open parking spots.

Sigh. Argh, that didn't help.

At least Sophia's doing well with her practice. And hey, she's got a book on demonic protection. That couldn't possibly go wrong in any conceivable way, could it?

Help.

CHAPTER 26
WE'RE ALL A LITTLE BIT EMO

We made it to Monday without any severe catastrophes. Honestly, it's making me nervous. A demon this bent on revenge not doing anything only means he's building up power for something big. Gonna go out on a limb here and assume the 'big bang' when he finally makes a move is going to be something much worse than yoinking Sophia's dress in the middle of school.

Worry about the demon is distracting. The writing class is intolerably boring and dry today. Professor Black is trying her best to let her kookiness add some life to the material, but there's just no way to talk about 'office writing' in any way that sounds even remotely interesting to people with a pulse. Honestly, if not for her, I'd already have given her a mental compulsion to just pass me for the semester and then skipped the rest of the classes. A big reason I don't is it would make me feel guilty. Every other student is stuck suffering through this class.

To be fair, it's not *that* boring. Sure, it's dry, but after the crazy paranormal things I've gone through, it's extra tedious. Kind of like how I imagine professional race car drivers get bored only doing fifty-five on the highway. Once you get used to speed, normal is boring.

I'm being metaphorical by the way. I'm never going to drive that fast. It's not safe.

Besides... I can fly.

Speaking of flying...

After class is mercifully over, I hit the sky. Need to clear my head and stop letting the circular worrying of when badness is going to happen chip away at my ability to be happy and enjoy unlife. I can't go on bracing for catastrophe at any second. It's not sustainable. Sooner or later, it's going to drive me nuts. Sure, life can be dangerous. Being able to deal with unexpected badness is way different from knowing there's something after my family with no clue when it will strike.

Suppose the only logical course of action for me to take at this point is to ask Sam to arrange a meeting for me with Olmaz. Maybe he'll be able to tell me how powerful this problem demon is. If I can't take the bastard on myself, we'll have to hope Olmaz is more powerful than him plus willing to get involved. If Olmaz is not powerful enough to get rid of this other demon, he might be able to refer me to a demon who'd play assassin for me.

Problem is, what would they charge? Would their price be something I can pay or might it end up being worse than living in fear of torment? I know Sam's been trying to tell us that demons aren't evil. At least, no more so than humans. Still, I can't help but worry one powerful enough to get rid of our problem is going to demand Sophia's soul or something. Why her? She's the most outwardly 'innocent' person in the family. Yeah, I'm stereotyping demons. Does that make me a bad person?

My mind is balancing moods a bit heavy for me.

I've got about an hour before my family is going to start wondering where I am. If I'm thirty to sixty minutes late getting home from class, they'll assume I stopped to feed. The moodiness demands a bit of silent reflection. It's tempting to stop by Glim's rooftop and talk. Nah. I kinda want to be alone right now. Also, being around me is starting to become unhealthy. I don't want the demon to notice him and add him to the list of people I care about who need to be attacked.

Hmm. It's been a while since I got my emo on at the Space Needle. That sounds like an idea. Not necessarily a *good* idea, but it's something. I'll sit there and brood, staring down at the city for a while and see if it makes me feel better.

Hey, it works for Batman, right? The silent brooding over the city thing. Besides, periods of emo brooding happen to all of us—vampires I mean. It's part of the package. The whole 'creature of the night' thing.

Let me have this.

I fly to the Space Needle, which isn't too far from school. Of course, when you can fly at more than double highway speed limits, anything within the same city isn't 'too far' away. I'm being a moody little brat just looking for some time to sit here feeling picked on and overwhelmed... so I fly in to land with my head down and my hair over my face.

Not the best thing for maintaining situational awareness. But hey, this is the top of the Space Needle. There shouldn't be anyone up here to see me.

"Holy shit!" yells a guy half a second after my sneakers touch metal.

I jump back and let out a shriek like a strange man just barged in on me stepping out of the shower.

Hey, it's not entirely different. This is my special personal place, after all. Even if it is technically someone else's private property. They don't use the roof for anything. I lock stares with an older dude sitting with his legs dangling off the edge. Okay, to most people, he's not 'older.' He's 'dad age,' a little younger than my father but not by too much. Hair's a bit shaggy, dark brown. Looks like he hasn't shaved in a week. His clothes give off the smell of beer and something stronger, though the alcohol isn't on his breath.

At the moment, the shock and WTF-ness of seeing me fly lights up his expression, chasing away the heavy doldrums of deep depression. It's still there in his eyes. This guy's given up. Most people don't sit at the edge of the space needle roof with their legs hanging over the side unless they're contemplating ending it—or seriously effing reckless.

I'm a derp. Trying to play it off casually, I blurt, "Oh, crap. You startled me."

"Are you real?" The man stares at me. "Did I just see you flying?"

Dude gives me the perfect opportunity. All I have to do is say 'of course I'm not real. You're imagining me. People can't fly', then jump off the side and vanish. I don't do that because my gut tells me this guy's going to take a serious shortcut to get down if he's left by himself. Not sure how a mortal got up here, but... here he is.

"It's complicated." I take a step toward him. "Do you wanna talk?"

He recoils from me, seeming afraid... and his ass loses its grip on the sloping roof, sending him sliding off the side. Without even thinking, I dive forward as fast as my undead reflexes can propel me —which is pretty damn fast. My chest slams into the metal as I seize hold of him by a fistful of flannel shirt. My flight power helps me stomp on the brakes and stop sliding. He dangles, all his weight supported by my left arm, for a few seconds. Yeah, he screams but it's not too loud. Like, he's not freaked out about dying, just wanted a few more minutes first.

Ugh.

Is it unethical to mind control someone to stop contemplating suicide? There's a question for the ages.

I pull him back up, dragging him far enough onto the roof to avoid the more severe part of the slope. He shouldn't slide off by accident again. If the dude goes for the edge, it's going to be on purpose. Plus, there's enough room for me to play goalie again. Maybe I can't save this man's life for good, but I can stop it happening tonight. If he ends it when I'm not around, it won't feel like my fault.

"Whoa," rasps the guy. "What the crap is going on?"

"I'm old enough to hear bad words. You can drop an f-bomb if you want."

"Are you an angel?"

Gawd, the cheese. "No. I'm not."

"You're pretty damn strong for a scrawny thing." He glances down at where I'm still holding a fistful of his shirt.

"Yep. So, umm." I let go of his shirt and shift around to sit cross-legged. "Want to talk?"

He sits up, hands braced against the roof behind him. The grinding noise of the gears in his brain is almost audible. "Did I fall asleep and is this a weird dream?"

"Nope. You're awake."

"Did you come up here to jump, too?"

"Nope. I'm doing the Batman thing." I gesture off to one side. "To sit here feeling moody and sorry for myself for a little while, pondering my feelings of being apart from society by using the physical distance of high altitude as a metaphor for emotional separation and aloofness."

He blinks.

"Too much?" I scrunch my nose. "Yeah, you're right. A bit too heavy handed. Seriously, though... if you want to talk about it, I have at least an hour before I need to be elsewhere."

The guy looks at me for a minute or so, not speaking, then glances off at the city. "It's fine. You don't need to worry about my problems."

"You're in my emo brooding spot," I say. "I can't get my sulk on with you here. Besides, I think my problems are probably pretty minor compared to yours."

"What the heck could be so wrong in your life?" He shakes his head. "You're a kid."

"I'm eighteen," I deadpan.

"Uh huh."

"Seriously. I am. Honestly, I'm nineteen. Just stopped getting older a year ago."

He starts to chuckle, then makes this weird face at me. "Wait, you sound serious."

"I am. You saw me flying right? Just roll with it and don't ask too many questions or government people in black will shove a turkey baster up your butt."

"What the hell...?"

"I'm being metaphorical. They don't use real turkey basters." I smile. "They have these weird buzzing electrical gadgets that—"

"Right..."

"Come on, man. Talk it out? I'm not good at this sort of thing." I offer a hand. "By the way, I'm Sarah."

He glances down at my outstretched hand. Not sure if he feels awkward introducing himself to a 'kid' or he's afraid I'm going to drag him off into the sky somewhere. Finally, he decides to briefly squeeze my fingers more than shake hands. "Steve."

"Hi, Steve. Look, I know you have no idea who I am, but... if whatever put you on this roof tonight is something I can help fix, I'll try. If it's like some chemical imbalance in your brain, all I can do is take you to the hospital."

Steve grumbles, then hangs his head. "Not your problem to worry about. And what could you possibly do to help?"

"I can't answer that until you tell me what's wrong."

He stares down at the city for a long few minutes. The mood in his eyes shifts ever so slightly as if the reprieve of talking to me is a welcome delay of tonight's inevitable conclusion. "Don't expect you could understand, but I lost my kids."

I gasp. "Oh, no..."

"Not like that." He sighs. "They're alive, but they may as well be dead to me. My ex-wife got awarded sole custody. She made up a bunch of bullshit about me, and the damn judge believed every word of it. I'm not allowed within 200 yards of my kids because everyone thinks I hit them."

"Ugh. I'm sorry."

"The bitch," says Steve, raising his voice, "doesn't even want Lucas or Leo. She never even really liked them. She can't be responsible for them. Amy's so immature she can barely take care of herself. She's got no ability or even interest in taking care of actual children. The only reason she's doing this is to hurt me. I don't even know what the hell I did to make her so damned spiteful. Lost my last appeal today. It probably didn't help that I came unglued in court and yelled at the judge. Really looked like the sort of asshole who'd hit his kids. I'm not. I would never do that. I love my boys!" He breaks down, crying into his hand. Tears slip through the hairs on his unshaven face, glinting in the moonlight. "The lawyer said we have to wait years to try again, if at all. It would probably take Amy doing something for us to even have a chance."

"Doing something?"

"Yeah, like getting caught with drugs, getting arrested... something bad." Steve wipes his hand across his mouth. "She's going to hurt them. I know it."

Eek! I shift closer to him. "Your sons are in danger? You think she's going to hurt them?"

"I don't think she's going to take them out and drown them or something drastic like that." Steve squeezes his hands into fists. "But the neglect. It's going to screw them up for life. She treats the boys like they're unwanted burdens she could do without. Maybe she even gets off on tormenting them like she does me. What kind of woman gets off on making people suffer?"

I purse my lips, thinking of Petra. "I've met one like that. How much danger are your sons in?"

"Who knows? If Leo got into bleach or something, she wouldn't notice until it was too late." Steve eyes the edge of the roof. "So, help me, I was *this* close to killing her. Yeah, I'd have been in prison but the boys would be better off."

"You didn't go through with it?" I ask.

"No. As bad as Amy is, killing her would traumatize Lucas and Leo." Steve's lip quivers. "I don't know what else to do. I failed my kids. Couldn't protect them."

I rest a hand on his shoulder. "I can help."

"Yeah, sure, kid. Good luck trying to change my mind." He scowls. "The bitch won. She destroyed me. Maybe if I'm dead, she won't feel the need to keep the boys and she'll put them out for adoption. It's the last thing I can think of to do in order to protect them from her."

"Wait." I pull on his arm. "Talking you down isn't what I meant by helping. I can actually help. If I can get your boys back to you, would you want me to do that?"

"The hell are you talking about?"

I smile. "Assuming you're not lying to me and everything you said about your ex-wife is true, if she really is a danger to those boys... I can fix this. Would you still want to throw yourself off the Space Needle if you had two boys to take care of?"

"Are you nuts? Of course not. They're my whole life." Steve frowns. "But you're a kid. What the heck are you going to do to fight a ridiculous justice system who thinks the mom is always right no matter what kind of horseshit she makes up?"

"I think you just had a bad lawyer." I shrug. "Tell you what. Go home tonight. Give me three days before you give up again, okay?"

Steve stares at me, 'yeah right' practically tattooed on his forehead.

"You saw me flying, didn't you?" I raise an eyebrow. "Three days won't kill you."

He scratches his cheek, making the beard bristles rustle. "I suppose I can hang on for a few more days. Still can't imagine what the heck you're going to do."

"Just trust me, okay?" I smile. "Oh, I'm gonna need some info. Where's your ex-wife living now?"

"She got the house. The house I freakin' built when I was twenty-five. Not even allowed near the property now." He scowls.

"You built it? Like literally?"

"Yeah. I'm a contractor. Got my own business." He flicks dirt off his jean leg. "Used to be so damn proud of myself. Certified electrician and a contractor. I'd give it all up to get my sons back safe from that witch."

"Hey." I poke him. "Witches are nice. Don't use the word like that. Give me a chance to fix this for you, okay?"

"Sure." Steve pulls out his wallet, takes out a business card marked 'Stephen Holland – Electrical and General Contracting'. It's got an address and phone number on it. "That's the house."

"Okay. What's your phone number?"

"The cell number's on the card."

Derp. So it is. "Okay."

"Don't call the main number. The bitch will answer."

"Got it." I tuck the card into my pocket. "Okay, Steve. I need to see you get down from here in one piece. Tonight is not your night."

He reluctantly stands when I pull on his arm. It takes me giving him a mild compulsion to 'have faith' and give me the three days to suspend his urge to leap to his death enough to get him moving. Ugh, this poor guy. While I'm in there, I double check his story. Yeah. He's legit. The dude's a devoted father. He really thinks killing himself might get Amy to give up custody of the boys, who would be much safer in foster/adoptive care than with her.

Society thinks demons are evil. Demons have nothing on humans.

After escorting him safely through the inner workings of the Space Needle to the ground level, I'm reasonably confident he's not going to do anything rash tonight. My demon problems seem way more manageable now.

But first, guess it's time to get my spandex suit on.

CHAPTER 27
NO CAPES!

Yeah, that's me. Superhero vampire girl.

Sigh.

It's almost tempting to run around in a spandex costume, if not for the whole 'trying to stay under the radar' thing. This is my compromise. I don't feel guilty about not roaming around looking for people in need of help because if I trip over someone who does need help, I will do what I can. Any traditional vampire who knew me as a mortal would never have given me the Transference. I'm the sort of person who thinks 'I have this power; I need to use it to help everyone.'

Not exactly great for maintaining secrecy.

Huh. Maybe if Natasha's idea ever takes off and vampires go mainstream, I could get away with it.

Not for many years, though. People aren't ready for us.

So, here I am, lurking in the weeds outside a house in Federal Way. It's a nice, quiet suburban neighborhood. This is exactly the kind of house the people in a cute Stephen Spielberg movie live in before all hell breaks loose. Lights are on in three rooms. The bigger windows flicker and flutter like someone's watching television. The other illuminated windows aren't so bright, suggesting the lights are on in different rooms on the back side of the house.

The thing about mind reading is, it doesn't prove actual truth.

Stephen truly believes what he told me. He's not lying. While it might be true, it also might only mean he's crazy and delusional. So, I'm not kicking in the door to slay the evil bitch queen and rescue the two kids without doing a little snooping first. And no, I'm not here to kill anyone. The worst thing I plan to do to this woman if she's everything Stephen says is to give her a mental compulsion to surrender the boys and give up custody—then leave him the heck alone.

Hey, not every 'superhero' deed needs to be worthy of a Michael Bay action scene.

If there's one thing vampires are good at, it's stalking and sneaking.

I make my way across the yard to the house and start looking in the windows. There's a thirtyish woman in the living room wearing a tank top and sweatpants. She's watching TV, some sort of action movie. Oh, I think it's one of the Daniel Craig 007 movies. Not sure which one, though.

The place looks reasonably neat. No messes.

Okay...

I can hear activity from the kitchen, so I zip around to the back-yard. Most houses I've seen tend to put the kitchen in the back. Not sure why they do that, but hey. It's a thing. Sure enough, the kitchen windows overlooking the yard are brightly lit.

While the living room was nice and tidy, the kitchen is a bit of a mess. The only person in the room is a black-haired boy about Sam's age. Stephen told me his sons are ten and six years old. This must be Lucas. He's standing on a chair positioned close to the stove so he can see into the pot and stir whatever's in it. Smells like boiling water and salt. I spot a box of spaghetti noodles on the counter nearby as well as a jar of sauce. The kid's wearing a T-shirt, jeans, and white socks.

Time for a math problem: hardwood chair plus socks plus pot of boiling water.

Ack.

Sure, the kid might be fine, but there's way too much of a chance he could end up in the hospital, scarred for life. Am I overreacting? I've seen Sam wipe out while wearing socks in our kitchen before. Granted, he wasn't trying to cook while standing on a polished hardwood chair.

Why the hell is that woman letting him do this? Oh. Wait. Stephen says she's super neglectful. Since I've only got his opinion to go by right now, I assume she couldn't be bothered to get off her ass and make something for the boys to eat. Lucas looks hungry. Like, seriously hungry. No, he's not starving away to nothing... but the look in his eyes. I'm guessing he hasn't had lunch today, nor a decent meal for some days.

He reaches for the box of spaghetti noodles and nearly topples off the chair. Shit! If he doesn't go face-first into the boiling water, he's going to crack his skull open on the floor—and probably pull the boiling water down on top of himself when he falls.

I dart over to the back door and let myself in. Locks? What locks?

Lucas is too freaked out by almost taking a dive to notice me entering the kitchen behind him. The last thing I want to do is startle him right now. Unfortunately, the best way I can think of to avoid him getting hurt is probably going to scare the crap out of him. Still, a jump scare is better than severe burns or a cracked skull.

I sneak up behind him and grab him with both arms.

"Aaaaaah!" shouts Lucas, squirming.

He doesn't fall off the chair since I'm holding him.

"Easy, kiddo. I'm here to help."

Lucas keeps wriggling, though not quite as hard. "Get off me!"

"Okay. Stop squirming. I'm going to put you down. Just don't want you to fall and get hurt."

He breathes hard for a few seconds, then goes limp.

A smaller boy, also with a mop of unruly black hair, runs in from the hall. He's in a Batman T-shirt, Iron-Man briefs, and white socks. He stares at me holding Lucas, not sure how to react. A stranger in the house is pretty scary to kids, but I'm not exactly the most threatening looking of people—unless I sprout fangs and make my eyes glow red. Maybe he thinks his mom hired a babysitter.

"Hi, Leo." I smile at the six-year-old.

"Are you gonna put me down?" grumbles Lucas.

"Yeah." I take two steps back, dragging him off the chair he's standing on, then set him on his feet. "Sorry for scaring you. You're standing on a wooden chair with sock feet right in front of a pot of boiling water. That's super dangerous."

Lucas gives me this look of annoyance, shame, fear, desperation, and a bit of anger. He doesn't seem to be able to speak while he's trying to sort out his emotions. Kiddo doesn't want to cry in front of a strange girl. He's more scared at being grabbed by a stranger too strong to get away from than anything that might've happened to him with the stove. Now that he's looking at me, though, his fear is fading.

"Who are you?" asks Leo.

"My name is Sarah," I say in an almost whisper so Amy doesn't hear me. "Your dad asked me to check on you."

The boys' both light up. (Metaphorically, I mean. They're not glowing. Sophia did not conjure them from mushroom dust.)

Leo's happiness melts to sorrow in mere seconds. "We're not allowed to see him. Mommy says he's a big asshole."

Oof.

If my mother heard a boy his age drop that word, she'd turn into the librarian spirit from Ghostbusters. The scream would shatter windows.

"He isn't," whispers Lucas. "Mommy just hates him."

"Why?" Leo picks his nose.

Lucas shrugs. "I dunno."

"What do you guys think of your dad?"

"He's awesome." Lucas finally loses his battle with stoicism. He's not *crying*, though tears stream down his face. "I miss him. I don't know why he had to leave."

"Mommy says he doesn't want us anymore. We're too bad." Leo stares down at the floor. "I don't wanna be bad."

Grr. Bitch. I grasp the boys' hands and gaze into their eyes. "Your mommy is not telling you the truth. Your dad loves you a lot. Like, a real lot…" I almost say he loves them more than his own life but, nah. I'm not going there. They don't need to know that.

Leo starts crying. "I'm not bad?"

"No. You're not." I smile at him, then peek into his head.

He thinks his mother is always 'too busy' for them. She barely acknowledges the boys are even in the house. Leo thinks his father decided to hate him and his brother and he hated them so much he left the house and never came back.

Why? Why would this woman tell her sons that? Good grief. Evil.

A little mental surgery later, Leo believes his parents had a fight and his father had to go somewhere for a while despite not wanting to go away. He no longer remembers being told his father hates him. I do the same for Lucas, though the older boy didn't believe his mom. He rejected her claim Stephen hated him. Good.

Seems the kids' memory agrees with what their dad told me. When he isn't working long hours with his contracting business, he's all about spending time with the boys. They don't have many fond memories of their mother. She's just this 'woman who happens to be in the house with them.' About the only nice thing I can say about Amy is she doesn't actively abuse them… at least not physically. Mental cruelty and neglect for sure. Their beds haven't been made or changed since Stephen had to leave.

Okay. This is done.

Ideas form in my mind.

"Lucas, don't worry about the stove. I'll fix you something to eat." I stand. "Can you take Leo and go to your room for a bit?"

"Okay." He takes his brother by the hand and leads him off down the hall.

I follow them most of the way into the hall until they veer left onto the stairs going up. I keep going straight and storm into the living room.

"What the hell is wrong with you?" I blurt.

Amy screams and jumps off the sofa, spinning to gawk at me. "Who the hell are you and what are you doing in my house?"

Not wasting the time. I wallop her with the Derp Hammer and dive into her thoughts. Hmm. Doesn't look like anything super pathological going on here. It's just a case of this woman being thirty-three with the mentality of an entitled seventeen-year-old. She can't handle responsibility. Doesn't *want* to handle responsibility. She figured marrying a successful contractor would let her continue living a carefree life, not having to do anything. Just go out and party with her friends, watch movies, goof off, and so on. With the divorce thing, she's had to get a job... and she's furious at Stephen for that. As if he's 'stealing' her time by forcing her to support herself. As far as the boys are concerned, she thinks of them as annoyances that impede her ability to have free time and fun. She'd just as soon drop them off at an orphanage and forget they exist, other than she wants to make Stephen suffer. She knows he's a devoted dad and the separation is killing him, so she did as much as she could to convince the judge not to let him be around the boys. According to her, it's his fault she has to work and can't just have fun all the time. Every bit of her life that didn't turn out as idyllic as she imagined it would is his fault. Mostly, it's all the 'adult responsibility' stuff she didn't expect to have to deal with.

Ugh.

Okay, bitch. I'm not going to feel the least bit bad about punching you in the brain. Metaphorically I mean. Time to set up this scenario. I root around her memories looking for things to work with. Aha. The parents. Her parents spoiled the crap out of her. This explains much. They live in California, have a decent amount of money. Her mom never had to work. She doesn't even know how her parents feel about the grandkids. She's aware Lucas has been cooking for himself and his little brother. Amy mostly orders out or nukes microwave meals for herself. At least she buys groceries for the kids, such as it is. Chicken nuggets and spaghetti.

Yeah, I gotta do something.

Right. So... here we go. Need to make this look like a situation the cops or whoever shows up to investigate will be able to process without scratching their heads too much due to unexplained paranormal influence. I hammer the concept into her mind that she is not going to keep the boys away from their dad anymore. She doesn't care about the boys. She can let them go be with their dad. She wants freedom from responsibility; she gets it.

I also give her an irresistible urge to go back to her parents' place, gathering all the negative feelings she has about Stephen, having to work a job, and everything else she dislikes about her life and channeling it into a sense of this house. She does not want to be here. She doesn't want half ownership or any money for the house. Just go home to your parents and let them support you. Find some other dude who is just as shallow as you are... and hope he's had a vasectomy so no more kids get caught in the crossfire.

The last thing I do is implant a compulsion to contact the family court and confess to lying about Stephen. She is going to be truthful and admit she made up the accusations of domestic abuse purely to ensure the kids got taken away to hurt him emotionally. She's also going to abandon the kids home alone and immediately take herself to California. Right now.

Oh, that wasn't the last thing. Oops. I delete myself from her memory. Then, I disconnect from her brain.

Amy stands there in a fog for a moment. Then, like her panties are full of angry fleas, sprints out of the living room. I head to the kitchen and finish making spaghetti. By the time it's ready to eat, Amy's on her way out the front door with a couple of fat, overstuffed suitcases. She gets into her mini-SUV and drives off, on her way to her parents' house in California. So what if it's like a nine-hour ride. My compulsion will keep her alert enough not to crash. She might pass the hell out as soon as she arrives, but that's not my problem.

Time for phase two.

"Lucas? Leo?" I call. "C'mon to the kitchen."

The boys wander in a moment later.

"Where's Mom?" asks Lucas.

"She left, and probably won't be back." I sigh. "Sorry."

"It's okay. She didn't want us, anyway." Lucas frowns. "What happens to us now?"

"Your dad's going to come home. Eventually." I point at the table. "Sit. Eat."

"Eventually?" Lucas scrunches his nose. "You said he wants us."

I nod. "He totally does. There's just some stupid legal stuff going on. You might have to stay at a place for a few days while that gets sorted out, but you're going to end up back here at home with your dad when it's all over."

The boys grin at me.

They scramble into their chairs and devour the spaghetti. When they're done eating, it's time for more mind powers. Feels a little wrong to charm kids. Alas, this needs to be perfect. Can't have one of them slipping up and talking like it's an arranged scheme or anything. They also can't remember seeing me here.

As far as Lucas and Leo will know, their mother just randomly decided to nope out of there and leave them alone. I give them a memory of Amy saying she's going to her parents and won't be back, making her seem consciously aware the boys will be left alone at home without an adult. When the cops talk to the boys, they will clearly state their mother intentionally abandoned them with no intention to return.

This may or may not get her in legal trouble. Can't say I'm terribly worried about that.

Next, I 'program' little Leo to call 911 and tell the dispatcher that their mother just abandoned them and he's scared, and wants his daddy. While the six-year-old wanders off to the phone, I send Lucas to his father's former home office room to use the business line to call his dad and tell him the same story—mom left saying she won't ever be back. Kids wouldn't care that he's been ordered to stay away from the house. I'm confident Stephen won't get in trouble once it all comes out in public that Amy lied.

Also, the boys believe Lucas cooked the spaghetti. I let him remember he almost slipped and fell off the chair, so he's got a lingering fear of trying to cook like that again. He's going to tell his dad, cops, or anyone who'll listen how his mom wouldn't make food for them and he almost got a face full of boiling water trying to eat.

Am I laying it on a bit thick? Maybe. I just want these two little guys to have their dad back.

I might be a vampire, but I'm not a monster. Can't leave two kids this age home alone. I lurk out of sight and wait with them. A police car arrives in a few minutes. I'm a fly on the wall in the living room. Neither the boys nor the two cops notice me there, watching as Lucas and Leo explain their mother decided to abandon them and leave. Both kids repeatedly tell the cops their mom lied and their dad never hits them. The woman cop asks if there's anyone here with them. Lucas says no, but he called his dad and he's coming right now.

No idea what the cops would normally do in a situation like this. I poke the lady cop in the brain ever so slightly to encourage her to let Stephen stay here with the boys. She'll probably find something about the keep-away order in the system if she checks. The woman's going to ignore it because the boys are so convincing about how much they love and want their dad.

I hang out in the house until Stephen shows up. Poor guy almost crashes his truck into the police cruiser in his haste. Watching him hurry over to the house only to have the boys charge out the door and clamp hug him is too much. Those videos of military people coming home after months and surprising their kids get me every time. This is exactly the same sort of feel.

Stephen seems like a completely different guy than the one I saw atop the Space Needle.

Yeah... I think they'll be okay. Might be a tedious few days for them while the legal bullcrap gets sorted out, though it feels right.

I slip away out of the living room and go down the hall as Stephen starts talking to the police about his situation. After slipping quietly out the back door into the yard, I leap into the air and fly toward home, still a bit choked up.

Not every catastrophe a superhero fixes is stopping the end of the world, but it's the small stuff that matters most. Maybe I really should get the spandex outfit.

"No capes!" I say, trying to do Edna's accent.

Yeah, I'm a dork.

CHAPTER 28
WAR

Monday always brought an unwelcome shift away from the weekend.

Sierra would never be caught dead in public hugging a plushie or teddy bear, so she had to make do with her bookbag. To any other kid on the bus, she simply wrapped her arms around it to prevent it from falling over. Inside, she tried to find comfort in holding something, dreading today would be the day it finally happened.

Every morning she went to school could be the last morning she went to school... or at least the last morning some of her classmates went to school. Everyone said 'it can't happen here.' Those words didn't comfort Sierra. She knew. Every student or teacher who ended up being shot at school all believed 'it couldn't happen there'—right up until it did.

She fidgeted at one of the zippers on the side of the backpack, wondering how much of this fear came from her being crazy. None of the other kids seemed afraid all the time, like her. Did they hide it well or had something gone wrong in her brain? Not even Sophia appeared to be phobic of school.

Blah. She's so innocent she doesn't understand how evil some people can be.

Twelve felt simultaneously like a child and not. Seventh grade. It became a blurry area whether the shooter would be a strange adult looking to do the most evil thing possible—or one of the students having a meltdown. Up until now, she totally feared an outside threat. The older she and her classmates got, the more likely one of her classmates could turn out to be the killer.

All the stories from the news stuck to her brain like Post-It notes. Girl says no to a date request. Boy shows up later with a gun. Kid has a meltdown at home, brings a gun. Kid is just plain nuts, brings a gun. Sierra didn't necessarily fear guns; she feared crazy people. Mom was still terrified of guns. She didn't even like that *Call of Duty* depicted them so realistically.

No, guns didn't bother Sierra. If everyone shooting at each other was an adult, part of an organized military, and signed up for battle... that was different. A war where everyone consented to participate didn't give her nightmares. A war where one insane jerk went hunting the most defenseless, innocent prey he could find kept her up at night and made it impossible to eat much for breakfast on a Monday.

The start of the week scared her the most since it represented being yanked out of the relative safety of home and forced into the functioning world. Thursdays bothered her the second most. Fridays came close to Mondays for fear. Lots of shooters liked to do their thing on Monday or Friday. Thursday happened to be close to Friday. She got nervous on Wednesdays sometimes since not too many shootings happened in the middle of the week, which made her worry someone would try to be unique.

Off the top of her head, she couldn't think of anyone here who'd be likely to snap. Sure, the school had its jerks. None took things far enough to make her afraid of them. And now, she didn't really have to be scared. If one of her classmates brought a gun to school, she'd make sure he couldn't hurt anyone. If some strange man stormed into the school with a rifle, she'd break him in half.

Yet, for some annoying reason, Sophia's magic couldn't chase away the fear.

This is my Fuzzydoom. She grumbled. *It doesn't make any sense I'm scared of some jerk with a gun now.*

She looked up, startled by a sudden shudder in the bus. It had merely stopped at the school.

Weird. Ride seemed fast.

Sophia, sitting next to her, bounced up to her feet like a happy blonde rabbit, eager to do 'school stuff.' Sam, to her right at the window, waited patiently for her to get up first. Sierra couldn't move. She felt like a death row inmate about to leave her cell for the last time and go to the chair. If she went into that building, she would die.

The oppressive dread only lasted a few seconds.

Stop being a little kid. Maybe they're right. Maybe it won't happen here. She closed her eyes and exhaled out her nose. *For every kid who thought it couldn't happen and died, there's thousands where it didn't happen.*

Sierra stood and shuffled after the last few students. Her hesitation made her and Sam the last two kids to leave the bus. Sophia waited for her by the curb. Her siblings fell in step on either side of her as they walked toward the school entrance.

Everything looked normal. The usual cliques of kids clustered here and there, hanging out before classes started. They had about sixteen minutes to themselves before first class. Since Sierra and her siblings all happened to be in different grades, they wouldn't see each other again until lunchtime.

She tried not to worry so much about her fears and tried to concentrate on a far more likely problem: the demon.

"Soph," whispered Sierra. "Can you do a little protection spell on us?"

"Umm. Yeah, I think so." Sophia flicked her hair over her right shoulder. "I'm still trying to make sense of the book I borrowed. It's not written in English."

The roar of a revving engine where the roar of a revving engine should not be set off Sierra's fight reflex. Everything around her slowed to an almost crawl as her attention shifted to a dark-colored car jumping the curb at the corner, less than twenty feet away from her.

Neither Sophia nor Sam showed any signs of having noticed the car coming right at them yet. With less than two seconds before impact, Sierra did the only thing she had the time to do: she shoved Sophia to the right and Sam to the left. Her sister went headfirst into the bushes along the sidewalk. Sam landed on the roof of a parked car.

Sierra's rail thin body wrapped around the front end of the speeding car. She vaguely noticed her face bouncing off the hood before sky filled her vision. Bushes erupted around her, leaving her staring up past tiny leaves and twigs at the clouds. A loud *whud* came from somewhere close by, the shock of impact so severe she felt it like a punch all over her body even though nothing else hit her.

People somewhere far away screamed.

Sierra blinked in shock. She lay draped across the thicker innermost branches of one of the school's fat bushes. A few sore spots on her chest, hips, and left shin didn't hurt too much. Several boys around her age appeared around the edges of the sky opening above, peering down at her. Upon seeing them, the strange sense of floating in a separate space, removed from time, ended.

"She's alive," said one boy, seeming surprised.

"Holy shit," whispered one of the boys looking at her. "Are you okay?"

Sierra wiggled her feet, squirmed a bit, then glanced down the length of her body. Nothing appeared to be broken, nor did she see blood anywhere. *I owe Soph big time. Holy shit.* "Umm. I feel okay."

Two boys grabbed her hands. A third grabbed her by the ankles. They lifted her up out of the bush and set her gently down on the ground. Almost thirty feet away, closer to the school, other students helped Sophia out of the bushes. Sam perched atop the roof of the car he'd landed on, staring at something in the distance.

Sierra sat up and looked to her left, away from the school.

A maroon Buick hit the big tree in the school's yard forty feet from her. Steam and smoke billowed from the crumpled hood. Leaf bits, acorns, or other 'tree stuff' covered the car. One seriously pissed off squirrel ran back and forth on the branches above it making noises.

Teachers tried, with minimal success, to herd students away from the crash site and get them into the building. Two women, Mrs. Aaron (who she once had for fifth-grade English) and Mrs. Page (her current phys. ed teacher) rushed over to where she lay on the grass.

"Oh my God, Sierra!" yelled Mrs. Page. "Don't move, honey. The ambulance will be here soon."

Mrs. Aaron knelt nearby and took her hand. The woman appeared ready to burst into tears, then seemed confused.

Some kids in the distance spoke—none too quietly—about how that car 'totally launched' Sierra.

"I'm fine." Sierra dusted herself off. "It didn't really hit me. Just looked like it did."

"Dear, you flew through the air," said Mrs. Aaron. "I saw it. I thought we were going to find you..."

"Sorry." Sierra broke her rule and hugged the teacher. Less than a minute after being hit by a car, no one would notice or care if she acted 'soft.' "I didn't mean to scare you."

Sophia and Sam jogged over. Neither appeared too worried, though smiled when they got close enough to look at her.

"You're bleeding." Mrs. Page dabbed at her forehead. "Though, it looks like only a few scratches from the bushes."

Sierra clenched her jaw. No way would a stupid bush be able to hurt her. If she did have cuts and scrapes, those totally came from being nailed by a car. Considering how far away Sophia crawled out of the bushes, Sierra had gone flying a considerable distance. No wonder Mrs. Aaron expected to find her all smashed up and dead.

"It must've looked way worse than it was." Sierra pulled her right leg up, knee to chest, then relaxed it before repeating the move with her other leg. Then, she stood. "I'm totally fine. Nothing hurts. It wasn't going that fast or something. I just kinda bounced off the side."

A teacher who'd run to the car to check on the driver belted out a brief scream of shock and dismay before backing away and yelling at students to go inside and not to go near the car or look into it.

Ugh. Sierra cringed. The car had been going much faster than she admitted. She'd have to alter her story to say it sped up after she bounced off it. Given the amount of damage to the front end and the teacher's reaction when she looked in the window, whoever had been driving the car probably died in a rather gruesome way. Even from where she sat on the ground, the splattery redness on the windows made a pretty strong statement as to the fate of the person behind the wheel.

Mrs. Page—who also happened to be an EMT when not teaching gym class—lifted Sierra's shirt enough to examine her stomach and ribs. The lack of any bruising appeared to surprise the woman. "Wow. Sierra, you are one amazingly lucky kid. C'mon. I'd feel much more comfortable if you got checked out at the nurse station before just sending you to class after that."

Some battles are pointless. "Okay. Umm. Did anyone see where my stuff went?"

"It's scattered everywhere," said one of the boys who pulled her out of the bush. "Your bookbag exploded."

"No, it didn't." Sophia held up the intact backpack. "You're making stuff up. Her bag is right here."

The boy's eyes fluttered. He mouthed 'WTF' without any voice behind it, then looked back at the grass where the contents of the backpack had likely been strewn about only a moment before.

Wow. Her magic not only saved my life, it's making it much easier for me to lie about being weird.

Sierra suspended her rule a second time, hugging Sophia right there in front of everyone. The teachers and other students who had not yet been chased into the building likely interpreted it as a 'grateful to be alive' hug. In a way, they happened to be right. None of them could know Sierra experienced such a surge of gratitude for what Sophia did she acted mushy in public.

"Amazing," whispered Mrs. Page to no one in particular. "Craziest thing I've ever seen. I thought for sure today was about to be the worst day of my life."

Mrs. Aaron sniffled. "I'm not sure how I would've handled seeing what I expected to find in that bush."

"Thanks for running over to help me." Sierra managed a genuine smile at the teacher. "I'll go to the nurse now. I don't need an ambulance though."

Mrs. Page hurried over to the car to check on the driver.

Sierra blinked, surprised that the teachers didn't insist on escorting her to the nurse's station. Then again, they had a gory crash scene to keep students away from until the police got there. She rolled her shoulders, checking once again to make sure nothing hurt too much. Mild soreness spread pretty much everywhere. She'd definitely taken a hit. No part of her truly hurt. The ache barely registered as even 'annoying.'

Sophia and Sam followed her down the sidewalk to the school, past a dozen or so teachers in various states of disbelief and panic. Even Principal Weber emerged from her office, a rare sighting indeed. The grandmotherly woman didn't pay specific attention to Sierra, so she likely didn't know exactly what happened yet.

Not waiting to be in the spotlight, she hurried through the door into the school building.

"Are you really going to the nurse?" asked Sam.

"Yeah. I don't want to get in trouble or attract more attention." Sierra swung her backpack over her right shoulder. "Thanks for fixing my stuff."

"No problem." Sophia smiled. "Are you really okay?"

"Yeah. Little sore."

Sam hugged her. "You took that car head on."

"Yeah. I know." Sierra rubbed her jaw. "Got a real close look at the hood. Umm, guys, if I get a little squishy later tonight when we're home, don't make fun of me."

"Squishy?" Sophia blinked. "Your bones aren't gonna break later on."

"Not that kind of squishy." Sierra smirked at her. "Squishy like I might be unusually nice to you. Possibly a small bit clingy. I would've been dead right there if you didn't enchant me."

"Oh. That kind of squishy." Sophia sighed. "I know it well."

"Yeah." Sierra put her arms around her siblings. "Are you guys coming to the nurse with me?"

Sophia nodded. "Yes."

"I saw a demon," whispered Sam.

"We know." Sierra chuckled.

"I mean, I saw one in the car right before you threw me to safety." Sam paused, rubbing his arm. "Thanks, by the way. I'm a lot squishier than you are, and not in the 'cries over kittens' sense of the word squishy."

Sierra gave him a brief squeeze despite wanting more of a hug. They were still in public after all. Overt displays of mushiness were way too embarrassing now that the adrenaline started to wear off. "You think that demon tried to kill me?"

"Kill *us*," said Sophia. "It tried to kill all three of us, because that's Mom, Dad, and Sarah's worst fear."

Sam narrowed his eyes. "We're at war."

"Yeah." Sierra scowled. "Stupid demon. How do we fight something that's stuck in another plane?"

"Working on it." Sam kicked an abandoned pen cap down the corridor. "What are you going to tell the nurse?"

"That the car just grazed me. I bounced off. Or maybe I should play dumb. Tell her it all happened so fast I don't really know."

Sophia nodded. "Go with that. Easier to keep your story straight."

CHAPTER 29
THE WORST POSSIBLE PLACE

Mom's screaming wakes me up a little early.

The last time I felt like this, Ashley and I got the brilliant idea to stay up without sleeping all weekend. We did it... but holy crap did we crash *hard* Sunday night. Both of us missed school the following Monday. If this is anything even close to what a hangover is like, I'm glad I'll never experience one.

She's yelling 'what' a lot, like someone is giving her unbelievable or horrible news. Weird that should make me open my eyes at... what the hell time is it? I manage to look toward my desk and see the clock. It's 9:42 a.m.

Whiskey Tango Foxtrot.

In an instant, the clock jumps ahead to 2:48 p.m. I no longer feel hung over or exhausted.

Ahh. Much better.

Mom yells something. Hmm. Maybe I'm not fully awake since I didn't make out what she said. She sounded pretty upset, though. I stumble out of bed and make my way upstairs. By the time I reach the kitchen, my body's fully out of sleep mode so I am not stumbling along like a broken android.

"Chill out, Mom. I'm fine," says Sierra from the living room. "Sophia's enchantment made me tough, remember?"

Wait. Mom? She's home at this hour? Did she have the day off work?

"I've got a bigger bruise than she got." Sophia fake huffs, like she's not really upset.

"Sorry," says Sierra.

"Don't you dare apologize for saving my life," chirps Sophia.

Saving her life? What to the what? I rush through the house to the living room. Sophia and Sam stand by the end of the sofa. Sierra's sitting in Mom's lap, hugging her. Holy monkey nuts, Batman. Something is seriously wrong.

"What happened?" I leap the sofa back and land seated next to Mom, staring at my older kid sister. "Are you okay?"

"Yeah." Sierra sighs.

"A demon jumped on some random guy and tried to run us over this morning." Sam explains how they were walking from the bus to the school entrance when a big old car nearly plowed into them. "Surprisingly, the driver isn't dead. He's really messed up though."

Mom appears equal parts confused and upset. She wants to be angry at someone, but isn't sure where to direct the rage. Also, Sierra's openly showing physical affection. Mom's not about to do anything to ruin that. It's kind of like having an aloof cat who hates being held. When you're finally allowed to give skritches, the world can explode around you and you'll ignore it. Sooner or later, the cat will have had enough and wander off. It's important to savor the time the cat tolerates being in your lap.

"Jonathan, we simply must do something." Mom shoots a pointed look at Dad. "I can't handle some demon from another world threatening us anymore. This is getting serious."

"You're right." Dad rubs his chin. "I should probably not go anywhere near the backyard grill until this thing is dealt with."

Mom shakes her head in disbelief. "You're not serious."

"I am. Who knows what might happen if I try cooking out there. I like having eyebrows." Dad wiggles them.

Sam smiles. "You don't need a demon's interference for your eyebrows to be in danger at the grill."

Sophia and Sierra muffle laughter.

"I did not overdo it with lighter fluid on purpose that time." Dad holds up a finger. "The squirt thing broke and I didn't notice it."

"But, Dad..." Sam fakes an exasperated sigh. "You're the one who taught me never to squirt without watching where the stream goes."

That even gets Mom to chuckle despite her nerves over Sierra's not-so-near-miss.

Whatever Dad prepared to say, he decides against it, his expression going serious. "I agree with your mother. This situation is escalating to the point where I'm concerned it would burn off a bit more than eyebrows."

"What can we do?" Mom squeezes Sierra.

"Not exactly sure yet." Dad gets this air about him like a project is brewing. Uh oh. He's either about to somehow come up with a way to fix this... or he's gonna waste a few hundred bucks at Home Depot.

My sister's facial expression is... tolerant. Okay, she's not upset. She's putting up with the clinginess for Mom's benefit. Mom's the one who needs a doll to hold. Hey, we have eight of them in my room now. Not sure they count as 'comforting' though. Wait, I'm wrong. We don't have eight of them in my room. Three are on the second recliner, watching us. They weren't there when I walked in.

My afternoon is full of crazy war planning.

Dad, Mom, and the Littles all toss around ideas for how to fight this demon. Everything from putting salt around the house to Sophia trying to make enchanted amulets of protection to Sam hopping on Max's shoulders and riding the hellhound into battle. All of it sounds stupid until I remember this stuff is real.

Unfortunately, no idea stands out as a clear winner by the time Sophia needs to get to dance class. For the first time in her life, she kinda doesn't want to go. Understandable given what happened earlier. However, she succumbs to guilt because she's got a relatively important part in an upcoming recital and doesn't want to let her dance class friends down.

The 'rents are too upset to focus on much of anything beyond demonic war planning, so it's me who takes her to the dance studio. At least it's significantly closer than downtown Seattle. I'll have enough time to make it to class, assuming I don't skip tonight for a 'family emergency.'

As usual, I drive like a little old lady. Whenever I've got one of the Littles in the car, I'm hyper careful. Maybe I should go a bit faster to avoid being pulled over as suspicious. If all a cop can see of me is my head and shoulders, they're going to think I'm too young to drive. Can't charm my way out of that if the sun's up. Better to avoid the hassle entirely. Not saying I'm overly short. Just... sitting in a car doesn't exactly give anyone looking at me from the outside much of a view of my whole body.

We make it to the dance class without a problem. I've been here often enough for the other parents to recognize me and make pleasant conversation for a few minutes before everyone ends up being reabsorbed in whatever portable distractions they brought along. Phones, Kindles, physical books, whatever. I don't know how any of them can read in here. When the kids aren't stretching or doing training exercises, the music they dance to is kinda loud. Honestly, this place is even worse than the taekwondo school Sam goes to. It's less grating, though. Music is still nicer on the ears than thirty kids screaming their lungs out.

Tonight's class looks more like a rehearsal than just a class. The kids all have costumes on. I really don't understand the whole translating literature plays into dance numbers thing. This is supposed to be some kind of mash up of *Rapunzel* and *Tangled*—but only dance. There are no speaking parts. Baffles me. I mean, if those stories weren't already well established in society's collective psyche, no one would know what the hell was going on, right? How does 'interpretive dance' even work? I don't interpret anything from people moving around, swinging their arms, or whatever. Yeah, dance is pretty to watch, but 'telling stories'? I don't understand. By dance geeks for dance geeks or something to that effect I suppose.

Maybe I'm not supposed to understand how it works.

And oh, yeah. Sophia's got an important part, all right. She's Rapunzel. I think she got the part for two reasons. One: she's blonde and has unusually long hair. Two: she's the smallest kid in here so the easiest one to put on wires and haul into the air. By smallest, I mean lightest. She's not the shortest, though she's definitely the thinnest. Yes, they have a wire rig here in the dance class. I'm not entirely sure where in the story Rapunzel is supposed to be flying around. Maybe it's a dream sequence? Or maybe they're just going to use the wire rig with a cardboard 'tower' to simulate her being way up high without having to build an actual tower that will hold her weight.

She's barefoot in a white Disney Princess dress with a circlet/crown of flowers on her head. My kid sister totally looks like a giant wingless faerie. Shockingly, Sophia's having a blast. She's not scared at all of being up in the air. Maybe she got over any fear of heights with me carrying her around, flying all over London.

The door opens. It's not entirely normal for someone to arrive this late for class. I glance over, as do most of the parents. A not-quite-thirty woman walks in sporting a mop of incredibly fake red hair. The maraschino cherry coloration sets off immediate recognition: Natasha, the 'vampires should go mainstream' wingnut Wolent asked me to spy on.

She pauses by the door, glances my way, and smiles.

Got a bad feeling. She doesn't look threatening, but then again, neither does Sophia. Sophia could mess some people's stuff up big time if she wanted to. She tends to mess things up *unintentionally*, though. Come to think of it, she's getting better. It's been a while since I got smacked in the face by a giant void octopus.

I hop up from my chair in the waiting area and fast-walk over to Natasha. "What the heck are you doing here?"

She chuckles. "I could ask you the same thing. Relax. I'm not looking for sweets."

Sigh. "Are you following me?"

"Nah. Just spotted you randomly and decided to take a closer look." She watches the kids for a moment, then smiles at me. "That little blonde sprite is cute. You didn't look like the type to keep a pet. Mind if I ask what the story is?"

Ugh. "She's my sister."

"Really?" Natasha raises both eyebrows. "She's mortal."

"Duh. We all start off mortal, right?" I shrug. "Well, except maybe the Oblivare."

"The what?"

I bite my lip. "This isn't the best place to talk about that stuff. I can explain them later if you really want to know."

"You're taking your mortal sister to her dance class?" Natasha makes an 'aww' face at me like I'm some sort of stray kitten. "That's adorable. Do you do it often? I assume you make her forget you still exist after."

"Often enough, and no... I live at home."

She stares at me. "You what?"

"Long story, but I am still with my family pretending to be normal."

"That's almost tragic." Natasha lets out this long, slow sigh. "Wouldn't it be much easier on you if we didn't have to hide?"

I shrug one shoulder. "Taking my kid sister to dance class would be a lot more difficult after being burned at the stake."

"You're so convinced it will result in violence?" She folds her arms.

"I am. Humanity is not ready." I lower my voice. "There is a significant portion of the population who would gladly kill anyone who has the wrong skin color, or worships the wrong deity, or loves the wrong type of person."

"They are idiots."

"Yes. Agreed." I nod. "They are only idiots because humans are all humans inside. We're literally an entirely different sort of being. You are suggesting the mice come out of the walls and live openly with cats who occasionally eat them."

Natasha smirks. "Yeah, but we don't kill them. Cats eating mice are a bit more permanent."

"True. If you're here to try convincing me to support the idea of going mainstream, I'm afraid you're not going to have much luck." I stuff my hands in my pockets. "All I want to do is keep my head down and avoid attracting attention."

"But you—" A spurt of blood explodes out from Natasha's chest.

An instant later, the report of a gunshot comes from the parking lot.

The girls—and both boys—in the dance class all start screaming. More shots come in the door, shattering the glass. Bullets hit me in the shoulder, chest, left thigh, and right shin before I'm able to summon the coordination to jump out of the way. Natasha throws herself to the left. She lands on her front, then yowls in pain.

I hit the floor on my left side and go sliding. None of the kids or parents think I'm dead because I'm making noise. It's a roar. Mostly. Anger mixed with pain. Two pale guys in black leather jackets adorned with patches depicting pentagrams, goat-heads, and other diabolical imagery race into the dance studio at vampire speed. One's tall and thin with long dark hair. The other guy's got a buzz cut and a crummy little goatee that looks like a shoe polish stain. He's four cheeseburgers away from counting as pudgy—and he's also pointing two handguns at me.

The kids keep screaming. Some dive to the floor, others run for the back door. Sophia's stranded on the wire rig, ten feet in the air, flailing her arms. She's as helpless a target as a paper cutout at a firing range. Though, I don't think these two are here for her. They're after me. Shit! A room full of kids. This is the absolute *worst* possible place for a vampire fight. Ignoring the little burning embers from bullets in my body, I fling myself upright and charge the two diabolist vamps.

My primary goal is shoving them outside before someone in this room who can't shrug off a bullet wound gets hit. Rifle dude swings his weapon up to block me. I end up grabbing the gun and pushing on it, shoving him back out the door. Pistol guy swerves around me, dashes into the room, and grabs Alexis Snow—that ten, err, now eleven-year-old with the formerly awful tiger mom. She screams as he pulls her off her feet by a fistful of her hair, arching her back so her chest sticks out.

The vamp is raising one of his handguns to point-blank her in the heart while chanting in some creepy not-English language.

Oh, fuck.

I ram my foot up into rifle dude's groin as hard as I can, then sprout claws and launch myself at the guy about to, uhh, 'sacrifice' Alexis. We collide eight tenths of a second before he pulls the trigger. I ram him aside with enough force to make him miss. Mostly. The bullet tears a slice across the outside of the girl's arm. Better than shooting her in the heart but still. I am furious. I totally lose any care for who sees what and go full enraged kitty all over this guy. Two dozen tweens watch in horror while I rip most of the skin off this asshole's face and chest. The whole time, I'm growling in a voice too deep to be human, eyes glowing red, fangs out.

Somewhere behind me, 'noises of generalized violence' inform me that Natasha is attempting to deal with rifle guy. Can't tell who's winning or what's going on except that no one is shooting. That's probably a good thing given there are so many children here—or not. The rifle fires a few times rapidly. Zings and pings from wild ricochets come from both sides. I whip my head to the left to look. The tall diabolist vamp and Natasha are wrestling for control of the rifle, which is pointing sideways to them—right into the room full of kids.

The guy who tried to kill Alexis, despite having almost no skin left on his face or chest, still has enough fight left in him to catch me with a mother of a right hook. Yeah, that's a broken nose. I land thirty feet away among the parents, breaking one chair and scattering several others. A few parents sit there, frozen in total shock, staring. Some scream and recoil from me. Yeah... dammit. I can't blame them. I do look like a monster right now even if I'm trying to protect their kids.

Son of a bitch. This is bad.

"Stop!" shouts Sophia, her voice ragged from emotion.

The dance class goes completely silent in an instant.

I sit up out of the mess of chairs. Everything is frozen. Time has stopped moving—except for me. On the left by the door, Natasha's in the middle of performing a spinning reverse foot sweep. Rifle dude's legs stick out in front of him. He's half a second from landing flat on his back. Three small knives stick out of him that hadn't been there before.

Dreading what I'm going to see, I shift my gaze right toward the room. Ryan, the skinny elf-like boy with the big, burly biker dad lays on his side almost directly beneath Sophia, clutching his chest. Blood seeps through his fingers. Oh, no! He's been shot. I'm no doctor but the wound is so close to his heart it looks like he's got about ten seconds left to live. I want to scream an F-bomb as loud as I can but I'm too heartbroken at the expression on his face to make a noise.

Alexis is much less severely hurt, but she's screaming and sobbing. Kids all around the room are frozen in place, all either ducking for cover where they happened to be or making a run for the exit. Ms. Ramirez, the dance teacher, is slumped on the ground dead, blood oozing from her throat. What the hell? I didn't even see anything go her way.

"No!" yells Sophia, waving her arms around.

Debris, blood, ripped costumes, children, parents, chairs, and everything in the room floats up and swirls around. Five bullets unstick from inside my body and fly out—yes, that is painful as all hell, but it's brief. My wounds close. Ryan Bowman flips up onto his feet. A burst of blood appears behind and in front of him, rapidly compressing back into his chest an instant before a tiny bullet flies out of him and goes back to rifle guy. That boy's almost scrawny enough to be an honorary Wright. His costume kinda reminds me of Flynn Rider from *Tangled*.

Another bullet zooms out of Ms. Ramirez, bounces off two columns, then the ceiling on its way back to the rifle. The dance teacher pivots upward off the floor back to her feet.

Three more bullets that miraculously didn't hit anyone emerge from the walls and go back to the weapon.

Sophia left me out of the time spell to a point. It's not reversing time and memory for me. I jump into the air to get out of the way as parents drift back to their seats and the chairs I knocked over bounce back into position. The guy I clawed the shit out of gets all his skin back. His shirt and leather jacket reconstitute to an undamaged state. He and the other asshole go flying out the doors, which rapidly un-shatter. Watching a billion tiny glass shards leap up from the floor and become solid again is pretty mesmerizing.

Sophia's glowing. Nimbuses of purple-pink light surround her hands and feet. Actually, her entire body is surrounded in light, it's just brighter at the ends of her limbs. The way she's hanging there on wires certainly adds to the epicness of the moment. Yeah, she's totally gone super-powerful little anime girl.

More shocking than watching the past fifty-ish seconds rewind, Sophia looks *pissed*, not terrified. I swear I've never seen her look so genuinely enraged before. Of course, she's stuck hanging on wires, so the glower on her face is kinda reminding me of a housecat picked up against its will.

Natasha reverses out of her foot sweep. The bullet hole in her chest disappears, and she ends up standing right where she was before the shooting started. I rub the heel of my right palm into my eye. Holy crap. I stare at Ryan. He's so small and cute. The boy's standing right beside Sophia like he's trying to protect her or get her down off the wires... and he's going to die in a minute. Wait. No. Sophia reversed time. There's no rule stating that everything *must* happen the exact same way when she lets go of her hold on the cosmic clock. I've got maybe ten seconds before those two diabolists open fire. That's plenty of time to grab the boy and drag him out of here.

Or, I could maybe not be an impulsive moron.

I should turn the tables and ambush those two guys out in the parking lot *before* they shoot.

The instant I look toward the door with murder in my eyes, Sophia calls my name.

I look at her.

"Wait." She gazes into the distance, then nods as if responding to a mental conversation. Klepto appears floating in midair right in front of me, clinging to my katana like a tiny grey koala bear on the side of a tree. Sophia gestures both hands at me. "It's dangerous to go alone. Take this."

Wow. I can't believe she made a Zelda joke after what just happened. Oh, hang on. Technically, it didn't happen. Only she and I will remember what almost occurred here tonight. That's definitely for the best.

I grab my sword. "Thanks, Klepto."

"Mew!" The tiny cat teleports over to Sophia's shoulder.

"Go forth and stop those buttheads, young adventurer!" Sophia folds her arms. "I'll just, uhh, hang out here." She swishes her feet around to make the 'hang' pun more obvious.

"Oof." I shake my head.

"Hurry. Get over to the door." She waves both hands in a shooing motion. "Spell's about to drop. I can't keep holding it up for much longer."

She doesn't have to tell me twice.

I rush out to the parking lot. The two diabolist vampires are frozen in place, halfway out of a beat-up old car they drove here in. Moving traffic goes by on the road at the far end of the lot, a clear demonstration of the range limitation on Sophia's time magic. I don't bother playing fair and waiting for the chrono-bubble to dissipate. If I can take these two jerks out before they can move, I am not going to feel guilty. Katana high, I fly-charge at them.

Alas, the time stop fades away. However, I'm so close when they resume moving that the double-handgun guy's got zero chance. He has just enough time to scream, "Shi—!" before I slice his head off at the neck. Rifle guy lifts his weapon to take aim at Natasha through the doors. He blinks before pulling the trigger, twitching as if startled. To him, I disappeared from the alcove inside as though I teleported.

"Looking for me, dickhead?" I ask.

"Yow!" he shouts, swinging the rifle around to point it at me across the car's roof.

I jump into a flip over the car, uncurling sword-first out of my tucked posture to ram the katana into his chest. Gravity pulls me down on top of him. I grab the rifle in my left hand, keeping the barrel pointed away from me and into the air as we crash to the pavement. He gurgles, coughing up blood and wheezing. It takes a vampire a few seconds to lose consciousness after having their heart split in two. In that time, he summons the strength to shove me away. Thankfully, he's rapidly succumbing to his injury and lacks the coordination to get control of his weapon enough to fire a shot before he's out cold.

No noise. No one calling the police.

I right myself in midair, turning being thrown into flying, then swing around, zip back over to him, and swipe a slash through his face, cutting both his eyeballs in half and doing a whole bunch of brain damage. Crazy how easy this katana can pass through a skull with a vampire's strength behind it.

He's effectively unconscious.

Pity for him and his buddy that Follows Rules Girl is too distracted right now to pay attention to what I'm doing. She's on the floor, sobbing and clinging to Ryan Bowman's dead body. No, the kid didn't really die. He damn near almost did though, because of these two.

Like one of those guys who picks up litter in the park, I stab the severed head of pistol guy on the end of the katana and fling it into the car. It hits the door on the other side with a dull thud and plops to the floor. Then, I chuck the bodies into the back seat out of sight. After a look around to make sure no one's aware of what happened... I erase the memories of an incredibly startled soccer mom. She saw me go all John Woo on those guys. I'm in luck. She didn't really believe her eyes. Good. I reinforce the idea she imagined it and send her on her way.

I sit on the hood of the beat-up car, pull out my phone, and call 'Mike'.

A different man answers. "Hello?"

"Mike?" I ask. "It's Sarah."

He pauses for a second. "Ahh. Yes. What's up?"

"I'm sitting on two problems who could really use some sunlight. Can you send some people? I'd deal with it myself, but I've got other matters of the sisterly kind to worry about at the moment."

"What happened?" asks Mike.

"Diabolists. Same crew that made the sefil. Two of them just tried to shoot up a dance studio full of kids. They kinda lost their heads. I'd say I have no idea how the heck they found me here at my sister's dance class, but I'm guessing they had... demonic inspiration."

He's quiet again for a few seconds. "Understood. Sit tight. Help is on the way."

"Thanks."

I hang up, feeling more than a little like Vincent from *Pulp Fiction* after calling in The Wolf.

Wow. I made a phone call to get rid of the bodies of vampires I killed... and make sure they stay dead for good. How on Earth am I going to explain this to Mom?

Natasha turns around in a circle, making a WTF face. After spinning four times, she spots me sitting on the corner of the car hood and fast-walks out of the studio over to me. "How did you do that?"

"What did I do?" I ask, not totally sure what she means.

"You disappeared. I've never seen a vampire move *that* fast." Natasha glances back at the dance studio, then at me. "You got all the way out here so fast I didn't even see a blur."

Speaking of the dance studio, everything going on inside is normal. The kids are going through the routine of their Ra-Tangled-punzel mash-up like nothing ever happened. Whew. No kids are hurt. No parents are permanently scarred from watching me shred a dude.

"Oh. That." I pat the car hood beside my butt. "Two diabolists showed up to get revenge on me. Not entirely sure if they meant to kill me or torment me by gunning down a bunch of kids." I shudder at the thought. Really do *not* want to know what would've happened if the one guy managed to kill Alexis while chanting crazy ritualistic nonsense. My imagination fills in a thought: Alexis's body turning into some kind of giant demonic monster that goes on a rampage. Or, maybe the guy would've absorbed a power boost. Whatever. I don't want to know.

One thing I am sure of: those two have lost their passes to the gene pool.

"That's crazy," whispers Natasha.

"Seriously. You have no idea."

I try to give her a brief explanation of what happened while omitting certain key details I'd rather not become public knowledge. Those details are Sam and Sophia having 'powers.' I'm not trying to brag, though I do make it sound like getting rid of the sefil was all me and Ashley. I'm really not bragging. I stress how we 'got *so* lucky' and almost died. No way do I need vampire society thinking of me as the 'sefil hunter' and calling my name if another one of those damn things ever happens to exist.

Six minutes after I make the call, an unassuming black Cadillac pulls up. Virgil and Stan, both in neat black suits, get out.

"Sec," I mutter to Natasha, then slide off the hood. "Thanks for coming."

"Not a problem." Stan walks up, greeting me with a nod. "What's the issue?"

I appreciate him not calling me 'sweetie' or 'hon.' At the same time, it almost seems weird to feel like an equal or at least a respected adult. I explain what's in the backseat, what the two diabolists almost did, and that I'd be grateful if they'd arrange a sun bath. Or incineration. Crematorium ovens work just as well as the sun and they're on a much more flexible schedule.

Natasha's nuclear red eyebrows tick up a few notches hearing me casually request the permanent destruction of two vampires. They tick up another notch when Virgil and Stan are all like, 'yeah sure, no problem.' Her giving me the 'who the hell is this girl who can order permanent death'? stare is more embarrassing than anything. I don't get a thrill from having power, or even the illusion of it. This is not me getting off on some power trip. No, this is me crying to Arthur Wolent about two meanies who tried to hurt me and letting him do the dirty part.

Stan leans into the old car. He pulls out a silenced Glock and pumps a shot into something. I imagine he's shooting rifle guy in the head just to make sure he stays asleep. Other guy's beheaded, so it's not necessary to give him a lead vitamin.

After that, he hops in and starts the old car.

Virgil gets back in the Caddy, and both cars make their way out of the lot and off down the street.

Natasha gawks at me.

"What?" I ask.

"You just ordered two vampires destroyed."

"For what they did... err, I mean almost did? They deserve it." I start walking toward the dance class. "I didn't really order it. Just requested. Big guy makes the call on that. Pretty sure he's going to do it. They are diabolists."

Natasha fast-walks to catch up, then keeps pace beside me. "What the hell is a diabolist? And why do you keep talking like those vampires shot up a bunch of kids? They never made it out of their car."

"Diabolists use magic that steals powers from demonic beings and the realms they inhabit." I glance at her. "Do you believe in magic?"

She pauses when we reach the doors. "Umm. I don't know. Should I?"

"If you want to. Might be happier not knowing." I wink. "Let's just say some stuff happened, then magic made it un-happen. I can't go into any more detail than that."

"Right. Maybe I should forget it." She exhales. "Yanno, I think I'm just gonna go back to what I was doing. You're not going to change your mind about the going public thing, are you?"

"Not now. Maybe in a few centuries. Ask me again when mortals are done killing each other over tiny differences."

She chuckles. "Okay. Uhh, take it easy, huh?"

"Trying to."

Natasha waves and walks down the shopping center sidewalk.

Meh. No. I don't think she was following me. Probably did just happen to be here and saw me. She's nothing to worry about, though she did seem rather surprisingly good at fighting. Oh well. I go back inside to watch the remainder of the rehearsal.

Not long after I sit back down, something even more Universe-breaking than a time rewind happens. There's a point where 'Flynn' and 'Rapunzel' are supposed to kiss. I'm expecting Sophia and Ryan to do this stage kissing thing where they just lean real close to each other for a moment... only Sophia really goes for it. She totally kisses him for real.

The look on Ryan's face is priceless. He was apparently expecting a stage kiss too.

Some of the kids laugh. Some clap. Two get the giggles.

Sophia's blushing hard when she pulls back, though that is not a face of regret. She knows what she did... and she'd do it again.

Oh, shit. No wonder she looked so angry.

My kid sister has a crush on Ryan Bowman.

CHAPTER 30

PROTECTIVE STEPS

Sam lay on his side in bed, staring at the digital clock on his dresser across the room.

The instant it clicked to 11:00 p.m., he peeled back the covers and got up, excuse locked and loaded. If the 'rents caught him, he simply had to use the bathroom. His mission had a high degree of success since he did not need to go far: only to Sophia's room across the hall and down a little. No need to change. Pajamas would be fine for this.

Blix hopped on his back and gave a thumbs-up.

Sam crept to his door, gingerly turned the knob, then peeked out into the hall. Dark. Quiet. The only light came from under Sophia's door, a dim pink glow from her nightlight. His youngest sister tended to be afraid of the dark and couldn't sleep in a room without at least a little bit of light. Sierra, as well as him, had the exact opposite problem. Light made it difficult to sleep.

Samuel Wright was not afraid of the dark.

He was mildly apprehensive about various things that might be hiding in the dark, but the darkness itself did not scare him.

Just in case, he backed into his room and grabbed a Nerf dart gun. If any demons tried to attack him, they'd regret it. Like 007, Sam crept out of his room and made his way down the hall, on high alert as if he'd infiltrated an enemy command center. He kept his gaze glued to the parents' bedroom door. If the knob twitched, he'd change course to the bathroom.

In under a minute, his toes sank into the pink-glowing carpet by Sophia's door. There he stood for the span of a breath, listening. The girls whispered to each other inside. No sound came from the parents' room other than Dad breathing heavily in his sleep.

Mission success.

Sam knocked twice, waited a second, knocked once, waited two seconds, then knocked three times.

"Dork," droned Sierra. "You don't need a spy knock."

He opened the door and hurried inside before closing it, then whispered, "You have to know it's me and not a demon."

Sierra sat on the floor in one of her fancy nightgowns. Sierra more or less dressed like him: PJs. Only, hers were kinda plain. Plaid pants and a blue shirt. Sam had Minecraft stuff all over his PJs. Much cooler than boring old plaid.

His sisters sat on either side of a ritual circle Sophia made from construction paper, yarn strands, random beads, buttons, coins, and a few small animal bones she'd probably got from the mystics.

He hurried over to sit with them around the circle.

"This won't take long." Sophia smiled. "I've worked out a way to cast a spell of protection against the demons attacking our worst fears. I'm going to do some magic. While I do it, you guys have to think about your worst fear."

"We don't have to say it out loud or anything?" asked Sierra.

"No," replied Sophia a little too fast. "We don't."

"You don't have to be embarrassed." Sam squeezed her hand. "My worst fear is something bad happening to you guys, Mom, Dad, and Sarah. Darryl and Jordan would tease me for being lame if I told them, but I don't care. I think Darryl's worst fear is a giant centipede."

"That's kinda silly." Sophia tilted her head. "Giant centipedes don't even live in this country. Or do you mean like a D&D giant centipede the size of an alligator?"

"Now *that* would be scary." Sierra shivered.

Sam shook his head. "Nah. A real giant centipede. They're like the size of a cucumber."

"You probably don't need a spell." Sierra chuckled at Sophia. "If your worst fear is just losing your clothes at school. That's not a big deal."

Sophia's cheeks reddened. "You should talk. You didn't even want to take a bath with me in the room."

"Not the point." Sierra poked at one of the small bones on the rug in front of her foot. "I mean, you're more afraid of being embarrassed than someone hurting you? Or us? Or Mom and Dad?"

"Umm." Sophia looked down. "I guess."

"Maybe she's too innocent to think about really bad stuff being possible." Sam pointed his Nerf gun at random shadows, ready to blast any demon that showed itself.

"Or she's just refusing to go there," said Sierra in a dry tone.

"Yes. I'm refusing to go there." Sophia clapped. "Can we not?"

"Ohhhh..." Sierra pointed at her. "I get it. By concentrating on your worst fear being something so small, you're trying to trick the demons."

Sophia cringed. "No. I'm really most afraid of something stealing my clothes when I'm out in public. That's super embarrassing. Everyone would laugh at me and make fun of me for the rest of time."

Sam raised one eyebrow. Sophia didn't lie very well. Perhaps he had misjudged things when he accepted her worst fear being public shaming. Loss of her clothing wasn't a specific fear. He figured it would bother her just as much, or even more, to go flying headfirst into a trashcan in the cafeteria. A room full of kids all laughing at her expense was the *real* fear. The exact mechanism of humiliation didn't specifically matter.

However... it seemed another dread lurked beneath the surface. Sierra's statement felt right. Sophia hid her true fear. Maybe she did want to trick the demons. Perhaps she simply couldn't bring herself to say it out loud. For the purposes of the spell, she only had to think about it, anyway.

Sam held his hands out to his sisters. "Okay. Let's do it before we get caught."

"We're not going to get in trouble. Relax." Sierra rolled her eyes.

"Mom told me not to do magic after bedtime." Sophia whimpered.

Sierra nods. "Yes. But this is important. It's not like you're doing something lame. We're protecting ourselves."

Sophia closed her eyes. "Okay. Let me concentrate."

"I can't believe you kissed that kid at dance class," whispered Sierra.

"That is the exact opposite of letting me concentrate." Sophia blushed, though smiled.

Sam cringed. The *last* thing he wanted to hear about was kissing. "Demons can be anywhere."

"Right. Sorry." Sierra took a deep breath, then let it out. "Okay. Do it."

"Concentrate on what you fear the most." Sophia spoke in a trancelike voice.

Sam closed his eyes, picturing some unknown tragedy happening to his family that he failed to protect them from. He couldn't bear to think about everyone being dead, so he imagined himself called to the principal's office at school where that weird Mrs. Weber who always stared at people and rarely spoke worked. She'd tell him his whole family died. He'd been scared of death ever since Scott murdered Sarah. Before she came home, he'd been convinced something else would happen to each member of his family until only he remained. His oldest sister returning had been the most awesome thing ever. Even better that she turned into a vampire with a bunch of cool powers.

A sniffle came from Sierra.

Sam cracked open one eye.

His middle sister trembled where she sat. He'd never seen her look so scared before, nor crying like that in near silence. She'd told him when he asked about fear what she dreaded most: being caught in a school shooting. It sounded like a reasonable fear for someone their age to have. Those drills really were scary. Sierra took it a bit far, though.

She thinks about it too much. Maybe I can find another demon friend and ask them to guard the school until she's not a kid anymore.

Sophia also appeared to be on the verge of tears, though she didn't tremble. Sam suspected her 'greatest fear' not to be a fear at all, but a deep sadness. Probably the same as his: losing his family. They'd all been through some crazy stuff. Between vampires, demons, ghosts, magic, and other unknown creatures, his family certainly experienced a degree of danger most mortals never knew of.

We can beat them. Sam puffed out his chest. *It's wise to be concerned, but we don't need to be scared all the time.*

Time passed in silence.

Eventually, Sierra calmed. Sophia opened her eyes and leaned slightly forward to look at a bit of paper. "Our fears haunt us from shadows distant. Against your evil, we are resistant."

"Does it *have* to rhyme?" whispered Sierra.

"Shh," whispered Sam. "Let her finish."

"You cannot hurt us from far away," recited Sophia. "With magic strong you're kept at bay."

Sam's hand tingled where he held his sister's. Seconds later, the same tingles happened with Sophia's hand.

"Okay," whispered Sophia. "Now we all have to say 'our fears are not for you to take,' three times together." After a brief pause, she nodded.

Sam chanted, "Our fears are not for you to take" thrice, along with his sisters.

Two of the crayons in the ritual circle exploded into colored powder, sounding like tiny firecrackers.

Sierra jumped, nearly letting go of their hands. "Eek!"

"It's okay. It's trying to scare us."

A heavy *thud* shook the floor from the parent's room, like Dad falling out of bed.

Sam's eyes widened.

"Fake," whispered Sophia. "Trying to scare us."

Blix, perched on Sam's head, nodded. "Yeah. Fake. Just noise."

Sophia created an aura of light around herself, which spread over Sam and Sierra. The magical glow lingered for several seconds before fading out. "There. Done."

"Nothing happened." Sierra examined her hands.

"You're not going to see anything." Sophia smiled. "It's a defensive spell."

"How long is it going to last for?" asked Sam.

"Umm. About two weeks." Sophia leaned to one side, grabbed the old book, and opened it. She looked over a few pages, flipping rapidly back and forth until she found something. "Yeah. Two weeks. We'll need to do this again if the demon is still bothering us by then."

Sam folded his arms. "It's not going to stop in two weeks."

"How do we destroy it for good?" Sierra frowned. "I don't want to get hit by another car... or worse."

"Yeah... or have Soph get pantsed at school." Sam chuckled.

"She can't get pantsed at school. She doesn't wear pants." Sierra gestured at her. "She's all about dresses. Besides, it's not gonna get her at school. Her costume's gonna disappear right in the middle of the stage during the production when there's a whole audience watching—and Ryan's right there."

"Eep!" Sophia grabbed her face in both hands. "Don't even say that!"

Sierra cringed. "Sorry. Just trying to make a joke. So, umm, what's the spell gonna do? Are we immune?"

"Protect us." Sophia shrugged. "I'm not sure exactly how. It makes it 'much harder' for the demons to affect us in negative ways. Whatever it does, it's way better than not having it."

"Sam..." Sierra looked at him. "Can you talk to Olmaz? Ask him if he knows how we can get rid of this bastard thing."

Sophia gasped at the language.

"Yep. I'll ask him tomorrow right after school." Sam picked his Nerf gun up off the rug in preparation to go back to bed. "I'm not allowed to open doorways to Hell after bedtime."

CHAPTER 31
VAMPIRES AREN'T REAL

S am wanted to bring his Nerf gun to school.

He didn't, though. The teachers would not be amused if they caught him with it. He couldn't exactly tell the truth about why he did it. Perhaps he'd get lucky, and they'd dismiss it as childishness. Then again, in fourth grade, Dustin MacLeod got a three-day suspension because he made a finger gun gesture... something about 'zero tolerance' for anything even remotely resembling a gun. Dad said they should call the policy 'zero sense' instead.

Sam held on to a bit of anger toward the entire school system over how it had traumatized Sierra with active shooter drills. It felt like some giant bully liked to scare her and he couldn't do anything about it. He also considered the drills pretty much worthless. About the only thing they did successfully was condition the kids to think of school as a dangerous place where they could die at any minute. Some teachers even said seriously bone-headed things, like suggesting if a gunman made it into the room, everyone—including first graders—should charge *at* the guy and fight.

He didn't act on his annoyance, mostly out of confusion. For one thing, kids charging toward a shooter vs. just sitting there passively while they're mowed down didn't sound like it would make too much of a difference. Even if it sounded stupid, Sam preferred the 'go down fighting' feel to the suggestion.

Odds favored nothing would happen. The thought of how unlikely it would be for a shooter to show up at his school allowed Sam to free himself of the constant fear that practically crippled Sierra. And now, he had friends. If anything *did* happen, he felt confident either Olmaz or Mel would make a school shooter wish they'd never gotten out of bed that morning. He also had Blix with him. While the imp couldn't do the whole 'drag their soul down to an eternity of torment' thing, imps were amazing at making machinery and gadgets malfunction. Blix could effortlessly turn a school shooter into a 'school puncher.' The guns would fall to pieces before the jerk could fire a single bullet.

Sam tried to reassure Sierra nothing could happen at least twice a week since he started making friends with demons. If she took any comfort in it, she didn't show it much. He hated seeing his second oldest sister scared. Sierra talked a lot about how she'd kick the ass of anyone trying to attack their school, but he suspected she remained terrified despite having almost vampire like levels of strength and speed.

Instead of bringing his Nerf gun—since he didn't want to end up suspended or expelled—he settled for a homemade slingshot. That, he could hide easily in a side pocket of his backpack. It didn't really matter how powerful of a weapon he used. Even Nerf darts would kill demons if he wanted them to. Heck, he could use a water pistol or throw a Frisbee and pretend it's a magical spinny blade thing like from that movie *Krull* Dad loved so much. Whatever magic he had would work no matter what type of 'weapon' he used. It only needed something as a means of focusing.

He would still likely get in trouble if a teacher discovered the slingshot, though it wouldn't be as severe as something 'gun shaped.' Also, he wouldn't be stupid. The slingshot would stay out of sight unless a demon showed up. Sam knew better than to show it off to his friends.

Since he could feel the presence of demons, he didn't need to spend all day with his head on a swivel. If one came close enough to mess with him, the hairs on the back of his neck and arms would stand up. For the most part, he acted normal all day at school, finding it a little more boring than the average Wednesday. The middle of the week tended to be the slowest day, as if all his teachers experienced a 'crap, it's not Friday yet. Ugh!' mood.

Eventually, he found himself out of school for the day and over at Darryl's house, hanging out in his friend's room playing Xbox. Sam preferred the PlayStation, generally speaking, but the Xbox had some exclusive games they could only play at Darryl's. Not that Sam resented anything about his life whatsoever, but going to Darryl's was cool. Mr. Linton earned a lot of money, way more than his parents combined. His job involved banks and money, or maybe stock market stuff. Mrs. Linton was a doctor who worked at a hospital. Something serious like cardiologist. Both Darryl and his sister Miranda basically got whatever they wanted. They weren't 'spare Ferarri' rich by any means, though Miranda acted like it. Thankfully, she left the boys alone for the most part.

Sam kinda pitied Darryl in a way. His dad worked more than he spent time at home, and even when the man was around, he obviously favored Miranda. He treated Darryl just fine, though the older sister got extra helpings of attention and could do no wrong. The rivalry, almost hostility that hung in the air between Darryl and his sister bothered Sam the most. He couldn't imagine acting like that toward one of his sisters.

Still, Darryl wasn't a jerk about it. Most of the animosity came from Miranda for some silly reason. It made no sense what she could possibly be jealous of since she got the most attention already. The girl loved to talk down at Darryl, almost acting like his second mother who had the right to order him around.

Mrs. Linton leaned into the bedroom. The woman looked so much like her daughter, it's as if reality ran Miranda through an aging app on an iPhone. She seemed a little younger than Mom and significantly younger than Darryl's dad. Both she and Miranda had the same long, dark brown hair and wore it in pretty much the same style. "Boys? It's about that time."

Sam glanced down at the Xbox game controller decorated in

pixel-camo between his hands. It didn't really feel like he'd been here that long already. Still, the alarm clock on his friend's dresser showed the time as 5:57 p.m. He had three minutes to get home before Mom considered him late for dinner.

Fortunately, Darryl didn't live too far away. Sam could run through the swath of woods in a straight line and make it on time instead of following sidewalks the long way around to the cul-de-sac.

"Ack!" Sam reflexively paused the game and dropped the controller. No real point pausing it since the console would be shut off. "Thanks, Mrs. Linton."

"Dinner's almost ready, hon." She smiled at Darryl. "Go wash your hands."

Sam, Jordan, Ronan, and Darryl hurried out of the bedroom. Darryl veered to the right on his way to the bathroom while Sam led the way down the stairs to the front door. The Lintons did not have a 'no shoes in the house' policy like home. However, Sam always kicked his shoes off anyway out of habit.

He paused by the door to put his sneakers on while Jordan and Ronan kept going. By the time he stepped outside, his friends had already vanished into the trees.

"Huh. Weird." Sam shrugged.

It seemed a bit odd for them not to wait. However, this close to dinnertime, they probably both ran home as fast as possible to avoid getting in trouble. Ronan couldn't run directly home due to the distance involved. He'd be going to Sam's house to take a mirror home... or maybe he'd stay and eat there. Mrs. Lawrence had a nice new job that paid her much more than she used to make. Unfortunately, it also ate up a lot of hours. On nights when Hunter had to work and wouldn't be home to feed Ro, he stayed over.

Wednesdays weren't usually one of those nights. Hunter ought to be home to watch him.

Not wanting to be late himself, Sam wasted no time wondering why his friends took off and left him there. He sprinted into the woods, following the same route he always took. At the big, cracked tree near the center of the patch of forest, it occurred to Sam that he couldn't remember if he did his homework yet. Most of the day before going to Darryl's felt like a blur. He grumbled to himself, assuming he still had a bunch of homework to do and the rest of the night would be shot to heck.

This 'enthusiasm' to spend the rest of the time he had left before bed on school stuff slowed his sprint to a trudge. Hands stuffed in his pockets, he meandered across the small, forested area between several cul-de-sacs and emerged slightly off course onto the wrong part of sidewalk. Normally, he went directly to his backyard, hopped the fence, and entered the house via the door to the kitchen. Tonight, he'd somehow veered off to the side a little and found the street leading to his cul-de-sac.

Not a big deal. Just added another forty seconds of time.

I must be distracted by something.

Sam punted a small rock off the sidewalk onto a strip of grass not belonging to any particular house, then trudged down the street toward home, where a most unusual sight greeted him.

Six police cars, lights flashing, sat parked at his house, one of them in the driveway. A bunch of cops stood around by the porch. The front door hung open, allowing the repetitive flash of a camera snapping inside to leak out into the world.

Sam froze, staring at the scene playing out in front of him. His house looked like the cold open from a show like *Law & Order* or CSI: Miami. Perhaps CSI: Cottage Lake.

His heart beat faster, making him feel lightheaded. Did vampires attack? It must've gotten out of control for the cops to be here. For a moment, he stood at the end of the sidewalk by the point where the cul-de-sac met the street, staring across the big open circle of black paving at his house and all the flashing lights.

A guy in a plain button-down shirt who looked a little older than the uniformed officers walked out the front door. He appeared to be crying.

Heaviness welled up in the pit of Sam's stomach. Dread fell on his shoulders, nearly pushing him over forward. He managed to take a step, then another, heading across the cul-de-sac in an almost trance, a night wasted on homework, the furthest thought from his mind.

When he got within twenty feet of the driveway, he caught sight of a bloody white sheet covering a small body behind the living room couch. A tuft of blonde hair poked out from one side. Horrified, Sam hurried forward, building up to a jog, then a sprint. He wanted to scream out for Max, ask the hellhound what happened, but grief wedged like a cork in his throat, keeping him silent.

Thump!

Sam's face collided with something dark, neither hard nor too soft.

He bounced back, startled at the sight of a uniformed cop right in front of him. The dude had come out of nowhere, intercepting him and blocking his view of home. He looked fairly tall. Athletic. Neither old nor young for a cop. The guy sorta reminded him of the liquid metal terminator.

"Sorry, kiddo. Can't go in there," said the cop. "Pretty bad scene in there. Whole family's been murdered. Real shame. Go on home."

Sam took a step back, feeling like he'd been slapped in the face. The idea of his whole family being wiped out left him momentarily speechless. His jaw twitched. Tingles raged at the corners of his eyes. Not much really made him cry, though the dam prepared to break. He couldn't believe this could happen. Not like this. Not while he'd been having fun at his friend's place.

"I live here!" yelled Sam. He tried to dart around the cop, but the guy caught him and pushed him back. "Let me go!"

"You live here kid?" The cop winced. "Oof. Sorry, li'l man. Damn. Going to have to call CPS. I can't let you go in there. Your parents and sisters are all gone. Someone went hog wild with a shotgun in there. It's a real horror show. The blonde girl barely has a head left. Still have no damn idea why the sick bastard rammed a wooden stake through some of the bodies. Anyway, you can't go in. Takes one hell of a mess to make Detective Lopez cry like that."

Sam glared up at the cop. Tears didn't come. No, this didn't feel right. Not at all. What sort of jerk cop would tell a ten-year-old boy his family got murdered in such plain, uncaring terms? The guy sounded so blasé about it. A uniformed officer wouldn't say a damn thing to a boy his age. No, they'd distract and stall him with bullcrap and ice cream until someone from CPS showed up to break the news gently.

Blix! Where are you?

He waited a three count. No sign of the imp.

Fists clenched, Sam reached out mentally, trying to summon Blix like he could summon Mel or Olmaz. Nothing happened. Not even a mental answer.

Sam frowned. *Okay. Something's messing with me. This isn't really happening.*

He glared up at the cop. "Nice try going for my worst fear, but this is not believable. There is a lot wrong here, but the biggest error you made is a shotgun can't hurt my oldest sister. What happened to her?"

The cop examined his fingernails. "Hunters got her first. She's been incinerated. They shot your old man when he tried to get between them and the tiny bloodsucker. Sick bastards pinned her to the wall with a stake like a bug in science class."

"What are you talking about?" Sam scoffed. "There's no such thing as vampires."

"Sorry, kid. Some people know." The cop flashed a faint smirking grin. "You're an orphan now, bud. It's not as bad as it sounds. I'm sure you'll find a foster home that won't beat you too badly. You are a bit of a smartass though. Might want to dial that back a bit."

Sam reached for the slingshot pocket on his backpack, absolutely intending to drill a rock into this cop's forehead.

The officer's amusement abruptly shifted to an expression of 'oh crap!', which confused Sam since he hadn't taken the weapon out into view yet.

A reality ripple appeared to Sam's right, a few feet away. Shimmering white energy spread out from a point like a stone fallen into a pond. At the center, a small imp claw poked out, grabbing the side of the tiny hole. A second hand appeared and grasped the other side. The hands shoved outward, widening the tiny breach. Blix, waist deep in an opening a mere ten-inches wide, stuck himself halfway out and reached toward him.

"Sam! Come!"

He whipped the slingshot up and fired at the 'cop.' An ordinary chick-pea-sized pebble he'd found in his backyard blasted through the man's head like a rail gun slug moving at ten times the speed of sound. Rather than blood or gore, black gunk trailed upward in a pin-straight line following the impossibly fast rock. The fake police officer made a face of absolute confusion, then fell over backward, his body stiff as a mannequin.

Sam grabbed Blix's little hand.

The imp pulled him off his feet. Sam yelled 'whoaaaaa' as he flew headfirst into the tiny hole and careened down into endless black-ness, waving his arms and legs. Right as he got the idea to yank his shirt off and conjure his wings, he crashed into something soft.

Sam jolted, finding himself in the cafeteria at school. He sat hunched over a table, using his backpack full of books for a pillow. Sleep crumbs fused his eyes mostly shut. Blix sat on the table beside the bag, invisible to everyone in the room except for Sam.

"You had a fake real," whispered Blix. "Other place. Not here. Not dream... but not real."

"Ugh." Sam pushed himself up to sit, then wiped his eyes. "I get it. So much for that protection spell."

Blix flashed a fanged, toothy grin. "Spell help. You not believe faster. Not emotional wrecking."

He yawned. "It got into my head because I'm tired. We stayed up too late on a school night."

"Yes." Blix nodded. "Try to sad you to death. Not work."

A momentary pang of dread came and went. Sam sat taller and peered across the cafeteria. Four tables away, Sophia—perfectly alive and not under a bloody sheet—sat there talking to some of her class-mates. Sierra, two tables past her with the seventh-graders, sat by herself, also napping on her bookbag.

Whew. Sam narrowed his eyes in anger. *Okay. Now I'm really mad at this butthead demon.*

CHAPTER 32
HER DEEPEST DREAD

Sophia walked along, gazing down at her feet.

The glitter embedded in her dark purple ballet flat style shoes sparkled in the late afternoon sunlight. Her pale pink frill socks bounced in time with her stride. She gripped the straps from her backpack out of habit. The older girl who picked on her briefly in first grade for being so small hadn't tried to pick her up by the backpack in years. Sophia had to be one of maybe eight kids in the entire school past third grade who actually wore their backpack properly. Most kids tended to just swing it over one shoulder.

Made it through the day without the demon stealing my clothes. She exhaled. *Yep. He's going to do that to embarrass me and I'm going to cry. My worst fear is having everyone laugh at me because my clothes disappeared in the middle of class.*

She reached the end of the sidewalk by the cul-de-sac and stepped down onto pavement, swinging wide into the street so Mr. Niedermeyer wouldn't be tempted to come running out the door to yell at her. Sometimes, he even shouted at kids who were on the sidewalk in front of his lawn. He didn't own the sidewalks. Unlike Sarah or Sierra, Sophia never felt tempted to antagonize the guy by walking back and forth on the sidewalk because it's public property.

After stepping inside her house, Sophia stooped to pull her shoes off, then removed her socks. Except on really cold days, she didn't like wearing socks in the house. It made them dirty plus she tended to slip and fall over in the kitchen. Also, cold days demanded thick, fuzzy socks. These thin frilly things didn't do any good for warmth. She wore them because they looked pretty.

Sophia tucked her flats into the shoe rack by the door, then turned toward the stairs, intending to go up to her room—but froze in place.

Mom and Dad sat on the sofa beside each other, holding hands and making almost the same faces they had on the night they told Sophia that Sarah had been found dead. A heavy mood hung over them.

She dropped her bundled-up socks.

No. No. No. No. No.

Tears rolled down her face.

"Soph?" asked Mom in an overly gentle tone. "Come here, sweetie. There's something we need to tell you."

Dad cleared his throat, seemingly fighting a difficult battle to avoid losing his composure.

No. No. No. No. No.

Sophia shook her head rapidly, trying not to believe her eyes. She didn't go back in time. Sarah wasn't dead. Well, she was... but not *dead* dead.

After a moment of her not taking a step, Dad got up and walked over. Without a word, he scooped her up into a hug and carried her to the sofa, where he sat again with her in his lap. Mom took her hand.

"There's no easy way to say this." Mom looked down. "You know things have been getting increasingly crazy these past few months."

"Yeah," said Dad, his voice cracking.

Her parents did not appear to be going through the same speech they did *that* night. She hadn't gone back in time to relive the worst night of her life.

"Sarah has decided to leave, in order to—" Mom choked up.

"No!" shouted Sophia.

Mom took a breath, then continued. "She wants to protect us from stuff like the demon, vampires, all the craziness."

"No!" Sophia burst into sobs, pounding her fists against Dad's shoulders. "Please, no! I don't want her to go away!"

"Sweetie..." Mom squeezed and relaxed her grip on Sophia's hand repetitively, as if working a stress ball. "It's hard, but... for the best. She's asked us to decide if we want her to alter our memories so we think she died that night or just make us forget she ever existed at all."

Grief weighed Sophia's voice down too much to speak. Her attempt to shout 'no' resulted in a wail nowhere close to words. She stopped pounding on Dad's chest and bawled into his shoulder, sobbing as hard as she did the night they told her the older sister she *so* looked up to and loved was gone forever.

Dad sniffled, rubbing a hand up and down her back. "It won't be painful once she makes us forget. Would you rather think she's dead or just not have any memory of her at all?"

Sophia refused to answer the question because she couldn't bring herself to consider it. In between sobs, whenever her voice managed to cooperate enough, she cried out 'no' or 'I want her to stay' or a desperate attempt of 'I'm going with her.'

Almost pain nibbled at her left ear.

Klepto licked her ear twice, then nibbled again on her earlobe, tugging.

Not now. Please leave me alone. Sophia lapsed into hard sobbing again.

A faint kitteny growl flooded her left ear, then another nibble—this one harder.

"Ow! Stop!" Sophia wailed. "What are you doing?"

Mom tilted her head, flashing a fake smile. "I'm sorry, Soph. It's better for everyone."

"Mew, mrrrrf!" said Klepto—right into her ear.

The mew plus a noise like a purr combined with a meow translated to the kitten telling her to think about Sierra getting angry at the PlayStation. Specifically, Klepto thought about the word Sierra sometimes shouted so loud the neighbors heard it. The one that started with 'bull' and ended with being grounded off video games for three days if Mom got wind of it.

Sophia sniffled back her tears and wiped her eyes. "Crap."

"Mew," said Klepto, thinking *yeah*.

Mom and Dad sounded far too okay with the idea of Sarah going away. How many times had Mom *ordered* her to stay and not even consider leaving? Sophia made no secret of how much she adored her oldest sister. If anyone in the family would be totally destroyed over losing Sarah as much as her, it would be Mom. Dad would be a wreck, though he could probably still find a way to function after the loss. Mom, not so much.

Sorrow burst into anger.

Stupid demon! It knows! It saw right through me. She scowled. Her worst fear did not actually involve being caught randomly naked at school. Not like that would ever even happen again. The nightmare she sometimes had of being suddenly without clothing in class was just a dream that's not ever supposed to happen for real, a subconscious manifestation of social anxiety and fear of embarrassment. It's not supposed to be literal because it's so super unlikely to ever happen.

Her worst fear, in fact, wasn't embarrassment in public, but losing her big sis. Of course, she dreaded harm befalling anyone in her family... but something about Sarah. Some kids had security blankets. Some developed imaginary friends. For whatever reason, Sophia latched onto Sarah instead. Even those rough times in the months before Scott stabbed her when Sarah always seemed to have better things to do than spend time with her kid sister, Sophia tried not to feel like her big sis hated her.

The demon knew. Despite all her attempts to misdirect it by repeating her fake worst fear over and over, it still knew.

Sophia growled to herself. "This is fake." Duh. She smacked herself in the forehead. "Of course it's fake. I walked home from the bus stop alone. No Sierra. No Sam. They're not even here."

"What are you saying, sweetie?" asked Mom in a tone of voice thick with malice that sounded way too much like the Other Mom from *Coraline*. "Is something wrong?"

"Get out of my mind!" shouted Sophia.

Her surroundings shifted in an instant. The living room at home became her first period math class, head down on her arms crossed over the desk. A few kids sitting near her snickered. Somehow, Mr. Walters hadn't noticed she fell asleep in his class. She hastily adjusted her posture, sitting up straight and widening her eyes.

I'm awake! Please don't notice I passed out.

The teacher continued writing some math problems on the whiteboard. Perhaps her entire nap took place while his back had been turned. According to the clock, she'd only been in the room for six minutes. Her school day just started.

Ugh. We stayed up too late. No wonder Mom wants us going to bed early.

A shadow moved out from behind the teacher's desk. Not the silhouette of a person, merely an amorphous blob of darkness. None of the kids in the front row—on either side of Sophia, who also sat right up front in the middle—noticed it. She assumed this due to the lack of screaming and pointing.

There you are! Sophia growled under her breath and thrust her right hand out toward the shadow.

As much as she'd ever wanted to destroy something in her whole life, she wanted to smash the thing that gave her such a horrible nightmare. Or daymare. Or whatever the technical term was for a transitory quasi-reality saturated in strong negative emotions with the potential to literally harm her.

In her haste, she neglected to concentrate on any particular means of destruction. Her magic, and the universe, took the path of least resistance when left to fill in the blanks. Rather than an obvious fireball forming around her hand and going flying—which generally didn't really happen with magic outside of movies—a nearby wall outlet by the wastebasket exploded, releasing a searingly bright electrical arc into the shadow.

The demonic entity burst into a shower of greasy black smoke and inky ectoplasm.

Now most of her classmates screamed. Lights flickered. Screams came from other classrooms. Someone in the distance yelled about fire.

"Oops," whispered Sophia to herself, her voice drowned in the chaos.

The fire alarm went off a moment later, adding an electronic whoop-whooop-whoop and strobe lights to the already intolerably loud chaos around her.

Trying to act as casual and unguilty as possible, Sophia shuffled along with the rest of her class as they rapidly evacuated the school building and gathered in the yard outside. Since it hadn't been a fire drill, and seemed like a real situation, no one stopped to grab their coats from the back of the room. She folded her arms, shivering in the mid-September breeze.

Klepto appeared in a flash and curled around her neck, a warm fuzzy ball of purring.

Thanks.

Eventually, a whole mess of fire trucks showed up.

It took a bit over ten minutes of standing around after the fire department arrived before the students stopped respecting class groupings. No one expected to be going back into the building any time soon like for a fire drill, so the kids spread out into friend clusters, or clique groups, or the loners just kinda standing off to themselves. Most of the voices around her discussed if they'd be going home early. A few kids said they saw flames shoot out of electrical plugs. One boy said the garbage can in his classroom burst into flames for no apparent reason.

Sam and Sierra came jogging over to her.

"What did you do?" whispered Sierra.

Sophia bit her lip. "Do I look that guilty?"

Sam nodded. "To us. Yes. But we know you."

"Drat." Sophia closed her eyes. *It was not mischief. I did good. I blew up a demon. No reason to feel guilty. I won't get in trouble.* She exhaled, then pulled her siblings a few paces away from any other kids so they could whisper about crazy stuff. "Saw a demon in my math class."

"Heh." Sierra snickered. "Figures it would be in *math* class. Evil attracts evil."

"I like math," snapped Sophia in an indignant tone.

Sam folded his arms. "I thought I felt something. Been looking for it all day."

"All day?" Sierra blinked at him. "It's not even nine yet."

"It tried to get me in the cafeteria right after we got here." Sam frowned. "I felt it there, but couldn't see it before it ran away. Too many people in the caf. What happened, Soph?"

She stared down. "I fell asleep at my desk and it gave me a nightmare."

"Nightmares aren't that bad." Sierra bit her lip. "I mean, they suck, but it's over as soon as we wake up. I guess the protection spell changed it so the demon gave us nightmares instead of doing stuff for real like sending another car at me."

"Maybe." Sophia scratched at her arm. She didn't really know what the spell did. Maybe the demon would've tormented Sarah so bad she would've decided to go away thinking it best for the family, but because of the protection magic, it only happened as a nightmare.

"So, what was your nightmare?" asked Sierra. "You get pantsed in gym class?"

Sophia stared at the ground.

"You're gonna lie." Sierra put an arm around her. "I know that face. Just be honest. I swear I won't make fun of you."

"I'm being childish," whispered Sophia. "I'm afraid if I say it out loud it might happen. My real worst fear isn't getting pantsed. It's, umm... you're gonna think I'm lame."

"We already think you're lame." Sierra grinned. "Our whole family is lame. No one thinks we're cool."

"I think you guys are cool." Sam smiled. "And I don't give a butt what anyone else thinks of us."

Sophia laughed, unexpectedly finding the comment funny.

"Okay. I'm really afraid that Sarah's going to think she's gotta go away to protect us... and make us forget she exists."

Sierra's expression fell flat. Her slightly older sister seemed worried.

"Sarah's not gonna leave." Sam shook his head. "Mom made her swear."

"Not unless the demons get into her head or they scare her so much she thinks we're all going to die if she doesn't." Sierra shivered.

Sophia tapped her foot, trying to think of a way to protect Sarah from demons.

"Also, you enchanted yourself." Sam poked Sophia in the side. "Sarah *can't* make you forget anything. You're also forgetting how that stuff works. The stronger a thing is in someone's head, the harder it is for vampires to delete it. It's really hard to make people forget their families... unless they don't really like them."

"We don't have that problem." Sophia grinned, slightly choked up.

"Ugh. Stop it. You're gonna make me do something mushy in public," muttered Sierra.

Sam and Sophia chuckled.

"You killed it?" whispered Sam.

"I think so. The spell caused a whole bunch of electricity to jump out of the wall and fry it." Sophia made an explosion gesture. "It went splat. Smoke and slime."

Sam flashed an 'aha' face. "That's why the whole school went dark. The main circuit breaker tripped... or melted."

"Sparks came flying out of the plugs in my class." Sierra waved her hand about excitedly. "The wastebasket caught fire."

Blix's voice came from Sam's backpack.

"He said you just sent it home." Sam sighed in a 'yeah, figured' manner. "But that specific demon won't be able to come back here for a long time."

"That's good, right?" Sierra raised both eyebrows.

"Kinda. The sefil demon's got tons of minions. He'll just send another one. Stay alert." Sam patted the little pocket holding his slingshot.

"Attention students," called Principal Weber over a bullhorn. "The fire department has just assured me the building is safe to enter. Everyone, please return to your classes."

"Wow." Sophia blinked. "She *can* speak."

Sierra groaned. "Already? That wasn't much longer than a fire drill."

"Guys..." Sam patted his sisters on the shoulder, one hand each. "Stay alert. It's going to try again."

CHAPTER 33
TOO REAL

Sierra set her chin in her hands, elbows on the desk, and stared blankly into space.

The room still smelled like burning paper. A dark stain marked the wall where the wastebasket had been. No one freaked out too much about the little fire set off by sparks leaping from the power outlet into a plastic bucket full of paper. Dad attempting to grill in the backyard made bigger flames. Mrs. Burke put it out herself with a fire extinguisher from the closet before the alarms even went off. Seems the fire department took the whole waste-basket out just to be safe.

Social studies bored the crap out of Sierra. Dad sometimes joked about how when he was a kid, they called the class 'history,' but the school boards responsible for educational content kept watering things down so much, they couldn't call it 'history' anymore for the same reasons Velveeta couldn't legally call itself cheese. The powers that be don't want to teach kids anything that might empower them to question or challenge the government—or paint the country in a less than perfect light.

Most of her classes bored her. Mom said she was bored in school because she's too smart for it. The classwork was trivial, so she's not engaged. Of course, the idea of trying to test into advanced classes didn't appeal either. That would mean work. The more her mind wandered, the more she wanted to go home and draw. Sarah had an amazing idea the other day. Making video games only required tons of math if she wanted to be the person programming all the guts of the game engine. That's only one part of it, though. Someone's gotta do all the character design, the level design, making all the artwork. She didn't need math to do art. She also liked comics and anime and stuff like that.

Dad told her that creative people tend to feel out of place in the 'school-to-office' factory pipeline. Sierra definitely felt out of place, like a mouse sitting in a cage hoping no cats walked by that day.

She felt pretty safe from the demon, at least. Sam and Sophia both fell asleep. Neither one of them had the nerve to break rules like she did. Sierra took steps to protect herself. She snuck into the teacher's lounge as soon as they got off the bus that morning and helped herself to some coffee. Nope. No sleeping in first period for her. She even had two good excuses ready for being caught. One: they don't have coffee in the middle school cafeteria, so she had to use this machine. Two: no one ever told her she wasn't allowed to use that coffee machine.

Everyone just sort of assumed that students weren't permitted to wander into the teacher's lounge and fix themselves a cup of coffee. No one ever actually said out loud she couldn't.

Fortunately, the room happened to be empty, and she got in and out before any teachers showed up. Not that she looked forward to yet *more* school, but at least when she made it to ninth grade, she could get a cup of coffee right from the cafeteria there. She bristled at being considered 'too young' for stuff like coffee, or staying up late, or driving, or whatever. That Sophia's magic might keep her twelve years old for an unusual amount of time irked her. However, being thought of as a 'child' longer than normal was a small price to pay for not feeling helpless. She could keep up with vampires now. At least, baby vampires. Good enough. She'd suffer the indignity of being thought of as a kid for a while longer. If the magic even did that. Sophia didn't know for sure… or maybe she did but chickened out of telling her.

I should promise not to be mad and tell her she can be truthful. If I'm going to stay twelve for years, I need to know. Something like that's going to require mental preparation.

She leaned back in her chair and peered down at her chest. Still nothing. Checking herself in the mirror every day didn't seem to be encouraging her body to develop any faster. Some of the girls in her class group already sorta had boobs, or at least the beginnings thereof. Not her. She couldn't care less about vanity or if the boys looked at her. The instant she noticed something developing, she could relax about the idea of being stuck as a tween for an extended period. Alas, her body refused to give her a clue.

Crap. If I'm gonna be stuck like this… should I like, fake it so people don't ask questions? She squirmed at the idea of wearing a bra and padding it with socks or whatever. Sarah always grumbled about how much she hated bras. Mom wasn't too fond of them either, but unlike Sarah, she wore them anyway, something about work decorum. Mom bought Sierra some 'training bras,' but she didn't bother with them much. What, exactly were they supposed to 'train'? Did someone invent them to train girls to get used to putting up with having a torture device strapped around their chests for the rest of their lives or did they supposedly 'train' the boobs to do something?

Somehow, that turned into the idea of 'trained boobs' doing tricks, barking, and begging for dog treats in her mind.

Sierra laughed out loud.

Class stopped. Everyone looked at her.

"Ms. Wright," said Mrs. Burke. "Do you find the Declaration of Independence humorous?"

"No, Mrs. Burke," droned Sierra.

"Then perhaps you'd like to enlighten the class on what you find so amusing that you laughed in the middle of class?"

"Uhh, no thanks." Sierra blushed. "I'll just take the detention, thanks."

Mrs. Burke shook her head. "Please, at least pretend to be paying attention, okay?"

"Sorry, Mrs. Burke." Sierra shrank in her seat.

Her social studies class didn't get any more exciting. Sierra remained as motionless as possible, like a prey animal waiting for the pack of lions to move on. In this case, she waited for the rest of the class to lose interest in staring at her. A random laugh in class hardly amounted to the most embarrassing thing that could befall a kid. She probably wouldn't get teased over it. At least Mrs. Burke let it slide without detention or pressuring her to explain why she laughed.

"All right. Everyone go to page forty-two in the textbook," said Mrs. Burke. "Read through to the end of page forty-five. You've got twenty minutes. Then we'll be discussing why John Hancock made his name so big."

"Giant hand cock," said a boy somewhere to the left, before snickering.

Most of the class chuckled, except for Sierra.

"That's an hour, Daniel." Mrs. Burke frowned. "See you after school today."

Daniel groaned.

Sierra opened the textbook to the appointed page. It talked about the signing of the Declaration. *Yeah. Sure. A bunch of rich white guys who murdered a whole bunch of Native Americans and owned slaves wanted to be 'free from tyranny'.*

Deep silence settled over the classroom as all the kids read, or at least pretended to be reading.

Minutes later, three loud bangs echoed in rapid succession from the hallway outside.

Sierra nearly wet her pants when a fourth gunshot went off. Glass shattered somewhere. Terrified shrieks of children filled the air. A few kids around her also screamed. Some tried to shush the others, whispering about 'remember the drills' and 'we gotta be quiet.'

Mrs. Burke jumped out of her chair, zooming to the classroom door. She grabbed the special locking thing and went to ram it into the bracket by the knob—but the door flew open before she could, smacking her in the face and knocking her on her ass.

A relatively young man, all in camo with a motorcycle helmet on, stepped in, brandishing a rifle.

Without the slightest bit of hesitation, Mrs. Burke rolled back to her feet and threw herself at the guy, trying to tackle him out of the room. Two shots blasted out of her back. Lifeless, the teacher collapsed to the floor.

All the kids around Sierra screamed. Some begged. Some hurriedly whispered at their smartphones telling their parents they loved them. Some ran to the back of the class and started trying to break the windows out.

Sierra couldn't move. She sat there like a statue, paralyzed in terror, staring at the faceless guy.

She'd imagined this moment happening every day for years. Ever since she'd first tasted vampire blood, and the power it gave, her imagination changed. She'd put herself into the scene as a superhero. She'd fly out of her chair and kick ass, just like playing *Call of Duty*.

The man pointed his weapon randomly at the class and fired. Blood sprayed from the cluster of students in the left side of Sierra's peripheral vision. She couldn't tell who'd been hit, only that the screaming got louder.

The tremendously loud *boom* snapped her out of her panic.

Growling, Sierra jumped out of her chair and ran at the gunman. She had the speed to be on him before he could even react to her moving. She had the strength to kick his balls up into his throat and break both his arms, maybe smash his jaw.

Only... she didn't.

He turned to face her as she charged in no faster than an ordinary girl, tilting his head in confusion. Sierra belted out a war cry and hurled herself at him. The man caught her, grabbing a fistful of her shirt in his left hand. All the punches she rained on him bounced off his Kevlar, too weak to bother him. A hint of 'what the hell are you trying to do' peeked out from under the insanity in the eyes lurking behind the plastic visor of his bike helmet.

What the f—

The man threw Sierra to the floor on her back, then stomped on her chest, pinning her down under his left foot. Without a word, he swung his AK-47 up so the tip of the barrel hovered less than an inch away from her nose. Her heart stopped.

Sierra broke out of the waking nightmare at her desk. She jumped out of her chair, screaming and flailing. Her foot caught the desk leg, bending the steel. She spun left and right, desperate to get away from the rifle she still believed was about to end her life... only it hadn't been real.

She found herself curled up on the floor of her social studies class, shaking, sobbing, and sorta growling.

Everyone gathered around her, looking concerned. Even Daniel Rios, the boy who relished every opportunity to tease or make fun of anyone, appeared worried.

"Hey, you okay, Sierra?" asked Daniel.

"She almost got hit by a car yesterday," said Kimberly Kirstein. "Don't pick on her."

"Almost?" Kevin Murphy whistled. "She got thrown like fifty feet."

"Ms. Wright?" asked Mrs. Burke in the softest voice she'd ever heard come out of the woman.

Sierra couldn't stop crying. She tried her best to look stoic, which didn't really do much. No voice wanted to come out of her. She couldn't make herself say a word, only stare through the crowd of students surrounding her at the door... waiting for the shooter to burst in.

CHAPTER 34
NOT OKAY

Something super weird happens to me.

I wake up at 12:31 p.m. Nothing feels weird, nor do I feel unusually groggy or stiff. There's no hunter looming over my bed with a stake and crossbow at the ready. It's bizarre for sure. I've never been able to wake this early without a damn good reason since becoming a vampire. Something external must be at play here. Question is what. And how bad is it?

Oh well. No sense lying here in bed wondering. It's clear I am not going to fall back to sleep after a few minutes, so I get up. Suppose this is a good time to get the vacuuming done, since no one is trying to sleep now. Well, no one but Ashley and Chloe and no amount of vacuum noise will wake them up.

I head upstairs, then go to the second floor with the vacuum, intending to start at the top. Only... looks like the Littles were in an extreme rush this morning. The bathroom is an absolute shambles. Ugh. Vacuuming can wait.

Even more odd than my unnaturally early awakening, the tub's got a glowing layer of ruby dust all over it. As far as I remember, Sophia hasn't used ruby dust for magic since she enchanted Sierra. Also, my bath bombs don't generally glow. Third problem: I can't wipe it off. The dust doesn't seem to really be there. It's an illusion or something. Or maybe it's out of phase with reality. I dunno. This is above my pay grade. My seemingly futile attempt to scrub the bathtub seems to abruptly work. Despite the glowing glittery residue ignoring the scrubby sponge, it all disappears at the same time like a video game task. Instead of the sponge making clean trails in the luminous red substance, I just do the 'cleaning animation' for a few seconds over the same small area and the entire tub looks clean. It's like the little peasant guys in RTS games hammering at a wooden framework for five minutes and it suddenly turns into a completed building.

Yeah, definitely not normal.

I'll ask Sophia about it when she gets home from school.

I tidy up the bathroom, vacuum the upstairs hall, then go downstairs and get started on the living room. Maybe I'll peel the sofa cushions and run the covers through the laundry. Yeah, it's been a while since the sofa got some love. I head down there and start unzipping the cushions.

The phone rings.

"I got it," I yell like a freakin' nine-year-old, to Dad, who's working in his little office down the short secondary hall out of the living room.

I zip to the kitchen and grab the cordless from the charging base. "Hello?"

"Hello. Mrs. Wright?" asks a woman.

"Umm, no. This is Sarah. Mom's at work. Can I take a message?"

The woman pauses. "Is your father available? This is Principal Weber from North Lake."

"Yeah. He's here. What's up? I'm eighteen if it matters."

"There's been an incident with your sister. Would your father be able to come pick her up?"

I glance at the clock on the stove. It's a few minutes after one.

Shit. My mind races trying to imagine what the reason for the call is. Did the demon do something? Did Sierra lose her temper and break some kid in half? Did Sophia try to help someone with magic and turn the entire school into a giant donut?

"Yeah. Do you need to talk to him or can I just tell him we need to go to the school right away?"

"It's all right to ask him to come pick her up," says the woman. "I can explain the situation when he arrives."

Hmm. The woman sounds concerned, not angry. This isn't good. "Okay. We'll be there as soon as possible."

"Thanks, dear."

I hang up and yell, "Daaaad!"

LACK OF INFORMATION about what exactly happened makes Dad nervous on the ride to school.

We take his new Sentra, obviously. It's the nicer car and, well, he's driving. Better he does it since I'm on borrowed time. I shouldn't be awake at this hour, so I'm afraid of spontaneously passing out at any moment. To avoid working ourselves into a panic, we don't talk much about what we think is going on. The only thing I say is that Principal Weber sounded more concerned than angry, so I don't think Sophia or Sierra did something bad—or got hurt.

Dad parks in the closest possible space to the entrance, ignoring the sign 'reserved for teacher of the year.'

We get out of the car and run inside. Dad leads the way into the office.

The trio of older office ladies look up at him.

"Hi. I'm Jonathan Wright. Got a call from the school about picking my daughter up? No one's told me anything about why, though."

The nearest woman, who's a bit heavyset with curly blackish-grey hair, perks up. "Oh, yes. I'll let Mrs. Weber know you're here. You can find Sierra at the nurse's office. Go back out into the atrium, turn left as you face away from this office, and it's the second door on your left."

"Thanks." Dad nods to her.

I offer a weak smile to the office ladies, then turn on my heel and follow him.

We enter the nurse's station. It's a moderately large room that sorta looks like a miniature emergency room with an exam table, cabinets, and medical stuff. An open archway in the back leads to a smaller office containing two desks and one nurse.

Sierra's sitting on a padded bench with her back against the wall separating the nurse's office from the clinic area. She looks fine, merely sullen as hell. It's difficult to read her expression. The look could mean anything from 'I almost died' to 'I'm going to be expelled' to 'I did something so damned embarrassing I can never again show my face in this building.'

Upon seeing her alive, unhurt, and as normal as Sierra gets, Dad relaxes with an audible release of air.

That noise coming out of him makes Sierra look up. As soon as she sees us, she bolts off the bench and zooms into a hug, clinging to Dad and trembling.

Oh, shit.

This is not like her at all.

A squeak comes from the nurse's chair as she stands. Sierra hastily forces herself to seem calmer, lets go of the cling-hug, and tries to act all casual and normal.

A short black woman in medical scrubs walks up to Dad, introducing herself as Melodie Davis. "You're Sierra's father?"

"Yes." Dad nods. "What's going on? No one's told me anything yet."

"It looks like Sierra suffered a panic attack in the middle of class." Melodie smiles reassuringly at Sierra. "She's medically fine right now. From what her teacher told me, it sounds like she had a doozy. Fell out of her chair in such an extreme state of panic she kicked a dent in the desk leg. It's pretty unusual for anyone to be strong enough to do that... but in moments of extreme emotion, it's not unheard of. Though, I suspect something else happened. Your daughter's leg would be bruised if she'd kicked the desk hard enough to bend it, and I didn't see any sign of an injury."

I bite my lip.

Sierra looks down, ashamed.

"Hmm. Panic attack..." Dad shifts his weight.

"It can happen to kids who've never had them before. Is everything all right at home?" asks Melodie.

"Fine as far as I'm aware." Dad manages a weak smile. "Things have been pretty normal for us lately."

It's good he added the 'for us' at the end. Stops him from telling a lie.

"I already told you, everything's fine at home." Sierra stuffs her hands in her pockets. "It's the stupid shooter drills that are freaking me out. I thought I heard a gunshot in the hallway. Why do you guys torture us with that bullshit? Not like kids are going to do anything to stop a gunman."

Melodie offers a sympathetic wince. "I'm sorry, hon. I'm a nurse. I've got nothing to do with that policy. I agree with you, though. It's traumatizing."

She pulls Dad off a bit to talk about considering the idea of having Sierra see a therapist. Principal Weber arrives and joins the conversation. Sounds as if Sierra happened to be sitting quietly in class, then flung herself to the floor, freaking out like a gunman had just stormed into the room. It took her over ten minutes, staring and shaking in the nurse's office before she could speak. One panic attack isn't necessarily a huge deal, though it's going into Sierra's school record. Since the nurse and principal are far enough away from us so they can speak with Dad and not have Sierra listen in, my sister edges closer to me.

"Wasn't a panic attack."

I put an arm around her.

"Okay, maybe it was. But... it didn't just happen to me. The damn demon did it to me." Sierra cling hugs me. "I saw it happening. A guy barged into my class with a gun. The barrel was right in my face. I woke up like the second before he killed me."

Bastard. I grumble. "Just a dream."

"Not exactly. If Soph didn't cast that protection spell, I might've really died."

Dammit. She understands the pseudo-reality thing with demonic hallucinations. An unusual urge shifts my attention to the principal. There's something off about how she keeps glancing over at Sierra. Grr. Stupid Sun. Without even realizing it, I divert power from shields. In seconds, it feels like I've gone from a comfortable temperature to the Sahara desert in mid-August. Evidently, Sierra had a pretty serious freakout in class. Principal Weber thinks Sierra is legitimately insane and is worried *she* might turn out to be a school shooter. She's already making plans to find an excuse to expel or transfer my kid sister—or if those fail, get CPS involved. Seems suspicious. Something is making her focus on Sierra with negative attention. Ack! Nope. I mash the delete button. My sister's episode wasn't *that* bad. No need for her to do anything else. No CPS. No trying to get her sent to a mental hospital for evaluation. Deleted.

The instant my need to fix this is satisfied, I drop offline. A haze of smoke surrounds me. I feel more thoroughly roasted than if Jeff Ross did a one-hour monologue about me.

"Ms. Weber?" asks Melodie. "Are you feeling all right?"

The principal stares into the Eighth Dimension for another twenty seconds, then looks around as if she forgot where she is or why she's in the nurse's station. "Yes, Melodie. I'm fine. Too darn busy. If you'll excuse me..."

Both Dad and the nurse blink in surprise as the principal abruptly walks away right out of their conversation.

"She's fine now as far as I can tell." Melodie smiles. "Though it's likely not a bad idea to let her talk to someone."

"All right. We'll definitely look into it. Thanks." Dad shakes hands with Melodie, then walks over to us.

The nurse pauses there a moment looking at the door where the principal went, shaking her head in confusion and disbelief.

Sierra stops cling-hugging me as soon as the nurse might look our way.

"It's been suggested I bring you home to remove you from the environment that's causing your stress trigger." Dad traces one finger over Sierra's forehead, moving her hair off her eyes. "The choice is yours. Do you want to have the rest of the day off or go back to class?"

Mom hurries into the nurse station, then stops short, blinking at us. "Oh, Jonathan? You're already here. They didn't mention anything about calling you."

"Yeah." Dad tugs Mom into a brief hug and gives her a little kiss. "Sorry if you tried to call me. Ran out of the house so fast I left my phone."

"I wasn't sure what happened. The school called me, too." Mom looks Sierra over. "Is she all right?"

"Yeah," drones Sierra. "If it's okay, I do wanna go home. I'm still kinda freaking out."

"What happened?" asks Mom.

"I'll tell you in the car... or after we get home." Sierra folds her arms, head down like she's still ashamed.

Mom raises an eyebrow. "Did the crimson faerie show up in the middle of class?"

Sierra almost smiles. "No. That would've been less embarrassing."

"Allie..." Dad leans closer. "Bit more serious than that. She had a panic attack."

"I didn't... really," whispers Sierra. "Something did it to me."

Mom gets this 'oh, it's the supernatural crazy' expression. "Right. Okay, we can talk about it at home."

We exit the nurse's station. The 'rents stop at the school office long enough to sign her out of classes for the rest of the day. I suggest riding with Mom so she's not lonely. Sierra wants to ride in the same vehicle I'm in. Dad's okay flying solo and encourages us to go with Mom since she's got a much bigger vehicle.

To avoid having to repeat herself, Sierra doesn't say a word on the trip back to the house.

Once we're gathered in the living room, she tells us—through tears—about what she saw happening. By the time she's done with the story, she's gotten her composure back, though she's still got a death grip on my and Dad's hands.

"So, I guess I really did kinda have a panic attack, but it's not my fault. If the demon didn't force me to see that, it wouldn't have happened." She grumbles. "I can't believe I froze like a little kid."

"Froze?" asks Mom.

"Yeah. I just sat there, almost peed my pants. Couldn't move." Sierra scowls. "I mean... I'm as strong and fast as a vampire. I could've broken that gun in half and shoved it up his ass. But... I froze."

"Sierra..." Dad nudges her shoulder. "You *are* a kid. Not a super-hero. There are tons and tons of stories about soldiers—grown adults—who freeze in combat. You shouldn't feel weak because you panicked when someone pointed a gun at you."

"It's your worst fear," I say. "Like beyond that even. Almost a phobia. The damn demon is doing it. Making it worse."

"Yeah. I know, but if it happens for real, and I freeze like that..." Sierra shivers. "Oh, no wonder I was so slow and weak. Just a night-mare. It wanted me to feel helpless again."

Dad scoops her into his arms like he used to do to us when we were five. "You are still a kid. You shouldn't be talking about freezing in combat. Good grief, what is wrong with our society?"

"Carl Sagan's show and *Firefly* get cancelled after one season, but *Duck Dynasty* goes on forever?" I ask, trying to lighten the mood. "That's what's wrong with society."

Mom shoots me an unamused stare.

"Tragic," says Dad. "Not what I meant. Though, I wonder if there's a connection. It's definitely a society problem. We're like the rats in the Ratopia experiment as it spiraled out of control. This is the part where the animals started killing and eating each other."

"Eek. Dad... That's gross." I cringe.

"No one's eating anyone." Sierra shrugs. "At least, I didn't see any zombies at school."

"Where are you going with this, Jonathan?" Mom wipes a hand down her face.

"Society continues changing in ways that make it more and more intolerable to exist within its boundaries. Like being in a social pres-sure cooker." Dad makes a pensive face, trying to remember some-thing. "Calhoun. That's the guy. He did a bunch of 'rat utopia' experiments back in the Seventies. Gave the rats everything they needed. At first, paradise. But it rapidly led to overpopulation and then a whole bunch of crazy evil stuff. The rats turned on each other

and got way out of control. He theorized that as the global population of humans grew, we'd do the same things as his rats did. People
didn't take him seriously, but I'm starting to wonder if he had a
point."

"This isn't you coming up with another fancy way to say guns
aren't a problem?" Mom rolls her eyes.

"Saying guns are the problem oversimplifies it." Dad shakes his
head. "I'm not arguing because I am pro-gun. I'm debating because
taking such a narrow approach in an effort to solve a much, much
more complicated problem isn't going to help. Even *if* anyone could
manage to get politicians to suspend the Second Amendment and
make gun ownership illegal—and trust me, there's more a chance I
will give birth to a winged pig than that happening—it wouldn't
fix it."

"It definitely couldn't hurt," snaps Mom. "Only the police should
have guns."

Dad holds up a wait hand. "Let's imagine for a moment that our
politicians weren't beholden to financial donations or corporations
and a national gun ban happened. Do you think we'd suddenly be in
Mayberry with Andy Griffith smiling his way down the street? In the
short term, you'll see a drastic drop in mass shootings, yes. However,
it's the illusion of a fix. The same factors that drive people to commit
those heinous acts will remain, and the fabric of society will
continue to rot. I hate to resort to one of their talking points, but it's
not wrong to say that this country had a whole bunch of guns back
in the 1950s and 1960s and you didn't see the same sort of mass
shooting events then. Society has changed in not-good ways. Fixing
this is a complicated process that can't be done in one quick, easy
step that fits neatly into buzzwords for political slogans."

"So, you're pro-gun now?" Mom sighs.

"No. I'm pro 'intelligence.' Do civilians need military grade
weapons? Of course not. But taking a weapon away from a violent,
insane person doesn't make them cease being a violent, insane
person. I'm saying it would be best if we, as a society, could fix the
issues that are turning people into psychopaths who lash out at
everything around them."

"Guys," I mutter. "Can we table the politics?"

"It isn't politics. It's societal stability." Dad sighs. "You're right though. Not the time for it."

Sierra closes her eyes. "I think I'm good. I got the freeze out of my system this time. Maybe I only froze because I knew it was a fake nightmare. If it happens for real, I'll be okay."

Mom squish hugs one of the sofa pillows. "If it happens for real, I *won't* be okay."

"Can I say something obvious that no one is even thinking about?" I hold up a hand.

Mom, Dad, and Sierra look at me.

"What?" asks Mom.

"Sam is at the same school. With Blix. We also have Coralie around somewhere." I smile. "Not only do we have an Oracle advanced warning system, if anyone ever did really show up at their school with intent to do harm, Blix would feel it coming, tell Sam, and he'd drop the flaming hammer of Mel on them. It would, in all probability, be over before Sierra even knew someone brought a weapon onto school grounds."

"Oh, umm." Sierra blinks. "Wow. I didn't even think about that." She lets out a long breath. "Maybe I don't need to be quite so worried about it then."

"It's okay. I think Mom is worrying enough for you." I lean against Mom.

"Garden variety psychos aren't an issue." Dad purses his lips. "But after what he did to Sierra today, I've had just about enough of this damned demon."

"Oh boy." Sierra cringes. "I hope this ends better than the time you tried to save money by not hiring an electrician."

Dad fakes a look of offense. "Rewiring a circuit breaker box is more complicated than stomping on a demon."

... and the next thing I know, I'm in bed. I sit up, feeling baffled. Did that just happen?

"Dad wants me to tell you that you passed out on the sofa." Chloe peers over at me from the dollhouse. "Mom's not happy she saw you sleepy, but you're not in trouble."

I look at my hands—normal—then at the clock. Almost four. Guess my body needed to make up for lost sleep. My brain chews on the events of the afternoon. Gradually, it starts to make some sense. If I hadn't been there to tweak the principal's mind, Sierra—and my family—would be stuck in a huge mess. Something woke me up so I could be there for her. Hmm.

Gotta be magic.

CHAPTER 35
BREAKING OUT THE BIG GUNS

Going to college is starting to feel like a pain in my rear end. When I got the bright idea to 'act normal' and do this to help my parents cope with my death, it never occurred to me I'd be constantly involved in wild situations. This is probably why most vampires don't have day jobs. Well, aside from the 'day' thing. Classes are an obligatory imposition on my time I could really do without. Wouldn't be such a big deal if the Universe allowed me to exist in peace.

It's not easy to pull myself away from home after what happened today. It hadn't only been Sierra who had the metaphorical poop scared out of her, though she got it the worst by far—which is kinda weird to think about. Sam, I expected would take any sort of attempt to mess with him in stride. The boy's as unflappable as a ten-year-old can be. In fact, he's pretty damn ballsy by adult standards. If any of the Littles would end up a crying wreck because of something a demon did, I figured it would be Sophia. I mean, 'horror' movies where the creature effects are so bad they look like 1980s store-bought Halloween costumes give her nightmares.

Sam and Sophia returned from school at the normal time. Sierra spent her bonus time in her room drawing. She's taken a renewed interest in it and it does seem to calm her down. Me bringing up the Oracle and demon thing appears to have helped her as well. As much as she doesn't like to admit it, the part of her still very much a child likes feeling protected. The same way it's wrong for Lucas Holland to need to cook his own meals at age ten, it's wrong for Sierra to feel it's her responsibility to protect herself from a school shooter. She's now got something between her and a crazy dude with a rifle. So what if it's a demon.

Should we be concerned some of her drawings look like Olmaz stomping on a dude with a gun?

Nah. It's a form of therapy. Speaking of which, Mom's going to bring her to see a therapist at least a few times. She wants it documented in case something else happens at school. I don't think she has any plans to sue them over the shooter drills. More like she doesn't want the school accusing her of not taking their concerns seriously and having CPS check on Sierra. Of course, none of us believe she's going to have another panic attack at school without a demon assaulting her mind.

So, anyway... the situation at home—aside from Dad being in a weird mood—were normal enough for me to attend my 'Rise of Modernity' class. The material is interesting enough to take my mind off things, like my Dad planning something that's going to end in disaster. Not sure exactly what's on his mind. Hopefully, I will return home and still have a house.

My house still exists.

Good.

It's 10:14 p.m. Do you know where your vampires are?

Waking up early and forcing myself online while exposed to sunlight left me famished. I stopped for a bite on the way home, but otherwise rushed back to the house as fast as I could fly. Everything appears normal. Nothing's on fire, glowing, levitating, or existing in an altered phase of matter.

Mostly.

The chaos begins when I reach the living room.

Dad's pacing around by the coffee table with his red headband on, the enchanted one Sophia gave him for his birthday. It looks perfectly ordinary, but it's giving him something. Not exactly sure what. Probably strength, speed, endurance, or whatnot. Maybe the magic in it lets him turn puns into demon-slaying weapons. But yeah, he's got the headband on. Uh oh. Shit's about to get unreal. I mean, he's still wearing his polo shirt and khakis. There's not too much that's threatening about a 160-pound computer programmer in his mid-forties. He might be 170. Not sure. Whatever. He's skinny.

Mom, Ashley, Chloe, and the Littles are on the couch watching him pace around. There's also a giant cardboard box on the coffee table. It's longish and rectangular, similar in shape to a five-foot-long stick of butter. I don't smell butter, so the carpet is safe.

"Aha! You're home." Dad grins.

"Are you okay?" I walk up to the back of the sofa and lean on it. "You seem a little... manic."

"Bastard got me, too. Had a nice little nightmare I am not going into any details about." He shivers.

I can imagine. Probably something about finding us all massacred. He and Mom have pretty much the same worst fear.

"This ends now." Dad pats the big cardboard box. "It's adventure time. We are going to kill a demon."

"Uh, Dad? The last time you said you were going to kill a demon, you were on your way upstairs holding a plunger."

"Sorry!" yells Sam.

Blix tilts his head and mutters something, sounding sad.

"No, dork." Sam laughs. "I took a big poop."

The imp falls off the sofa, laughing.

"Be that as it may,"—Dad points at me—"I'm not being whimsical this time. This is not a bathroom joke. I am absolutely, completely, and totally *serious*."

Sierra blinks. "Wow. *Three* adverbs."

Dad thrusts both arms into the box, causing an eruption of foam packing peanuts, and yanks out the queen mother of Nerf guns. The toy rifle is bigger than Sam, with all sorts of blinking lights and fancy accessories. It's mostly orange, with fluorescent green and yellow trim. He hefts it up in a Rambo pose, narrows his eyes, and tries to do his best Christian Bale Batman voice. "That demon is going to regret ever messing with us."

"You're serious?" deadpans Sierra.

"Absolutely." Dad holds his chin high.

"Completely and totally even," adds Sophia.

"Targeting sequence initiated," says a robotic voice from the Nerf gun.

Mom stares at him like she can't believe her eyes.

"Whoa." Sam gawks at the Mecca of Nerf weaponry. "You bought a Nerf Galaxy Commander Ultimate Edition!?"

"Yes, I did." Dad nods once. "And it's mine."

"Aww," whines Sam.

"You aren't big enough to even lift that monstrosity," says Sophia. "It's bigger than you are."

"It's plastic!" Sam gestures at it. "I can lift it."

Dad models the 'weapon' for us. "This is the biggest, fanciest, butt-kicking-ist complete Nerf assault platform available to humanity. This. Is. Serious."

"Well, it's not Sparta," mutters Sierra.

"That's a Nerf gun." I try not to laugh. "You spent a hundred dollars on a giant Nerf gun?"

"No." Dad holds his head high. "I did not spend a hundred dollars on this piece of magnificence." He pauses a moment. "It retails for $299."

"Plus taxes," adds Sierra.

Mom buries her face in her hand. "I married a giant nine-year-old."

"Aww, come on Mom." Sierra gently elbows her. "You know boys never *grow up*, they just get facial hair... and start to smell bad."

Sophia seems to be taking this oddly seriously. She doesn't look like she's about to laugh. Chloe isn't paying much attention to anything but the doll she's holding. Giant Nerf guns are 'boy stuff' which she couldn't care less about. If he'd pulled a giant Barbie dreamhouse—or a toy skeleton—out of that box, she'd be over the moon. Ashley's tittering.

"Okay, Dad... you're forgetting one small detail." I stretch to my right and pat Sam on the head. "The Nerf dart thing only works for him."

"The boy enchanted the darts already. They should work on demons, even if it's me shooting the gun." Dad swings the monstrosity around, posing with it.

"Oh, now I know what it reminds me of... those big guns from *Aliens*." I snap my fingers.

My father peers down at the thing, gets this 'oh wow, you're right' gleam in his eyes and slightly alters his stance so he looks even more like a colonial marine heavy weapons operator.

Sam scampers over to the box and rummages. "Dad, you're forgetting the targeting module."

"Oh, drat!" He holds his left hand out toward the boy.

My brother fishes this gaudy plastic headband with a single amber eyepiece out of the packing material and passes it to him. Dad takes one look at it, realizes it's never going to fit an adult head, then offers it back. "Might be better if you wore that. My aim's good enough. You could use the extra visibility."

Sierra leans toward me and whispers, "We're doomed."

"Go back to the dart thing." I float up and over the sofa back, landing to sit between Ashley and Sophia—who promptly leans against me. "I thought the way any sort of 'weapon' could hurt demons no matter what it is was like a 'Sam thing.'"

"Umm. Dad's part of the family, right?" My brother scratches the back of his head, scrunching one eye half closed. "I had to get it from somewhere. Besides, Blix is sure Dad shooting darts will work as long as I'm kinda close to him and I want it to work."

Sierra whistles. "That thing is really impressive, but I think it's too big and unwieldy."

"I've said that to a guy or two before." Ashley snickers.

Dad looks about ready to drop dead.

Mom shakes her head.

Sophia, Sierra, and Sam make confused faces at her.

"You dated a guy with a big Nerf cannon?" asks Sam.

"Yeah." Ashley cackles. "I think he put the batteries in backward because it fired too early."

"Subject change," says Dad in a singsong voice.

Sierra reaches out and fiddles with a little decorative control knob on the side of the Nerf weapons platform. "This thing is neat, but I think you should've gotten a paintball gun instead. More ammo. How many shots does that monster hold? Paintball hopper's got hundreds."

"Uhh, ten," says Dad, seemingly embarrassed.

"That enormous thing only has ten shots?" I almost laugh.

Sam winces. "It's amazing but it can't be perfect."

"For $299, you'd think it would hold more than ten darts at once." Mom frowns.

"It's all bling but no sting," says Sierra while flashing a suburban kid's idea of what gang signs look like.

Sophia holds her hands up like a conductor about to lead a symphony. "I can fix that."

"Oh crap. Brace for it!" Sierra dives into the sofa, pretending to be scared.

My Barbie loving pink-mageddon sister channels her inner Rambette. Multicolored magical lights form around her hands, then leap at Dad. Neon green plastic stuff grows out of the side of the giant toy cannon. Over the span of about two minutes, the expanding plastic takes on the form of an ammo backpack like from the movie *Predator*, only loaded up with a bunch of Nerf darts rather than bullets. A flexible plastic feed chute runs from the bottom of the backpack to the side of the gun above the trigger. She grows a gyroscopic balance mount out of the side of the ammo pack, really making it look like the big guns from *Aliens*. Naturally, she did that on purpose since Dad was already channeling Vasquez.

"There." Sophia nods.

"Soph..." Sam gives her side eye. "There's a reason no one makes actual Nerf guns with ammo backpacks. The foam darts are too light. They won't feed properly."

She holds up a finger. "There are two things in the Universe that freely ignore the laws of physics, gravity, and inertia. One is a two-year-old who does not want to be dressed. The second is magic. Trust me. It will work."

"I likey," says Dad. He test aims around the living room. "Maximum demon carnage, zero chance of unwanted casualties. And it looks cool."

Sierra grins. "You look like *Dork* Nukem."

"I still can't believe you spent almost three hundred dollars on a toy." Mom makes a face at him like he's nuts.

Dad takes on a commando stance. "This is not a toy. This magnificent assemblage of plastic, electronics, and foam is a minor price to pay for the safety and security of our family. This is the instrument of our freedom from demonic oppression."

Sierra and Mom both facepalm at the same time.

Dad wags his eyebrows at me. "Since you're home, it's time. Ready to go to hell?"

Hmm. No idea what he's planning... but I do know I'm not ready... yet.

"One sec. Be right back."

I rush down to my bedroom and rapidly strip to my underpants, then throw on some old jeans, a beat-up shirt I won't miss, and the closest thing I have to combat boots. Finally, I grab the two most important fashion accessories: my katana, and a red headband. After tying the headband on, I hurry back upstairs to stand behind the couch, sword resting back over one shoulder.

"Okay. Now I'm ready."

"Yes!" Dad grins from ear to ear at me, pumping a fist. "Time to go kick some ass."

CHAPTER 36
STRAIGHT TO THE BAD PLACE

We all head downstairs to the basement, standing in the large, main space.

Better to do this downstairs where the windows are both small and massively tinted. Strange glowing magical lights from inside our house might get the neighbors asking questions we don't want to answer. The room is mostly empty now except for beige carpet, the washer and dryer, and Dad's old ping pong table no one's touched since I was eleven. It's not really usable at the moment due to all the boxes and stuff piled up on it.

Sam marches around in a circle, his bare feet squishing the form of a ring into the carpet. He's carrying his sneakers in his left hand, his Nerf rifle in the other. Sierra's got her sword—which is very much a real weapon. She, too, is holding her sneakers, otherwise wearing a raspberry-colored T-shirt, jeans, and raspberry-colored socks. Sophia's armed only with a stealth attack kitten and extreme cuteness. Her white dress is midway between plain and frilly. She's also barefoot but isn't carrying shoes. Ash has gone full preppie in a turtleneck and skirt. Like Sophia, she's barefoot and not bothering to carry shoes. Dad and I are the only two people with footwear presently in the house. Mom doesn't seem to care we're breaking her rule. She's still in her work skirt-suit. Pretty sure her stockings are going to melt if she tries walking around hell without putting her shoes on, though she left them upstairs.

This is all a bit distracting for her. She's not thinking too clearly.

Oh, Chloe's here, too. Kiddo's wearing one of her fancy doll dresses. No shoes for her either, though she's got a cute anklet of pink plastic flowers. Wait a minute. Chloe's here. What the heck are we doing?

"What the heck are we doing?" I repeat out loud.

"I'm opening a portal to a tangential demi-plane where the demon who's messing with us is," says Sam matter-of-factly. "We're going to go down there and kill this butthead for good. I found him."

"So, you're sending us to hell." I exhale.

Sierra glances at me. "Sare, it would be faster if you and Ash just kissed and started making out."

Ash laughs with a hint of 'eww.'

"What?" I blink, feeling the same way. "Why would I do that?"

"Because you'll go straight to hell." Sierra grins. "At least, according to Uncle Hank."

Mom laughs.

"He's such a jerk," whispers Sophia, rolling her eyes.

"Umm, so you're serious about this? We're really going to hell?" I glance at Chloe.

Dad holds up the enormous Nerf weapon. "I'm as serious as I've ever been. This crap is stopping tonight."

Sierra blushes a tiny bit, smiling at Dad. It seems what happened to her at school today *really* got him angry. Our father isn't exactly the 'beat the shit out of anyone who gives his kids a hard time' type of guy. He might want to be, but his physique isn't capable of cashing those checks. However, fate's given him the ability to be the tough guy—with a Nerf cannon—for once, so he's taking it.

"Right. Umm. What about Chloe?" I ask. "It's probably not a good idea to bring her with us."

"We can't leave her home by herself." Ashley fidgets. "She's only seven."

"I'm mature for seven." Chloe flicks her hair off her shoulders. "And I have Barbies."

Heh. "Still..."

Chloe shrugs. "If you want me to go with you, that's okay. I won't see anything down there scarier than the asshole."

Mom flinches. Not sure what bothers her more between a kid her age using words like that or any mention of the child's abusive father. Also, I kinda doubt demonic demi-planes are incapable of being scarier than the mortal world. Case in point: five-headed nopeasauruses. I think most reasonable people would consider a three-ton spider-dragon-whatever a slight bit scarier than a drunk bastard. Though, then again, it's relative. To her, an image of her dead father might be worse than a huge furry monster.

"I can ask Mom to watch her?" Ashley tilts her head. "It's not *too* late yet. How long do you think this will take?"

"Going to an outer Abyssal realm to finish off a weakened demon?" Mom rubs her chin. "Can't be any worse than suffering through a deposition hearing with Grant Marley."

"Who the hell is Grant Marley?" asks Sierra.

"One of Lockheed Martin's lead attorneys." Mom frowns. "We think he was born without human limitations of needing sleep, food, or having any sense of respect to the idea that other people have lives outside of work. Every time he's part of a case I'm on, he makes everything ten times more work than it needs to be, trying to trip the opposition up on technicalities or bury them in paperwork. Even if we end up on the same side of the table, it's *so* damn tedious just waiting for him to exhaust all his motions and processes."

Okay, maybe Mom *can* kill a demon or two.

"Be right back." Ashley takes Chloe's hand. "C'mon."

"Lemme grab some stuff!" The kid darts into my room, returning a moment later with the haunted doll, Rebecca, as well as a fistful of Barbies in a tangle of fake blonde hair and partially worn doll clothing. "Okay."

Ashley and Chloe zip across the basement and go up the stairs.

"Ash!" shouts Mom. "Please grab my shoes when you're on the way back."

"Okay!" yells Ashley from somewhere upstairs.

Sam keeps pacing in a circle. Blix levitates above the midpoint of the ring my brother's stamping into the carpet. He's got his legs folded and arms out in a tiny Buddha pose. A few minutes later, Ashley runs down the stairs and hands Mom the sneakers she wears while driving back and forth to work. White New Balance. With pink accents. Office power footwear. Or something like that.

"Thanks, hon." Mom smiles at her.

"No problem."

"You're not bringing shoes?" Mom glances down at Ashley's bare feet.

"Nah. The ground's probably going to be hot enough to melt sneakers... I can just float."

Mom twitches.

"This realm isn't overly hot," says Sam in a toneless voice. "Just about done. Everyone inside the circle if you want to go."

Dad jumps in.

Ashley, Sierra, Mom, Sophia, and I all step over the footprint circle.

Six seconds later, our basement disappears.

We're now standing in a strange desert-like place. The sand is indefinably somewhere between beige and grey, not a natural color. Jet black rocks ranging in size from my fist to small Toyotas jut out of the ground all over the place. Patches of fire burn seemingly without reason here and there. The landscape is full of small 'forests' of dead, blackened trees that look more like roots growing up into the air. Here and there, signs of ruined buildings stick out, giving the place an aesthetic that makes me think of what ancient Greece would've been like a few decades after someone dropped nuclear weapons on it.

It isn't 'rivers of magma' hot, though it's definitely bikini weather... and humid.

The sky is a nauseating shade of pale green the likes of which I haven't seen since I was about eight and we visited Dad's grandmother. All the cabinets in her kitchen were painted the same color. I guess this shade of creamy green was the 1950s best attempt at

Weight Watchers. Paint your kitchen this shade and you'll lose most of your appetite. Clouds obscure just about everything above us. Angry is the best word I can come up with to describe what's going on in the air. Either we're about to get the most epic tornado ever witnessed by human eyes... or the sky is transforming into a St. Patrick's Day mint milkshake.

I'm not sure which idea scares me more.

"Whoa," says Dad. He takes a few steps off in a random direction to put his foot up on one of the rocks, like Riker from *Star Trek TNG*.

Mom pulls her sneakers on, then hurries over to stand beside him. Whatever. I guess we're doing a thing here. Dramatic pose before it starts or something. I approach and stand to Dad's left. Sierra moves up beside me. Sam drops his sneakers, steps into them, then runs over. Neither Sophia nor Ashley react like the ground is too hot to walk on barefoot. They join our little group photo op, too.

This is, after all, *my* family we're talking about. This shouldn't be a picture. We should be a spoof painting done in a Frank Frazetta-ish style like the movie posters for *National Lampoons*. The idea of some artist trying to make my dad look buff and heroic might've made me chuckle except for the fact of us standing in hell. And yeah, I know this isn't 'hell' in the strict sense of the word. Hell is something religious wingnuts made up to scare people with. Or, I dunno. Maybe someone way back then got transported to one of these demi planes while on LSD and thought he saw stuff.

Whatever. I'm going to continue calling this place 'hell' because a four-letter word is much easier to say.

Blix crawls up off Sam's back to perch on his left shoulder. He's like this little capuchin monkey with fangs, bat wings, and a bladed tail. The somewhat oversized head and big eyes makes him cute. Okay, cute *now*. The first time I saw imps, they freaked me out. Well, I suppose they say beauty is sixty percent personality. Those other imps definitely had been freaky.

"Which way?" asks Sierra.

"Oom narixa," rasps Blix, raising one of his spindly arms and pointing off to the side.

If the direction we're facing is north, the imp's indicating northwest. I have no idea which way we're actually pointing or if the concept of compass directions means less here than the opinion of any man who thinks they know what's best for women.

Sam points in the same manner as Blix. "He's over there."

"Are you sure this is a good idea?" asks Mom.

"I am absolutely certain." Dad nods. "That I have no clue... if this counts as a good idea."

"Can't be worse than when you tried to fix the upstairs toilet plumbing," says Sierra. "Talk about a total shit show."

Mom sighs.

Dad's expression is mixed between indignation and pride. He's proud of her for the pun.

"I still wanna know how he managed to get blasted with it." Sam squints "I thought it was only explosive on the way out, not once it's already in the toilet."

Mom's face turns almost the same color as the sky.

"It didn't blow up out of the toilet, Sam." Dad shakes his head. "I was in the basement, replacing a pipe. Gravity did the awful work."

"Yaaaah!" screams Sierra.

I spin toward her in time to see her sword taking the head off an enormous black snake. My sister appears to be moving at normal speed, spinning with the follow up to throwing beyond-human strength into her weapon. As willowy as she is, the blade pulls her around so much she has to flow with it or she's going to end up on the ground.

One severed snake head glides in slow motion into the air, tumbling end over end. It's about the size of a fat honeydew melon. The remainder of the snake body's as big around as a deli bologna log, sticking up out of the ground near her. I turn, following the snake head with my gaze.

Naturally, it hits Sophia in the chest. She reflexively catches it.

Three... two... one...

My smaller sister lets out a scream of disgust capable of shattering all glass objects within 100 meters. Once she runs out of air, she randomly chucks the disembodied snake head into the air. It comes back down to land on Mom's head, then slides off into her grasp. My mother is not impressed. She smirks at it. Her utter lack of bother seems to further freak Sophia out.

"Eww! Mom! Gross! How can you touch that?" wails Sophia.

"She has experience wrestling enormous serpents," deadpans Ashley.

Dad looks like he wants to overact being proud, but it's too awkward. Umm, no. I don't even want to think about that.

"Ash!" I swat at her. "That's the parents you're talking about."

What happens next shocks the crap out of me. No, not a hydra or giant tarantula. Mom wags her eyebrows at Dad like she's not disagreeing with Ashley.

Oh hell. Where's the hole in the ground to swallow me now?

"Sophia," says Mom in her overly calm 'mom voice.' "After you've been responsible for four infants, it takes quite a lot to gross you out."

Sierra yells again like she's an actress in a lame Kung-Fu movie.

She lops the head off another big snake that sprouted up from the ground. This time, she cut a bit lower. The severed bit includes two feet of serpent body plus a head so it's too heavy to fly far and plops to the ground near her.

"We should probably move," says Sam. "Those aren't snakes."

Mom peers down at the head she's still holding. "It certainly looks like a snake, just a bit larger than normal."

Sophia shivers, averting her gaze away from the dead creature.

"What are they then if they're not snakes?" I ask.

Blix babbles at Sam.

"They're the serpent-headed ends of tentacles attached to a demon bigger than Mom's Tahoe." Sam glances at Blix. "He says the other sixty tentacles are coming after us."

"*Sixty!*" yells Sierra. "Shit!"

"Onward!" calls Dad as he breaks into a jog. "It's not running away if we're traveling *toward* our objective."

Mom tosses the snake head aside and hurries after him. The rest of us waste no time and get moving. Klepto leans out from under Sophia's hair to hiss at something behind us. Blix gives a middle-finger salute to it as well. Yeah, there's quite a bit of snake hissing going on back there. I'm hoping a demon the size of a Chevy Tahoe that's buried itself in the dirt isn't the fastest creature in the universe.

"Let me take point," I say, hurrying to get ahead of Dad.

Mom gives me a worried, confused look.

"Because I've got a sword. Dad's heavy ranged support. He shouldn't be up front."

"Good point," say Dad and Sam simultaneously.

"Dork." Sierra sighs. "We are not characters in his D&D game."

"Aren't we?" Sophia manages a weak smile. "I'm the mage. You and Sare are fighters. Dad's being silly and using a D20 Modern character in a fantasy setting. Sam's a summoner."

"What am I?" asks Ashley.

Sophia glances at her. "Umm. Monster girl. Tiefling sorceress maybe."

"She doesn't have magic," says Sam in a flat tone.

"No, but she's got powers to charm people." Sophia grins.

"I'm not sure that works on demons." Ashley holds out her hands like she's trying to extend claws, forgetting she didn't get them in the vampire powers lottery. "Crap. So much for being monster girl tonight."

Sierra gazes at the darkening sky. "Oops. We did it again. No one rolled a healer."

"What's Mom?" Sam glances over at her.

"Mom," says Mom, "has no idea what any of you are talking about."

I cringe inside. Honestly, Mom should've waited for us back home.

Sam and Sierra have a brief discussion of how to 'label' Mom right now in terms of D&D character archetypes. She's not really fitting any of them.

"She must be the gamemaster." Sierra shrugs.

"Then she'd have limitless power." Sam scratches his head. "Her limitless power doesn't really extend outside the house."

A "mew" comes from under Sophia's hair, followed by a camera flash of bright purple light. Seconds later, the kitten appears hovering in front of Mom, clinging to the handle of her big cast-iron frying pan, which in total defiance of physics, levitates.

Dad stops walking to face Mom. "Yon furry squire doth present you with the epic weapon, Impslayer."

Blix raspberries at him.

"It's okay," whispers Sam. "She only wallops bad imps with it."

"Mom's cast iron isn't a magical weapon." Sierra rolls her eyes.

Sophia steps over and grasps the handle of the floating frying pan. Her hair rises up off her back as if she's experiencing a mild breeze that only exists for her. Silvery-white light spreads up from where her fingers touch the handle, enshrouding the entire frying pan with a sublime glow.

"It is now," says Sophia.

"Wow." Sierra shakes her head. "A magical frying pan. This is almost as lame as that time Dad ran an 'April Fool's' D&D campaign where everything was silly."

Sam raises both eyebrows at the glowing cast iron. "What did you do to it?"

"Umm. It's basically a +4 frying pan of demonslaying." Sophia flashes a cheesy smile. "At least, that's what I tried to do."

"Not a +5?" Sierra blinks.

Sophia folds her arms. "What kind of GM gives low level characters +5 weapons that easy?"

"Ones who want their players to get out of the campaign alive," I say.

Dad eyes Mom, then the pan, then Mom. "I'm not sure how a plus enchantment translates to the real world. We're not following game rules."

"It will help her fight." Sophia grins. "She's not taking sword classes like Sierra, nor does she have vampire reflexes."

"I dunno." Sam resumes walking. "She clubbed the heck out of those imps pretty easy. I think Mom took a double specialization in frying pan."

Mom grasps the 'weapon', making a face at us like 'did you kids *really* take my prized, beloved cast iron pan to hell? The way she's holding it makes me think she's mostly trying to protect the pan from harm, not wield it like a weapon. "I played varsity softball in high school. Swatting those imps out of the air wasn't hard."

"I'm kinda shocked you can just casually create greater magic items like that." Sierra blinks.

Sophia waves dismissively. "It's only a temporary enchantment. Permanent ones are *much* harder. It's also a lot easier to do in this place since the rules of reality are super different and favor magical things."

We trek across the strange landscape, following Blix's pointing finger.

I'm not really sure if we actually went to a demi-plane or just somewhere in Nevada and the special effects department is green-screening out the cacti. The terrain is pretty similar to hard-pack desert with all sorts of meandering ravines and mini-canyons. They look like the paths streams might have carved into the earth, though any water has long since disappeared.

"Incoming," calls Dad. "Two o'clock, high."

"What?" Sierra blinks. "It's not two yet."

"Yeah." Sophia peers up at him, confused.

Dad sighs. "It seems I need to teach you guys about old technology. Clocks used to have hands that went around in a circle. I'm using 'two o'clock' as a referential direction to the way we are facing. Twelve is straight ahead. Two is slightly to the right."

"Oh. Weird." Sierra chuckles. "You said clock hands, I was imagining these little gremlin things like my alarm clock coming to life."

"I can make that happen." Sam grins.

"Please don't." Sierra raises her sword after catching sight of something in the air. "Oh, crap! Incoming!"

"I already said that!" Dad raises the giant Nerf gun.

Sam nods at Blix and holds out his hand. The imp pokes my brother in the fingertip with a claw, sorta like he's taking a blood sugar test. Sam then reaches his poked finger out and makes a blood smear on the back of the Nerf cannon so Dad doesn't see him doing it. He makes no effort to hide this from Mom, who squirms. Pretty sure she's not fond of the idea of my kid brother using blood magic. Also, Sam's not hiding it from Dad out of fear of getting yelled at. He wants Dad to feel like he's helping all by himself.

I think this is why that Nerf gun is going to be useful against demons.

Creatures descend on us from the sky. They kinda resemble imps, if someone squished their entire bodies up into their heads. Basically, these goobers are imp heads with wings sticking out the place where a neck should be. Their heads are about double the size of Blix's... and they spit little fireballs at us.

Lovely.

Sierra scrambles back and forth trying to go after anything low enough for her to reach. She looks like a four-year-old trying to whack the pinata at a party for older, much taller kids.

Dad opens fire, flinging a barrage of peach-colored Nerf darts into the air. He looks so silly. The Nerf cannon sounds ridiculous... kind of this clicking plus a pneumatic puff noise with each shot while built-in speakers play cheesy fake laser blast noises. Though, as hilarious as he looks, the attack is astonishingly effective. Any flying-imp-head that makes contact with a Nerf dart explodes like a water balloon full of raspberry pudding.

Sam's *much* smaller Nerf rifle has a similar effect, though he's shooting single shots at a much slower rate of fire. He also has a bit more trouble hitting the zooming imp heads. Not that Dad is a master marksman. He's simply throwing hundreds of Nerf darts into the air. The mini demons are flying into them more than he's accurately targeting anything.

Unlike Sierra, I don't have to obey the law of gravity. I fly up and start chasing these little bastards. Smacking them with a katana isn't too difficult for me. *Hurting* them on the other hand is a challenge. Feels like I'm whacking coconuts with a sword that's much too light to do the job. Most of the time I make contact, I swat the damn thing away like a winged softball rather than slice it. The one or two that came close enough to the ground for Sierra to hit seem to take more damage, but not enough to destroy them. Her sword is heavier than mine. Katanas are slicing weapons, not hacking weapons.

The imps spit a hail of golf-ball-sized fireballs at us. Sophia sticks both arms up into the air like she's trying to get something off a high shelf at the supermarket. Most of the incoming fireballs start bouncing off in random directions. Their flight pattern kinda makes the image of an invisible dome appear around us. Some do make it in. Everyone except for me and Ashley (who are flying) absorbs a few hits. The fireballs leave black marks on clothing but don't seem to be doing too much more than causing yowls of pain.

This makes me worry it's not really a physical attack and might be doing something less visibly obvious.

Sophia rakes her right hand at the sky in a clawing motion. Three of the flapping horrors freeze as if time stopped for them, then fall to the ground with dull thuds. At this, a handful of the demons appear to consider her prime threat number one and dive bomb her.

Sophia screams.

Mom, who's already right next to her, raises the cast iron. Her expression of determination briefly goes to shock as she jerkily swings at the first imp-thing to get close. The way she moves totally looks like the frying pan is in control, just pulling her around. She wallops the fiend heading at Sophia square in the face. Two comparatively large wings tumble around either side of the pan and keep going forward while the remainder of the creature (its giant head) explodes in a shower of purplish red goop.

My mother's gaze darts to the next closest imp. She clobbers it out of the air, ending the demon with a wicked overhead wallop. Slimy residue hits the ground with so much force it splatters over everyone. The third time she swings the cast iron, her motion appears intentional and no longer janky. She's either adjusted to the frying pan doing most of the work or they've developed some sort of cooperative relationship.

Ashley zips around in the air with me, chasing imps. I swear part of her has to be cat. She's got this manic look in her eyes like a kitty chasing a laser pointer dot. It's really tragic the universe decided she doesn't get claws. I'm not going to ask where the Bowie knife came from. She doesn't collect knives. Gotta be a gift from Klepto. Anyway, fast-moving flappy things in the air seem to tease some animal instinct out of her. She's aiming for wings, too. Her knife isn't too effective on the stupidly hard skulls of these fiends, but it sure slices the hell out of the bat-like wing membranes.

Ooh! Good idea!

I swap tactics from trying to play imp baseball to serving up an order of wings. Whenever she or I take one out of the sky, Sierra runs over and stabs it through the head into the ground. That seems to finish them off. The ones she kills don't explode. Seems that's a side effect of the magic Sam and Sophia are using... or at least the magic Sophia put into Mom's frying pan.

Gonna be difficult to explain to the grandparents why the pot is glowing next Thanksgiving. Oh, wait... she said it's a temporary enchantment. Mom's prized cast iron is going to go back to normal soon—unlike us.

Ash and I might've escaped the majority of mini fireballs, though we look like we marched in a Diwali parade where they ran out of every color but purple. Dad's relentless Nerf machinegunning set off splats all around us. By the time the last of the flying heads is gone, we're a mess.

I land among my family and sigh.

"Are you okay, Sarah?" Mom twirls the frying pan over her hand like Red Sonja doing a flourish with her sword.

"Yeah. Just... purple." I grumble. "It's the second corollary law of supernatural combat. Any fight with demons *will* result in someone being covered with goo."

Ashley sets down beside me and stuffs the knife in a sheath that's now on her belt. I swear that wasn't there ten minutes ago. "What's the first corollary law of supernatural combat?"

"If vampire claws are involved, someone is losing all or most of their wardrobe." I frown.

Dad and Mom laugh awkwardly. They know I'm being silly, though it's silliness based on past experience. It's embarrassing enough to end up naked out in public, but if it happened in front of the 'rents, I'd probably go full Dalton and become a recluse living somewhere in the remote parts of the UK.

Sophia waves her arms around. A few hundred Nerf darts rise up off the ground, gather in a cloud, then float over to Dad. The top of his ammo backpack opens and the tiny foam missiles all go back into it in a neat stack. A much smaller bundle of darts floats up to Sam and drops at his feet. He promptly gets to work repacking his magazines.

I suppose that's one big advantage to using Nerf: Dad and Sam can keep using the same ammunition over and over.

Yes, my kid brother is wearing a bandolier of eight bright orange plastic Nerf rifle mags. He's like a little kid playing Rambo. Okay, he *is* a little kid playing Rambo. We wait for him to reload the mags then stick them in his bandolier. Not sure where the bandolier came from. Sophia must've conjured it when I wasn't watching. Or maybe he had it back in his room and Klepto fetched it.

"Oops." Sam leans over to Sophia and whispers.

She nods at him. The kitten vanishes and returns with a strip of red fabric hanging out of her mouth.

"Thanks." Sam takes the cloth and ties it around his head. "There. Now I'm ready."

Dad beams with pride.

We make our way deeper into the desert. Sophia is kind enough to magically clean us of purple demon goo. Good. That stuff was sticky and oily. Yes, both. Don't ask me how something can be sticky *and* oily at the same time. It doesn't make sense, but it happened in this place.

A group of six demons charge over the top of a hill in front of us. They're about Sierra's size in terms of height, but significantly stockier. All are armed with spears or javelins that resemble straightened spinal columns tipped with onyx sword blades. Oh, I bet those are tails from larger dead demons.

Probably not a good idea to get stuck with one.

Sierra lets out a war cry and charges.

"Sierra Renee Wright!" roars Mom. "You are not allowed to charge alone into battle against demons! Especially when you are outnumbered! Get back here!"

My sister isn't going to stop.

She's not scared of these things. I hope she's not making assumptions that prove wrong. Also, I'm not waiting to find out, so I launch myself forward. Ashley's right behind me. Sierra is fast, much faster than a mortal ought to be. However, she can't fly. My flight speed can top out like 140 MPH if I'm really pushing myself. That's way faster than even I could run on the ground.

The three of us reach the demons at roughly the same time.

Sierra 'matadors' out of the way of a thrusting spine spear, then shoves herself in close, almost chest-to-chest with the demon. Smart. Really damn hard to use a polearm when you're in such close quarters. She hilt-punches the demon in the nose, steps on the spear, and jumps over its head, slashing it as she goes.

Two of them go for Ash.

"Eep. Never had two guys trying to stick me with their bones at the same time before." She evades their strikes with the grace of an elf, then yanks the knife back out of its sheath. I'd say she looks like a suburban white girl trying to act like a tough gangster girl but... she's a lot more intimidating than you'd think for someone who's never fought with a knife before.

I ignore her comment and attack a demon that's about to stab at Sierra's back.

These things turn out to be slow. Well, slow to me. They're moving about as fast as an athletic mortal with training. I split its head in half down the middle as Sierra does this Matrixy maneuver. She dives off her feet into a spinning logroll, swinging at the demon's knees while she's rolling over in midair. No, she can't fly. She's just moving so fast she's quicker than the speed of gravity. After severing both of its legs at the knee, Sierra finally succumbs to gravity and flops to the ground.

Ashley bum-rushes a demon, ripping her knife down its face and chest before grabbing its bone spear away from it like she's confiscating a dangerous weapon from a little kid. Two of its fingers break from the force with which she disarmed it. She's never taken even one martial arts class and, as far as I know, never tried to get into combat with a spear. She did, however, cheerlead our first two years in high school. She can drum majorette the hell out of that spinal spear. Hey, that's not much different from kung-fu, right? Lots of spinning and fancy moves.

Her mesmerizing display of spinning makes me expect her to go full on Liu Kang, but nope. Fanciness ends with the twirling. Ash goes full on cavewoman and wallops the demon she disarmed with it like a club. The hit sends the diminutive creature backpedaling, leaving it wide open for her to stab it in the heart. Assuming, of course, they have hearts.

Sierra and I mop up the remaining ones without much difficulty.

Yes. Vampires cheat. Magically amplified tween girls like Sierra cheat, too. Our strength and speed advantage makes this fight feel like we're just beating on mannequins for practice. Fine with me. These are demons working for (or controlled by) another demon who's trying to destroy my family. I don't care about fairness or honor here.

The rest of the family catches up to us a full minute after the last of these six demons is a twitching mess of gangly limbs on the ground. Dad seems mildly disappointed they're all dead before he got close enough to use his Nerf gun. That is one major disadvantage to Nerf compared to actual bullets. *Way* less range.

"Sierra," says Mom.

"Sorry. I know it was dumb to take on six demons by myself. I promise I won't do it again." She swats her sword at nothing to sling black blood off it. "Unless there's no other choice."

Blix chatters.

"He says we're here." Sam nods toward the crest of the hill where those six demons came from. "Boss demon's on the other side."

Dad pats his extreme Nerf cannon. "It's time for the final confrontation. You guys ready for the boss fight?"

"I'm out of healing potions," says Sam in a blank tone.

Anyone outside our family hearing him would think he's serious. He's not. Healing potions do not exist. Though... Starbucks mocha lattes come close.

We regroup, take a collective deep breath, then march over the hilltop.

Ahead of us, the ground descends into a shallow but massive crater. At the center of an enormous depression shaped a bit like a contact lens stands the ruins of a stone building. The area around the building is a rectangular stepped pit about the size of a football field. In it stands an obviously demonic creature. He looks more or less like a human man of indeterminate age who's been barbecued. Patches of his body simply don't exist, fringed with ashy tendrils. I say his age is impossible to determine because of the whole barbecue effect. He doesn't have enough skin left to tell if it's wrinkled or not. At least he's not naked. I'm not sure if the 'furry black skirt' type thing he appears to be wearing is actually clothing, demon fur growing out of him, or rotten entrails covered in fuzzy black gangrene.

I also don't really want to know. It looks like a skirt made of goat fur. Whatever it really is, I'm going to believe it's a worn garment and not actually part of him. It's difficult to fight while wanting to throw up.

Oh, he's got wings, too. They're massive, batlike, and tattered to hell. Long, curving black talons sprout from the bend in each wing. They're too thin and long to be effective as anything other than decorative. The horns sticking out of his head are thicker and might be usable as weapons if not for the physical awkwardness of trying to use them. They stick straight up. He'd have to bend over and come running at us. Way too silly. Nah, those horns have to be a mark of rank or station.

Naturally, he's got a long prehensile tail, too, tipped with an onyx-colored blade roughly the size of a Roman gladius.

"No wonder he spoke through the backyard grill," says Sierra. "He looks even more burnt than Dad's last attempt to barbecue chicken."

Sophia sputters—that's her laughing but trying not to.

"Ouch," says Dad in a voice like *The Tick* being triumphant.

"Be nice," whispers Mom.

"I *am* being nice." Sierra glances at her. "That guy is *more* burnt than Dad's chicken."

"Truth," says Sam.

Sierra looks up at Dad. "And I'm teasing. The chicken wasn't bad at all."

Dad grins.

Perhaps our biggest problem, though, is the army of smaller

demons surrounding him. I'm not *too* worried. They seem to be the same type of demons as the ones who charged over the hill. Slow—to me—and fairly easy to kill. The only fly in that ointment is, even slow opponents can be dangerous when there are 400 of them.

The sefil demon appears surprised at our presence. Due to his lack of skin, it's difficult for me to tell if his expression is because he's worried we're here to kill him or simple shock that we happened to be stupid enough to land right on his proverbial doorstep.

"Wow." Sierra looks around at the desolation. "Why do demons live here? Do they just stand around all day? Isn't he bored? Like, there's no PlayStation or anything to do."

Deep, resonant laughter seems to come from everywhere. The sefil demon's chest bounces as if he's the source of the noise. Welp... he's done being surprised.

The minion demons closest to us stop milling around like a bunch of eighth graders at lunchtime and all turn to look in our direction. One by one, they blur and change. In seconds, an army of Sophias smiles at us.

"What the crap?" barks Sierra. "Why do they *all* look like her?"

Wow. She almost sounds offended.

"Because Soph is cute and defenseless." Sam flicks the safety off his Nerf gun.

Sierra huffs.

Sophia makes a 'hey, I'm not *totally* defenseless' face at him.

Dad squeezes Sierra's shoulder. "You're cute, too, sweetie."

Sierra's face is stuck somewhere between indignation, embarrassment, and a smile.

Sam raises his Nerf gun at the demon swarm. "It's trying to confuse us, thinking we won't be able to attack Sophia."

Dad steps up beside Sam, his huge cannon giving off a plastic rattle. "I have no qualms shooting any of you with a Nerf gun. If I make a mistake and hit the real Sophia who isn't a demon copy, the dart will just bounce off."

"This demon really isn't that smart, is he?" whispers Ashley.

"Whatever intelligence he has is being obscured by a blinding need for revenge." I rest the katana back over my shoulder. "There's also the demonic arrogance of him thinking he can't possibly lose to a group of mortals."

Dad peers back at us as the army of Sophias make their way up the crater toward us. "So, how do you want to play this? Tactically or just Leeroy Jenkins it?"

"What the heck does that mean?" I blink.

My father whistles. "Drat. I keep underestimating my skills at teaching you pop culture."

"Dad," drones Sierra. "Pop culture to you is history class for us."

"Ouch." Dad cringes.

"It's okay. You can teach us about Leeroy Jenkins later. I really do wanna know." Sierra smiles at him.

Dad gives off a sense of pride again. "Well, basically, it's what you did before. Just charging in. Leeroy Jenkins is essentially 'get 'em'."

"Get 'em?" blurts Sam, sounding frustrated. Since his voice carries obvious emotion, I know he's acting... or quoting a movie. "That's your plan? 'Get 'em?'"

Dad cackles. "*Ghostbusters!* Love it!"

I exhale out my nose, surveying the throng of cute little blonde tweens coming to kill us. "Wow. This is like a twisted horror movie where *The 300* meets *Sailor Moon*."

"'Get 'em' it is," says Ashley. "Be careful not to hit the real Sophia."

"Kinda easy there." Sophia folds her arms. "I'm not carrying a giant spine spear... and none of them have a kitten on their shoulder. These guys really are stupid."

"Meeeeew!" roars (sorta) Klepto, pointing one paw forward.

"What did she say?" asks Sam.

Sophia adopts a 'wizard's combat pose.' "She said 'get 'em.'"

CHAPTER 37

WEAPON OF LAST RESORT

"On three," whispers Dad.

"Wait." I furrow my brow.

"For what?" asks Mom.

I point the katana at the approaching Sophias. "Feels like I should shout something epic before charging into battle. Can't think of anything."

Sam chuckles.

Sierra glares at me like I'm a dork. "How about, 'die, you miserable bastards?'"

"Not bad. Lacks something, though." I sigh. "Whatever. No time to waste coming up with something appropriately cinematic."

Since I have no better ideas, I raise my katana, yell, "This is Sparta!" and charge.

"For Hufflepuff!" shouts Ashley before following me.

Yeah, that tracks. Totally her.

Sierra opts for the tried-and-true simple barbarian scream. No words. Just raw fury and bloodlust as she raises her sword and sprints down the hill. Though at her age and size, she sounds like an aggressive Girl Scout Cookie seller trying to get on the porch before the door slams and less like an ancient Celtic warrior.

"Let's rock!" shouts Dad before cutting loose with a storm of Nerf machinegunning.

The barrage rips the fake Sophias to pieces in a spray of severed limbs and purple slime. It's like playing a video game that's been edited to meet Nintendo's 'family decency' standards with the utmost minimum effort: they just changed the blood purple without actually reducing any of the gore. Yes, it's disturbing to see hundreds of copies of my little sister being shredded like that. Two things break the illusion enough for it not to give me nightmares. One: none of the Sophias look scared. They just keep smiling eerily like something out of a horror movie with a killer little girl. Two: when they die, the screams of agony do not sound anything like Sophia's voice. Each demon gives off a polyphonic wail, five voices crying out simultaneously, a sound several octaves too low for her to produce.

I rush at the line, telling myself over and over again that these are not my kid sister. My biggest worry is—unlike Nerf darts—my katana would absolutely wreck the real Sophia if I mistakenly hit her. An idea hits me after I cut two of them down. These things are demons. They don't smell like strawberry pie. Yes... the real Sophia has a scent like if you took a Hostess fruit pie with strawberry filling and microwaved it for thirty seconds so it's nice and warm and... ugh. Now I really want one.

Mortals smell like what their blood will taste like to me. Kids tend to translate into various sweet items like chocolate, fruit pies, candy, and whatnot. No, I am not tempted to bite Sophia because she smells like a warm strawberry pie. If the craving ever got so bad I couldn't resist, I could easily go get an actual strawberry pie and enjoy it. Behold the great, fearsome power of the Innocent bloodline.

These goobers are so slow to me, I have plenty of time to sniff at them before committing to an attack. It's not pleasant. They smell like old sneakers left out in the rain for a few months.

Sierra is caught up in the moment. She rushes into the fray at full speed, ducking and weaving around the demons in a continuous ballet of gore. Several of the fake Sophias end up stabbing each other in their haste and confusion trying to hit her.

Dad appears to be focusing his fire toward Sierra, trimming

down the numbers threatening her. The endless stream of Nerf darts cuts them down like my father's using a garden hose to disperse creatures made of soap suds. Sierra looks like she went for a swim in a pool of purple finger paint.

Time is kinda meaningless to me at the moment amid the chaos. I'm not sure how long it takes, zipping around and slashing at demons before I reach stairs. Oh wow! We've pushed the minion army back to the football-field-sized pit. It's basically a stairway on all four sides, leading down about fifteen feet to the bottom.

Right as I start fighting my way down the stairs to the flat stone floor at the bottom, the minion demons revert to their normal forms. Guess the big guy figured out turning his cannon fodder into fake Sophias isn't making us all decide 'oh noes, we can't hurt something that looks so adorable' and go right home.

Speaking of the big guy, he's only about sixty feet away now.

And... as many minions as I've seen go down, there are still hundreds of them forming a ring wall around the main demon. Dad's continuing to pump Nerf darts into the crowd, blasting them to bits. Sam isn't shooting at the minions. He appears to be trying to snipe darts at the big demon. Alas, being ten years old, he's kinda short. His shots keep hitting minion demons since he can't shoot over their heads.

It now occurs to me that a rather crazy amount of fireballs and javelins are flying out of the minion army toward my family. Most of that's been going right over me, Ashley, and Sierra, since we're in the thick of it, mingled among the outermost minions. I gaze up at a passing spine spear, following its trajectory with my eyes as it comes down toward Mom, Sophia, Dad, and Sam. The spear deflects off another invisible shield dome.

Ooh. Nice! Sophia's on defense.

Mom's standing right by her, playing goalie. Looks like she's taken out a whole bunch of minion demons who made a run for the real Sophia like Ewoks trying to disable the shield around the Death Star. In fact, right as I look at her, she smashes one over the head so hard its entire skull disintegrates in a shower of purple gloop. The way the spindly arms flail for two seconds before the dead demon falls over is kinda hilarious.

"Grr!" yells Sam. "There are too many of 'em."

"Ow! You little shit!" yells Ashley. She pulls the tip of a spear out of her stomach, breaks it, then stabs the front end into the face of the demon who impaled her.

Sierra roars. I spin toward her, ready to assist.

A demon's grabbed her from behind, lifting her off her feet and pinning her arms. She mule-kicks both sneakers into the face of the demon preparing to stab her, breaking its neck with a sickening crunch. The last time I heard a noise like that, Mom snapped a bundle of raw spaghetti noodles in half for some crazy recipe she found online. The demon staggers side to side waving its arms, its head dangling behind its back like a bowling ball on a string.

Sierra rams her head backward into the nose of the demon holding her. Another crunch. It promptly loses its grip on her—and gets run through by the spear of another demon that had been trying to kill Sierra as she falls to a seated position on the ground. She grabs the spear and pulls herself into the air, kicking the new demon under the chin so hard its head flies clean off.

Okay, she's got that handled for now. I have nine problems of my own.

Mannequins are dangerous opponents when there are lots of them. My sword can only be in one place at a time. As easy as they are to kill, a few manage to hit me. The attacks are relatively shallow, grazing strikes due to the fact I am not sitting still. The spine spears sting almost as bad as vampire claws in the way that a bee sting is almost as painful as a gunshot. It hurts more than it should, though it doesn't make me feel like I'll be nursing sore wounds for a week.

Sam rips off his shirt and throws it to Mom. His conjured demon wings erupt from his back giving off a *fwoof* noise like a spring-loaded umbrella made of leather. The boy leaps straight up into the air and starts shooting over the minion ring at the big demon. His first dart gouges a big scoop out of the demon's left shoulder—damn close to a head shot.

The big guy roars in anger-slash-fear. A scary number of minion demons sprout wings and leap after Sam. Crap. So much for trying to fight my way through to the center. Also derp. I'm a moron. I can fly. Why the hell was I charging in on the ground? Guess I got caught up in the whole '*Braveheart*' feel before the attack began. Grr. No time now. I gotta keep them off Sam.

Rather than shoot at the big guy, Sam's got other problems. He flies backward, rapidly shooting Nerf darts at the throng of minions going after him. Ashley jumps up with me, chasing the ones going after my little brother. Blix hovers next to Sam, handing him spare magazines every time he runs out. I have no idea where the imp got a World War II army helmet from.

With Ashley and I in the air, Sierra's stuck on the ground by herself. This forces Dad to concentrate entirely on keeping her from being overwhelmed, leaving him no opportunity to try shooting the big guy. Here's hoping his Nerf cannon's batteries don't die on us from overuse.

Mom stands sentinel in front of Sophia and Dad, going full Jackie Chan with the frying pan. It's the craziest, silliest Kung-Fu movie I've ever seen—in no small part due to watching my mom kick ass. She's almost channeling Uma Thurman from *Kill Bill*. It's... weird. But cool.

Ashley and I do to the demons chasing Sam what a pair of angry feral cats would do to a roll of toilet paper. Demon bits rain to the ground. I'm being slightly more surgical about it since I have a sword. Ashley's manic knife swings are making a damn mess.

The rest of the flying demons abruptly divert course and race back to the ground.

For an instant, I think they're afraid of us... then I realize the even more surprising truth. Sierra's almost punched through the ring to the big demon. He's pulling reinforcements down to protect himself from my scrawny kid sister. Guess it's true. Size doesn't matter. At least, it doesn't matter when magic is involved.

Sam's okay now, mostly.

"Ash, cover Sam."

"Got it!" chirps Ashley. She flashes a manic fanged grin at me.

I'm glad this goop is purple. Otherwise, if she'd been covered in red stuff, that would have looked utterly psychotic.

I dive out of the sky, heading right for the big demon. He's preoccupied with Sierra being so close and doesn't see me coming. Unfortunately, my aim is slightly askew. Instead of cutting his head off, my katana hits his left horn. With a *clank* like I swatted a crowbar against a steel railing, my blade severs the horn at the demon's temple. A seventeen-inch piece of dense demon bone sharpened to a deadly point falls to the dirt. Momentum carries me to the ground in front of the demon in a cool three-point superhero stance.

Can't help it. I waste two seconds looking at the blade, afraid it suffered a massive nick. Whew. No damage.

Luck is mine. The big demon is shocked I cut his horn off for about the same amount of time it takes me to check my sword and stand up. He glares down at me. I meet his disdain with defiance. He's not *that* much taller than me. Only like two feet.

"Remember me, asshole?" I slash for his throat.

He leans back, suffering only a minor paper-cut to the neck. He pivots and swats me with one of his wings. It's kinda like a giant grandmother clubbing me with a collapsed umbrella. The attack shoves me aside while not doing damage or even hurting much. This demon is significantly more potent than the minions. He's fast. Fighting him is going to happen in real time. No big deal. I actually know what I'm doing with a sword. I've fought other vampires before—ones older than me—so I can keep up with a real fight. Having a katana is still a big reach advantage over claws, even if his claws are six inches long.

The chattering of Nerf machine gunning continues behind me.

Darts fall on the big demon from Sam taking pot shots out of the sky. For the most part, the demon evades his attacks, though the occasional dart tears holes in his wing membranes or melts a gouge in the side of his arms.

Ashley and I attack this demon in a pincer move: her behind, me in front. He spins into a blur of flailing claws and wing strikes. I score a superficial hit on his torso once or twice. Ashley gets a piece of him, too, sticking her dagger in sensitive places. It's obvious whenever she hits him because he roars in agony.

Hmm. Pain seems to be slowing him down a little. Time to go

tactical. A few seconds after she sticks him in the kidney area, making him flinch, I sprout claws on my left hand and take a swipe across his undefended stomach. The slashes are shallow but they make him scream louder than ever. Yeah, vampire claws are something else, all right. They can even make the most wicked demons cry out in agony. Only other thing I know powerfully painful enough to do that is the Kars for Kids ad jingle.

This is good and bad. Good, because pain seems to be making him lose focus and accuracy. Bad, because it's pissing him off and I think he's getting stronger.

I take a clawed elbow to the face, knocking me over backward.

Yep. He's getting stronger.

He lures Ashley with a wing in the manner of a matador teasing a bull, then spins into a tail strike when she falls for the bait. The super flexible tail smacks into the back of her calves like a two-inch-thick bullwhip, swatting her off her feet. She catches herself with flight, hanging in place upside down for half a second before zooming straight up and avoiding the demonic claws going for her heart.

He's open! I launch myself at him, stabbing up into his chest from behind and left. The tip of my katana bursts out his left pectoral region. If he has a heart, I've impaled it.

The demon glances down at me like 'what the hell are you doing?'

Aww, shit.

I see the backhand to the face coming. Got a split second to choose between abandoning my weapon—it's really in there good—or taking the hit to avoid being disarmed. Not really a choice. If he hits me, I'm going to be disarmed anyway. Grr. I jump back, ducking the huge hand passing inches above my skull. He roars, eyes burning with orange fire. Uh oh. I think I've gone and made him angry.

He comes after me in a flurry of blind fury, swinging again and again. Claws the size of daggers slice the air, making audible hissing sounds as they miss me repeatedly by millimeters. I keep dodging, going around in a circle.

Ashley drops out of the air behind him, grabbing her knife in both hands and ramming it into his back before yanking it downward all the way to his belt. Yeah, it's a belt. This close to him, I'm sure he's wearing an actual skirt. Don't want to know what type of being the leather or fur came from. The demon throws his head back, howling in agony like he just smashed his pinky toe into a steel bedframe at two in the morning.

I grab my katana and pull... but it's not budging at all.

Sierra zooms in from the side, chopping her sword into the demon's right thigh. The blade sinks into the charred red, blackened flesh only about half an inch. "Crap. He's harder to cut than steak Dad grills."

"I heard that!" shouts Dad.

Of course, she's kidding. Dad thinks 'well done' is a crime against humanity. He also thinks 'cooked' is too much to ask. One of these days, he'll find the sweet spot where steak no longer counts as 'raw' to a reasonable person. What he calls 'rare' is the beef equivalent of sushi.

I tug again on the sword. It's stuck good. Apparently, I am not destined to become the Queen of Camelot.

The demon swats Sierra's legs out from under her with his tail while simultaneously introducing the back of his right hand to my face. I hit the ground, sliding, seeing stars. Oof. Is this what it's like to be Chris Brown's girlfriend? Gah! My head is spinning.

Sierra, as she cannot fly like Ashley, eats the ground alarmingly hard. Fortunately, the noise coming out of her is a growl of anger, not a mewl of pain.

"Mew," says Klepto, really close by.

I shake off the dizziness and sit up. The kitten's standing right next to me beside my katana. Tarlike black gunk covers the entire blade from hilt to tip.

"Ooh! Thank you!"

"Mew!" Klepto vanishes in a pink-violet flash.

I take a quick inventory. I think I've got a dislocated jaw, at least one broken rib, and a sprained ankle. Ashley's apparently suffering a broken leg from the tail strike. She's not putting any weight on her left foot. We're both kinda ripped up and looking weary. There are still enough minion demons in a ring to keep the hail of Nerf darts from Dad away from the big demon. Damn. They're freaking endless.

Sierra rolls back to her feet and stabs up at the demon's chest. He pivots, letting the blade score across his stomach, and grabs her by the neck, lifting her off her feet. Her face reddens as he slowly squeezes, intending to break her neck while making it take as long as possible.

Dammit! I fling myself off the ground into a flying charge, sword up over my head, aiming for that wrist.

Mom comes out of nowhere, smashing her cast iron pan into the back of the demon's head.

A bell-like *claaaaang* echoes over the barren landscape. I swear the big demon makes the most Homer Simpson 'duhhhh' face I've ever seen.

"Get your damned hand off my daughter, you bastard!" shouts Mom.

I slash downward, my muscles screaming from vampiric power, desperation, and raw anger. A painful jolt rocks the katana in my hands when the blade makes contact. Feels like I whacked a brick wall with an aluminum baseball bat. It hurts badly enough, I expect my wrists to shatter. However, the blade slices cleanly through the demon's forearm. Sierra drops to her feet and staggers back a few steps. The demon's severed hand hangs around her neck, a macabre fashion accessory.

She scrunches her face in disgust, grabs the hand, and flings it off.

The back of the big demon's skull appears to have been partially liquefied. Still, he doesn't seem worried, merely annoyed. Scowling at Sierra, he shakes his stump of an arm... a mass of wormlike tendrils burst forth, twist around, and solidify into a new hand. Took him less than two seconds.

"You gotta be—" Sierra cuts her gaze to Mom. "Can I drop an f-bomb?"

"Go ahead, dear. This is an appropriate moment." Mom nods.

Sierra shifts her stare back to the demon's new hand. "You gotta be fuckin' kidding me."

"I don't think he's kidding," says Ashley—right behind him.

The demon spins, swatting her aside as she slashes him across the back. She eats dirt about fifteen feet away. Again, the demon gives off an anguished wail of pain from the gouges she tore open across his kidneys.

Huh. That knife is hurting the demon a lot more than it ought to. Oh crap. Sam did something to it, didn't he? If Mom finds out he cut himself to 'put the juju' on Ashley's dagger, he's going to be in huge trouble.

"Worth it, and oof. That's a broken shoulder," mutters Ashley. She gasps in managed pain. "Everything we do to him, he's just regenerating."

"On the bright side, there *do* appear to be noticeably fewer minions," calls Dad.

"He's making more of them," shouts Sam from the air.

Oh hell. This is not going to end well for us if we keep doing things the conventional way. "Soph, freaking do it already!"

"You know not what you ask of me!" yells Sophia in a nervous tone.

I become aware of another broken rib. Yeah, I'm not going to be able to keep this up for much longer. "Stop being melodramatic and just do it already!"

Sam distracts the big demon away from mauling Mom and Sierra with a rapid-fire pelting of Nerf darts that forces him to raise both arms to shield his face. The darts blast small chunks out of his arms, but the flesh regenerates almost as fast as it's disappearing. Wisps of ash fly off the wounds, which glow like embers from internal heat. I make the nauseating realization that this demon is in a constant state of being consumed by flames and regenerating. No wonder he looks like Freddy Krueger left in the furnace too long. Oof. Guess that explains why he's such a pleasant dude to be around.

Sophia holds her arms out to either side. She does this *Sailor Moon* like spin, then points generally toward us.

A black spot the size of a manhole cover appears on the ground a short distance to my left, right at the inside of the minion ring. Huh. Weird. The minion demons are still in a ring, they're not breaking formation to come inward after us. You'd think... well, maybe he wants the shield against Dad's Nerf barrage. As fast as that thing spits foam darts, it might actually be able to kill him before he can regenerate.

Furry blackness starts to squeeze up from the black hole Sophia summoned.

With a pneumatic *fwoomp*, Fuzzydoom pops up into being, rapidly fluttering his tiny little wings. One might be confused as to how a ten-foot-wide orb could have fit through a hole so small. Well, for one thing, he's almost all hair. For another, he's the product of Sophia's three-year-old brain coming up with a nightmare. It's going to make about as much sense as the average car commercial on TV.

"Your aim's off," yells Sam. "Fuzzy's too far away from the big guy. He'll never catch up to him."

"He's not even trying to," wails Sophia. "I told you! I can summon him here, but I can't control him. He wants to kill us, too!"

With the big demon still busy trying to keep Sam from shooting him in the face, Sierra decides to act. Quiet as a mouse, she sets her sword down, then runs up behind the demon to grab his long tail in both hands. The instant she's got a hold of him, she lets out this barbaric roar and yanks him off his feet, swinging him around and around by the tail before 'She Hulking' him right at Fuzzydoom.

The big demon barely has time to look confused before he crashes into the furry orb—and simply vanishes.

All the minion demons burst into clouds of dense black smoke, sinking to the ground.

"That's it?" Ashley blinks. "Just... gone? No explosion of goo?"

"How... anticlimactic." Dad tilts the Nerf cannon up and blows across the barrel.

Fuzzydoom seems to be on his way to destroy Mom, though it's kinda hard to tell given how slow he glides.

"Guys!" Sophia flails her arms, looking terrified. "We have to run for our lives before Fuzzydoom gets us, too!"

Sierra, dusting her hands off, strolls back to where she dropped her sword and picks it up. "Don't you mean we should lazily meander away for our lives?"

"Whatever." Sophia sighs. "Come on. Get away from him. We have to get out of here. I can't send him away, only bring him to wherever I am."

Dad gazes off into the distance.

I limp over to him. "What? Do you hear something?"

"Not yet. We just destroyed the big boss demon." He raises one eyebrow. "I'm waiting for this entire demi-world to collapse."

"That doesn't always happen." Sam drops out of the air beside us, then folds his wings.

Mom makes a face at him. She's not entirely thrilled with the boy having demon wings, even if they aren't really part of him, only temporary magic. I dunno. I think they're kinda cute.

"Do we need to fight our way back to the spot we entered from?" asks Sierra.

"Nope." Sophia runs up to us. "We just have to get far enough away from Fuzzydoom so I have time to cast the spell."

"How long will it take you to cast the spell to take us home?" asks Dad.

"Umm..." Sophia bites her lower lip, doing mental math. "About twenty seconds."

"Okay, so..." Sierra glances at the bizarre creature. "We need to get about four feet away from the pom-pom of doom."

Sophia's face turns red. Not sure if it's anger or embarrassment. "Stop!"

"What?" Sierra shrugs.

"Making fun of him." Sophia looks down.

Sierra gives me a 'is she serious' glance before looking at her. "I'm not making fun of him. Well, not entirely. He really is super slow. Why does it bother you that I make fun of him?"

"Because." Sophia stomps. "It makes me feel stupid and silly for being afraid of him. And I think if I stop being afraid of him, he might stop existing."

"Wouldn't that be a good thing?" I put an arm around her. "He really is dangerous."

Sophia shrugs. "Yeah, but if Fuzzydoom stops existing, then we couldn't use him to help us get rid of even bigger problems. He's at least so slow we can keep away from him."

Dad turns the Nerf cannon's power switch off. All the lights go out. "She should send Fuzzydoom to the offices of the executives who cancelled *Firefly*."

"Seriously." I bow my head. "Now that would be a public service."

"Sophia," says Mom. "You are not to use any nightmare creations of yours—or anyone else's—to kill television network executives."

"Yes, Mom," says Sophia.

"Can we go home now?" Sierra looks down at herself, covered in demonic goo. "I feel so funky."

"Yeah." Sophia holds out her hands. "We just need to form a ring."

CHAPTER 38

A HELL OF A MESS

We reappear in our basement... which is full of smoke.

For an instant, I panic, wondering what Chloe got into while we were away—then I remember she's with Mrs. Carter. Also, Chloe isn't the sort of kid who'd play with matches if left unsupervised. The source of the smoke becomes apparent after a moment of standing in it.

A circular patch of carpet—the entire area inside the path Sam walked before—is simply gone. The rug at the edge of the disintegrated part is full of scorched black lines forming mystical-looking glyphs and patterns.

Mom freaks out if one of us walks around the house with sneakers on because she doesn't want us messing up the rugs. Also, shoes track in germs and stuff from outside. She's not a super germophobe in most ways, but the rugs are like her weird little thing. For some odd reason, though, it doesn't set off her germ thing if one of us goes outside barefoot then comes inside without taking our feet off. It's just shoes that make her squirm. Maybe it's legit OCD?

She gawks at the destruction for a few seconds before this manic look of a mental break spreads across her face and she launches into this yelling tirade, giving it to all of us—except Ashley because she's a friend and Dad because he's an adult. Mom yells at us like we decided to randomly light fire to the rug for fun and amusement.

Sophia bursts into tears right away since she's just that sensitive.

Sam, Sierra, and I just kinda watch Mom melt down. It's obvious she's overwhelmed and doesn't really mean it.

"... replace all the carpeting down here... and it's going to come out of your allowance, young man." Mom gives Sam her 'I'm so disappointed in you' face.

The boy doesn't flinch.

"Why do you think he did it?" asks Sierra in a droll voice.

"Because." Mom flails. "Those markings look demonic and there are no kittens involved. Nothing's pink."

"Mom? Are you done?" I put a hand on her shoulder.

She stares at me. For an instant her eyes burn with the 'how dare you talk to me like that' fire. Then she gets this 'oh, uhh... derp' expression, glances down at Impslayer, then back at me. "We went to hell, didn't we?"

Sam relaxes.

Sophia sniffles back her tears, seeming almost shocked to discover Mom wasn't really angry at us.

"Yes. We did." I pat her shoulder. "We *all* kinda messed up the carpet. But the demon that's been trying to kill us, who hit Sierra with a car and gave her an anxiety attack? He's dead. I think a hole in the carpet is a small price to pay for getting rid of that threat."

"Sarah." Mom looks down. "This is not a 'hole' in the carpet. That's an eight-foot swath missing. I don't think 'hole' is the right word."

"It's nothing we can't fix. Don't take it out of Sam's allowance. I'll cover it." I smile. "I've got a few bucks in the bank."

"Can't Sophia just fix it?" asks Sam.

Mom holds her hands—and frying pan—up. "Umm. No, it's fine. I'd rather pay for a carpet service than have our entire house teleported into a random demi-plane."

Sophia huffs. "I'm not *that* bad at magic."

"She is getting better." Dad pats her on the head. "What story do you want to give the carpet service, dear?"

Mom stares at him. "Well... we could, uhh..."

"Tell them some demonic cultists broke into our house?" He points at the mystical 'writing' in scorch.

"I am reasonably sure I can fix this." Sophia walks around the damaged part of rug. "Repairing stuff is easy. Well, easy as far as magic goes. Want me to do it?"

"Umm." Mom presses a hand to her face, thinking. "How sure are you that you can fix it and not set off a catastrophe?"

"Nine out of ten." Sophia smiles. "Already had the catastrophe the other day."

"What?" Mom lowers her hand just enough to peer over it.

"Umm. I tried to do some protection magic and a piece of it ran away. I still don't know what it did." Sophia bites her lip. "Something weird might have happened. Could be in the house, could be with the neighbors. Dunno."

"The bathtub was glowing the other day, but it stopped." I shrug. "Could that be related?"

"Umm. Maybe." Sophia scrunches her nose in thought. "I'll check it out as soon as I'm done down here."

Dad chuckles. "I'm sure we'll figure it out what that runaway spell did soon."

"All right, dear. Go ahead and magically repair the carpet. But be careful."

Sophia cracks her knuckles. "Can everyone please move away from the burned part?"

"Shoes!" calls Mom, before hurriedly pulling her sneakers off.

I float into the air and remove my boots.

"Mom," says Sam. "Ashley and Sophia were walking around the demonic realm barefoot. Their feet are dirtier than our shoes."

My mother makes a baffled face at him. I think she realizes on some level that going outside barefoot tracks in just as many germs as shoes are capable of, but it doesn't bother her. It's not like she makes us wash our feet at the door. The disconnect makes her eye twitch twice.

"Are there bacteria in hell?" asks Dad.

Blix shrugs.

"We're all pretty funky." Sierra sticks out her tongue before sprinting for the stairs. "I'm gonna take a bath. Call firsts!"

Sophia watches her go with this expression of 'but wait, I'm gonna...' She shakes her head, sighs, then waves her hands around. All the demon goo, dirt, and other funky stuff peels away from us and gathers in a floating blob a little smaller than a basketball.

"Do not flush that down the toilet," says Mom.

"I won't. Dad? Bucket please."

He hurries off, returning soon with a big orange Home Depot pail. Sophia drops the mess in the bucket, then turns her attention to the floor. Gradually, the burn marks fade away. Two minutes after she began to concentrate, the giant patch of missing carpet shrinks until it's whole again.

Mom stares in awe.

Sophia opens her eyes and lets her arms drop to her sides. "Is that okay?"

"Yes, it is." Mom hugs Sophia. "I'm sorry for not trusting your abilities. You really are getting quite good at this stuff."

"Thanks, Mom." Sophia squeezes her back.

I feel like I got hit by a truck. Ashley looks like she feels like she got hit by a truck. I'm going to go lie down and let my bones knit.

About forty minutes have passed since we returned from not-quite-Hell.

We've collected Chloe from Ashley's house. She's happily playing with the haunted dolls. She and Mrs. Carter had a great time. She quite adores Ashley's mom. Not only is Mrs. Carter a wonderful, sweet person, she knows about vampires. Chloe doesn't have to hide anything while visiting her.

I'm farting around on the computer in *Skyrim*, still sore all over but no longer in anything that qualifies as actual pain. Ashley's reading another graphic novel. Both of us are kinda hungry. We'll probably go out to bite someone soon.

"All right, dear," calls Mom from the second floor. "You've been in there long enough."

Wow, Sierra must really be enjoying her bath. She's not usually a 'sit there and soak for an hour' type girl. She considers it boring, time stolen away from playing video games. Ooh, yeah. I need me some peaches and cream bath bomb time. Like. Now.

"Sierra? Don't ignore me," says Mom, sounding worried and annoyed in equal parts. "Sierra? Answer me right this second or I'm coming in there."

It's totally not like Sierra to ignore Mom entirely. Something's wrong.

I pause *Skyrim* and stand.

"Sierra?" yells Mom, calling for her. "Where are you?"

I rush upstairs in a blur. Mom's standing halfway into the bathroom in the second-floor hallway, looking around.

"What happened?" I ask.

She looks at me. "I don't know. I thought Sierra was taking a bath. It's about time she got out of the water, but she's not even in there. Strange. The door was still closed."

I lean past her to look into the bathroom. Smells like a bath in progress. Sierra's clothing's thrown all over the floor. Her pajamas sit on the sink stand, neatly folded. Okay, that's strange. She wouldn't have left the bathroom without putting her clothes back on or changing into the pajamas she obviously brought into the room with her intending to wear post-bath.

"Dear," says Mom. "Am I seeing things or is the bathtub glowing?"

"Oh, yeah. It was doing that the other night. The ruby dust... or an echo of it." I shrug. "Tried to clean it but it's like it wasn't really there."

Mom gives me a flat look. "Something happened."

"Sophia?" I yell. "Did you have a chance to check the bathtub yet?"

"No," yells Soph from her bedroom. "Sierra was in there. I couldn't."

I lean my head out of the bathroom and shout, "Can you come here for a sec please?"

Sophia scurries out into the hall, all ready for bed in her nightgown. She looks so normal it's like we never even crossed planes to fight a demonic army. "What's up?"

"I think something weird happened to Sierra." I point at the bathtub. "Any idea why the ruby dust is glowing?"

"Eep!" Sophia ducks between me and Mom into the bathroom. Her attention jumps first to the pajamas and the clothes, then she gawks in horror at the bathtub. "Oops."

"What did you do?" asks Mom.

"Remember when I said some magic ran away from me?" Sophia cringes, bright red in the face. "I think it got absorbed by the enchantment residue on our tub, empowering it to do something."

Mom blinks. "Are you saying our tub is magical?"

"Yes." Sophia nods. "But it's just from exposure to magical energies. It doesn't have any power... unless, uhh, it's charged."

I bite my lip. "And you charged it?"

"I didn't mean to." Sophia grinds her toes into the bathroom rug. "In a way, it's probably a good thing the tub soaked up the magic. That means it didn't leave the house and do something weird to someone else."

"Wait..." Mom pinches the bridge of her nose. "I took a bath last night. Your father showered this morning. Sam bathed last night, too. Why didn't anything weird happen to us?"

"Umm." Sophia fidgets, squishing her toes into the bathmat for a moment. "I think because Sierra's a magical creature now, she resonated with the enchantment residue. You guys are normal. Well, not *normal*." She fake laughs. "You know what I mean. Or maybe because I used the tub to enchant her originally, she's got a connection to it somehow."

"What happened to Sierra?" I ask.

Sophia stoppers the sink and runs a few inches of water into it. She leans forward, gazing into the tiny pool. "Uh oh. She's gonna kill me."

As far as I can see, the water in the sink looks perfectly clear and unremarkable.

"Are you feeling sick, sweetie?" asks Mom.

"I'm not gonna throw up. I'm scrying." Sophia keeps peering into the water. "It's like a crystal ball. Crap. There's nothing there that looks like a doorway for me to make a portal."

"Soph. Out with it. What happened?" I poke her in the side.

"I think everything in the tub—water, soap, and Sierra—fell through the bottom and landed somewhere outside. She looks really angry."

"Where is she?" I ask.

"Umm. I dunno. Looks like she's way up high somewhere in a city. She's freezing." Sophia stares up at me. "Read my mind."

I peek into Sophia's thoughts. Sierra is curled up in a ball, naked on the roof of the Space Needle, shivering and scowling. A huge smear of wetness surrounds her, where all the bathwater ran off the side.

Shit. She's soapy and wet. If she doesn't freeze into an icicle, she's gonna fall off. I know she's incredibly tough thanks to the enchantment. She *might* survive the fall. Those are *not* dice I want to roll if I can avoid it.

"On it. No time to explain." I race out of the bathroom, grab a blanket from the closet, then dive headfirst out the window at the end of the hall.

It's night, so gravity is not a problem.

I set a new record for personal flight speed. By the time I reach the Space Needle, Sierra's given up on being helpless and stranded. She's trying to rip open the steel maintenance door that would allow workers onto the roof to do stuff. She's already broken the knob off and has left multiple dents in the steel. Holy crap! Did she get stronger? Or is this just desperation talking?

Her lips have already turned blue and her teeth chatter rapidly.

I fly around into her field of view. Don't want to startle her. She'd either punch me hard enough to break something or freak out and fall. Slippery soapy skin doesn't have a lot of traction on curved steel. Oh hang on... she looks dry already.

The instant she sees me, her face runs the gamut of emotions from wanting to sob, to being furious, to adoring. Now that I know she's not going to be startled by my sudden appearance, I zip over and wrap the blanket around her. She cuddles herself up in it, still shivering.

"Thanks," rasps Sierra past chattering teeth.

"Are you okay?"

"No. I'm freezing my ass off. I'm stuck naked on the roof of the goddamned Space Needle."

"You're not naked anymore. I brought a blanket."

"Technicalities." She leans against me. "Don't let me fall. Please."

I scoop her up, wrapping the blanket around her like I'm trying to contain a cat who really doesn't want her claws trimmed at the vet. "Wouldn't dream of it."

"What happened?" She squirms, trying to snuggle tighter into my chest. "A minute after I sat down in the tub it's like the bottom opened up and dumped me out onto this freezing-ass metal roof."

"Wait... it happened right away? You've been stranded on this roof for like forty minutes?" Eek. No wonder she's dry.

She squirms. "Has it only been forty minutes? Felt like two hours. Crazy no one heard me scream when my butt hit the ground. The bath was almost too hot, and in an instant, my ass is on ice cold steel."

"Someone might have." I take off, flying almost straight up. "Better get out of here before someone comes to look."

"Grr. Bitch."

"What?" I gasp.

"Not you. Sophia. She's mad at me for beating her to the bathtub."

"Oh." I shake my head. "She's not."

I explain the runaway magic going into the bathtub and lying dormant. That glowing red dust had to be a sign the tub was 'armed and ready to fire.' I also tell her Sophia thinks there might be some sort of magical connection between her and the tub. "It didn't do it to anyone else."

"Why did it put me on the Space Needle?" Sierra scrunches her nose.

"Would you have preferred the mall?"

She shudders in 'oh hell no' for a second, then goes thoughtful. "Actually... at this hour? Yes. It would've been closed. No one there. Warmer than out here. Hiding places. Stores I could've broken into and grabbed something to wear. Did we really get the demon or did he do this?"

"We got him." I put on my most melodramatic 'so serious it's funny' voice. "There's no coming back from Fuzzydoom."

She laughs. "Okay, so why the Space Needle then?"

"Umm. Either sheer randomness or it's my fault."

"How is this your fault?"

"Both the bathtub—with appropriate bath bombs—and the Space Needle are places I find peaceful and relaxing. Maybe the magic somehow created a bridge between them. I dunno. Totally guessing. That makes about as much sense as anything."

"Our life is really weird now." She sighs.

"Yeah. It is."

Sierra grins. "But it's kinda cool."

"I'm surprised you're not freaking out more."

"Bleh. No one saw me, so I can pretend this never happened." She shrugs one shoulder. "No point freaking. By the way, thanks for the save before I got frostbite. Probably would have gotten frostbite without the enchantment."

"You're welcome, and yeah, forty minutes up here in September? Good chance."

"Am I in trouble for going out after bedtime?"

"Be serious."

Sierra chuckles. "I am. Mom flipped out over the rug. She's not coping well."

"Meh. She's coping well for Mom." I grin. "How much of a badass was she? Frying pan of doom."

"Seriously. But she cheated. Magic weapon." Sierra smirks.

"Hah."

She shivers again. "Hurry up and get home. I need to warm up.

Uhh, is the tub safe again or is it going to yeet me to Seattle again every time I use it?"

"Probably safe. It only had a little magical charge from the stray energy. Sophia's checking it out now." I spot our house in the distance and alter course for the backyard. "Was the tub kinda glowing when you got in?"

"Yeah. Duh. Stupid of me, right? I should've asked Sophia why it was glowing first." Sierra frowns. "Got too obsessed with getting in there first. Guess I deserved this lesson in humility."

"Nah. Tween siblings are supposed to race each other to the bathroom." I hold my blanket-mummified sister close and glide in through the same second-story window I leapt out of. Mom is still standing by the bathroom door.

Sophia walks out of the bathroom. "All fixed. It won't do that again."

I set Sierra down on her feet. "Any idea why it did it?"

"Best I can guess is the stray magic I let go was infused with my fake greatest fear." Sophia blushes slightly. "But, it wouldn't have done it to me unless I wanted the magic to activate. The magical link to Sierra just made the spell fire off automatically."

"Are you all right, hon?" Mom looks Sierra over.

"I'm okay, Mom. Little cold. Can I finish my bath?"

Mom raises an eyebrow. "Finish? You were in there for—"

"About two minutes," mumbles Sierra. "I was stranded on top of the Space Needle most of the time."

Mom looks at me. "I trust you're going to explain what just happened?"

"Yeah. C'mon. Let her warm up." I nod down the hall.

"All right." Mom shakes her head, but follows.

Sophia goes back to her room. Sierra turns on the water in the bathroom.

I head downstairs to attempt defining the crazy for Mom.

Yeah. How messed up is it that Sierra falling out the bottom of our bathtub and landing atop the Space Needle is *not* the weirdest thing my family did tonight?

CHAPTER 39

YOUR EVERYDAY RUN-OF-THE-MILL BOMB DELIVERY

T hursday is shockingly normal. Nothing even remotely weird happens.

Well, nothing weirder than Chloe talking to dolls who reply to her.

Yes, I had a nice long session with a P&C bath bomb after everyone not a vampire went to sleep. No, the tub did not yeet me out into the world in my birthday suit. It didn't even glow.

I wake up Friday afternoon to a text message from a Mike. Ashley and I now use the term 'the Mikes' to refer to the group of mortals who liaise between Wolent and the outside world. It's kind of a *Men In Black* type deal, like the movie, not the actual PIBs. As long as they work for him, willingly, they're aware of stuff. As soon as they want to quit or get fired, they'll lose all memory of vampires being real or what they did for the past however many years.

Wolent's got a job for me tonight. The request to 'FedEx a spicy burrito' is code for him wanting me to blow someone up. Ugh. 'Mike' explains, when I call in, that there's a nest of relatively young anarchists who've been causing problems for Wolent's interests. When I say 'young' I'm not talking about teenagers like me. They're young as vampires, which means they've been undead for less than twenty years.

Damn. Talk about conflicted. The idea of firebombing people is totally opposite to who I am—or maybe who I used to be. Mortal me would've had a mild panic attack even being in the same room as an explosive device. It isn't like this is trivial to me now. This bomb is designed to kill vampires. If it goes off in my face, I'm not going to shrug it off with mild charring like something out of a *Bugs Bunny* cartoon. Somehow, though, I can compose myself enough to function while carrying such a thing around.

As contrary to the fiber of my being as it is to be an assassin, two reasons get me to go along with it. First, the target is vampires, not innocent mortals. Also, these vampires are attacking us at random. By 'us' here, I mean the society vamps, which presently includes me and Ashley. Apparently, these are the same miscreants responsible for Theo ending up in the morgue... and killing the mortals who got caught up in it. The dead mortals weren't completely innocent victims though. In a feat of self-destructive stupidity worthy of a *Jackass* movie, they saw a gunfight break out in close proximity and decided to join in. It's unclear to me whether or not the dead mortals acted in perceived self-defense or craziness, mistaking anarchists shooting at Theo and his friends for gang activity. Maybe they just saw gunfire and decided to participate because they really were that stupid. Who knows?

The second reason I'm inclined to be a good little junior vampire associate and do what Wolent asks is... I trust his judgement. If he thinks these anarchists are a problem significant enough to be dealt with by fire, then... well, I suppose they are. Of course, I'm no blindly obedient idiot. I'm not going to run down there, toss the bomb through the window, and run off. I am at least going to verify they don't have any captive mortals in the blast zone. That, and, well, maybe observe them for a short while to allow myself to believe they are as bad as Wolent's people say.

We'll need to pick the device up from Wolent's place before going. Mike wanted to drop it off this afternoon, but Mom doesn't want me bringing dangerous incendiary devices in the house. Go figure.

Everything seems fine and normal—and I do enjoy my 'no classes Friday' like an ordinary teenager... at least a teenager when all the friends she knows are busy at work or school. I get my girly on and spend time with Sophia, Sierra, and Chloe. Lots of hair brushing and girl stuff happened. Surprisingly, Sierra happily devoted like thirty minutes to working a brush through Sophia's blonde mane. Yeah, Sierra's *really* grateful to her sister for the enchantment. Not only did it save her life—that car would've... don't even wanna think about it—it's given her super powers.

Of course, there's a complication.

Not with my sisters, with the bombing mission.

Our targets are expected to gather at their meeting location around 1:30 a.m.

The hour isn't a problem for vampires, after all. No, the issue is Chloe. At that time, the 'rents will be asleep. Aurélie is still in Louisiana. I don't really have anyone capable of babysitting. Ashley's insisting on going with me. I mean, we *do* make a great team. That morgue run would have been a serious pain in the ass for me to pull off without her charm powers hiding us from the workers. I'm not quite skilled enough to go full Dalton and hide myself from both people *and* cameras while retaining enough mental capacity to do much else. Ash has a point. Odds of doing this successfully are much higher with her along.

Besides, she decided to take the plunge into vampirism to be able to do stuff with me. We're still the same people, just instead of going to the mall for the occasional diversion from hanging out at home, we go blow people up or break into places.

Hmm. Maybe I could ask Glim to keep an eye on Chloe. Haven't seen him in a while. I grab my phone to call him. It starts ringing before I can unlock the screen. The caller ID says Mike.

"Hey, I'm about to leave the house," I say... ever so slightly impatient sounding.

"Hello, Sarah," says Mr. Wolent himself.

Eek!

"Uhh, I mean, sorry for running a bit late. I'm kinda scrambling to find a babysitter for Chloe. Normally, Aurélie would keep an eye on her. I think I have it sorted. Just gotta make a call."

"You think?" Wolent chuckles. "If you like, I can keep an eye on her. You've got to stop by to pick up the food, right?"

By food, he means 'spicy burrito,' which, of course, means firebomb.

And whoa. Mr. Wolent wants to babysit? Was that a note of amusement in his voice? He seemed almost hopeful I'd accept the offer. Huh. Weird. It came off too genuine to be something dodgy like handing her off to St. Ives for more tests. No, I really think he kinda wanted to see her. Maybe he's decided to be curious about a vampire child. Whatever sense moms have to defend their kids tells me this is not a bad idea. Yeah, I know, Chloe isn't my kid and I'm not old enough to be anyone's mom. Still, though.

"Okay. We'll be there in a few minutes."

"Wonderful. See you soon." There's a smile in Wolent's voice as he hangs up.

Again, weird. He kinda sounds like Grandpa Sheridan (Mom's dad) talking to one of the Littles when he's got a surprise gift for them. Maybe he bought her a dress or something. A doll perhaps? Chloe has that effect on adults. She just gives off a similar mood to a starving stray kitten on the side of the road. The tragedy of her mortal life's etched into her eyes. Almost everyone who sees her thinks she looks sad and wants to squeeze her.

She's not sad. At least not anymore. The kid doesn't act emo at all. Just... looks it.

"Slight change of plans," I say.

Ashley glances up from the dark shirt she'd put on and been fiddling with for the past few minutes. "What's up?"

Chloe peers over the dollhouse at me.

"We've got to do a little delivery job for the boss," I say. "It's too late at night for the 'rents to watch Chloe, so... umm, Mr. Wolent invited you to play at his house until we're done."

The kid flattens her eyebrows. "That crazy bitch isn't going to put me in the stupid microwave again, is she?"

"No. This sounded pretty sincere." I smile. "I think you might've gotten to him."

"Huh?" Chloe's expression softens. She tilts her head. "What does that mean?"

"I think the old guy might be warming up to you." I grab my boots. "It's good if he likes you. Means we're much safer."

"Is that why you blow people up for him?" asks Chloe. "If he likes you, you're safe?"

Ashley snickers.

"Well. It's more complicated than that, but kinda yeah." I exhale. "It's not all blowing people up. And when it is, it's bad vampires. Vampires who cause really bad trouble that puts us all in danger."

"Is he gonna ask me to blow anyone up?" Chloe stands out from behind the dollhouse.

"No. You're too small." I walk over and take her hand. "The only responsibility you will ever have is to not let mortals know you're a vampire. Oh, and have fun. You get to play and be carefree forever."

"Like us." Ashley grins. "Except for the sometimes having to blow people up part."

Chloe laughs. "Okay."

~

We fly to Arthur Wolent's mansion.

"Hello, ladies." Aziz bows in greeting then opens the front door for us.

Chloe gawks at him, almost the way you'd expect a kid to react to meeting Santa Claus. She continues staring in awe at Aziz until we go inside, then leans backward to keep staring at the door. If not for me pulling her along by the arm, she'd have fallen on her back.

As soon as the door closes, she gazes up at me and whispers, "Is that Maui?"

Ashley clamps a hand over her mouth, making OMG eyes at me.

"He does kinda... sorta look like Maui." I smile. "But that's Aziz."

"Aww, don't ruin it for her." Ashley sticks out her tongue.

Chloe gives me a suspicious face. I think the child believes Aziz *is*

Maui from *Moana* and I'm trying not to admit it. The guy's almost big enough. I mean, his physique is inhumanly large. Side effect of being a Beast I suppose. When I say his biceps are bigger around than my waist, I'm not exaggerating. They really are. They have almost the same hairstyle, too.

We arrive at Wolent's office at the end of the extravagantly decorated hallway. Per tradition, I knock once to announce myself, then open the door and walk in. The door isn't locked, which means we're allowed to walk in.

The study is surprisingly empty. No Paolo. No Stefano. Those two are usually neck deep in Wolent's backside. Strange not to see them here, conspiring about something or another. Vanessa Prentice reclines in one wingback chair, the only other person in the room. As much as I suppose it's possible to be, she's basically Wolent's girlfriend. Honestly, as shallow and beauty obsessed as she comes off, she's not really a bad person. She treats me just fine, nice even. Ashley says she's the 'other kind of redhead.' Ones like Ashley are 'aww how cute' type girls. Vanessa's basically a live version of Jessica Rabbit, only her chest isn't cartoonishly large and she has an actual waist.

"Umm," I say. "Hi."

Vanessa waves.

The curtains in the back of the room flutter. A dark blur zooms from there all the way over to us in the blink of an eye. There stands Arthur Wolent... wrapped up in a voluminous Dracula cape with a high collar. He leans up to Chloe, whips the cape off his face, and says, "Bla-bla-bla!"

I'm too shocked to move.

Chloe squeals in delight, zips into the air and flies circles around him. "Bla-bla-bla!"

Vanessa makes a face at this spectacle. Seems like she thinks Mr. W is being silly, though the cuteness kinda gets her.

So that was his big surprise. The Dracula cape. Heh. How about that? I think Chloe really did get to him.

A mortal dude who looks a little familiar—as in I've seen him around here before but never spoken to—approaches and hands me a large white object. It resembles some sort of kitchen gadget one might buy from the Sharper Image catalog. Rice cooker? Electric kettle? Himalayan salt-infused electric air ionizer? Weird blender? No damn idea what it's supposed to be. I know it's the bomb. They've disguised it to appear like a small appliance.

"When you push the on button,"—Mike indicates a huge, one-inch-wide round rubbery white button on one face of the device with the same circle symbol they put on almost everything these days to indicate the power switch—"the device will detonate in two minutes."

"Is there a way to turn it off?" asks Ashley. "If something goes wrong?"

"No." Mike shakes his head. "Once you push the button, you will have no choice but to get away from it. We don't want the targets disabling the device."

I blink at it. "Wait. You wired a big, obvious rubber button on the side of the device to an unstoppable detonation process? There's no safety? What if something bumps into it?"

'Mike' smiles. "We expect you to be careful with it."

I stare at him.

He chuckles. "I am teasing. Yes, there is a safety. Set the dial to ten before you push the button if you want it to activate."

'The dial' means an ambiguously labeled analog plastic switch in the middle of the front face. It's got numbers going from one to ten. Currently, it's on three. Kinda reminds me of the 'toast done-ness' selector on Mom's fancy toaster. How appropriate a metaphor here.

"Okay. Set to ten and push the on switch." I nod once. "Got it."

Mr. Wolent and Chloe roam around the room pretending to be Dracula and Maven-as-a-child from *Hotel Transylvania*. It's kinda adorable. The vampire boss of Seattle's basically acting like a cute grandpa... one who'd blow up your house if you wronged him.

I pat the side of the bomb. "Okay. We're on it."

CHAPTER 40
INCONSPICUOUS

Ashley and I fly to the industrial area of Seattle near the docks. Our target property looks like a disused small warehouse. The place is in decent enough shape. I say disused because it's covered in 'commercial property for lease or sale' signs. Doesn't seem to be much activity going on inside.

"Is this the place?" whispers Ashley.

I take out my phone and look at the pictures Mike sent. Someone took them earlier this afternoon before the sun went down, out the window of a car as they drove by. "Yep. Looks like it."

"Okay, Ash. Can you hide us from vampires?"

"You know I can." She smirks. "Remember the hellbillies?"

I snicker.

"I walked right in there and they didn't know... until I tried to grab the scroll." She frowns. "As long as you don't try to grab something one of them is really attached to, or like, start a fight, we should be fine."

"Does leaving a bomb count as starting a fight?" I glance down at the 'appliance.' Still can't say what it's supposed to be. It's going to give those anarchists a big dose of 'healthy ions'. Or maybe unhealthy ions.

"Possibly. We might have to run away when you hit the button." Ashley flashes a goofy smile. "We'll find out."

"One thing I love about you is the confidence." I chuckle.

"I sound confident?"

"No, you sound like you don't know what will happen and aren't really concerned." I grin at her. "That's not confidence. It's reck-lessness."

"Fair." She raises her arms and lets them flap against her sides. "I'm impulsive. Blame the hair."

Impulsive is one word for it. Her going vampire seems like a rash decision. But... it's probably the most well-thought-out thing she's ever done. She stewed over it for half a year. Also, Aurélie would never have gone along with the plan if Ash didn't truly want it.

"Okay. Ready. Let's do it." Ashley strikes a martial arts pose. "Ninja unicorn mode active."

I have no idea what a ninja unicorn mode is. This is, of course, Ashley, so unicorns are bound to be involved somehow. We might be here to kill vampires, but she still tries to put the 'cute' in execute.

We float up and over the security fence, then walk across the small parking area to the office door. Missing letters on the glass are still visible as cleaner spots that spell out 'Carlisle Shipping and Storage.'

Voices inside, all men, murmur in conversation. Distance plus a closed door make it difficult to understand them. Sounds like they're discussing sports. I pull the door open and enter a small waiting area with a reception desk. A calendar hanging on the wall behind the desk shows March of 2014. Hmm. This place hasn't been dormant for *too* long.

Following the sounds of conversation, I cross the recep-tion/waiting area to another door, then go down a hall past several offices to the main warehouse room. Most of this building's interior space, despite the building being three stories tall, is one giant room. Steel shelves in long rows hold only dust. One lonely little forklift stands against the far wall. To my right, past an assortment of lockers and storage cabinets for workers' gear, the corner appears to be set up like a break area. A beat-to-hell sectional couch frames off a little 'room' by a small television. There's a table in the middle, a mini fridge at the corner, and six vampires lounging about.

The TV's showing some manner of sports commentary show. One of those things where former athletes too old to play anymore put on suits and talk about the current generation of guys. Nothing I've ever cared to pay attention to.

All six vampires are wearing various combinations of jeans, leather vests, jackets, and steel chain jewelry. They look like random, nameless gang punks who give the main character a hard time in an Eighties action movie. It's so bad I find myself staring at the ceiling and wondering if I'm dreaming. Maybe I've got a new demon playing games with me thanks to Dad's love of Eighties cinema?

Meh. More likely these vampires are forty years old and stuck in the Eighties like Dad. Maybe they have no fashion sense. Other than their crime against style, they look pretty normal. Two of them kinda give off skinhead vibes, though. If mortal me ever saw these guys anywhere, she'd have walked rather fast in the opposite direction.

Gee, I feel stupid standing here holding this fake appliance.

If one of them sees me, do I run away, sprout claws, or pretend to be a door-to-door salesgirl and see if they're interested in the Thingamajig 4000—guaranteed to roast any vampire to perfection in four one-thousandths of a second.

None of them look at us.

So, they're a bit scary. That's not really a reason to kill them. I mean, hell. That boy in Sophia's dance class, the one she's got a crush on? His dad looks like a huge biker. I'd have been terrified of him, too. Turns out, the dude's a big teddy bear. His son wants to go to dance class instead of karate, and he's totally supportive of that. Really cool.

"Screw the Redskins, or whatever the hell they're calling themselves now," says one guy. "In fact, fuck football entirely. It's all part of the machine. We need to burn it all down. Once those elitist cocksuckers go up in flames, we take out the rest of the traditionalists... then the city is our playground."

"Yah." One of the skinhead guys thrusts his arm into the air and headbangs as if listening to hardcore thrash. "Gonna purge it all."

A guy reclining on a part of the couch, staring up at the ceiling, gives off an annoyed sigh. "You morons are forgetting the tiny little problem of Wolent being old as shit. How exactly are you planning to survive killing him?"

Ashley squeezes my hand. The look in her eyes says, 'these guys are assholes.'

I nod.

"Got that sorted." The guy who hates football laughs. "While the five of you have been sitting around in here jerkin' off, I laid the groundwork for the master plan."

"Master plan he says," mumbles a punk in a blood-stained biker vest, sitting on the opposite end of the couch from the ceiling starer.

"It's in motion. Got some mortals wound up like toy soldiers. Bringin' all the pieces together." He draws his hands in toward his chest, making fists. "All comin' to us. You know how those scumbags have that fancy little party once a month at their fancy little hotel?"

The other five nod and/or make noises of agreement.

"Well, next time they all do that, we're gonna roll up on the place with a big ass truck full of boom boom." He makes a quiet explosion sound effect. "Ought'a be enough to take out the entire hotel. Every one of them old bastards is gonna be gone."

"That's going to kick the hornet nest." Ceiling starer sits up. "Lots of mortal casualties."

"Who gives a shit?" Football-hater waves dismissively. "It'll get blamed on religion or politics."

"Only thing that sucks about this plan," says bloody-vest guy, "is we gotta wait like three weeks before they throw another one of them parties."

"Truth." Football hater scowls. "To hell with rules. We're gonna flip that undead kingdom bullshit on its ass."

"No... no you're not," I whisper, then look down at the 'appliance'. Yeah, Wolent was right. These guys are a *serious* threat. They're going to truck-bomb the Fairmount Olympic and kill hundreds of innocent mortals at the same time they attack us? No way.

I twist the mysterious setting dial to ten, then push the power button. The 'appliance' doesn't beep or anything. No lights come on. It gives absolutely no indication anything happened. I did, however, feel a faint click under the big rubbery button, so I'm sure I activated the mechanism.

Trying to stay calm despite holding instant death, I walk closer to the break area. Ashley follows, clinging to my arm. The guys keep talking about how 'awesome' it will be once they've destroyed all the traditionalist vampires and nothing will stop them from being the kings of the night—whatever that means. These guys sound kinda like the Oblivare, who miss the days when vampires terrorized peasant villages.

I set the appliance down on the mini fridge by the corner of the sectional. Good a place as any without having to walk in and among the vampires and get close enough to kiss one. Thanks to Ashley, they still haven't even looked at us.

Not wasting a second, I backpedal five steps, then spin around and fast-walk to the door leading to the office part. Ashley scoots after me. As soon as we're in the hall and out of direct line of sight of the anarchists, a heavy sense of relief falls over me. That relief doesn't stop me from speeding up to a run.

We hurry down the hall, dash across the waiting room, and run outside before leaping the fence and stopping on the sidewalk on the opposite side of the street. Despite what we just did, I feel about the same as a kid who just threw a water balloon at a passing car, then ran away from the angry driver.

For a moment, we stand there watching the building in silence.

"Wow. That was easier than I expected," whispers Ashley.

I wince. "Yeah. Right. Something is going to go wrong."

We keep watching the building. Nothing happens.

"Maybe they found the bomb?" She raises an eyebrow. "Did you set the dial right?"

"Yeah. To ten just like Mike said. Hmm. Dunno. No one's screaming or rushing outside." I shrug. "And it doesn't have an off button. I don't think they noticed it sitting on the f—"

A thunderous *boom* goes off. A blinding orange glow floods most of the warehouse windows an instant before they shatter outward. Half a second later, a concussive blast wave washes over us with enough force to knock me back a step.

Ashley waves her arms for balance, then laughs. "I think they noticed *that*. Let's get out of here!"

CHAPTER 41
FOLLOW UP

Consciousness filters across my mind.

I open my eyes to the sight of my bedroom ceiling. Not sure what's the most difficult thing for me to believe really happened: my whole family went into a demonic realm and fought a demon. I firebombed a warehouse of anarchist vampires plotting to blow us up. Arthur Wolent had a blast—of a non-incendiary kind—amusing Chloe for an hour. She now kinda thinks of him as grandpa.

Weirder and weirder she goes, down deeper and deeper the rabbit hole plunges.

It's Saturday. I'm in no hurry to go anywhere or do anything specific. This is the exact kind of perfect teenager with no responsibilities day I love. The best part of being a vampire is flying, but permanent teenagering is pretty close to the top of the list of cool. Oh, shit. Am I stuck thinking of the same exact music and fashion as cool as right now? Like in thirty years, will I be a nerdy lame geek? Or does being an eternal teenager mean I'm going to constantly evolve to think of whatever teenagers of the era think is cool?

Ugh. Guess I will find out eventually. No point worrying about that now.

And it's not like I have a social life. Who cares what anyone might think of the music I like.

"I'm hungry," says Ashley.

"We fed last night."

"I know. Not that kind of hungry." Ashley pushes herself up and looks at me through a curtain of bedhead red. "I want waffles. It's Saturday morning."

"Ooh. Good idea!"

"Waffles!" cheers Chloe.

Yes, we are diabolical creatures of the night.

Or creatures of the lazy Saturday afternoon. Waffles everywhere quake in fear at the mere thought of us.

We meander upstairs.

Mom's in the midst of vacuuming the living room. No sign of the Littles, which means Sam's at Darryl's place. Sierra and Sophia probably went over Nicole's. Or maybe Dad took them somewhere like the mall or whatever.

I head to the kitchen and yank the freezer open. Ack. We're out of frozen waffles.

Ashley checks the cabinets. There's pancake mix, but we don't have a waffle iron.

We look at each other.

"Do you want waffles bad enough to leave the house?" I ask.

"Ugh. Not ideal, but yes. I do. My craving was kinda for *real* waffles, anyway. Frozen would've been settling." Ashley sets her hands on her plaid-shirt-covered hips.

The vacuum cuts off. A moment later, Mom enters the kitchen. "Good afternoon, you two." She smiles. "Did you have fun last night? Noticed you went out kinda late."

"Nah, not really fun." I twirl my hair around a finger. "Just had to drop a bomb off with some dangerous Lost Ones who wanted to wage war on the traditionalists."

Mom blinks. "Oh. Well. How did your bombing mission go?"

"Fine. Incinerated them all, and we got away without a scratch." I smooth my hand down the front of the long T-shirt I slept in. "Didn't even suffer wardrobe damage."

"Are you girls staying in today or is there anyone else you need to light on fire?" asks Mom.

Ashley whistles. "Conversations I never imagined having with Mom for $400."

"Right?" I chuckle. "We're gonna run to IHOP or something and get waffles. But yeah, I think we're staying in tonight."

"Probably." Ashley scrunches her nose. "I mean, what could we possibly do tonight to follow up on bombing anarchists?"

I shrug one shoulder. "I've got a little homework."

Dad leans in the archway from the hall and wags his eyebrows. "How about a movie?"

~

fin

ACKNOWLEDGMENTS

Thank you for reading Vampire Innocent #17!

Many thanks to all the readers who like spending time with Sarah and her increasingly-more-strange family! Without your continued support, this series wouldn't have made it to book 17.

Also, thank you to Lee Sheridan for editing. As always it is a great pleasure to work with you!

Finally, I'd like to thank Alexandria Thompson for her wonderful cover design.

Sarah's story will continue in book 18 hopefully on the sooner side of later.

About the Author

Originally from South Amboy NJ, Matthew has been creating science fiction and fantasy worlds for most of his reasoning life. Since 1996, he has developed the "Divergent Fates" world, in which *Division Zero, Virtual Immortality, The Awakened Series, The Harmony Paradox, and the Daughter of Mars series* take place. Along with being an editor at Curiosity Quills press, he has worked in IT and technical support.

Matthew is an avid gamer, a recovered WoW addict, Gamemaster for two custom RPG systems, and a fan of anime, British humour, and intellectual science fiction that questions the nature of reality, life, and what happens after it.

He is also fond of cats.

Visit me online at:
   Facebook: https://www.facebook.com/MatthewSCoxAuthor
   Pinterest: https://www.pinterest.com/matthewcox10420/
   Goodreads: https://www.goodreads.com/author/show/7712730.Matthew_S_Cox
   Email: mcox2112@gmail.com

OTHER BOOKS BY MATTHEW S. COX

Divergent Fates Universe Novels

Division Zero series

- Division Zero
- Lex De Mortuis
- Thrall
- Guardian
- Harbinger
- The Shadow Fixer
- Neuroshock

The Awakened series

- Prophet of the Badlands
- Archon's Queen
- Grey Ronin
- Daughter of Ash
- Zero Rogue
- Angel Descended

Daughter of Mars series

- The Hand of Raziel
- Araphel
- Ghost Black

Virtual Immortality series

- Virtual Immortality
- The Harmony Paradox

Prophet of the Badlands Series

- Prophet's Journey
- Prophet's Mercy

Divergent Fates Anthology

~

(Fiction Novels - Adult)

The Roadhouse Chronicles Series

- One More Run
- The Redeemed
- Dead Man's Number

Faded Skies series

- Heir Ascendant
- Ascendant Unrest
- Ascendant Revolution

Temporal Armistice Series

- Nascent Shadow
- The Shadow Collector
- The Gate to Oblivion
- The Queen of Discord
- The Burning Alchemist

Vampire Innocent series

- A Nighttime of Forever
- A Beginner's Guide to Fangs
- The Artist of Ruin
- The Last Family Road Trip
- The Phantom Oracle
- How Not to Summon Demons
- Ordinary Problems of a College Vampire
- A Vampire's Guide to Surviving Holidays
- An Introduction to Paranormal Diplomacy
- A Vampire's Guide to Adulting
- How to Stop a Vampire War in Six Easy Steps
- Ancient Vampire Death Cults and Other Annoyances
- Hunting Vampires for Fun and Profit

- A String of Seriously Unlucky Events
- The Summer of Completely Usual Strangeness
- Demonic Crisis Management for the Modern Vampire

Standalones

- Wayfarer: AV494
- Axillon99
- Chiaroscuro: The Mouse and the Candle
- The Spirits of Six Minstrel Run
- Sophie's Light
- The Far Side of Promise anthology
- Operation: Chimera (with Tony Healey)
- The Dysfunctional Conspiracy (with Christopher Veltmann)
- Of Myth and Shadow
- The Girl Who Found the Sun

Winter Solstice series (with J.R. Rain)

- Convergence
- Containment
- Catalyst
- Catacombs

Alexis Silver series (with J.R. Rain)

- Silver Light
- Deep Silver
- Silver Quarrel
- Silver Crucible
- Silver Heart

Samantha Moon Origins series (with J.R. Rain)

- New Moon Rising
- Moon Mourning
- Haunted Moon

Vampire For Hire series (with J.R. Rain)

- Moon Master
- Dead Moon
- Lost Moon
- Vampire Destiny
- Infinite Moon
- Vampire Empress
- Moon Elder
- Wicked Moon
- Moon Blade

Maddy Wimsey series (with J.R. Rain)

- The Devil's Eye
- The Drifting Gloom
- Dark Mercy
- Primal Wrath

Samantha Moon Case Files series (with J.R. Rain)

- Blood Moon

Immortal Operative (with J.R. Rain)

- Broken Ice
- Broken Wing

Four Elements series (with J.R. Rain)

- The Elementalist
- The Black Rose
- The Wakefield Curse

Witches series (with J.R. Rain)

- The Witch and the Hangman

Zeb Clemens series (with J.R. Rain)

- The Beast of Devil's Creek
- Wanted: Undead or Alive

~

Young Adult Novels

The Eldritch Heart Series

- The Eldritch Heart
- The Cursed Crown
- The Sapphire Soul

Evergreen Series

- Evergreen
- The World That Remains
- The Lucky Ones
- Nuclear Summer
- The Nuclear Frontier
- The World We Make
- The Threat Unseen

Progenitor Series

- Out of Sight
- Out of Mind

Diary of a Teenage Fey

(Short story series)

- Elder Horror
- The Hag of Barrow Falls
- Babysitter's Nightmare
- Lharakki
- Bauble for a Soul
- Simulacrum
- Amorphous
- Manticore

Standalones

- Caller 107

- The Summer the World Ended
- Nine Candles of Deepest Black
- The Forest Beyond the Earth

~

Middle Grade Novels

The Adventures of Ubergirl series

- My Dad is a Mad Scientist
- Aliens Ate My Homework
- The End of all Halloweens
- Dr. Infinity and the Soul Smasher

Tales of Widowswood series

- Emma and the Banderwigh
- Emma and the Silk Thieves
- Emma and the Silverbell Faeries
- Emma and the Elixir of Madness
- Emma and the Weeping Spirit

Standalones

- Citadel: The Concordant Sequence
- The Cursed Codex
- The Menagerie of Jenkins Bailey